We finally find a book concerning real people in contemporary China. Believable characters, wit, romance, conflict, grief, and growing faith make it exceptional.

—Caroline Bales, Instructor of Social Studies, Georgia State University

China's Hope is a must read for all global human rights advocates.

—Ann Vining, President of Georgia Nu chapter of Alpha Delta Kappa, International Honorary Educational Organization

The characters in China's Hope draw the reader into intriguing stories. I could not put it down.

—Maxine Drinnen Chesser, Retired Executive Director of CampFire USA Georgia Council

CHINA'S H⬡PE

Barbara Howell

CHINA'S HOPE

BARBARA NOWELL

Tate Publishing & Enterprises

Published by Tate Publishing & Enterprises, LLC
127 E. Trade Center Terrace | Mustang, Oklahoma 73064 USA
1.888.361.9473 | www.tatepublishing.com

Tate Publishing is committed to excellence in the publishing industry. The company reflects the philosophy established by the founders, based on Psalm 68:11,
"The Lord gave the word and great was the company of those who published it."

Book design copyright © 2010 by Tate Publishing, LLC. All rights reserved.
Cover design by Kandi Evans
Artwork by Lynda Stephenson
Interior design by Stefanie Rooney

Published in the United States of America
ISBN: 978-1-61663-082-9
1. Fiction, Christian, General
2. Fiction, Contemporary Women
10.04.05

ACKNOWLEDGMENTS

The author wishes to thank all of those whose encouragement and prayer made this book possible. Many thanks are also given to Robert for his patience and support, to Lynda for her encouragement, and to Annette, Evelyn, David, Laine, and Margie for their valuable assistance.

FOREWORD

From the beginning to end, *China's Hope* presents a scenario of intrigue involving family life including both marital and parental love. The tragedy and horror of human trafficking, one of the world's oldest problems, is explored as it plays out in the lives of five different individuals whose dreams and futures were suddenly and cruelly altered by people who were determined to seek personal financial gain at the expense of the captured ones. Set in rural China where 80 percent of the population live, *China's Hope* demonstrates how different life in the countryside is from life in large cities.

Modern China exhibits great economic progress and is establishing its place on the international scene. The plight of Chinese females is a problem that continues to cause concern around the globe. For those of us who live where society's mores and laws dictate equality for females, it is difficult to understand how people tolerate this behavior. Five uprooted individuals bond in the midst of cruel treatment. Although they live in a vastly different cultural setting from their upbringing, these women adapt to their current circumstances. Haunting questions develop as the drama unfolds. Who are the people in my midst that are facing this kind of persecution? Am I respecting both genders equally? What is the source of my inner strength?

God's transforming power plays a large role in the lives of these females and with those who associate with them. The power of the Christian faith in the lives of individuals can change people even when they are in captivity. It is possible for slaves, empowered by the Holy Spirit, to impact society as they live out their faith in a real-life situation.

Throughout her life, Barbara Nowell has demonstrated passion and concern for the peoples of the world. In this story she gives the readers a glimpse of what is in her heart. In addition to characterizing the plight of women in China, the author clearly communicates that no situation is hopeless, regardless of how extreme it appears. The story challenges the reader to take seriously the way that every individual is treated in all parts of the world.

—Dr. M. Rodney Webb
Associate Pastor to seniors and missions,
Briarlake Baptist Church, Decatur, Georgia

PEACEFUL HOME

Somewhere in southern China, the silent gray sky offers scant light in the square, one-story farm home constructed with locally made bricks and a sun-bleached, clay-tiled roof. A thread of smoke rising from the chimney announces that someone is awake and working inside the house where a lit candle shines through a south-facing window. The sun has not yet shown its face on this day that will shatter this peaceful home.

The twenty-three-year-old farmer's wife has already risen to begin her day. She finishes preparing rice cakes with dried plums. After eating one, she sets enough out for her family and carefully packs the remaining cakes into a willow basket as a gift for her second uncle's family. On top of the rice cakes, she places a soft cushion that she made for her grandfather, who spends part of each day sitting under the branches of a peach tree. This cushion, fashioned of goose down and covered in bright blue cotton cloth, will soften the hard wooden stool on which the old man sits.

Her movements are graceful and sure as she works with the confidence of an experienced housewife serving her family. She places her almost two-year-old son's shoes next to his bed and her three-year-old daughter's shoes and hairbrush beside hers and smiles at the charming sight of her sleeping children. In her eyes, Shimmering Sunrise and small Strong Wind are perfection in flesh resting in quilts made with loving stitches by their young mother.

Gently waking her husband, she gives his shoulder a caress. "Pride of His Father, I am leaving now. Breakfast is ready. Please make your son wear his shoes. I will return from second uncle's house as soon as possible."

Pride of His Father is an ordinary man who tills his land as his family has done for generations. He works hard but never seems to finish with the demands of farming without the benefit of animals or motorized vehicles to ease the burden of his labor. He knows how fortunate he was to win the hand of his lovely Silk Fan, and his pride in her increases as they work and rear their children together.

Her parents named her Silk Fan, but the poetry of her name fails to describe what her husband has discovered, that his lovely wife supports him and their children with a strength that is better described as tempered steel.

She wears her hair cut two inches below her ears in a simple style, which frames her attractive face and fits her busy schedule. According to the custom, her clothes should be sent to her by her mother each year, but the tragic events of her country's history have deprived her of both parents and a brother. They were accused of the crime of being large land owners, and all three died in the years following this accusation, which removed order from this ancient land. Since she has no mother to send her clothing, Silk Fan sewed her own cotton suit of a medium-weight gray fabric. It has long slacks and a slightly baggy coat with two squared pockets. She spends little time on herself yet always seems to be tidy. She wears her best outfit.

Leaving home before the sun fully lights her way, Silk Fan fingers the newly emerging buds on her plum tree and walks quickly across the familiar land. She carries a willow basket of her own making, filled with gifts. As she walks down the road of a nearby village, she notices an empty plastic bottle lying beside the narrow dirt road. What silly worker has put his water bottle aside and forgotten it? Her frugal nature is offended. She notes the poorly constructed homes of mud walls, dirt floors, and thatch roofs and recognizes how meager living conditions are here. Walking through the paths between diked rice ponds, she notes the remains of winter vegetables still growing where rice will soon be planted in flooded pools. It is her familiar world.

The morning dew dampens her shoes, collecting dirt as she walks, but this does not concern her. She is on a mission.

A rooster with beautifully colored tail feathers crows from the roof of his thatch-roofed shed. His owners are still sleeping. A white cat belonging to someone in this place meows at Silk Fan and begs shamelessly.

Today, when she needs a babysitter for her little ones, she misses her parents again. Her destination is the home of her mother's brother, Brave Warrior. Silk Fan needs her cousin to watch her two small children whiles she works beside her husband in the spring planting of the legume field.

The neighbor's young people who work in the city return with all sorts of toys, gadgets, and things. They even listen to music on tape players. But Silk Fan's family has no such luxuries. As she walks the path between two rice ponds, she listens to the wind playing music in the reeds growing there, and she sings an old folk song, one she sang to her children as a lullaby last evening.

THE STARS IN THE SKY DANCE
FOR JOY EVERY NIGHT

"Hello, Mr. Tax Man. Greetings to you."

"Hello, Mrs. Farmer. May I sit here with you while you shell your peas? I have come to see how wealthy you are."

"Oh, sir, I tell you no lie. I'm the wealthiest woman I know. My well gives sweet water. Let me draw you a cup."

"Indeed, your water is fine. Thank you for the drink."

"My husband is a wonderful man, planting and harvesting our food."

"Does your man plow with an ox?"

"No sir, no ox have we, nor goat, nor cow, nor mule. We walk on strong feet and grow what we eat. Oh, how wealthy we are."

"Mrs. Farmer, how many gold coins have you?"

"Gold coins? We have none. But the sunset each night is painted in pink, purple, and gold, and grander than any painting hung in a hall. Each night we sit and watch this display of colors and gold. I am the wealthiest woman I know."

"Give the name of your machines if you will. A truck, a plow, a bicycle, a corn grinder, or such."

"Look around, sir. No machines have we, and none to break or repair. But we eat what we grow, and my back is strong as I grind my corn on a stone from my grandmother's mom I do."

"What a lovely heritage to have."

"What a wealthy woman I am. Mr. Tax Man, you have not asked about my greatest treasures. My husband loves me! My next treasure is young but grows each day. We have a son! We are the wealthiest people I know. And the stars in the sky dance for joy every night, seeing how wealthy we are."

Content as the poor woman in the folk tune, Silk Fan smiles to herself as she finishes singing.

SECOND UNCLE

At midmorning, Silk Fan arrives at the peasant village of her relatives. Many of the homes remain essentially unchanged for six to nine generations. The houses display the many skills of their inhabitants with kiln-baked bricks, finely smoothed concrete, and bamboo frames for windows and doors. From a short distance away, she spies the sun-bleached tile roof and smiles. A thin blue vein of smoke escapes from the chimney. The old house now lived in by Second Uncle Strong Warrior and his family holds tender memories for Silk Fan. It is the home of her grandfather and was the childhood home of her deceased mother and first uncle. She finds the familiar sights comforting.

The sturdy house has four rooms that may have led to the accusation that her family was too wealthy. Her grandparents and their grandparents for generations worked the land. But the accusers came to envy any who had more materially, and the prosperity of the family was enough for charges when jealousy ruled the minds of incompetents.

The sturdy walls of the old home indicate the type of work its owners practice. There is a washtub hanging from a large nail, and lower down two hooks within a child's reach. Anchored high on the southern side are smooth bamboo poles that serve for drying laundry. A stack of corncobs and stalks declare that there is still fuel available for the stove, even at this time of year. Baskets hang high under the eaves, and a window faces the south for warmth during wintertime.

Silk Fan knows that newly sharpened tools stand in the shed in readiness for the planting season. Two wooden benches shine silver with age near a plain, wooden worktable. She remembers that her second uncle built the table to allow his wife and daughter working comfort.

A single stool is positioned beneath a gnarled, old peach tree. Long bamboo poles, stripped of their sparse side limbs, lie under the work table, ready for many uses by gifted workers.

The pig sty is empty now, but she knows that it will hold small pigs for fattening as soon as the spring litter is born on his neighbor's farm. A shelter to one side of the house pens their brown chickens and speckled geese.

She is pleased to see the bright blue paint on the heavy, old door. She is sure that this bit of brightness is for the benefit of her aunt. Silk Fan likes to observe the tenderness with which her second uncle treats both his wife and his daughter. She knows that her aunt is the daughter of town people and had a good education before she married her uncle. In those days, his family enjoyed a good reputation and prosperity. The old home, now inhabited by three generations, is comfortable, warm, and loving.

As Silk Fan enters the path bordered with berry bushes, she notes the figure of a man crouching over a bucket, with a brown dog in close attendance. Second Uncle Strong Warrior is feeding his dog, Sergeant. The dog and her relative both turn to greet her.

"Ah, Silk Fan, I am glad that you have come this morning."

"Ah, Second Uncle, you look well."

"Silk Fan, you are a beautiful girl."

With a laugh, Silk Fan replies, "Second Uncle, this girl is now a married woman with two children."

"You are still a beautiful girl."

Auntie hears her and exits the house. Her face lights up at the sight of Silk Fan. "We are so glad to see you. Please forgive your uncle if he still thinks of you as being the age of our Quiet One."

"Hello, Auntie, I brought you some sweet rice cakes with plums."

"Thank you, dear one, we will enjoy them." Auntie's hair is drawn back from her pleasant face. "How is your health?"

"I am well."

"How is grandfather?"

"He is up and about every day. He will come out soon to sit under the peach tree."

"And how is my pretty cousin?"

Auntie laughs at the compliment. "She is a happy girl, busily growing."

They all smile. She is their only child, their pride, born late in life when Strong Warrior returned home from government service.

"Tell us, Silk Fan, how are your little ones? Is your son walking well now?"

"He walks, runs, and climbs. We are fortunate to have healthy children."

"How is small Shimmering Sunrise?"

"She is a very loving child."

"And Pride of His Father? Is he well?"

"Yes, he is well. He is anxious to begin the spring planting. He has already cleared the lower field."

As soon as the polite greetings are made, Silk Fan states the purpose of her visit.

"I was hoping that I could return home with a young mother's helper. She can watch my little ones while I assist Pride of

His Father with the spring planting. Can you spare Quiet One for a week?"

"She would like to see you and go with you to care for your children. Of course, she is in school now. She is singing in a spring concert on Friday, and the students have been working hard on learning the words of the songs. Perhaps next week will be a better time. I am sure that Quiet One will be glad to come help you with your little ones."

"I appreciate that, Auntie. How is her schoolwork progressing this year?"

"She always does her assignments, but the teacher does not work the class hard enough. She is only a local girl and does not have enough training."

Silk Fan knows the problem of untrained teachers and does not want to upset her aunt, so she moves slowly to speak with her grandfather, who is emerging from the house dressed in rumpled pants and a comfortable flannel shirt.

"Greetings to you, Grandfather."

"Hello, my dear child." The patriarch is now stooped and tanned.

Silk Fan makes a slight bow with her head in a traditional salute of love and respect. He reaches over and pats her hand.

"I see that you learned family lessons well. Do you remember walking down the rows in the vegetable plot helping me plant each year?"

"Grandfather, my memories of my time with you are part of the joy of watching things grow. I brought you a gift, a soft cushion for your comfort."

The old man smiles and places the blue-covered cushion on top of the stool where he daily sits outside.

Second Auntie rushes to bring Silk Fan a thermos of water and urges her to sit and rest.

"I know that you will not stay long. Refresh yourself on this food and water while you visit with Grandfather. Let me get some things together for you. Our nuts were especially good this year, and I am packing a ring of apples for you."

Second Uncle rejoins them with a basket full of small packages of wrapped seeds. Sitting down on the ground next to Silk Fan, he begins a farmer's dialogue while Grandfather looks on. He is a head taller than his father, and his strong face has also begun to weather.

"These cucumbers are very early bloomers. Do not allow them to grow too large. These melons are not the ones we usually grow. A friend swapped them with me. Here are some apple seeds Auntie wants you to have. You know how to plant them. This is winter squash."

Silk Fan interrupts, "Second Uncle, I have winter squash. Save those for selling."

She is afraid that he is being too generous with her. Second Uncle nods his head and puts that package aside.

"Do you need sweet greens?"

"Yes, please. You know what my favorite is. Do you have any yellow peppers that are mellow, not hot?"

"You know that I would save some for you. Here are both hot, red, and mild yellow peppers. There are some beans and greens."

"Oh, Second Uncle, these are wonderful. You are always too good to me."

Silk Fan repacks her gift basket, and then she fills her pants and jacket pockets with the remaining seeds.

"I must begin my return trip home. My son can run faster than his father."

"We understand, dear. We will bring our daughter to you next week."

"Thank you both for the gifts. I feel so rich having relatives like you."

"Good-bye 'til next week."

"Until next week."

Silk Fan slips the basket on her arm and begins her return trip at a quick pace.

Perhaps I will arrive home in time to cook some dried apple pies for Pride of His Father, she thinks.

When she comes to a point where the path parallels the great Chian Jung River, she smiles. She likes to watch the people at work in the nearby fields, watch the boats, and feel the churning power of the wide river. A chilling wind from the river blows her hair. Something disturbs her serenity. A figure of an older woman kneeling by the water's edge startles her. The working woman dressed in warm clothing is bent over, writhing and groaning. Soft-hearted Silk Fan notes the woman's face wrinkled in distress and immediately comes to her aid.

"Are you ill? May I call someone for you?"

Bending down to help the ailing woman, Silk Fan is suddenly grabbed by strong arms and smothered by an odorous rag. She hears the footsteps of another person running from the nearby field, and she is dragged by two strangers to a small boat on the river.

Her homemade basket lies on the ground, spilling out its treasure, mute witness to its vanished owner.

ATTACKED AND BOUND

When Silk Fan awakes from her attack, she finds herself tied, with the strong odor of drugs around her face and hair. Through foggy eyes, she sees a boatman methodically rowing upstream. The regular beat of the waves make a sloshing sound on the side of the fishing boat where her head rests. This noise annoys her beyond reason, and she shakes her head to make the pain and odor leave, the noise stop, and her familiar world return.

What a strange dream! I am in a boat with water splashing next to my ear, and my head is in the middle of a clanging brass gong. Oooh! Strong rope is cutting into my wrists. I cannot move my hands. I am tied! Where am I? Silk Fan, try to remember—how did you get in this place? Do I know this man?

Shaking her head again she realizes that she is not dreaming but experiencing her own nightmare. She stretches against the rope in an attempt to sit up but is unable to move.

"Why are you doing this? Let me go. I have done nothing to you. Untie my hands."

The boatman gives no answer.

"Who are you? Where are you taking me?"

There is no answer.

"I have no money. You have taken the wrong person. I am the wife of Pride of His Father from the next village. We do not owe any money. You have made a big mistake."

There is no answer.

"Perhaps you know my family here. My grandfather is well known in this area. His name is Gift of Wisdom. My second uncle is known by the name of Strong Warrior. Do you know him? Anyone in this area can tell you my name. This is a big mistake."

Again, there is no answer.

The hard-faced boatman bundled in a dark knit hat and heavy jacket with ragged sleeves appears to be a working man returning to his family, but he does not go home, and he does not take his captive passenger home. Seeing the hopelessness of her situation, Silk Fan begins to scream, "Help!"

Without changing his expression, the boatman takes a foul rag and rudely stuffs it into her mouth.

As she struggles for breath and strains against the bonds, Silk Fan worries about her family awaiting her return. *My poor little ones, what must they think? Oh, Pride, please hurry. Please find me.*

After most of the traffic on the river has ceased, the boatman steers toward the shoreline, straining his eyes in the dark. When he sees a truck parked beside a market road, he steers toward a dock.

The driver of the truck speaks briefly with the boatman. Together they drag the bound young woman out of the boat to the rear of the farm truck. Someone startles her by offering her water and bread.

"Please untie me. I am bound so tightly that I am numb."

A man's hands untie her ankles, but this time her knees are tied together. Before Silk Fan can drink her water, she hears the motor roar alive, and she is thrown into a mass of cut pine boughs. After feeling around in the dark for the bread, Silk Fan begins eating her first food in hours, determined to stay strong.

She twists, strains, and fights her bonds. *My knees are bound, my water fell over when this awful ride began, my hands, feet, and my head still hurt, a pine branch is sticking into my back, and I don't like the looks of this driver!*

Silk Fan's strong will turns inward. *You are just braiding mats! Think about your real problem! Think about where these people are taking you. This is a long ride. Where are these men taking you? And why?*

She does not want to think about the answers. In her heart she knows. Eventually she dozes.

The first light of morning reveals places she has never seen. *How will I ever find my way back home? Oh, my good husband, my little children, how can you forgive me for being so naïve and trusting? I didn't even think about the fact that I am still young and salable. Every time I use pine boughs for the rest of my life, I shall remember the sharp jabs on my back and feel myself bound and horrified at this fateful day.*

The truck stops and two men pull her from the truck. Silk Fan strains to see the place as she is drug to the door of a small storage shed and shoved inside.

Silk Fan hears a gasp. "Who are you? What do you want?"

The young housewife is surprised to hear a girl's voice answer hesitantly, "I am Walks with Grace. Who are you?"

"Please untie me. My name is Silk Fan. My legs are tied, and my hands do not move."

"You are tied up? Oh, you poor dear!"

A tall figure emerges out of the shadows. She looks over the newcomer suspiciously and bends to untie her bonds.

"Thank you. How long have you been here?"

"I'm not sure—perhaps three days. I was on my way to classes at the university when two strangers knocked me down. Then, pretending to help me, they grabbed me and brought me to this shack. What do these men want? I have done nothing illegal."

"This is very frightening. I may know, but it is too awful to say. I must warm my hands. Those bandits kept me tied up for so long."

"Why do you think that we have been captured?"

There is a pause before Silk Fan speaks. "I believe that we are to be sold as prostitutes, singsong girls, or as wives."

"This cannot be! I am a good girl. My parents have arranged my marriage. I am engaged to marry a fine young man from a family in town. His parents already love me."

Silk Fan sighs sadly. "Do they ever allow you out of this hut?"

"Every evening I am allowed out a few minutes to relieve myself, and they give me something to eat. Then those men shove me back inside here. But do you really think that we are to be sold? That is against the law!" The captive girl continues, "I believe that there is something in the water. It has a strange taste."

"Then it is true. We are to be sold to other men."

From the small tool shed comes a loud, piercing scream followed by moans of grief. "Oh dear, Pride, please take care of our babies. Will I ever see you again?"

But no one outside the hut hears the screams. No one hears the groans nor sees the tears. Hours pass slowly in the shed.

"Why do these men not marry girls from their own region?"

"Since you are already in this sorry business, I shall tell you things about China's shame. You are a valuable part of this country. You are one of the most valuable jewels in this ancient land of ours."

"But why do you say that? My family is not rich."

"You are valuable because there are not enough women to provide for all the men who want wives because these people have murdered their own daughters."

Gasp! "I do not believe you! How can anyone kill their own daughters?"

Staring into space with her hands tucked under her arms for warmth, Silk Fan sighs. "It is true. Horrors have happened in China. We live in frightening times."

"I do not understand. Why would anyone murder their own daughter?"

"You must know that people have preferred boys for a long time, but I do not understand it either. I only know that people in authority made laws that families are allowed only one child. Many awful stories are heard. Of course the babies still come. Parents try to hide the new babies, or give the babies to others, or run away, or leave the country. It is useless. The government authorities will not listen. Many tiny babies and even unborn babies died. There is still much grief."

"You are just making up these horror stories to frighten me. I do not believe you!"

Silk Fan does not answer the accusation. She simply continues speaking in a dull voice with tired eyes, telling the story she knows to be true. "Most of the people in China are farmers, growing food. When so many farmers protested these cruel laws, explaining to city officials that children are needed to work on the farms, the laws were loosened, and many farming families are now allowed two children. It is still true that most families want at least one boy. The disposable children are always girls."

Walks with Grace stands up and stomps her foot. "Why do you say such bad things? I do not believe you. My father is a farmer with four children."

"How many children do the younger families you know have?"

A puzzled look crosses the student's face, and then she sits slowly, shaking her head. Silk Fan watches a puzzled look cross the student's face as she slowly sits down in the dirt, shaking her head.

"Can there possibly be anything worse than this situation which you are describing?"

Silk Fan gets to her feet. "We must try to escape! Are there

BARBARA NOWELL

any tools for digging? Is there a weak place in the walls? If we wait until daylight, it may be too late."

Both young captives move around the walls until a man's voice booms with a crude greeting. "Get out here, you worthless mud carriers. You are going to have company."

The loud guard is new and more frightening than the last silent ones. He roars rudely at his own joke. Walks with Grace shudders as she stands close enough to smell his offending body and strong tobacco odor.

Taking the hand of her new friend, she leads her outside. "You will only have a few minutes to go to the latrine. Come with me."

A second man hands them a basket containing fruit and bread. The men sit down where they calmly eat their food.

"What's going on? Who's there? Someone untie me. Please."

Walks with Grace and Silk Fan run toward the pleading voice to find a third young victim blindfolded, bound, and sitting in the dirt. They untie the newcomer and help her to her feet while the two men look on in detached boredom.

"You are uncivilized animals. What is wrong with you? Get her some water!"

The guards continue eating and ignore the outburst by Silk Fan.

"What is happening? Why are we here? Who are those awful men?"

"These are not the same men who stole me."

All three turn to look at their captors.

"You are correct. They are two different men."

"But who are they? Why?"

The men finish eating, and the younger of the two yells, "Time is up. Get back in your barn, you worthless cows."

The older, heavier man has a whip made of rope, which he slaps in his hand in a threatening way. He says nothing, only grinning menacingly at his prisoners.

Walks with Grace takes the hands of her new companions

26

and leads them back into their jail. The windowless shed now appears more inviting than the grinning face of the new guard.

"Please tell me where we are. I am so afraid." Covering her dusty face with her hands, the newcomer cries aloud, "What is happening?"

Comforted by her new friends as she settles down on the earthen floor sniffling. "I'm so dirty. Those smelly men are so mean. I want to go home."

Silk Fan walks around the small building, looking for openings in the wall or holes between the wooden boards. "Walks with Grace, what is this stuff over here?"

"I do not know. It is not mine."

"Come over here to this crack of light. These seem to be schoolbags for holding books, pencils, and money."

"Yes, I understand. I have mine with me."

All three crowd together to inspect the pile of small bags. Some are empty and some heavy with books, papers, discarded along with sweaters, a testimony to the cruelty of the secrets this shed has witnessed.

"Why are they here?"

"To whom do they belong?"

"Why are there so many schoolbags?"

"Where are these girls now?"

Silk Fan sinks down on the ground in shock. "It is what I feared the most!" She stares into nothingness in reluctance to believe what she now knows to be the truth.

"Would someone please tell me what this is all about? Why are these things our concern? And why did that vulgar man bring me to this place? "

"What is your name?"

"I am called Beautiful Moon."

"Forgive us, Beautiful Moon, we may not have much time. Allow Silk Fan to tell what she thinks. Please my friend, tell us what dreadful things you suspect."

"Yes, tell us why we are here."

"Oh, this is a desperate situation. I think that we have been kidnapped by an evil gang of men who will sell us as slaves or wives."

"No! Did you say wives? I am learning to be a baker. My parents promised me that I must approve of the man they choose for my husband. If I don't like him, I will not have to marry him."

Although she is one of the victims, Silk Fan feels like a powerless mother in this impossible situation. She sighs deeply. "If this is what I think, it is neither we nor our families who will have a say in the matter."

Disbelief and horror silence the two younger prisoners.

"We have to think. These pirates robbed other schoolgirls of their book bags, so that means that our things will also be left behind."

It seems the ghosts of other girls with shiny dark hair and innocent smiles haunt the crowded hut. *Were they distracted while memorizing facts for a history test that dreadful day? Where are these girls now?*

"Take anything you want and put it in your pockets or in your underwear."

Silk Fan bends down and begins looking through the homemade cotton carryalls.

"There may be some things in here that we may need very soon."

Beautiful Moon says, "I cannot take anything that belongs to someone else. When they return, their property should be here for them."

"My dear young friends, listen to me. These girls will not come back. We will not come back! They will never see their families again. We will not be allowed to see our families again! All three of us have been stolen and will be taken to a faraway district where we will be some man's property. Perhaps we will be a singsong girl, or a slave, or a farmer's wife, but we will probably never see our homes again."

"No!" Slapping her thin baker's hands over her own ears, trying to shut out the words too harsh to hear, Beautiful Moon screams in horror.

"We must plan on escaping, but even so, we need to have some things of our own. Now, do what I say. Take whatever you find that you can possibly use. You will have no money, nothing! I think one of these bags will fit around my waist. I'm going to place my seeds in it."

"What is a singsong girl?" Beautiful Moon asks the question in such a quiet voice that it is almost inaudible.

"It is a prostitute who is owned by ... " Beautiful Moon cries softly. She does not wait for Silk Fan's answer to be completed. She is in agony.

"We do not know when these pirates will return. What did you find?"

Walks with Grace is so angry. "This bag has eight copper coins. Just eight copper coins, and she was not allowed to keep them!"

Silk Fan tries again to instruct the girls. "That is right. Now take all of your own money and hide it under your jacket."

"What money? I only have a few coins for the train fare to classes," Walks with Grace cries angrily.

"Stop that crying. We must think." Silk Fan finds a flowered green bag. She fills it with several small items and, placing the string around her own neck, drops it between her breasts beneath her light jacket. The other two stand as if paralyzed, weeping and sniffling.

"I told you to get busy and fill your pockets with useful things. Do it now." Silk Fan speaks forcefully for the first time.

Tentatively Beautiful Moon approaches the pile in the dirt. "Here is a book of poetry. Does anyone want it? I can't take it. This is stealing."

Silk Fan tells the weeping girl, "Look at how many there are! The owners will never see them again. We are just the latest three of a large number of victims of this awful gang of criminals."

With tears running down her face, Walks with Grace bends down to search the bags. "Here is a notebook and a pencil."

"Here is another notebook and a pen," Beautiful Moon says timidly.

"Good. Now hide them." Silk Fan does not want to disturb them more by screaming.

"My slacks have inside pockets. My mother sewed them especially for coins." A weak voice quivers as Beautiful Moon joins the reality of her capture.

Walks with Grace concedes further. "If I had a needle and thread, I could sew one of these small bags inside of my slacks in just a few minutes."

"I shall search for a needle and thread. There must be a sewing project here somewhere. Here is something. It looks too large to be a school project, but it is white fabric and thread. What can it be?" Walks with Grace asks.

"Oh look! It is lovely fabric. There is too much material for tea towels. It is so large for a school project." Beautiful Moon lifts a length of white fabric up to examine it.

"This could only have been planned for a fine celebration tablecloth." Beautiful Moon, a girl of fine upbringing, recognizes the worth of the fabric.

"Perhaps it could have been for a hundred-day celebration for a baby. Those are wonderful parties where I live," Walks with Grace notes, "or it could be for a beautiful wedding celebration."

"Are we going to take a tablecloth with us?" Beautiful Moon asks incredulously.

Silk Fan, the practical housewife, is the first to recognize its worth. "None of us has any clothes. I shall make a lovely nightdress for one of us. At this time, our own clothing is much more important than the celebration of a baby's first hundred days on earth. You two play emperor's maids to decide which of you will receive it."

Silk Fan begins the work of cutting the length of lovely fabric with the only scissors they find, a small pair of embroidery scissors. In a few minutes, Beautiful Moon smiles and says, "I won, but I feel guilty. Is there not enough fabric to make each of us a short dress?"

"No," Silk Fan answers, "do not feel guilty. There is enough material to make one fine nightdress with sleeves. Perhaps we will all have some nice clothes when we arrive at our destination."

Walks with Grace retrieves another schoolbag. "Here is a heavy bag. It has two rice cakes, some notes on a vocabulary test, and two silver coins."

Silk Fan instructs: "Each of you, take a coin and hide it well. Eat the cakes. Now, keep looking."

"This has a comb and two hair clamps. I still don't want to take these things." Beautiful Moon whimpers.

"There will come a time when you will need something to sell in order to feed yourself or your baby," Silk Fan answers quietly.

"My baby?" Beautiful Moon stands with her mouth open in disbelief.

"Yes, your baby. Why do you think you are wanted? It is not for your fortune," Walks with Grace answers harshly as grief grips her being.

"Here, one of you, take this folder. It has paper in it for writing home if you ever get an opportunity."

"May I have that?" Walks with Grace asks eagerly.

"Is there any more food in any of those bags? One way criminals try to control their victims is to deprive them of food, money, and dignity. It is also a trick used by mothers-in-law. Remember that." Silk Fan tries to remember facts for their necessary education.

"Here is a belt. It is too large for me I think." Walks with Grace is tall and thin.

"Put it on under your jacket and slide this notebook under

the belt. Now, find what else you can use. You have space for a bag under the belt."

Silk Fan opens the small bag and counts the coins. "There is not much. She did have enough money to buy another train ticket."

"Why choose poor girls? We have nothing worth stealing."

Silk Fan answers with fervor, "Yes, Beautiful Moon, you do! You are what men commit crimes for. You are a lovely young woman who will bear him children."

The young baker gasps. "That's all he wants, a sex slave?"

"Now you are getting the idea. But that's not all they want. You are needed as a worker to support the household."

"How do you know so much?"

"I am married to a farmer, and we have two young children."

"Really, you are married? Tell them, and they will let you go free."

"I'm afraid not. These evil men are very dangerous. They are only part of a larger gang. They are unconcerned about anything except delivering us to those who have purchased us."

The two girls stare in wide-eyed horror.

A white cotton nightdress begins to take shape as Silk Fan sews a seam in the crisp, new cotton fabric. She works in the faint beam of light filtering in through the walls. "Now, my new friends, sit down. I have much to tell you. When we sleep, or eat, or eliminate, we must all three stay together. These men are not to be trusted. We do not want to be raped before we get wherever we are being taken."

Sniffles turn into sobs again. Ignoring the sobs, Silk Fan continues, "There is something I want to ask. If we can possibly escape, do you think that you could find your way home?"

Beautiful Moon's voice quivers softly. "No."

"You must pay attention to everything. Notice which way the roads lead. Watch for canals or rivers. Try to discover the name of towns we see. If there are police, or officials, or work group leaders, you must shout that you are being kidnapped.

Don't worry if you are threatened or hit. You must still shout out. This may be our only chance to get back home. The officials might save you. Perhaps they have been bribed and will do nothing."

"I will escape! I will not be some evil man's sex slave."

"Now about food, always eat when you have the opportunity. You do not know when you will get any more food. If the drink has a strange odor, just accidentally spill it."

"Won't there be other people in these homes? The old mistress will not allow the mean men to starve us." Beautiful Moon asks an honest question.

"Oh, you innocent beauty! Your mother-in-law, the old mistress, no matter how kind she might act, will be your 'prison guard.' It is she who will withhold her smile, her approval, and food, water, and clothes until you act submissive enough. She has much prestige and power, and she will make sure that you know it." Silk Fan tries to be patient.

"My mother did not say anything about mean people." Beautiful Moon does not really understand.

"It may be that you will have a charming mother-in-law who will welcome you into the house with warmth and love. Your dear mother knew about the other kind of mistress. She just wanted to protect you and give you a peaceful youth. It has always been this way in China. It is the old mistress who financed this sorry business."

Walks with Grace gasps, shaking her head in anguish.

"My mother said that my mother-in-law would be like another mother for me," Beautiful Moon says wistfully.

"She is the mother of her son, your intended husband. She thinks of herself as your boss and will protect his interest, not yours. She can make your life livable or unbearable."

"We won't have to kowtow to her, will we?" Walks with Grace pleads.

"Perhaps you will if you are sent as a slave in a large old family home in a remote place. Since the revolution, one does not see much bowing anymore. My own darling grandfather told me that in his childhood, everyone in the house, including his mother and brothers, had to stand with their hands at their sides and bow when his father came home at evening. No one even spoke until he was seated at the dinner table. You will be expected to follow whatever is traditional in that region."

"Silk Fan, what if she really is mean and I don't like her?"

"You must learn to be a good play actor. Calmly state what you want or need and pretend to be respectful. Remember that withholding things from you is meant to make you feel helpless and dependent upon her."

"This is too much!" says Walks with Grace.

"Let's not think about these things." Beautiful Moon is in the denial that follows shock.

"I now have the sleeves sewn into your nightdress. You will need to put it on under your jacket."

"Thank you." Beautiful Moon removes her jacket and blouse and blushes in modesty. "I shall appear as a stuffed toy," she says with a laugh.

"What can we do with all of this long skirt?"

Walks with Grace giggles. "Stand quite still and I shall fold it. We must not laugh, or those men will know that something is amiss. It must fit down under your slacks. Now put your blouse and jacket back on."

"We should all try to take more than one bag. We will need them for a hundred tasks. Look, when I roll it up, it will fit under my breasts."

"That is a good idea."

"Now you look like an old grandmother." They all laugh at the sight of Silk Fan's new image.

"It is so good to have a reason for laughing," Beautiful Moon says, smiling.

"There is a small amount of fabric left over. Shall I make two hand towels?" Silk Fan asks the younger prisoners.

Beautiful Moon answers, "I have the clean new nightdress. You should each have a towel."

Walks with Grace folds the new cotton to fit it in her underwear. "I shall hem it nicely when I arrive. I need something of my own. I do hope that you both will be living close by. We shall all need friends."

"I, uh, I have something to ask you, Silk Fan. If we are in the same town, will you be my sworn mother? You are so kind and so strong."

"Thank you, Beautiful Moon, but I will have no status. I will be just as you, a bought bride, and a new daughter-in-law in the house. Why don't we agree to be sworn sisters? We can agree to keep in touch if possible and be strong together. "

"Oh, this is so good. We will have family."

So the three young women, traveling against their wills to families not of their choosing, choose their own sisters. They solemnly vow to be sisters to each other.

"It is getting dark. I can barely see. This seems to be a ball of string. Why would a girl have a ball of string in her schoolbag? And what is this thing carved of wood?" Beautiful Moon is puzzled.

"Let us see. It is for a school project in a class on weaving fabrics, and this wooden piece is a shuttle." Silk Fan explains the bag's contents.

There is silence as they think about the student who was deprived of her freedom, her education, and even this basic tool for learning a woman's skill of weaving.

In the small hut sitting in the dirt, Walks with Grace says wistfully, "A woman. I still think of myself as a girl."

The three captives decide to make one last serious effort to escape while they do not hear their guards outside. The first digs while the second bangs on the walls, and the third works fruitlessly on the door hinge. As dark seeps in through the cracks between the boards, each gives up her efforts and lies down with dirty and bleeding hands, still prisoners.

After a long time, the frightened voice of Beautiful Moon repeats its childish refrain, "I want to go home!"

The sleep of the sworn sisters is interrupted before dawn by the sound of voices outside and the door lock rattling. An uncultured masculine voice barks out of the dark, "Get up, you lazy females. You have five minutes to eat."

Rushing to get up and follow instructions, they go outside into the misty air of dawn to wash their hands in the dew on the grass and wipe them on their clothing and then quickly divide the package of dried fruit.

A large hand shoves them. "Move! If you make any noise, you will all be gagged."

Walks with Grace is shoved in the direction of a path by a newly planted field.

"I want my bag of personal things and my books." She starts for the door.

"You will not need that now. You are finished with school and such. Now move!"

She walks quickly as a hand shoves her again. It is still dark as the five figures move through the shadows of a strange town. One forces coughing. One screams in fright at the growls of a dog. Both receive rough shoves for their noises.

"Where are we going?" Silk Fan demands.

There is no answer.

"I want to go home. My parents will be so worried," Beautiful Moon explains.

"Be quiet! Keep walking."

"I cannot see where I am going," Walks with Grace complains.

"Be quiet, you worthless females."

A rope whip whistles in the air and lands on a girl's back. It has the opposite effect intended. She cries out in surprise and pain, making much more commotion than her simple remarks have made.

Beautiful Moon turns about and cries, "Oh! That hurt. Why did you hit me with that whip?"

"You big ox! What is the idea of beating a simple school-girl?" Silk Fan demands of the strange man. "Here, here. He is an animal. Don't cry."

"I want to go home!" Beautiful Moon has never been mistreated.

Big Ox shakes his head at the problems he has in trying to herd female captives through a town without being noticed.

Silk Fan sighs. *If that scene does not awaken the town, nothing will.*

She takes the hands of Beautiful Moon and Walks with Grace. Each is aware that their baggy clothes hide their findings from the shed. Walking three abreast in the streets of this deaf town, they pass the empty stalls of butchers' markets, the woodworker's shop, and a barber's chair. Next, a colorful pile of clipped cotton threads indicate where a seamstress worked. Outside the smallest houses lie thin leavings of willow and bamboo. The basket weavers live here. Ahead of them a train station looms.

Big Ox growls, "Don't move! We will tell you what to do. If you yell or try to get attention, I promise you this. I will kill you! I have knives. You will not get away." He stomps toward the train ticket office.

The other pirate who has walked behind growls, "Sit down and wait."

Silk Fan thinks, *Oh, why did I not think of this possibility? I must try to escape while there is only one man to guard us.* As she arises, he returns with five tickets.

"Huh! Money is no problem; he just purchased five train tickets."

"We must go to the latrine." Walks with Grace speaks up and Beautiful Moon follows.

"Yes. I need to go."

"You worthless females! There is little time. Go now."

In a restroom in the train depot, Silk Fan explains excitedly, "I just realized that we did not discuss a possible escape."

"What do you mean?"

"We are going farther and farther away from home. We must try to get away from these men. If we get another chance like that, when one man leaves, I am going to run. You can help if you will just scream and run in different directions when he chases me."

"Oh, please take me with you," Walks with Grace pleads.

It will only work if we separate and run. We cannot all get away. I promise that I will not forget you." They hear the snap of a whip against the door.

As much as they drag their feet and dawdle, they still find themselves being pushed onto a northbound train. The group of five enters a car toward the rear of the old passenger train. Silk Fan looks about frantically. Beautiful Moon's eyes plead for someone to notice them. Walks with Grace deliberately stumbles to attract attention, but no one in this predawn business day pays any heed to the group, nor to the rough hand that guides the slight feminine shoulders into seats near the back in the section known as the "hard seats."

Big Ox moves to sit in the same seat with Walks with Grace. The other two are guided into the seat behind her. The man they have named Growler stands up in the aisle and snarls, "Just don't move. We are going to be here a while."

He leans over them so that they cannot leave, and his knife is visible.

One woman enters the car and sits down, but she is too preoccupied with her load of willow baskets to notice the desperate expressions on the faces behind her. Surely she will notice that none of the five is loaded with books or tools or produce to sell. She can save them from the horrible future they face. She takes out some dried prunes and calmly eats them, dashing the hopes of the three kidnapped victims.

A middle-aged man parks his overloaded bicycle outside their window and sets up his stand with neat rows of vegetables. The passengers watch him as if he were a puppet show designed to entertain them. A yellow dog yawns and lies down in the dirt. The captives watch helplessly.

Beautiful Moon sees the dog and says, "I wish that I could exchange places with that dog."

"Shut up." Big Ox is always rude.

Beautiful Moon begins to cry. Silk Fan takes her hand, looking out the window through her own silent tears.

Walks with Grace rises from her seat and announces, "I must go to the latrine."

"You just went. Now sit down."

Silk Fan decides to draw attention to their party before the train begins the trip. She stands up and shouts, "Why can't she go to the latrine?" She is quickly knocked down onto the back of the next seat, bloodying her nose. She cries out as blood gushes from her nose. She searches for the small towel. It is so painful that unbidden tears flood her face. As she realizes that her Pride of his Father has never hit her, she thinks, *Oh, Pride, please find me.*

Walks with Grace is pulled down into her seat and slapped sharply on her head.

"I told you to shut up!"

The victims have chosen the wrong time for their play for attention. The basket maker continues with her breakfast. The vegetable hawker does not notice the scene, and nothing has been gained. Silk Fan mops her bleeding nose with a small, clean cotton cloth that was a part of a school sewing project a short time ago.

"Now try to remember everything: the name of the shops, the crops, how the houses look, people, everything."

Beautiful Moon does not answer. She only nods her head. She has never been more than ten miles from her home. She is terrified. Walks with Grace has never been mistreated, and in the last few moments she and her new friend have both been struck.

Through how many towns have we traveled? Where are we now? Are we still traveling north? Will we get another chance to escape? What chance do I have without money in a strange place? Oh, Brave Warrior, please find me.

No answers came to the questions filling her mind, and no help comes for the three unhappy sworn sisters moving farther and farther from their homes. A young man in a green uniform appears briefly and does his business with new passengers. He leaves quickly to attend to more important passengers in more expensive sections.

All day and all night long they continue the ride in the train speeding away from home. The train moves steadily northward toward mountains, and then incredibly it moves right into the mountain, blanketing everything in blackness. The first time it happens, Beautiful Moon holds her breath. "We are running right into the mountain." She gasps. They are too frightened to laugh at their own ignorance of mountain tunnels.

At a rural town much like many others, Growler and Big Ox drag their companions out of their seats and shove them off the last car. No one seems to notice the desperate eyes pleading for help. People of all ages hurry past them. People in city clothes and farming clothes move shoulder to shoulder, each going his or her own way and ignoring the young girls dragging their feet.

Beautiful Moon is rudely shoved. She whimpers.

Walks with Grace spins around to protest loudly, and Silk Fan fakes a stumbling fall in the road in order to cause an attention-getting scene, but she is quickly kicked by the one they call the Growler. They all three cry aloud in protest and beg for help from the passersby.

A long-faced man with a load of caged chickens swings his load around the crowd of people impeding traffic and continues on his way. Two young women with their navy-colored bags snuggly hung over their necks stare at the spectacle for a moment but maneuver their bikes around the problem in the road. Girls busily talking and laughing pass by seemingly unaware of the plight of their sisters. Old men sitting at their doors continue smoking. *Do they understand?*

One old man in a faded Mao jacket and knit hat turns aside. He has seen this before. He will not interfere.

All that is said and done is wasted. They are pushed in the direction of a well-worn road leading away from the train station.

Silk Fan thinks, *Why would no one help us? Where are we going now?*

As they came to a small stream, Growler snarls, "Stay here. We wait."

The captives eagerly drink from the stream while Growler and the Big Ox look about.

Beautiful Moon tells her friends, "My parents would not allow me to drink from this stream without boiling the water, but I am so thirsty."

Silk Fan is watching their guards. "My friends, we must try to escape! The next time one of these pirates leaves for food or anything, we must be ready to run. There seems to be nowhere to hide here, but we did not do well in the villages. Whoever gets free must contact our families. Now tell me what you will do if only one guard is here. You must run! Run! Go south toward home; try to find that train!"

An unusual sight of a dark green van with smoked windows interrupts their discussion. At the stream where the incongruent group waits, it stops, and a front window rolls down silently. Growler motions for the captives to board the costly novelty.

Silk Fan notes Walks with Grace looking around desperately. *There is no one here to see us. Where did these horrid men get the money for such a luxury?* Reluctantly, they climb into the second seat of a van that still emits an odor of factory newness.

Silk Fan resists. "Stop poking me, you foul-smelling animal. I am going!" She steps inside to the jeers of the men. Beautiful Moon moves obediently inside the van anxious to avoid any physical contact with either Growler or Big Ox.

"Who is there? Please don't hit me again. I need to visit the latrine."

All three girls whirl around in their seats to locate the source of the pathetic pleas.

On the last seat is a fourth girl, bound and blindfolded. A fifth girl lies on the floor with her hands tied behind her.

"Please untie me."

Silk Fan reacts in vocal horror, "Oh no! This gets worse and worse!"

Walks with Grace is quick to assist. "I'll help them."

Silk Fan is furious. "You untie her! Aaiie! You monstrous animal! This girl needs to relieve herself. She is hog-tied. Don't you have a soul?"

As the two passengers are untied and helped out where they take a much-needed break, Silk Fan realizes that there are now two more men who are better dressed than the others.

"Time to move, you worthless females," one man warns.

The other man grins a vulgar smile and waves his woven whip.

One of the newest captive girls has trouble walking. "Would you please look at my feet? They will not work properly."

Walks with Grace takes the stranger's feet into her lap and discovers blue lines circling her ankles. "Your feet are cold because the circulation is cut off with these ropes. I will rub your feet. Where are your shoes?"

"After that mean man threw me down, I tried to run away. He took my shoes and threw them in a muddy ditch. That is when he tied me up and stole all my things."

The five captives become acquainted as the van moves slowly onward.

Beautiful Moon is startled at the condition of these two captives. "What happened to your face?"

Walks with Grace joins in. "Why is there mud all over your clothing?"

Silk Fan urges, "Shhhhh. Let them speak."

"I am White Flowering Tree. I am seventeen years old, and I am a senior in high school. When I was waiting on my bus, two men came from behind me and knocked me off my feet. They hit me in the head, tied me in a wheelbarrow, and covered me with straw. I do not recall many hours. I tried to run away when I was allowed to go to a latrine later. They took my shoes and glasses and threw them away."

She is interrupted by another confused voice. "What is going on?"

One of the latest captives asks in a childish voice, "Why has this happened to us?"

All three ask, "Who are you?"

"My name is Summer Rain, and I am thirteen years old and a student in technical school in the city. My family and my entire village were so proud when I was accepted into the fine school. I study many subjects, but business machines are my favorite."

"Oh my grief, she is only thirteen years old," Walks with Grace announces.

There is a pause in the conversation as they all stare at this, the youngest victim yet. As Chinese count years, she was thirteen because the year before birth is included, but she has only been on earth for twelve years. What can be said to explain this horror to a child?

"Tell us how you were captured."

"I was on my way home from machine laboratory after school classes. It was my first day to travel the train alone, so I was very foolish."

"What do you mean foolish?"

"My parents have told me not to speak with strangers, but this polite couple said that they could help me find my train."

In astonishment, Walks with Grace asks, "Did you say a couple? Are you saying that a woman captured you?"

Young Summer Rain bows her head in embarrassment and guilt. "Yes. The woman dropped her bundle. When I stooped to pick it up for her, the man covered my face with something.

He held me tightly, and it smelled awful. My elbows were tied together, and I felt so tired."

The motherly Silk Fan sympathizes. "Oh, you poor dear."

From the front seat of the van, a threatening voice yells, "All of you lowly females, shut up." The young man in well-tailored city clothes slings a braided whip against the second seat and snarls, "You are a sad sight of worthless mud carriers!"

Beautiful Moon gasps as if the whip has hit her. She cowers.

Silk Fan reacts like a mother tiger defending her kittens. "Look, you snake, does whipping girls make you feel big? You will never be a whole man."

"I said shut up!"

As the outburst draws the attention away from the last captives to the front seat, they realize that the original two men, Growler and Big Ox, are no longer with them. They are younger and better dressed than the two previous guards.

"The other monsters are gone," Walks with Grace states.

Beautiful Moon whines again, "I just want to go home."

Silk Fan demands, "Do you two men have names?"

There is no answer.

From the backseat, a brave new voice adds her bit. "They are too dishonorable to be given names."

"Be quiet, or there will be no food tonight for you cackling hens."

"Then you are so ashamed of your names that you will not name your fathers?" Silk Fan grows bolder.

The driver speaks covertly to his companion, who then turns around with no comment. Two girls write busily in their notebooks while the conversations turn to guarded whispers. In spite of their bravado, their fear of the men is real.

As the expensive motor novelty moves through village after village, the passengers in the rear seats give up trying to motion out of the windows. No one seems to see them. From the shadows inside the van can be heard a whimper, "I want to go home."

"Yes, I do too." White Flowering Tree and Beautiful Moon hold hands and cry.

The driver stops the motor and announces, "Your palace chair ride ends here. Now we will walk."

The five captives scramble outside to discover that they are in a field of half-grown grain. As the Half Man distributes flat bread and carrots, he threatens the hungry victims.

"Now don't get any ideas in your weak heads. If you try to run away, you will be caught and beaten. You can eat while you walk. Now move, you worthless mud carriers."

"Hey you, Half Man, have you always been so charming? I understand why you must steal a bride. No one in her right mind would consider you for a husband." Silk Fan moves deliberately away from his raised whip as the gang leader holds back the arm holding the whip.

"Listen, my friends. There is much I must tell you while we walk."

"What?"

"First, if one man leaves for any reason, we must all run. The second thing I want to tell you is this: you must keep on trying to contact your families. Bribe anyone you meet to take a letter to your parents. Go tell the police. Tell your work leader. Tell the cadres. Months from now you must still continue to try contacting your homes. You may not be certain that any letter actually arrives until you get an answer.

"Now remember, do not ask permission for anything. Just do as you please. These heartless people want to break your spirit. They may smile and tell you that you are one of the family now, but remember that they are slave traders, and you will only have the rights that you demand."

"I am so afraid." It is one of the newest captives, White Flowering Tree.

"Why do they want me? I cannot cook or bake bread. I only help my parents on the farm. I am only a schoolgirl. Will I be allowed to return to finish my school semester? I have earned an award this year."

Incredulously, White Flowering Tree shouts at Summer Rain, "You don't get it, do you? Don't you know what slave traders do?"

"Don't they capture people to do their farm work for them?"

Sideways glances are exchanged, and collective sighs escape their mouths. After a pause Beautiful Moon gently asks, "What has your mother told you about men and married life?"

"Mother said that she would explain it all to me when I am ready for marriage."

"Oh my grief, she is a baby!" Walks with Grace does not try to speak quietly.

Beautiful Moon begs, "She is only thirteen years old! Please tell her what is going to happen."

Silk Fan suddenly feels quite old as she takes Summer Rain's arm and says, "Come, my sweet innocent friend. Let me be your mother for a while. She would have prepared you if she had dreamed that you would be captured. You were taken to be the bride of some man somewhere."

The other girls walk ahead, discussing the innocence of Summer Rain. "Poor child. She is so young."

"She was raised by a proper Chinese mother to be a proper, innocent bride."

"Her mother victimized her!"

"No, her mother was protecting her daughter."

Silk Fan continues her instructions. "After the wedding and all of the guests have gone home, the bride is dressed in her wedding nightdress, and she awaits her new husband. When he comes, he caresses her breasts."

"Why does he do that?"

"Next—"

"Stop all that female chatter up there!"

"Relax. They are doing no harm," the older of the guards comments while he drives.

"No! No! I do not believe you!" Summer Rain stops in her tracks; her face is drained of its color. "You made up that to frighten me!"

Silk Fan stops ahead of her and extends her hand, inviting the young one to rejoin her. A whip cracks the air in Summer Rain's direction, but she ignores the growled curses and the whip too. "Move on, worthless one."

The youngest girl hurries to catch up with her other companions and demands in horror, "Do you know what she told me? She said that ... " Looking around and blushing, she is too embarrassed to repeat her newly learned knowledge.

Sympathetic Beautiful Moon says, "Poor child, she is so young."

A high-pitched voice is heard saying, "Do you know what she told me?" Nodding heads are her answer.

"Silk Fan will only tell you the truth." Beautiful Moon tries to console the youngest victim.

Another girl looks on and nods in agreement.

The thirteen-year-old asks hesitantly, "How do you know this to be true?"

Silk Fan gently takes her hand and explains once again. "I am a married woman. My husband is a farmer who at this moment is feeding two small children, who are wondering why their mother has not returned home in time to serve them dinner."

"Do you really mean that?" Summer Rain is naive. "Tell them that you are already married! They will have to let you go home!"

"These slave traders are not concerned with our plans, our rights, or our families. They are evil men who have been paid money to capture us. However, I will never stop writing to my husband and uncle and planning my escape."

"I never dreamed of such dreadful things. Oooh! I stepped on something. My foot is cut and bleeding." Summer Rain sits down on the dirt to hold her foot.

"Keep moving."

"Oh, shut up, you Half Man. Where are her shoes?" Silk Fan, the mother tiger, speaks.

"Do you want the feel of the whip again, you worthless female mud carrier?"

Silk Fan turns and speaks quietly, "If you strike any of us again, I promise you that you will have difficulty getting up, and your wife will wonder what has happened to your manhood."

He stares in disbelief at the unexpected vocal threat but stands still while the injury is examined.

"Comrade Gang Leader, what are your plans for our injuries? We need some cloth for a bandage."

The leader looks annoyed, but he removes a cloth from their dinner basket and hands it to Silk Fan. The bleeding foot is wrapped up in the bread cloth, and the sad procession continues.

"How much farther must we walk? It is so late. We will need the moonlight to see the way." Weariness has turned their tears into an honest, vocal complaint by White Flowering Tree.

Shortly ahead, a comical scene blocks the road. A farmer is screaming at a large pig that has fallen through the slats of a farm wagon. The wagon, which was built for lightweight hay, is no match for the weighty animal with its legs caught in the broken wagon bottom. The poor, frustrated farmer is so distraught that he stands beating and screaming at the helpless squealing pig.

Their desperate situation prevents the young women from seeing the humor in this noisy, ridiculous scene. Beautiful Moon runs ahead of her friends and pleads, "Oh, sir, please call the authorities. These men have taken us prisoners. Please help us."

Half Man comes forward with a fake smile on his face. "You silly woman, these jokes are not funny. Don't bother this man. He has enough problems."

He grasps Beautiful Moon's arm with enough power to break it and, smiling broadly, guides her on down the darkening road.

The exhausted farmer is knocked down where he sits, past thinking or acting rationally.

The exhausted farmer is knocked down where he sits, past thinking or acting rationally.

Silk Fan speaks calmly. "There are so many of us. Perhaps we can help you."

"I don't think so. I need a rope, and I have none."

"We have a rope. It is short, but we will be glad to give it to you in your need."

Half Man turns around to see the crowd, including the farmer, looking at him.

"How much do you want for your rope? You can see that I need it."

Half Man, the vain man dressed in his fine city clothes, is exasperated at being tricked into relinquishing his symbol of power, but wanting to move on without all of this attention on his captives, he answers, "Will two coppers be a fair price?"

"Two coppers is quite a fair price."

The girls all surround the cart and help the exasperated farmer free his animal.

Silk Fan turns as they are leaving and asks, "Farmer, what about your cart? Will you come back for it?"

"No. That sorry thing is good only for firewood."

"May I take the wheels for myself?"

"Enough!" The leader who has maintained some veneer of propriety in public shouts, "We must be on our way."

Ignoring the outburst, Silk Fan says, "Someone help me. I want the remains. They can be useful." White Flowering Tree realizes that this is a game of power that Silk Fan is playing with her captors, and she is still frightened.

"Good!" There are smiles as they ready themselves for travel again.

"Hey, slave traders, this is my bridal gift for my new husband; I shall not go empty-handed." Silk Fan grins broadly.

The gang leader looks in disgust at Half Man, who shakes his head and curses under his breath. "Now we will have to walk in the dark because you smart females wanted to play good neighbor."

From behind, a grumbling male voice is heard. "We are going to get rid of you very soon."

"I don't know why she keeps saying slave traders. I thought she said that we were wanted as wives."

"Dear, you still don't get it. We are to be bed slaves to some men who are too ugly to win wives on their own merits." Walks with Grace's anger is directed at Summer Rain.

White Flowering Tree's face cracks into grieving lines. Girls always anticipate their weddings as romantic events. There is nothing romantic about this trip and wedding that she fears. She cries quietly.

Summer Rain explains her solution to the situation. "I will just explain that I am too young to marry. Any reasonable family will return me to my home, where I will finish my education. Won't they allow me to return home?"

The question hangs in the air. It is such a simple question, but those who know the answer hold their tongues, reluctant to add to the anguish of their unsuspecting friends.

Silk Fan finally answers with a tired voice, "These are not reasonable people. They hire gangs to kidnap innocent wives for their sons. They are not honorable people. They prefer to pay thieves than to deal fairly with your families."

None of the girls responds to her answer.

The two men are squinting into the dark at homes along the way.

Beautiful Moon asks, "Silk Fan, is there anything else you wanted to tell us?"

"Yes. There is so much to tell you. You must try to come to market every single market day. Do not ask permission to come. Just smile and tell your jailer that you are going, and ask if she wants to come along. I will see you there."

The innocent White Flowering Tree asks, "What does she mean my jailer?"

Walks with Grace answers dryly, "She means your mother-in-law."

Silk Fan continues, "We will all meet every week. Perhaps we can also meet on laundry days. You must also find some means of making money and find some place to hide it. Keep writing letters to officials. You may get to go home again. Don't be discouraged, and don't let them break your spirit. Don't argue with anyone. They will not be fair or listen to you. They want to make you weeping, tired, and round-shouldered. Be strong!"

"I don't understand," whimpers Summer Rain.

"I want to go home." Beautiful Moon sniffles.

"Now, watch carefully where each of us goes. We will need friends in this heartless place of criminals."

As Silk Fan gives the young girls last-minute instructions and encouragement, the men search for the houses where they have been sent.

THE DELIVERY

The two kidnappers peer across the road, looking for a house. "We have missed one house. It should be right here! He said that it would be next to a field of wheat, the first house after a road called Glorious Prosperity Lane. Stop! We need to go back a bit. Go drag one of those worthless females back here."

Half Man grabs Walks with Grace by the arm and steers her three houses back to the way they have just come. He stops at the corner house and calls out at the gate entrance. A light brightens the house, and a handsome young man is followed out of the door by a short woman who fidgets nervously. She has on a clean outfit. She is expecting visitors.

The young man emerges in the lit doorway and speaks to the slave traders. "This is the right place. Come in."

All five young women stand frozen in the road. A rough hand shoves Walks with Grace in through the gate and ushers the other kidnap victims on down the dark unpaved road. No words of introduction are made. No traditional words or ceremonies are performed. The exhausted and frightened friends continue obediently down the road to their futures.

The young man and his mother stare at Walks with Grace. She is dirty, her clothing is wrinkled and travel-worn, but she holds her head up in educated dignity. "You will do nicely," says Black Pearl.

The next girl to be chosen, White Flowering Tree, is not hesitant in speaking to either of the people who claim her. When the door is closed she quietly says, "My feet hurt, and I am so tired. Please show me where I may bathe. Those awful men beat me and stole all my belongings. They even stole my shoes."

"It will all be fine. You will see." The mistress of the house takes White Flowering Tree outside to a side courtyard next to a darkened barn, where she is given a bucket of water and a sad excuse for a towel. When the mistress returns with a cake of soap, she finds White Flowering Tree soaking her bruised feet in the bucket while sleep has claimed the rest of her being.

"Wake up. You went to sleep while sitting here." The older woman leaves, and White Flowering Tree bathes with cold water.

Half Man no longer looks like a city man in his fine silk shirt. He did not count on his victims being so difficult to manage. Chinese women traditionally do as they are told. He is as tired and hungry as his four remaining "brides." "You big-mouthed, trouble-making female, you have caused enough problems. You are the next to go." No one answers.

A girlish voice betrays its owner as she loses her composure and begins to cry. "I wish my father were here." It is young Summer Rain.

Another voice in the dark sobs, "I just want to go home." Beautiful Moon joins the chorus of fear and grief.

The gangsters stop at an ordinary-looking farmhouse a short distance away and confer again. An older man comes to the open doorway silhouetted against a light. The two crying, young girls gasp as their guards confer with the older man.

A quiet voice is barely heard saying, "Please don't sell me to an old man."

Silk Fan addresses the captives. "I will go to the old man. It is indecent to ask this of young girls."

"You are late."

"Yeah, we had some delays."

"Whom do you have here?"

"See what you think. She is not as young as some."

There is no old mistress in this household to welcome the new arrival. This is obviously a widower seeking a replacement for his first wife. The man appears to be in his sixties, with thinning hair and a muscular body hardened by years of daily work in his fields. He moves surely toward the calm young woman who is thrust before him. Studying Silk Fan's tired face, he notes her wrinkled suit, uncombed hair, and erect shoulders to determine whether his money has been well spent.

"Sir, I want you to know that I am a married woman. I am the wife of Pride of His Father in the southern province by the Chang Jiang River. We have lived there for eight generations. My grandfather and my uncle will be glad to pay my ransom price. I have two small children who need me."

Ignoring her speech, the older man nods to the kidnappers, takes her arm, and moves toward the open doorway.

Silk Fan considers the other two younger girls when she decides to lift her head with a deliberate act of dignity as she walks into the strange house. She does not want the other victims to be dragged into their new homes kicking and screaming in protests against this grievous event of injustice.

The traveling party moves on down the dark, frightening road. They stop at a place only two buildings away.

"This is it. He said that it was the last of three houses crowded together."

A knock brings a young man and his mother to the gate bordering the dirt road.

"Hello. What do we have here?"

"Take your pick. Both are young and strong."

A look of horror twists two young faces. Beautiful Moon speaks to her companion, Summer Rain, "This is as bad as it could possibly be. We might as well be animals sold at the market!"

At a nod in the direction of Summer Rain, the young man turns back into the house while the mistress of the house takes the youngest girl by the dirty hand and leads her into the house. A candle in a clay pot is the only indication that anyone is expected this dreadful night.

"My name is Summer Rain, and I want to go home. My parents will be so worried. I am missing my classes at the city technical school. Please let me go home."

"Now, now, come in. You need a nice cup of water. Why are you so dirty and unkempt? You will be fine here. Let me take your shoes. Where are your shoes?"

"Your gangster friends took my shoes, beat me, and threw me in the dirt."

"Tsk, tsk." The mistress of the house merely clucks her tongue. "You may bathe and rest here. It is late now. Things will be better tomorrow."

The old woman helps Summer Rain undress and bathe with a new cake of soap. She makes no comment as she pulls several cloth schoolbags from around her neck and neatly folds her dusty school uniform in a pile on a bench beside her.

"Here is a clean nightdress. It is not new, but it will do. Come and lie down here with me tonight. We all need sleep."

"It is such a relief to get a bath and go to bed, but this is all a mistake. My teachers are expecting me in class."

The twelve-year-old schoolgirl is asleep before she closes her eyes. The young man of the house waits outside while his mother cares for Summer Rain. He enters his house and looks at the young girl lying in a heap by the side of his mother on the family kang. He has not yet spoken a single word to her.

The last of the slave traders' charges is the baker known as Beautiful Moon. As soon as her last friend disappears into a country home, she begins to weep again. The three walk a quarter of a mile before stopping again. Her sobs and grief are ignored. They pause at a house with neither a wall nor a gate. Two figures sit under a tree, their lit cigarettes giving proof of their presence.

"Hello."

"Who is there?"

"It is Swift Horse. We have someone for you."

The young man says, "We had just about given you up. Bring her in."

With a tear-stained face, the lovely girl known as Beautiful Moon is led into the square-shaped rural home. It is midnight.

"Hello. My! You have had a long trip, haven't you? You will be fine. It will all work out." Double Joy speaks the village mantra.

"May I have a drink of water?"

Surprised at the quiet voice, the old mistress takes her hand and moves the long brown hair aside from her dirty face and sees with alarm that she has a beautiful girl with lovely delicate features for a daughter-in-law.

The young man named Key Keeper smiles at Beautiful Moon while his mother goes to get a cup of water. She mumbles as she goes, "She is a porcelain doll, not a farmer's wife."

The following morning after the fateful trip, Silk Fan awakens early, as is her habit. Looking for the older man, she sees no one and hears only morning sounds. Still in her traveling clothes, she swings her legs off of the strange, hard bed and slips on her shoes.

He is gone. The cowardly man left early in order to avoid any conversation with me. There is almost no food here, and where is the latrine? The staged wedding will probably be today, so the place needs a house cleaning in preparation for any guests who might come. What a mess. Even a second wife should have a better welcome than this.

"Well! He could have done some housekeeping," she says

aloud to herself. "I wonder whether he is an absolute pig or just a spoiled old man made helpless by women waiting on him."

The house is built of yellow brick with wooden shutters and features brick floors with a brick platform kang for sleeping. There is only a single chair and table. The cooking surface is covered with grime, and piles of dirty rags and clothing litter the floor and one end of the kang itself. The walls are darkened with the accumulation of soot. Only one storage cabinet stands against a wall.

As she begins cleaning, her disgust surfaces. "This twig broom must have been made in the Ming Dynasty," she says to no one. After sweeping out the small home, she recognizes that the brick floor needs more than a good sweeping, so she goes searching for a bucket and water. After three trips to the waterspout and much splashing on her pants legs, she declares, "The floor may not be sanitary, but it is cleaner." Scrubbing the floor is the death of the twig broom.

My clothes should be washed early so that they can dry in the sun. There must be a washing pot here even if he has not used it. Hmm. No pot, no soap, and no fuel for a fire. I suppose that today is not laundry day. I must wash the clothes I am wearing! There must be one hundred years of soot from a thousand fires here on the walls of my new home.

My new home. Her shoulders drop in grief. She knows what the other "brides" do not know. She will never be allowed to leave. If Pride of His Father and Second Uncle Strong Warrior do not come for her, she must find some way to stay alive. It is only a dream that one day she might return to her husband and children.

"Do not cry, Silk Fan," she chides herself. "Crying will not help them or you." She begins wiping down the darkened walls. *Don't think, just work.*

Neglected little children and a tired and lonely man are all that she can imagine for the future back in her cozy home in southern China.

I must write a letter to Pride and tell him what has happened to me. Oh, Pride, what is the answer?

A familiar image of her three-year-old Shimmering Sunrise awaking with sleep in her eyes and straight black hair in her small face comes to mind and brings tears to her worried mother's mind. *I can hear her calling, "Mommy, where are you?"*

"Stop it, Silk Fan!" She shakes her head. "This is not helping!" She climbs up onto the kang and attacks the second wall with a fury.

"Hello." The old man comes in and looks around for her. He sees the pretty young woman standing on the brick kang, scrubbing the sooty walls with plain water. He puts down some packages. "I have brought some food. Can you cook?" He does not appear as old as she hoped. He does not smile, but he has a pleasant face with a firm jaw and a good profile. His clothing needs laundering, but he walks with confidence and has the muscular build of an active farmer.

Resisting the temptation to answer with a sarcastic reply, Silk Fan says nothing.

"Oh, I see that you are cleaning. My wife has been dead for a while, and I have no idea about such things. I guess it is rather dirty. Did you find what you need?"

"No. Do you have any whitewash or paint? And where are the cooking utensils? I found only one soup pot. Where will I find a steamer and some spoons?"

"Tomorrow is market day. Nothing much can be found today. If you can make do today, I'll see what I can find for you."

"What about wood for the fire?"

"We do not get wood here very often. I will have a boy bring some coal in today. Make something to eat. I will return this evening."

"I know that you need a wife, but I am not the one for you. I will have no heart for it. I will always love my legal husband. We have two very young children. There is no grandmother to care for them. Please allow me to return to my home."

Silk Fan speaks with composure and dignity. She is still standing wet and dirty on the hard-surfaced bed of the house.

He answers her a second time. "The deed is done. The money has been paid. I cannot allow you to return to your home. This is your home now. My mother and father are dead, so you will only have the care of the two of us."

"So you really don't want a wife. You have bought and paid for a slave. Is that how you treated your first wife?"

He ignores her comments and shows her the property. "The latrine is in the corner of the courtyard. Well, it is no longer a real courtyard. A few years ago, the authorities made us plant food in every spare place, even the courtyards. Those bricks against the back wall were pavement for the courtyard. I will replace them if you wish. Here are some cold vegetables."

He begins again to leave for the day when he is stopped by her question.

"Have you purchased any new clothes for me?"

"No."

"Will your family and friends bring wedding gifts?"

"Probably not."

"You have not made provisions for me."

He shrugs and says nothing.

"You have not even told me your name."

"I am called Hero of his People."

Silk Fan looks him directly in the face and asks, "Do you have a broom, a rake, and a hoe?" She is not ready to show any traditional courtesy to this man.

"Yes, tools are in the shed."

"Have you grown any herbs?"

"No."

"Do you keep chickens, ducks, or geese?"

He shrugs his shoulders. "No."

"I found no towels. Where are they?"

He does not answer.

"Are there jars for making jams?"

At this point, she knows the answer to her inquiry. She states her immediate needs.

"I will need a ball of small-sized hemp rope, some wool, and some fabric for sewing, and I need poles for hanging laundry."

"Woman, what is your name?"

"I am Silk Fan."

He nods. "Silk Fan, here is all of the money I have. Get what you need."

He takes several coins and two yuan from his pocket and leaves them on the only table. She makes no comment as he opens the door. She will not thank him.

"Where is the cleaning soap?" As he turns to answer this question, he almost falls over the broken old hay cart at his doorstep.

"What is this trash?" he asks in astonishment.

"It is mine."

Shaking his head, Hero escapes as quickly as he can. Frowning at the scrap of a cart, he hurries away.

Sitting alone at the table badly in need of scrubbing, she eats some dried fruit and thinks to herself, *It has happened. I really am a prisoner, and the entire village will guard me. He went off to the fields without a backward glance. The first thing I will do is write to my precious husband.*

She looks for paper—any paper—and cringes at what she finds.

At least there is work to be done. What a piggery! It is difficult to decide which is the most annoying, the lack of any sort of paper in the house or the disgusting condition of the neglected house! My young friends will be glad to see me this morning. It is too early for market. This is certainly an insignificant amount of money. I do not even know what day of the week today is.

Looking around for a hiding place for her money, she laughs. *This mess would discourage any thief.* Putting the money in one of her own schoolbags, she hangs it as high as she can reach from a nail in one corner.

Hmm, I remember that White Flowering Tree was taken to the house three doors down. It is probably not too early for visiting. I wonder what kind of people live there. I have waited long enough to go visiting, but I must look like a war refugee. Perhaps her mother-in-law will let me have a small amount of soap to wash my clothes and myself.

Silk Fan moves the broken cart away from the doorway and examines the outside of her new home and the courtyard. It groans with neglect. *I wonder if he is just totally lazy or if he has lost his spirit after his first wife died. Life could be very hard here if he will not even care for his own home.*

One side of the small shed at the far corner of the courtyard contains a few baskets and garden tools, while the right side contains the latrine. The sun filters in through the holes in the bamboo roof, and small birds have claimed space for a nest inside. Silk Fan speaks aloud to the startled bird that flies out a hole in the wall.

"How did you fare last winter, little bird? Would you like some company? Do you think a pair of fat geese could last the winter in this meager place?"

There is neither a fence nor wall on the side facing the road. The only living thing in sight is a mature fruit tree shading part of the oblong space. At the back corner boundary, she notices a small opening in a low wall. She looks inquiringly and sees another small courtyard adjoining her own. She knows that only the poorest homes usually share precious courtyard space. When she visits the next home, she meets White Flowering Tree, who is relieved to see her friend.

"Did you know that I am living right across the courtyard from you? We are neighbors. We will see each other every day. Won't that be harmonious?" White Flowering Tree smiles weakly and steps to stand near her friend as if for protection. She acts as if she is afraid to speak.

Turning to her unwilling hostess, Silk Fan introduces herself. "Hello, I am your neighbor, Silk Fan."

The woman in neat clothing answers, "My name is Pure."

Silk Fan says brightly, "May we see the wedding linens you have prepared for White Flowering Tree?"

Awaiting her answer, she gazes intently into the lined face of the older woman, knowing that she is putting her on the spot and that in most probability she has neither purchased nor made any items in preparation for her new daughter-in-law.

"Uh, well, we have not purchased any. We will get some," Pure says vaguely.

Silk Fan continues, "Well, let us see the wedding clothing you have prepared. She already needs some things for daily wear also."

"Oh, we did not know when to expect her."

Silk Fan carries her act further. "That is fine for now. I am sure that you will have some lovely things for her when the neighbors and family come to present their gifts at the wedding celebration."

The older woman just stares at this unexpected turn of events.

Silk Fan knows the reputation of many women expecting daughters-in-law. They do not plan on spending money on wedding celebrations, gifts, clothing, or anything else that will give the young bride an elated sense of her importance. The older women expect a servant, not a princess.

Even when legal brides travel many miles to arrive at their new homes, guests bring gifts and celebrate with traditional foods. The bride's parents usually provide her clothes, and if a bride price is paid, it is to be used for her furnishings. Since the bride's family was not consulted in this case, she has no special things, nor even necessities for her new married life. This is Silk Fan's message as she turns to White Flowering Tree and asks innocently, "Dear, what is your favorite color?"

"Pink is my favorite, and I like green, the color of apple leaves in spring."

"How pretty! I like pink and green also."

Turning to look at her hostess again, Silk Fan says sweetly,

"Now you know which colors to look for. I am anxious to see the pretty things you find."

Holding out her hand, she says innocently, "Have you finished eating? Let's go to see Summer Rain."

Silk Fan takes her friend's hand and walks out of the door of the house.

HERO SPEAKS

W hen Hero came home at noontime, he brought some vegetables and told me to prepare food for the evening meal.
I see no meat or rice. I want to have a hot meal waiting
for him when he returns because I want to discuss my leaving once
again. Perhaps there is some food in the root cellar.

Silk Fan emerges from the small dugout cellar with a pottery jar of honey, two shriveled carrots, and some very old, dried
peppers.

I shall simmer a tasty soup. The honey will make a nice accent for
these vegetables. That is the best I can do with no more commodities to
use. Surely there is bread here in the northern place. He did not bring
any rice, corn, or wheat. I wonder what this man has been eating.

After preparing the best meal she can manage with the vegetables he brought, she inspects the small house. Perhaps he will
not even notice, but it is much cleaner, and it even has a fresher
smell. When he returns, he will have a hot meal waiting for him,
and I will sit down quietly and explain my situation to him again.

Now what will I find to wear while I launder my dust-covered clothes? These are his clothes, but they will have to do. They will at least cover me while I wash my things. Even with no soap, my clothing will be cleaner.

Using one of the water buckets, Silk Fan launders all of the clothing that she has worn for the entirety of her trip northward. Her nicest outfit and her underclothes that were once clean and fresh are now the only ones she owns. She spreads them on the grass growing in the sunniest place in the courtyard.

Surely there is a private place for bathing. I shall have to make one later. For now, I shall close the door and wash one thousand miles of dirt from my body. I wonder how many miles we did travel.

Lifting one of the heavy buckets of water, Silk Fan takes it inside the house and begins her much-needed bath. The water is clear and cold, and she takes her time for a leisurely bath, but a vision of two laughing children keeps clouding her mind.

"Oh, Mother, that water is so cold. That is enough; I am not really dirty."

"Not dirty? The piggy is cleaner than you are today, Strong Winds."

Her little girl chimes in, "I'm not as dirty as the piggy, am I, Mother?"

"Perhaps not, my little Sunrise, but you need a bath also." It is the memory of an ordinary evening with an ordinary young mother performing an ordinary task. It is a vision that haunts and brings unbidden tears to her eyes.

Before she can claim her own clean clothing, he returns to find his house filled with the aroma of steaming soup.

"You have cooked dinner! It smells like a feast."

Silk Fan tries to smile as she answers, "It is ready. Do you want to eat now?"

"Yes, I do. Let us see what you have prepared." Hero washes his hands and sits in the only chair at the only table. Silk Fan sits on the brick kang and slowly eats a bowl of soup. Neither speaks throughout the meal.

When he finishes, Hero smiles. "So you can cook. That is harmonious."

She waits until he finishes his meal, tamps tobacco in his pipe, and lights it. She is tired and nervous, but she makes herself address him formally. Looking him in the eyes and then properly lowering her gaze, she speaks her request a third time.

"Mr. Hero of His People, I want to explain some things to you. I understand that you need a wife, but I am already married to my husband, Pride of His Father. Our two children are very young, and we do not have a grandmother to help with them. You seem to be a good man, and I am sure that there are widows who would gladly join you here in your home. I have a most serious request of you. I will stay here long enough to thoroughly clean your house and your courtyard, but I am needed at my own home. My husband and my second uncle will gladly repay all of your expenses if you will allow me to return to them."

Hero looks at his newly purchased bride. Slowly removing his pipe from his mouth, he answers her evenly, "You must know that what you ask is impossible. You will get used to living here. If you want, you can have another child. There is not that much work to do. There are only the two of us. My parents are now with the ancestors."

"My family needs me."

"Woman, I will not ask much of you."

Silk Fan strains to remain composed. With a face drained of color and energy, she looks directly at him and answers, "You ask for my whole life."

Hero turns his head away from her pleading face. He will not face her any longer. Hero has spoken.

Three times Silk Fan has explained about her married status, and three times this man has listened and denied her request. Reasoning with this man who purchased her will not be possible. She turns from the table and walks out of the door, looking for a place where she can grieve in solitude, but no such place can be found.

Sinking to the ground beside the rough bark of the tree on the far side of the courtyard, she leans her head back against it and sobs. Her aunt once called Silk Fan a triple joy; now she is to know triple grief. Angry, disheartened, and deeply grieved, she sits for hours in the courtyard alone. Still wearing the borrowed clothing, she is unconcerned about her appearance. The reality of her life overwhelms her now. Hugging her knees, she weeps; her tears drench the borrowed pants. She is helpless to change anything about her own future.

Moaning on behalf of her family in southern China, she cries more loudly. If this man named Hero dies tomorrow, would these hard people allow her to leave? She knows their dirty secrets of gangs of kidnappers who attack and steal innocent girls and women from their homes and transport them far away where they cannot be found. She knows why there is a shortage of wives. She wails, "I will never be allowed to leave this dreadful place."

As the moon rises in the sky, crosses the heavens, and pales in the light of the rising sun, Silk Fan sits against the tree, grieving for her family. Her shoulders hold the burdens of all of the young girls who are prisoners like she, a heavy burden of shame for her homeland.

After a night of deep sorrow, Silk Fan makes some decisions. Although the future looks bleak, work will now be the salvation of her sanity. If she could not return to her home family, then she could still claim something of herself. She could—no—she will farm, she will clean, she will cook, and she will sew. She will befriend the friendless. She will hold her head high, beg from no one, and live a useful life.

These uncivilized bandits have stolen her body, but they cannot steal her soul. She is still Silk Fan, daughter of an ancient house of China. She is determined to be what she has always been: an honest, talented, peasant woman, unafraid of work and determined to survive. When the sun rises to light the new day, she does not enter the meager house that must now be her home. Until the old man leaves, she will stay outside and find something useful to do. Taking a bamboo rake from the neglected shed, she attacks the far edges of the courtyard. *What must my family think? Would they know what has happened to me?*

After raking the courtyard area, Silk Fan walks to visit Summer Rain. She remembers that she took a folder of paper from one of the schoolbags.

"Greetings to you, Summer Rain."

"Greetings to you also, Silk Fan."

"How is your foot this morning?"

"It is no longer bleeding. It does not look serious."

"I am glad. Summer Rain, I have a need for something you have. Would you let me have some of the paper in your folder?"

"You know that you are welcome to it, my sister." They both smile at the reference to their sworn sisterhood.

Returning to her house, Silk Fan writes a letter to her husband:

Dear Pride of His Father,

I have some very bad news for you. I do not know whether or not you will receive this letter, but I must try to let you know of my tragedy. I was attacked and taken a very long way away. I am so sorry that I did not show more caution. I was tricked when I stopped to help an old woman. I was tied up and put on a boat moving upstream in the river, and then I was moved in a truck and then a train for a long way. We walked for two more days going northward.

Pride, I do not know where I am. This is a small farming village. Please do not be angry with me. You know how much I love you all.

Silk Fan

THE WEDDING

On the second day in this place so far from home, the five kidnapped young women prepare for their weddings. The villagers are meeting in the schoolhouse, waiting upon the arrival of a government representative who will officiate at the event. The school building is not a fine piece of architecture with columns and porches commanding respect, just a sturdy wooden building in the center of the village that serves as a school, courthouse, and meeting place for the small village. It is not well furnished but still has old-fashioned wooden benches. The kidnap victims and the families who purchased them meet in this building today. This is their first opportunity for all of them to meet together since their arrival.

While the village awaits the arrival of the government man who will officiate the wedding ceremonies, the young prospective brides sit together on a wooden bench in the school building.

White Flowering Tree is given an old, elegant robe as her wedding dress. The beauty of the robe is lost on its young wearer, who thinks of it as a used, out-of-date robe that her great grandmother might have worn. It is a frowning girl who seeks out her friend Silk Fan.

"Today is our wedding day. We should be joyful. My mother always said that she would send me from my home in happy clothes. She said that I would wear fine linens and something red for good luck. She promised me a new quilted jacket and pretty shoes. Just look at me now. I could be in an old opera. Silk Fan, please look at the back of my hair. The old mistress took my braids out and did something to it. How does it look?"

"Your hair is very pretty, White Flowering Tree. It is arranged in the way married women always wore their hair before the revolution."

"Do you know who these people are? Are they Hui people?" Beautiful Moon looks around the room.

"I do not know. Walks with Grace, do you think that they are Yi people?"

"I met some Yis at the university in my dance class. They were happy girls who liked music and singing and dancing. These people don't seem to be Yis."

White Flowering Tree studies local faces. "Perhaps they are Tu people."

Silk Fan frowns as she thinks of the next few hours.

"Please listen, my friends, I have something important to say to you."

All four of the younger brides gather around their friend Silk Fan.

"Tonight when he takes you to his bed..."

Groan. White Flowering Tree reacts.

"Shhh. I want to hear this." Walks with Grace shushes her.

"Listen. This is most important. The neighbors will be waiting to hear you."

Summer Rain asks, "Hear what?"

"Shhh, listen. When he takes you, it will probably hurt you. You must scream out in surprise and pain. When he has finished with you, wash yourself, and go to your courtyard and weep out loud for as long as you need to."

"What is she talking about?" It is Summer Rain again.

"This is a triple horror," Beautiful Moon speaks for them all.

"I wish that my mother had told me this," White Flowering Tree whimpers sadly.

"Please tell me what this private wedding matter has to do with the neighbors?" Walks with Grace demands a logical answer.

"Our land is so crowded that you will never have much privacy, but it is very important that you allow the neighbor to see and hear you cry tonight."

"Why?"

Silk Fan sighs. "The village wants to know that they have obtained unblemished goods. You want to prove that you are a virgin."

"Do you mean that the people will talk about us that way?"

Walks with Grace joins the conversation and almost shouts, "Wait one minute. We are taken from our homes, our property stolen, our lives destroyed, and they want proof of our virtue?"

"Please believe me. These people can be crueler than you can imagine."

Beautiful Moon listens with huge, disbelieving eyes. "How can it possibly be any worse? That is so disgusting."

The youngest, Summer Rain, asks quietly, "What is she talking about?"

No one answers her innocent query.

Silk Fan pleads earnestly. "Please remember what I have told you."

They are still girls, and so they put from their minds those things they do not want to think about. They inspect each other's wedding garments.

"Just look at us. We look like war refugees, not brides." Walks with Grace's anger shows.

"His sister brought me this outfit to wear, but I think that I

6

must return it after the wedding. I still have no shoes," Summer Rain says while looking down at her bare feet.

"At least someone thought to dress you for your wedding. I have nothing special to wear. I am still wearing my school clothes. Do you think that it is because the family is so poor or because they have no pride?" White Flowering Tree asks.

Walks with Grace answers through gritted teeth, "That family had enough money to purchase me from the gang of criminals!"

"Perhaps it is because the bride's family always pays for her clothes." Beautiful Moon clinches her hands together, not from cold but from fear.

Silk Fan is dressed in her gray outfit she wore on the long trip to this northern village. It is now clean, but it is not a wedding outfit. She sympathizes with them. "I am so sorry, dears. Hold up your heads. You are the prettiest brides they have ever seen."

Summer Rain says again, "I am so afraid."

White Flowering Tree says with tears brimming her eyes, "I wish my family was here."

Beautiful Moon repeats her wish. "I want to go home."

Walks with Grace says, "I still have not received a single wedding gift."

Silk Fan responds to them all, "You must keep telling him what you need."

"Silk Fan, he doesn't even talk with me. I do not believe that he knows my name." White Flowering Tree is miserable.

"Are you sure that this wedding is a good idea? We shall be legally tied to this foreign land of nightmares. We will never be able to return to our homes." Walks with Grace sees no solution in the weddings.

"My young friends, you must be brave. I am convinced that we would not be allowed to leave this place alive if we do not cooperate. From the start, we must demand that we be treated with respect. A wife is respected. A slave girl has no respect and no rights and still must serve her master in his bed."

"I do not see what difference it makes. I have not been treated with respect since my spring musical practice. It seems like a hundred years ago." It is the sensitive musician, White Flowering Tree.

"I thought that bed slaves and stolen wives existed only in stories." Summer Rain tries to understand the situation.

"We are being allowed to sit together now since the entire village is here to guard us." Beautiful Moon looks around at the full room.

White Flowering Tree answers, "My old mistress watches so closely that I had to write my letter to my parents while I sat in the latrine!"

"I had my letter written and hid it in my schoolbag, but it is not there now." Walks with Grace adds her comment.

Silk Fan explains, "She found your letter and burned it."

"I am just so afraid." White Flowering Tree and Summer Rain hold hands for comfort. "I am too."

Silk Fan gives her message one last time: "Remember that this may be our last chance to get away. This man has authority. Speak up to this government man!"

"What if he is like the policeman I spoke to? He refused to help me."

Silk Fan says earnestly, "All we can do is try."

"I want to go home," Beautiful Moon repeats her lament.

"We all want to return to civilization." Walks with Grace lifts her head defiantly.

"I want to go back to technical school." Summer Rain speaks firmly.

The official business begins. Parents and old aunts and uncles as well as wide-eyed neighbors crowd into the school building to see and hear.

He is only a minor authority, but he is still the authority on marriages here in this province. Every detail of his appearance is noted. He wears no uniform, except an official hat, but he wears his authority with an air of arrogance.

A local couple stands before him first. They are well dressed, and it is obviously a happy day for them. The young prospective groom's hair has been combed back with water, and the local bride's hair has been carefully curled, an unusual sight here. She is a local farm girl and turns admiringly to her chosen man, sure that she has the best choice of the entire village, and proud of his manly voice as he answers the questions.

Silk Fan states that she does not wish to marry Hero, but both he and the official laugh and reply that she is old enough and continue with the paperwork. Her protests are ignored as a joke.

The witnesses are hushed as this important ritual is dated and recorded in the government-issued notebook. Beautiful Moon, the loveliest bride, has long brown hair falling by her bowed head. She speaks so quietly that she is asked to repeat her name. She looks truly frightened, but the government cadre does not notice. His job is to write in his notebook and perform the brief ceremonies.

When it is the youngest girl's turn, she looks squarely at the well-dressed official and takes a deep breath. When asked her name, she announces in a clear voice, "My name is Summer Rain. My father is Middle Way. He owns a bicycle repair shop. My mother is Winter Rain. She is known for her silk weaving. I am thirteen years old, and I attend the city school of technology. My village is quite proud that I was chosen to attend this school. I do not wish to marry this man. I was stolen from the train station as I was traveling to class. I want to return to my home."

The crowd begins to shove and protest the fact that she has been allowed to continue speaking so long. The family that has paid for her is embarrassed and angry.

"Sir, what do you have to say to this matter?"

"She is just nervous. Her family made the proper arrangements."

"She appears quite young. What is her age?"

The uproar of protests from the crowd drowns out any one

voice. The marriage officer is proud of his position but has ridden into enough poor and remote villages to know what threats are behind every curve in the road. This is not a situation he enjoys. Local people still resent any interference in their affairs, regardless of the laws or guidelines. He raises his hand for silence and then asks everyone to leave so that he may interview the youngest and bravest of his problems for today. She stands motionless in the corner, showing more composure than either of them feels. He stands beside her and waits until all others leave the room.

The girl tells her story, "All of us here except the bride in the rose-colored suit with the small cloth buttons were kidnapped from southern districts. They have not spoken to our parents. These people have treated us shamefully. We are not brides. We are prisoners."

He looks perplexed, and for the first time he studies her face, her body, and her clothing. She cannot be twenty years old, the minimum age for marriage. She does not appear to be like any other bride he has ever seen. She is barefoot!

"Do you think our mothers would have allowed us to come to our weddings this poorly dressed?"

With shaking hands, Summer Rain removes a letter from under her clothing and hands it to the official. It is written in a schoolgirl's characters on cheap, lined school paper. She is aware that half of the village is watching through the window, but it never occurs to her to fear for the life of the official. She only knows that this is her chance to return to her home. "This is a letter to my parents. I am sure that they are quite worried about me."

The young official has his easy position because he can read. He does not know much about women's clothing, but this event is strange. Not only are the brides poorly dressed, something else is missing here today. There is no party atmosphere, and the brides are not smiling. None smiles except the one in the rose-colored suit. He believes this young girl, even if she had not written out her letter so carefully.

Summer Rain watches as sweat begins to appear on his upper lip. If he refuses the marriage applications of all five of these brides, he knows that he will not arrive safely back at home. He is aware of the practice of enslaving young women. That is one reason for his job. The purpose of the government policy is to postpone childbearing for five more years than was traditional in order to control the population as well as to utilize all these young women in the workforce. Here in the remote mountainous region, changes came very slowly. These people have brought brides to him today for legalizing their marriages.

He does not enjoy being in the middle of this situation. If his superiors discover the age of this schoolgirl or if her family succeeds in bringing other police here, it will mean trouble for him. He could lose this easy position and be forced to take a poorer-paying one, perhaps even a job requiring physical labor. This decision requires finesse. Drawing himself up to his full height, he admits the crowd standing outside. They all speak at once, and he again lifts his hand for order.

"Sir, I have reason to believe that this person is not of age. This violates the policy of our central government. A marriage to a child is not allowed."

The young man known as Mountain Climber came to the village schoolhouse today for his wedding. He is the first to comprehend the ruling. He followed the instructions of his elders, paid his city-earned money, and cooperated with the selection of his wife, and now an official with a notebook informs him that his wedding is not to be. He opens his mouth to protest, stuttering in disbelief.

The next person to understand rushes forward with a fury of words and protests, "Sir, this is my son, Mountain Climber. He is a fine farmer. Ask any person present. This marriage must take place. She is just nervous."

Before the entire crowd can begin its uproar again, the official announces that the other weddings will start presently.

Silk Fan walks to where Summer Rain stands and taking her hand says with a smile, "You have done it, my young friend. You are free. You will go back home!"

"Do you really think so?"

"You will stay at my house. Why are you crying? You are going home to your parents and friends. The official will contact your parents. You will be back home in a few days."

"Oh, Silk Fan, I told the official about all of us. Why didn't he let us all go free?"

"He is afraid. He is only one small man. We will give you letters to take back home with you. There is still a chance for us."

Silk Fan does not share her adult conclusions with the other brides but thinks her own thoughts as the ceremonies continue. *In an upside-down set of values, the victims will feel shame after this night, and their attackers will smile in victory. The most puzzling question left unanswered is why women who have not been treated with respect themselves so eagerly take part in the degradation and humiliation of other younger women.*

The five couples whose wedding applications have been approved stand in front of the government official in the neat clothes that have never seen mud or sweat stain. The brides are not as well dressed as he. The families and neighbors crowd shoulder to shoulder in the back of the room. They want no more problems. The ceremonies proceed with four of the five brides standing subdued and straight-faced through the formalities.

The official is eager to leave as quickly as possible while there is some confusion. Summer Rain firmly takes the hand of her friend Silk Fan and walks out of the building with her. The child gazes downward, refusing to look at the family who has paid their money to the gangsters for her life. If she had looked at her friends, she would have seen two young faces wet with tears. The third face is set in a stiff mask. Walks with Grace has been taught dignity.

Brides traditionally show a small amount of proper reluctance to leave their parents' home when going to their groom's family home, but this is not propriety, it is grief and horror.

The local couple moves on toward his family home, followed by a noisy group of family and friends. There will be food, laughter, songs, good wishes, and smiles at their home now. If they are lucky, some fireworks will splash the sky with lights. Every guest brings proper wedding gifts of linens, wine, kitchen utensils, candles, robes, and new tools. As the other three new brides go to the homes of their new husbands, some pretense of celebration prevails.

Walks with Grace receives a warm quilted jacket as a gift from her new husband's aged grandfather. It is not new, but it is still serviceable and pretty. He makes a traditional speech about what a happy day it is when a new daughter-in-law comes into the house. She smiles and thanks the dignified man for his kind gift. It is the only gift she receives this dreadful day. There is an awkward silence as water is offered with slices of dried fruit and thin crackers. After a time, the mother-in-law ushers her confused old father-in-law out of the door. Other arrangements have been made for the wedding night. The tall university student with the pleasant face looks perplexed. *I do not even have a nightdress.*

The newly married couple is left alone. Conspicuously absent are the brides' families and their gifts. Dressing a bride in the finest clothing affordable is an ancient custom ignored in this house. Her modesty is not considered, and her dignity is not honored. She is merchandise that has been bought.

When they return to the house, Silk Fan is surprised to find that they have wedding guests. Hero has said nothing about anyone coming.

"Hello. I am Heaven Sent, Hero's daughter. This is my son, Courageous, and my husband, Willing Worker."

Heaven Sent has large brown eyes and a center part in her hair that is brushed behind her ears. She wears a traditional garment in a yellow-flowered print. Her family is dressed in their best clothes, and they bring a gift to her father's new wife.

Silk Fan is astonished to discover that her uncommunicative Hero has a family. He quickly introduces Silk Fan and smiles at the boy of about six years of age who hides behind his mother's legs.

"We have brought boiled eggs and apple cider. This is for you."

Heaven Sent hands Silk Fan a gift of a willow basket filled with cotton towels. There is no place for sitting and entertaining guests except the one chair and the kang. Hero has made no preparations nor purchased any food or gifts for celebrating. They eat the refreshments Heaven Sent brought and visit briefly.

Surely they know the conditions of my coming here. Am I supposed to pretend that I am a normal bride thrilled with my marriage to this old man?

Summer Rain and the boy, Courageous, go outside to look for shooting stars. Heaven Sent asks Silk Fan, "Would you like for me to find a place for her to stay for the night? We have a friend, an elderly widow who will gladly allow her to stay with her until her parents come for her."

Silk Fan answers, "Thank you. I will see if she will do that."

At the home of the next wedding party, a small group celebrates.

White Flowering Tree's mother-in-law, Pure, who did not want to waste money on food for a party, smiles as she passes out platters of boiled bread to her guests. The groom stands proudly smoking a cigarette while the frightened bride sits alone on the platform bed of bricks. A prayer wheel spins endlessly. The family is happy with its good fortune. Only the bride is unhappy. White Flowering Tree still clasps her hands together tightly as she thinks, *Perhaps this is really a dream. Perhaps I shall wake up in my own bed in my parents' home.*

An old holy man in baggy clothes standing under a tree in

the family courtyard intones some ancient wish for a harmonious family and long life. He is given some coins before he moves on.

In another house only five lots down the road, the delicate beauty known as Beautiful Moon receives a wedding gift of eight candles in a wooden box wrapped in leather bindings. She knows that eight is a proper number for a gift. It is a lucky number. The food that some neighbors bring is eaten.

She smiles and thanks her sister-in-law for the gift and wonders, *Is this all of the gifts I will receive? Perhaps he will give me some nice gift to apologize for the horrors I have endured. He has barely spoken to me. Oh, I am so thankful that Silk Fan made me that nightdress from the tablecloth.*

With the papers officially stamped and the brief celebrations finished, the kidnapped girls from southern China begin their lives as married women.

Early the next morning, Pure, a new mother-in-law, is sweeping her courtyard when she notices an oddity by her door. There in a pile is a long braid of lovely black hair. Beside the braid lies her pair of scissors. She gasps in recognition of the meaning. If White Flowering Tree can no longer be the carefree schoolgirl wearing a long braid, then she certainly will not wear it as an announcement that she is a proud wife.

WEEK TWO

In the two weeks since Silk Fan arrived in this small farming village, she thinks of Hero of His People as her owner, not her husband. She does not honor him in traditional manners. She will not serve his meals properly, eat her meals with him, nor speak to him unnecessarily. She speaks in even, civil words but does not show his family respect.

When he sees her scratching a place to plant a few cucumber seeds next to their door, he informs her that he owns two private lots. One is usually reserved for wheat and the other planted in cabbages in the fall and mixed vegetables in summer. He is quite surprised to learn that his new wife has vegetable seeds in her possession.

"So you are a farmer, are you? You may plant your seeds in my cabbage field. I will take you there in two days."

Later, when he takes her to his cabbage field, she is amazed to see that he has plowed it. After smoothing her rows and carefully planting the seeds that her beloved second uncle gave her for her own farm, she remembers that many of her seeds now lie scattered on the ground where she was attacked.

He watches her plant her seeds and says, "If only half of these seeds produce, we shall eat better than most of my neighbors." Hero of his People smiles in satisfaction.

Seeing that she still has a few paper packets of seeds left, she looks around the field.

"What do you need now?

"I have some fine apple seeds. Do apple trees grow here?"

"For people lucky enough to grow them, apples earn a good bit of money."

"It will take a few years, but I might as well plant them. They are too nice to waste." *Surely I will not be here to see them produce fruit.*

He waves his hand in the direction of the northern end of his plot. "Why don't you plant your apple trees on the ridge at the far end of this field?"

She wonders if the wind will destroy her trees as she plants them high on the ridge. She finds space to plant five seeds in a row, where a plow could never climb. She has never seen such high, windy hills, nor planted in earth the color of yellow meadow flowers.

Returning to their home, she stoops to pick two different varieties of spring herbs. He just nods his graying head and smiles.

Keeping herself busy is a challenge for Silk Fan. She cleans and mends the garden shed and puts fresh wheat straw down on the earth floor in anticipation of a few fowl. After cleaning her house, she asks a neighbor where to find fresh reeds for making new bed mats. The woman does not answer. *Perhaps she is deaf,* she thinks. The kidnapped wife has no idea about the shunning practice of the village designed to force the new victim wives to depend upon their new families.

In spite of all of the neglect in her aged house, she still must look for ways to occupy her time. There seems to be no money for repairs, and this house is not difficult to keep. She decides to tackle what appears to be a pile of soiled clothing and rags that has occupied the corner of her house for too long. Even without a proper wash pot, she will have to launder the pile, finding it too discouraging to face this soiled heap each day. After filling her two buckets full of water and bringing them to her court-yard, she decides that she will wash everything in the soiled pile of fabric. *Surely most of this should be burned, but I shall wash it all before discarding any of it.*

He notices her activity and leaves to return with another man and a large black pot hanging between them. In the bot-tom lies a slab of homemade soap. He explains simply, "You might need this. I loaned it to a friend."

Before she can find fuel for her fire, a boy comes with an armload of wheat straw. Behind him walks Hero carrying a bucket of coal. Without a word, he lays the straw and coal in the center of the destroyed courtyard and builds a fire. Placing the pot onto the fire, he looks satisfied with his own efforts.

She smiles at the boy named Stands Strong and says noth-ing to Hero.

Hero instructs, "Get more water, and only stop when she tells you to." The neighbor boy continues to bring more water and carefully pours it into the big black pot.

Two hours later, Hero returns with four long bamboo poles used for drying laundry. Silk Fan maintains her silence and smiles only at the boy, not at Hero. Later, she will learn that her neighbors laugh at her efforts to wash her things right at her doorstep, since it is so much easier to use the canal.

She spends most of the day at this task. After drying the large collection of old clothes, rags and questionable linens in the sun, she brings in the stiff bundle and asks, "Which of these clothes do you wear?" Some of them seem too worn to be of any use; some were too dirty to come clean."

He chooses a few items and declares them his clothes. Then he explains a mystery.

"The weather gets very cold here in the winter, so I just put some of the old clothes and things on the floor to warm my feet."

"I see." This piece of information warns Silk Fan of the extent of the cold in this mountain village and another hint in how meager living conditions are in this place.

"Would you like for me to make you a pair of winter house shoes or a small rug? I can do either with this pile of discards."

The astonished man who has been a widower for too long answers, "Can you do that? I would like to have a warm pair of winter house shoes. What do you need for making them?"

"I will need a pair of scissors, needles, thread, a thimble, and some wool for warmth in the feet. And I need fabric for my own clothing."

Hero quickly removes all of the coins from his pocket and places them on the table where he eats his meals alone. "What a lucky man I am," he says aloud.

It is a few moments before Silk Fan realizes that she has willingly offered to help this man who paid criminals to kidnap her from her home and rob her of everything she loves. She shakes her head in amazement at her own words. After cleaning her cooking area, she pulls out the obvious rags and begins separating the pile of newly laundered fabric.

This can wait until tomorrow. I am tired now. I must have lost my mind. I just offered to sew for the criminal who paid for me. This pile will give me something to do while my dear second uncle's seeds sprout. I wonder if I can make a fresh cover for sleeping on that odd bed. How did anyone ever think of sleeping on bricks?

He will have a warm pair of winter house shoes, but they will not have any embroidery on them! Making his knee-length shoes will keep my hands busy.

The next day, Silk Fan smoothes pieces of worn-out bedding and clothing in two neat piles. She does not know why she made the offer to make him a pair of much-needed shoes, but she is to discover that this act of kindness will pay rich dividends. She is barely into the sewing project before she realizes that the small pair of scissors rescued from the schoolgirl's schoolbag will not serve to cut all of the layers of fabric she needs to complete her task. She must wait until she has sharp sewing scissors.

Realizing that this was never going to be a comfortable, well-furnished home, she decides that she cannot burn or throw away the remaining pile of rags and fabric. She has never worn rags but considers now the usefulness of the remaining discards. He makes no effort to purchase her any fabric or clothes for her own use. She shudders to think that it is because he has spent all of his money on her purchase price. This gives her much to think about as she slowly chooses the best fabric for Hero's shoes. As she carefully removes sleeves and smoothes the fabric into two layers, she saves the most complete shirts for other uses. *Are some of these things a woman's clothes?*

I will have to consider whether I am willing to wear his dead wife's old clothes.

Finding a woolen shirt that Hero has not declared his choice, she examines it carefully. The shoulders are torn, indicating to the talented young woman that it is too small for him. *This is salvageable for my own use if we do not have any more money soon.* As she views the pile, she reconsiders the use of each item. Some will have to be laundered two or three times more, but she keeps them anyway. She saves those pieces as she continues with the job of making something useful from discards. When finished, she has a clean stack of items that she can use if necessity proves as dismal as she imagines. She piles them in the corner of the kang from which they came, this time minus the accumulated dirt.

Taking a much worn and torn sweater to the light from her door, Silk Fan sits in the doorway to evaluate the strength of the old gray sweater. She pulls at several strands and decides that it is strong enough for reusing. *Knitting will keep my hands busy. I will begin knitting myself a wool hat. Pride of His Father will come for me before the snow falls.*

Working keeps her hands busy but not her mind. Winding the gray yarn into a ball, Silk Fan considers her immediate needs. She has the skill needed but no knitting needles. In her mind, her shopping list grows longer. The list is lengthy and expensive for even beginning to meet the basic needs of the meagerly furnished home. With a sigh, she wonders if these and other needs will ever be in her new home.

On market day later in that same week, Silk Fan thoughtfully considers her remaining seed packets. She has already planted all of the space that Hero allowed for her. Separating her treasures into two different groups, she speaks aloud, "I shall keep some of these to replant in case some seeds do not germinate, as I still have time for replanting this year. These I will part with. They are the only things that I have with which to bargain. I do not need them all, and I desperately need other things for my house."

Speaking aloud to her own ears helps her make the difficult decisions she must make in order to begin living in this new place. She carefully removes some seeds for replanting and leaves the rest of the pack for selling. Silk Fan does not realize that her reluctance to part with the extra seeds is an unconscious effort to hold on to the last symbol of her beloved home farm, but she is strong enough to realize that they are the only answer to her many needs. *Let me think, I need so much that it is difficult to decide what to ask for in exchange for my treasures.*

Taking one of her schoolbags, she places her seed packets inside and walks the short distance to the village marketplace. She is confident that someone will know the value of so many new seeds in this early spring.

She claims a position in the center of the wall where others will meet. Knowing that the other brides will come today, she spreads out her long mat beside her. On the faded schoolbag she lays out her vegetable seeds, as a noble woman displaying her jewels.

Two local women come by with their goods. They chatter while they spread out the items that they hope to sell. The first places a beautifully constructed bamboo birdcage holding a small finch with blue bars on its wings. *She must need money. Everyone considers the bird a fine possession.*

The other woman places a basket of brightly colored, hand-knitted long underwear in front of her. Neither speaks to Silk Fan.

A young woman brings a neatly tied bunch of slender bamboo poles. They will sell quickly today. New bean or cucumber plants will grow on poles such as these.

An older woman finds herself a place on the wall where people are standing about. She places four white eggs in her basket. They will sell today.

An older man wearing a once fine felt hat brings a splintered, wooden box and sets it down across the road, not with all of the women, but under a tree, where the older men of the village will congregate to gossip and play cards. Taking his time, he places his materials on the box and sits himself down with care. He is the respected village scribe.

Two young men come holding a large, steaming brass pot between them. A relative in a pink apron follows with a tin ladle in one hand and a stack of tea bowls in the other. They are the tea sellers. They will do well today. The two men leave the woman in charge of the family tea stand.

Two young women come with their mothers or mothers-in-law. They carry large baskets containing roots that were dug up in the hills above the village. The girls will visit for a while then go to draw water for the day. The older women are here to visit with their neighbors and to get the best price for their roots, favorites for traditional medicine.

A muscular young man wearing a plaid, woolen shirt comes next with a wide box full of baby chicks. A woman with a toddler on her back follows him. They hope to sell their new chicks today. A customer pays her money immediately and asks the seller to wait while she goes home to get a basket deep enough for her purchase of six of the peeping chicks.

A young couple comes by with several baskets for sale. Baskets are an inexpensive commodity, but there are dozens of uses for them, so if the price is low enough, they will sell. He is about to leave her when he sees the vegetable seeds spread out before Silk Fan. He asks if she will exchange some seeds for one of his baskets.

"No, sir. I do not need baskets, but I do need sewing scissors, cotton fabric, knitting needles, and new wool."

The young man is disappointed. He must sell some of his wares before he can purchase anything.

Silk Fan smiles and nods at the serious young farmer. Two of the women who have not spoken with the new brides exchange questioning looks.

Ignoring the tradition of snubbing new brides, the women both arise and go to see the display of seeds. "What kind of seeds do you have to sell?" It is plain that neither can read the labels.

"I have fine-running green bean seeds, good brown bush bean seeds, red and yellow pepper seeds, a few summer apple seeds, some squash seeds, and some melon seeds."

"How much do you want for your seeds?"

"I will exchange one packet for a set of knitting needles or three packets for a sharp pair of sewing scissors. I will exchange my apple seeds for ten needles and a spool of cotton thread."

The two local women exchange looks. This young woman knows exactly what she wants. She is not a typical bought bride.

"If you will save all of the pepper seeds for me, I will bring you a set of knitting needles."

"Do you have more than one set?"

"Yes, my mother-in-law has gone to be with the ancestors, and I have her set. I also have a set, and so does my daughter."

Silk Fan smiles and answers, "If you will bring me two pairs from which I may choose, then I will hold the pepper seeds for you for fifteen minutes."

The bird owner speaks next.

"I want the melon seeds and also the bush bean seeds. I do not think that they are worth a pair of scissors. I will exchange my lovely bird for three packs of your seeds."

"I do not need a bird. I need a pair of sharp sewing scissors." Silk Fan speaks politely but firmly.

The bird owner leaves and stands nearby as two men come over in a cloud of tobacco smoke. They discuss their childhood memories of food. "I remember eating yellow-meat melons at my grandfather's home. They were sweeter than honey."

"I remember eating some of those brown bush beans with onions and corn cakes. What good eating!"

The owner of the caged bird waits no longer.

"I have decided that I will give you my sewing scissors in exchange for three of your packets. I want the apple seeds and the bean seeds as well as the squash seeds."

"That is good harmony. The scissors must be sharp. I will hold these three packets for you for fifteen minutes."

Both women seem pleased with the agreement. The customer leaves in a hurry after asking her neighbor to watch her caged finch.

Silk Fan smiles at Walks with Grace, who arrives as the neighbor women leave.

"What a morning! If both of our neighbors return with their promised tools, I shall have had a successful morning. Oh, my friend, I have saved you some pepper seeds. I think that peppers improve any food on the table."

"Thank you. I shall find a place for planting them. Will you have any left after these two women claim their seeds?"

"Yes. I have two packs left that I plan to exchange for baby chicks."

Walks with Grace laughs and says, "You are a sharp swap artist."

Removing her two remaining seed packs from the display on her schoolbag, Silk Fan rises from the ground and approaches the woman selling the baby chicks. "Good morning. What breed are your chicks?"

"It is the kind we always have. They are brown with yellow legs." A few balls of fluff are drinking, and a few are walking in the water, but they all seem healthy to the southern farmer.

"I would like to swap four of your baby chicks for two of my packets of vegetable seeds. They are fine seeds. I have green beans and sweet melons."

"That is too high a price for my chicks. Would you accept two chicks for your two packets?"

Hesitating for the proper length of time for serious bargaining, Silk Fan agrees. Two for two will be a good exchange.

Smiling, Silk Fan returns to her post on the market wall and meets her first customer, who has just returned. "Here are my needles. Which do you like?"

Selecting a medium-sized pair of knitting needles, she gives her customer the desired pepper seeds. Next, she gives her friend three of the packets to hold. Taking the cotton schoolbag and the other two packets, she goes to claim her two peeping chicks. She chooses two lively ones and slips each down into her bag.

Other people are beginning to join the gathering. The second woman who offered to exchange her caged bird returns with her sewing scissors. She begins telling how fine her scissors are when Silk Fan touches the edge and dismisses her in midsentence.

"I am sure that they will do. Thank you."

She turns to give the woman her three chosen sets of seeds and says to Walks with Grace, "Please take my chicks, and do not allow that man on the bicycle to leave the market."

Her friend is startled to find herself guarding a pair of knitting needles, two chicks, and a pair of scissors. The next instruction puzzles her. Who is the man? What is happening?

She turns to see a stranger who has just arrived on a bicycle with a young girl perched behind him. He wears his best clothes for going to town, and she wears a poor child's faded dress. In her hair sits a large, pink flower. The lovely flowers grow in the hills, but why is this plain-looking child wearing it? Silk Fan is horrified at the sight.

The visitor purchases two bowls of tea and gives one to the child. He asks the tea seller where he may buy food. The tea seller does not readily understand his accent. He sees no food stands. Silk Fan forces herself to remain calm as she boldly addresses the stranger. "Would meat-filled rolls suit you, sir? I have some at my home if you will allow me a few minutes to get them."

He understands her speech. Perhaps he is a Wu man. "That would be happy harmony. We will wait for you here."

The pork-filled rolls were prepared for her noonday meal, but she will not eat them this noon.

"I shall return with your food in a few minutes."

Silk Fan leaves the area in a trot. She had no idea what the local custom was regarding adults running in public, but at this time, she is unconcerned about local protocol. She runs the last two blocks of her errand as fast as she possibly can. Retrieving all of her meager coins from her green cotton schoolbag hanging in the corner, she screams for Hero, who is in the courtyard evaluating how to reset the bricks. He is startled as he has never heard her raise her voice. Now she is running into the house and calling loudly.

"What is the matter?"

"Oh, Hero, give me all of your money! I will explain when I return."

He complies but has less than a yuan to give her.

She wraps the two meat-filled rolls and moves again. She is obviously disappointed with the amount of money and groans.

"This will never be enough." Turning quickly, she gasps, "Thank you, Hero."

Out of breath and distressed, she begins her return trip, running again.

Hero watches her leave and wonders about this latest surprise with his amazing new wife.

Slowing down, Silk Fan is relieved to see the man and his bicycle with the child still standing by the tea stand. Trying not to gasp for breath, she says as calmly as possible, "Here you are, sir. Enjoy the rolls." He thanks her and hands her ten coins in payment.

She nods, and making a great attempt at speaking in a casual tone, she asks, "How much do you want for the girl?"

"Oh, I do not know. She is my niece, and since both of her parents are now dead, she is my problem. I am keeping her brother, but I cannot feed a useless girl." Shrugging his shoulders, he continues, "Is there a singsong house in this village?"

"No. This village is too small for such a place. You will need to ride much farther to find a larger town for such a business."

"I will have to ride all day to find a town large enough to sell her. I have been traveling since morning."

Speaking as if this were the most normal business transaction in the world, she tells the stranger, "I will buy her."

"You will?"

Holding out her hand for him to see her coins, she asks, "Would you accept this money as payment? This is all of the money I have."

He looks at the money and considers how much longer he will have to ride to rid himself of his young niece. "If you want to take her, I will accept this." He pockets the coins. He is glad to find a customer for his unwanted niece. It will be years before she can marry.

Silk Fan states calmly, "I am going to need a sales receipt. Would you sign one? The scribe is there under the tree."

The well-dressed stranger speaks briefly to the orphan, who

holds everything she owns in a small, faded bag clutched tightly in her hands. She looks up at Silk Fan.

"Would you like to come with me?" Nodding her head, the thin child walks with the woman she has never seen to watch her official sale.

"Do you want to go with this woman?" asks the village scribe.

When the girl nods, Silk Fan gently removes the flower from her hair. Both the child's uncle and Silk Fan sign the dated document, and the stranger who has rid himself of an unwanted child pays the fee to the cigarette-smoking scribe.

The child's uncle rides off on his bicycle, which is lighter now. He does not look back. He eats one of the meat-filled rolls and slides the other one in a pocket, riding back home. Smiling her sweetest smile, Silk Fan leans down and asks, "What is your name?"

"I am called Humble."

"I am Silk Fan, and you are going to my house to live with me. Would you like that?"

The orphan child nods her head.

Silk Fan speaks softly, "Come with me. I want you to meet my friend." Taking the child's hand, she walks the short distance to the astonished Walks with Grace.

"Walks with Grace, this is Humble. Would you like to walk to my house with us? We are going home now."

Smiling at the new child and ignoring the neighbors, Walks with Grace picks up the knitting needles and scissors while Silk Fan gently lifts her bag of baby chicks. All three newcomers to this northern village walk back toward their new homes. All three carry small bags. Humble holds the hand of the woman called Silk Fan, who just this morning thought of herself as poor. Without considering her own limited resources, she saves an orphan child from a life of prostitution and gains a daughter. She does not labor over her decision.

"Walks with Grace, would you please show Humble where

my shed is located? These two baby chicks already have a warm place to sleep. Just place them gently on the floor."

While Silk Fan speaks to Hero about her purchase of an orphan girl, Walks with Grace escorts the quiet, thin child to the corner of the property, where they place the two chicks into their new quarters, the tool shed with holes in the roof and sides. Hero is astonished. He stops his bricklaying to watch them.

When Silk Fan brings an old pottery lid filled with water for her fowl, she finds Humble sitting cross-legged on the earth outside the shed, watching the baby chicks. The small chicks briefly examine their quarters and then close their tiny eyes. They are all three at home.

"Humble, thank you for watching the chicks. They will do well in this old shed. Would you like to help me cook some stew now?"

Silk Fan smiles and chats with her young adopted daughter as they cut up vegetables for their noonday meal. The child has little to say.

"When we finish making this food, we will begin sewing you a new outfit. We have a nice pile of fabrics we can choose from. Would you like a new pair of slacks and a blouse for school? I have saved some buttons we can use. We will also sew a warm pair of long shoes for you."

Hero of his People watches them and smiles.

The next day while Hero is in the fields, Silk Fan pens a second letter to Pride.

My dear husband,

How I wish that I knew whether or not you received my first letter which I sent with Summer Rain. Even the government marriage official agreed that she was too young to marry and said that she was free to leave. Her father and uncle came for her.

Now I must pay someone from another village to mail my letters. No one here can be trusted to mail them for me. Everyone here seems to know about the kidnapping conspiracy. There were four girls who were attacked and brought in with me.

At market today, I purchased an orphan from her uncle. She is too young for prostitution. I will give her to a local widow who has befriended us when I come home.

An old man purchased me. I am now his slave, but I will not kill myself. I will try to escape and return to you.

Your sorrowful wife,
Silk Fan

LAUNDRY DAY

In the first year of their capture, Walks with Grace looks for strangers who might be bringing her mail from home or officials who might come with word of her freedom. It is Tuesday, the day for geometry class at home, but here it is laundry day.

At the house of her owners, the tall girl removes her only outfit and slips into her quilted jacket and then wraps a bed covering around her bare waist. *I am almost naked, but my clothes must be cleaned!*

After stuffing her linens, dirty clothes, and those of her unwanted husband into a wicker basket, she follows Black Pearl down to the canal where her mother-in-law begins whining high-pitched, nonstop instructions and insults.

"Now first, worthless one, find a place where no one is working. Not over there, you stupid child. Find a better rock for scrubbing. Next, get each piece of your laundry wet. Use the stick to beat the soiled places. You are using too much soap. Just

CHINA'S HOPE

beat harder. Why are you washing your rags first? Don't you know anything?"

"Well, I..." Walks with Grace sighs and manages to hide her hurt. Intelligent and unaccustomed to such criticism, the young woman turns back to the cool water of the canal and continues to wash the clothing and linens just as she learned from her own mother. As a university student, she took care of her own laundry, study schedule, and money management.

The irritating rant goes on. "Well, get busy. Do as I do. Scrub each piece just so. Next, dunk it under the water and rinse it six times. Let me show you how to wring out the water. You are not paying attention to me! Stupid girl!" Her whine subsides to a mumble.

Why is washing dirty clothing such a problem? Back in southern China where the weather and the people were so warm and kind, laundry day was a pleasant outing. I wonder what tribe these people claim and why they are so unhappy. Perhaps they are Wei.

Walks with Grace looks across the way to see other women dipping their linens into the slowly moving water. Their naked young children squeal as they splash and play in the shallows. She folds her wet outfit, her husband's clothes, and her linens neatly into the willow basket. She finishes with a collection of rags, which she wrings out and places on top. There are none of her friends here today, just several of the neighborhood women. She begins her slow trek back up the hill toward her dreary new home, carrying a heavy load of wet laundry.

"Why don't you wait?"

"I have finished."

"What is your hurry? I have not finished and am visiting with the neighbors."

Quietly she answers, "None of them speaks to me. Why should I stay where everyone shuns me?"

"When you prove yourself, everyone will speak to you."

"So I will live in a village where everyone treats prisoner

97

brides with hatred? How shall I live in such an atmosphere? To die is my only hope."

"Hush, hush. Such foolish talk!"

Back at their house, Walks with Grace spreads out her wet laundry to dry and stares into space. She thinks of home and the young man who loves her.

Do my professors know why I am not in class? Will I ever see my love again? What must my true love think? How can I ever face him again? Will laundry ever be a pleasant time again?

THREE MONTHS
AFTER CAPTURE

In the three months since her capture in southern China, Beautiful Moon has not received any response to her letters that she sent with Summer Rain and a traveling merchant. There is still no word of comfort, nor has any family member come to take her home. She still wears her blue baker's uniform, faded by daily wear in the fields as she works beside her mother-in-law. One knee of her slacks was torn on her trip north, and she wears no shoes, in spite of the fact that the ground is rough. In years past, many poor people went barefoot, she knows. But Beautiful Moon, a city girl, thinks it primitive to go without shoes. Even though there is enough money for necessities in this home, the new bride's needs are not met.

Her mother-in-law, Double Joy, is up early, preparing food. She is anything but joyous as she says, "Get up, you lazy girl. We are going to the second mountain today."

Beautiful Moon tries to speak respectfully. "Oh? What is the occasion?"

"We are going to the old cemetery at Three Pines to honor our ancestors. Hurry up and help me pack the cabbage rolls I have made."

"I have nothing to wear. There will be other people there, yes? I still have no shoes. My clothes are not appropriate. I do not want to see people. I will just stay here for the day."

"Of course you will go. It will be mostly family."

Beautiful Moon smoothes her long brown hair back with her hands, picks up two baskets of food for the day, and follows her husband up the trail that leads to the high country. Double Joy, the mistress of the house, is the last to leave her house. She has changed her clothing from work clothes to a clean suit and carries food offerings for the dead.

The delicate young beauty wearing torn work clothes turns in astonishment from her glance at Double Joy to note that her husband is freshly bathed and wearing his other shirt. She sets her baskets down.

"You are both dressed for this event. Look at me. I am ashamed to go barefoot and in torn clothes to this place. It is not proper."

Key Keeper, the new husband, gives Beautiful Moon a puzzled look and says, "You look all right. Come; let us be on our way."

Like an obedient slave, she takes her baskets and follows him up a hill that drifts away from their village. He carries nothing in his hands. As they climb higher she pauses to admire the view, but the old woman will allow no such foolishness. As they reach a plateau where the wind whistles through the trees, the ancient cemetery is visible.

Walking the last rock-strewn yards, she is told how many family members are buried here. There is some entertainment in just being away from their house and seeing something different. This may turn out to be an interesting day, in spite of her clothing.

The old mistress seeks the best spot to spread out her meal. She settles on a large rock and then makes herself busy locating family graves and leaving offerings of small portions of bread neatly tied in leaves.

Beautiful Moon turns her head to look at her husband. They are so seldom alone. She smiles at him and wishes he would take time to visit and talk with her. Key Keeper does not appreciate either the smile or the treasure he has in his young wife. He has never learned how to treat women, and he has not had to court her or win her affection. He could be addressing an old friend or the neighbors when he says, "Wherever we sit, we will eat well today. I am hungry." He walks away to explore the ancient cemetery.

A tear rolls down her cheek. *How I miss having someone who will talk with me. Will he never want to spend any time with me except in his bed?*

More people come up the trail, some with children who play along the way, racing and hiding among the trees. A festive mood enlivens this day set aside for visiting and rest as well as paying respect to all of the ancients.

Others leave gifts of bread, fruit, flowers, or painted prayers on graves. The family of three sits down on the rocks to eat their prepared picnic. The old mistress offers her son, Key Keeper, the pork pies first. He takes three. Next, she serves herself two of the special treats. Beautiful Moon is served the remaining one. They eat their meal in silence. The food is good, but it is not like the food served at her mother's table. Beautiful Moon keeps thinking of mealtime at her home when her father laughed and teased her mother and people were happy.

A small group of relatives comes near, a young woman with a two-year-old son dressed in bright colors. The young mother wears a lovely yellow outfit, complete with fine leather shoes. Beautiful Moon has not seen any like them since she was in the city taking painting lessons. She watches the stylish young woman with her child until her husband in a silk shirt and belted trousers joins her.

Beautiful Moon gasps. She stares but cannot speak. She covers her mouth with both hands. *It is not real. He was one of them!* Her heart pounds furiously. *I know that man!* When she can trust herself to speak, she asks, "Mistress, who are those people?"

The old mistress barely looks up. "Oh, they are just cousins, Swift Horse and his wife, Laughing Stream. They live only a short distance away in another village."

Beautiful Moon is determined not to cry, but the longer she watches all of these people go about their day, the angrier she becomes. Finally, she can tolerate it no more. She rises and walks past the old women gathering to gossip, steps around the children playing on the rocks, and speaks to the smartly dressed young woman very near her own age.

"Hello. I am Beautiful Moon. Your suit is lovely. Have you had it long?"

"Hello. I am Laughing Stream. My husband bought it for me not too long ago. After he returned from a business trip, he brought me this suit and these shoes to match. He is so good to me."

As Laughing Stream bends down to dust dirt from her toddling son, a slim silk braid swings from her neck, suspending a single piece of carved white jade. Seeing the jade, Beautiful Moon becomes nauseated, but she controls her anger as she asks quietly, "Was the jade pendant an apology gift?"

Without thinking, Laughing Stream answers with a slight smile. "Yes."

"Did he call you a stupid pig and a lazy, worthless mud carrier?"

"Why yes, he did, but how did you ... "

"Does he beat you?" She stops tending her child and stares at Beautiful Moon. This conversation has ceased being idle talk between young wives and turned into rude, embarrassing questions.

"Why do you ask these things?"

"Because he called me these names when he tied me up and beat me with a whip."

Laughing Stream drops the cloth she has in her hand and stares in shock.

The captive wife from far away in the south has been trying to live in peace with a husband and family forced upon her. Today is humiliating enough before seeing the kidnapper the girls named "Half Man" because of his cruelty. She now vents all of her fury on his fashionably dressed wife.

"Where do you think your man got the money for such beautiful clothes and fine shoes? Did you ask him that? He did not make that kind of money selling cabbages! That business trip was a kidnapping trip to steal innocent girls away from their schools and families. Those empress's clothes were paid for by this immoral family to procure unwilling slave brides. Look at me! Your man beat me and stole everything I had. I have nothing! My friends named him Half Man because he was so mean."

Beautiful Moon breaks into unbidden sobs. "And you are wearing my grandmother's jade pendant. I braided the silk thread, just as she instructed."

"What are you saying?"

The crowd cannot ignore her sobs. They begin to come closer.

"The dark line is carved as a lizard sitting on a leaf."

Laughing Stream holds her pendant in shaking fingers. The lines are finely carved and can only be identified upon close inspection. This sobbing wife of her husband's cousin is telling the truth! She sits in shock watching the shabbily dressed relative cry. Her toddler son wanders away.

The man called Swift Horse brings his small son back to his wife and reprimands her, ignoring the ill-clad, crying young woman until she screams at him. "You are a pirate! You are a thieving excuse for a man! You beat young girls. You will never have enough gifts to satisfy your ancestors. You have brought shame to all of them. How can you pretend to honor them? You have no honor! You stole me from my parents' home, took all that I had, and your wife wears my grandmother's jade! How can you show your face in public?"

Shaking with fury, clinching her fists against her sides, she leans forward and spits out, "This is a crime against the peace! It is a crime against the good name of China!"

She shakes her head, grits her teeth, and continues in an unaccustomed scream, "I did not just fly in like a migrating bird and drop from the sky! My capture was a planned attack funded by this family! This is a crime against our nation, against innocence, and against me personally!"

Beautiful Moon looks directly at the silk-shirted kidnapper, thrusts her head forward, and points a thin, trembling finger heavenward. "This is a crime against girls and women the world over. It cannot be ignored. It is against the laws of the land and against the laws of decency. You are guilty of this crime, and *you* are not forgiven."

As Beautiful Moon's long frozen voice reaches a crescendo, she gets a hard slap to her face. Her mother-in-law will not allow her to continue. Her old voice is like stone saying, "It is such a nice sunny day, and you have spoiled it by your ranting."

Everyone on the mountain hears those screams. The holiday mood broken, people start to leave in embarrassment. This new bride has broken all rules of propriety with her rude screams. The gangster husband takes his son and roughly drags his well-dressed wife away. He says nothing. Their picnic basket and napkins lie scattered on the rocks.

Rather than reply to any of the charges, her mother-in-law busies herself with the task of gathering up her things into her basket. Key Keeper cannot dismiss the charges so easily. He stares as if to say: *What do I say? What can I say? Where did my lovely wife get such fire in her? She has been here three months, and she still thinks of me as a criminal!*

Sitting on the ground where Double Joy's blow has thrown her, she turns to her husband and says, "You are guilty of this crime, and you are not forgiven! You did not even allow me to say good-bye to my father."

Some people are still nearby. Double Joy hurries over to shush the barefoot girl who now sits on a rock sobbing on her drawn-up knees. "What do you mean causing such a scene? What will people say? You are a worthless girl. Get up!"

She does not get up. She sits rocking herself with her tears soaking her cotton slacks. No one comes to give her any comfort or say any kind words. As she has so many times in the last three months, she repeats, "I want to go home."

She means, of course, home to people who love and respect her, home to the south, where civilization and humanity reigned in her happy childhood, home to her aunt's bakery shop.

"You are all mad. Surely this is the land of haunting spirits. How can so much evil thrive? How can so many people be so cruel? Laughing Stream is wearing my grandmother's jade pendant. He took it from around my neck when he tied me up." She whimpers as tears run down her pretty skin.

The embarrassed mother-in-law pulls up a small seedling pine tree and threatens her with it. Her gutless son says something for the first time.

"No. Do not beat her. You go on home. I will wait for her."

The old woman mutters, "Worthless girl." She grumbles all the way to the crest of the mountain.

Key Keeper stands looking out over the mountainside. Everyone else has left. He still does not hold her nor wipe her tears. He never acknowledges the truth in any of her statements. He stands waiting on her until the sun approaches the horizon in the distance.

Finally, he says, "We will have to walk in the dark if we do not begin soon."

"Just leave me here. I belong among the dead. I have no hope. Let me die here. None will grieve my death. None will bring gifts to my grave. Please let me die."

Key Keeper does not answer except to take her arms and pull her to a standing position and turns to walk slowly.

"Come, it is time to go home." He walks her slowly toward the trail that leads to the only place he has ever lived.

The lovely bride who is known for her beauty stumbles barefoot across the stony ground, still sobbing after her husband, the stranger, down the mountain trail. He seems not to hear her moaning, "I have no home, only a prison."

The following week while sitting with her friends at a sewing lesson, Beautiful Moon is free to write. Her embarrassment and grief have opened the well of her creative talents. The young baker who has no oven finds paper and a pen and writes her thoughts.

LOSSES

I will never feel my father's hand,
Nor hear my grandmother's blessing,
Or wear her jade,
Or hear kind words,
Or laugh,
Or be dressed as a bride,
Or walk in wet rice paddies,
Or giggle with girl friends,
Or wear pretty clothes again,
Or wait with joy for my lover,
Or smile with pride at my man.

Beautiful Moon walks to Silk Fan's home and hands her the poem. She does not even speak as she delivers it to her friend for safekeeping. Silk Fan reads the latest of Beautiful Moon's poems and shakes her head. She recognizes the works as honest reflections of her grief and admires her creativity, but she worries about the future of this girl who only wanted to bake bread and marry a man of her approval. She sadly places the poem with her own latest letter to Pride of His Father. At this time, she lacks the money for stamps or envelopes and bribe money.

GRIEVING

The four captured brides are meeting at the home of Silk Fan to learn how to make meat pies rolled in a wheat crust. The three visitors bring a roll of pork sausage and a few vegetables that they will take home in tasty pies for their families. Humble is in school, so Silk Fan is their teacher this morning.

White Flowering Tree's mind is not on cooking. "Do you know who these people are? They speak so strangely that I fail to understand some things they say."

Grating carrots for her pies, Walks with Grace completes her task before answering her friend. "I fail to understand sometimes also. I must really listen in order to follow the conversation."

As she folds herbs, carrots, and onions into her circular pie shells, Beautiful Moon joins the conversation. "It is easy for me to understand. They want me to do something. They want me

to carry this, lift that, move this, cut that, load it, dig somewhere, empty something, and do it again and again."

"Do you think that they will ever say thank you?" White
Flowering Tree asks.

Walks with Grace adds, "Or say, 'You did that well'?"

Beautiful Moon places both flour-dusted hands on her hips
and pronounces, "They will smile and thank us only when the
moon and sun collide."

Silk Fan asks the question all want to know. "Do you think
we are still in China?"

Beautiful Moon shrugs her shoulders, and White Flowering Tree concludes, "We could be in Mongolia. These people do
not speak any Chinese language I understand."

They continue rolling wheat flour into even sheets and mix-
ing the sausage with herbs and vegetables while all four ponder
the questions. The sizzling pan releases fragrant steam when
the individual pies are fried.

White Flowering Tree complains, "His mother has yelled
at me three times already this morning. My own mother never
yelled at me. I hate this place and the people in it."

Silk Fan, truly concerned about the constant negative feelings and sanity of the stolen brides, speaks up. "My friends, this
grieving cannot continue. It is destroying us. Every single day
each one of us must think of something good. We must not stop
until we find something good."

"Something good? Like a train ticket to Hunan?" It is lovely
Beautiful Moon expressing her frustration.

Bitterly, White Flowering Tree retorts, "Something good,
like suddenly going deaf?"

Walks with Grace speaks out. "Listen to Silk Fan."

"You know that there is nothing good for us in this cruel
place," White Flowering Tree persists.

"We must find something pleasing. We must change our
thoughts. The widow says that the creator, God, made us in his
image. We can thank God that we are healthy. Think about the

breeze at evening. It is good. The cranes flying overhead are graceful. Stay busy with gardening, sewing, or children. These are good things." Silk Fan tries to smile.

"You are all my good friends," Walks with Grace joins in. "That is a good thing."

"These pies look fine. Learning to cook is good." Beautiful Moon smiles.

Silk Fan announces, "Next time we meet, we will speak about the good things you have discovered."

"My list will be very short." White Flowering Tree refuses to think positively.

"Please try."

As they depart to return to their separate homes, Beautiful Moon hands Silk Fan a slip of paper. "Here is another poem I have written. It is not about good things."

THE SNOW IS GONE
The snow is gone.
Cherry blossoms are in bud.
Grass turns from brown to green.
Herbs and wildflowers crowd the path.
Why am I the only one dead?

Beautiful Moon gives the verses she writes to her friend Silk Fan for safekeeping. They release her pent-up feelings of her anger, grief, and rebellion. This small project of finding something good in their lives is meant for Beautiful Moon as much as any of the others.

"Tomorrow, if it is clear, I am going to collect grass and small limbs for my fires. You are all welcome to come with me. Bring a knife blade and a harvest basket."

"Thank you, Silk Fan. You are the good thing in my day." Walks with Grace-thanks her friend.

My darling Pride of His Father,

I, along with the other captive girls, am trying to return home by speaking to officials. We spoke to the local cadre, the village chief, the elected committee, and a marriage officer as well as the schoolteacher. None of them will help us, so we do not know what to do.

One young woman named Beautiful Moon has tried to leave several times and is caught and returned severely beaten each time. On market days, we look for people willing to speak to us or take our letters out of this village where everyone seems to be our guards.

People here speak strangely. It is still hard to understand them.

I am being brave for your sake. Pride, I love you more than ever.

Silk Fan

SEWING LESSONS

hite Flowering Tree gives the bedding a shake, folds it, and hurriedly places it against the wall at the end of the family kang. This is one of the two mornings each week reserved for sewing. Her mother-in-law gives her prayer wheel a spin and sniffs in displeasure at the eagerness with which the young, captured wife prepares to leave, but she says nothing. This morning's absence allows a time of relaxation for her also, as it will be unnecessary to guard White Flowering Tree for a few hours. The entire village will watch as all four of the new bought brides meet at the home of the elderly Han widow. This is an opportunity for the mistress of the house to sit and smoke with her friends while they complain about the difficulties of having a daughter-in-law.

White Flowering Tree brushes her hair back with her hands and picks up her sewing supplies. Hurrying down the dirt road, she passes a toothless beggar woman and wishes she had something to give her. The thought comes unbidden, *At least she can sleep with whom she pleases.* A holy man who stands by a neighbor's wall appears to be talking to the air. She ignores his monotone recitation and moves by him. As she climbs the outside staircase, she hears feminine chatter. She greets the other seamstresses and realizes she is smiling. *Perhaps all life has not been stolen from me.*

Silk Fan is speaking. "It is difficult to imagine that the weather will be so cold here that we will need this heavy padding on our feet." Others nod in agreement.

"How I wish my mother could see my shoes. They really are going to be quite pretty," Walks with Grace comments.

White Flowering Tree shrugs her shoulders and adds, "I am glad my grandmother cannot see my work. It is not as fine as her sewing."

Walks with Grace looks up from her stitching and says seriously, "I have a question."

The widow asks, "What is it?"

"Why is everyone here so difficult to know?"

White Flowering Tree joins in her inquiry. "Yes, why are people so unfriendly?"

"Why is the whole village cold toward us? They speak to each other, just not to us. They do not approve of us."

White Flowering Tree explodes. "How can they disapprove of me? No one here knows me! No one knows where my home is. No one knows I write poetry. Not one person has asked what food I like. No one knows that my mother's name is Fragrant or that I play lovely, traditional music. No one knows that I like peonies, and no one cares!"

The upstairs porch is suddenly quiet. Once again the chatter has turned to a sad discussion. Each of the brides has a similar story. The widow, their sewing instructor, speaks quietly in her refined voice. "I believe I can explain this mystery to you."

"Please tell us." Silk Fan speaks first.

"Yes, tell us. We try not to offend anyone." White Flowering Tree is serious.

The elderly woman who was brought to this village with proper ceremony years ago as an honored, legal bride with many gifts remembers the shunning of her first year. "There is an old idea that you must be made to depend upon your family so that you will be faithful to them. After a year or two, when you are obedient and respectful enough, people will begin to speak to you."

White Flowering Tree understands immediately. "They plan to break our spirits!"

Walks with Grace almost whispers, "I understand. They will speak to us only when we have babies and cannot leave this place."

Silk Fan concludes, "That is incredible!"

Walks with Grace, the analytical university student, asks, "Why will we want to speak to any of these people who have been a part of such a cruel conspiracy?" Silence is the only answer to this appropriate question.

As the weeks pass, a pattern is established. The widow faithfully copies Bible verses from the speaker on her radio, who daily reads a new verse in a slow, deliberate voice. She and her helper, a neighbor named Diligent, prepare the verses for the benefit of the brides. Each sewer settles down with her many colored threads, decorating the outside of her winter shoes while listening to Diligent read from the collection of Bible verses their hostess saves so carefully. The brides bring the agreed-upon coins each lesson, and she in turn pays Diligent a small amount, reflecting the low value placed on women's skills.

Diligent needs friends because she has committed the crime of not producing a baby in the five years of her marriage. It has not occurred to the community to ask the unimaginable question; could it possibly be her husband's fault that no baby has come?

What seemed like a diversion or welcomed mental stimulation at first is now studiously considered. All listen intently. The subject of today's reading is love. Frown-crossed brows await the few verses to be heard today.

White Flowering Tree grits her teeth. *I know one thing. I*

am not willing to give up my one claim to myself, my anger! I have every right to be resentful and angry! These crude people with no morals, and no manners either, should be rightfully asking for my forgiveness.

Beautiful Moon is creeping slowly up the steps. As White Flowering Tree watches her friend, she decides not to voice her resentment while Beautiful Moon is being treated so shamefully. Arriving late because her latest battering has slowed her ability to walk, she holds her left arm to her body and grimaces as she sits on the wooden bench. The widow asks about her injuries, but the beauty with the dainty face doesn't speak. *It is obvious that she has been beaten again.*

White Flowering Tree jabs her needle into the side of her shoe, sewing on yellow chrysanthemums with a vengeance. *This truly is a mad place. Just when a brief hour removes the gloom, something brings it back with a thunderous storm of horror and pain! How could anyone treat this guileless girl with such cruelty? She only wants to go home.*

Beautiful Moon speaks in a quivering voice, "They made me come today." Their lovely young friend sits with her head bowed, holding her injured arm to her side. Her winter shoes are left untouched beside her. Tears run down Walks with Grace's face. After a while, she picks up one of Beautiful Moon's shoes and begins to hem the knee-high tops with neat satin stitches. Silk Fan takes her other shoe and threads a needle with a bright pink thread and then deliberately embroiders a rosebud, complete with a sharp thorn.

Silk Fan keeps her head down, unable to look at the pain-bound face of the fairest one of the brides. *If she tries to run away again,* they think, *she will at least have warm winter shoes.*

The conversation freezes as this new reminder forbids their speaking. Their needles move in and out. They dare not look at each other. They are trying so hard to hold in the tears, even screams. They all want to run away. How can they comfort poor Beautiful Moon?

The widow speaks, "Diligent, will you read to us? We will study love another time. I think we need something else today. Please find the papers where I copied the psalms. We want chapter three."

While the passage is being found, White Flowering Tree whispers, "Why did they make her come when she is in such pain?"

"Shh. She was sent as a warning to us all." Walks with Grace understands.

Diligent begins reading aloud in a clear voice, "The book of Psalms, chapter three."

"Oh, Lord, so many are against me. So many seek to harm me. I have so many enemies. So many say that God will never help me. But Lord, you are my shield, my glory and my only hope. You alone can lift up my head ... I cried out to the Lord and he heard me from his temple ... Then I lay down and slept in peace and woke up safely, because the Lord was watching over me. And now although ten thousand enemies surround me on every side, I am not afraid. I will cry to him, 'Arise Oh Lord!' Save me oh my God! And he will slap them in the face breaking off their teeth. For salvation comes from God. What joys he gives to all his people. Oh Lord, you have declared me perfect in your eyes, you have always cared for me in my distress; now hear me as I call on you again. Have mercy on me. Hear my prayer."

Psalm 3–4:1

Beautiful Moon speaks so lowly that she is almost not heard. "Could you please read that again?" All three of her friends nod to their teacher, who nods consent to her helper, who begins anew to read deliberately:

"Oh Lord, so many are against me. So many seek to harm me. I have so many enemies. So many say that the Lord will never help me. But Lord, you are my shield, my glory and my only hope. You alone can lift up my head ... " (Psalm 3:1–3).

Diligent continues to read the verses from the psalm slowly while all present weep as they pretend to sew.

Diligent puts her handwritten pages down and painstakingly copies the third chapter of the book of Psalms in neat black ink. No one asks that she be given any verses today. Each knows that Beautiful Moon needs the entire chapter for herself. Diligent wants to hurry to complete the assignment, but she knows this will only mar the characters. She copies all of the verses and the first verse of chapter four where Beautiful Moon stopped her.

Anger turns to fury. Hatred boils inside of White Flowering Tree, who does not speak but purses her lips and narrows her eyes in hatred against the people of this monstrous place. The wise old woman prays, "Lord, I have seen happier people at funerals. Please teach me how to help them." After two more hours, she says pleasantly, "I look forward to seeing all of you next time."

Silk Fan, Walks with Grace, and White Flowering Tree escort the battered Beautiful Moon back to the place she must now call home before returning to their own. It is a show of support, even if it is small. Diligent says her farewells and then leaves. She does not have to explain that it is not in her best interest to be seen openly with the kidnapped brides while her family honors the silent treatment of new brides.

Silk Fan is the first to arrive at their next sewing session. She does not need the sewing instructions but desperately needs the friendship of the other seamstresses in the twice weekly sewing circle. Her warm winter shoes are almost ready for the leather worker to sew the soles onto the leggings. After hemming the tops, she removes scraps of fabric from her bag and begins cutting out doll clothes. Unwilling to do this work when Hero is present, she takes this opportunity to begin her project.

"Have you finished your shoes, Silk Fan?"

"Yes."

"May we see them?" They are excited to see the first of their work completed.

It is Walks with Grace who first exclaims, "What beautiful work you do, Silk Fan!"

White Flowering Tree admits, "I fear that my work looks very childish compared to yours."

Silk Fan, the softhearted diplomat, answers, "Your shoes are very nice, and they will keep you warm too."

The widow asks, "What are you working on now?"

Hesitating a moment before answering, Silk Fan says, "It is a sleeping doll for my daughter at home."

Walks with Grace gasps and quietly begins to weep.

Her friends exchange glances and then ask, "What is the matter?" She cries all the more.

"I think I am pregnant."

"Ah, you poor dear." The motherly Silk Fan offers sympathy.

White Flowering Tree stumbles over her words, "Uh, I have something to tell you. I am too. I will have a baby next spring."

Unsure how to respond to this news, no one says anything for a minute. This should be a joyful day. These new lives are unwelcomed because it means that their kidnappers have won. The plan for captive brides is working. They are to be too pregnant to travel, too poor to try, and too involved with a baby to leave. This village of few girls now has wives for their sons, mothers for their grandchildren, and workers for their fields.

Silk Fan finally speaks. "We will raise these little ones together. I know how to make baby clothes. We must hurry with our winter shoes because we have much sewing to do. We will make pretty things for these new babies."

White Flowering Tree tries to explain her feelings, "I am still a schoolgirl. I don't know anything about babies."

Silk Fan is quick to answer, "We will all help you."

Bowing her head, she says, "I wish I could tell my mother." No one has an answer to that heart cry.

All four of the brides have written letters and paid travelers to deliver them. None has received answers. Were they all confiscated before they left the village?

Silk Fan composes another letter and encloses it in a package for her two children.

Dear Pride of His Father,

I am making our precious children toys so that they will know how much I love them. I am also spinning wool and will try to knit hats for them before winter.

I see your face in everything I do.

Silk Fan

BEAUTIFUL MOON

Her parents named her Beautiful Moon as a proper traditional name, but the name is unnecessary for drawing attention to the fact that she is truly a beautiful young woman. This week, she needs the advice of her older friend, Silk Fan, a farmer's wife who knows how to stay busy and make life a little more bearable.

Beautiful Moon has spent this week collecting branches for making a fence to enclose a mail order of baby chickens and ducks that should arrive shortly. She examines her scratched arms and work-worn hands. Silk Fan told her to ask for these chicks and ducklings, and she is glad to discover that no one has volunteered to help her because that means that she is free of the constant company of her critical mother- and sister-in-law. After assembling her supplies, she dutifully tells the old mistress where she will be. "I am going to see Silk Fan. I will return shortly." *I wonder when they will stop watching my every move.*

Silk Fan sits outside her doorway sewing. She places her sewing down as she sees Beautiful Moon approach.

"Hello, Silk Fan."

"Greetings to you, my dear friend."

"I have collected the sticks and rocks as you instructed me. Now I need help in building the enclosure. Can you spare the time to show me how?"

"Of course I can."

As they walk the short distance, Silk Fan tries to encourage Beautiful Moon, seeing her unhappiness. "You will enjoy having the small chickens and ducklings. They will grow quickly, and when the ducks are larger, you will take them down to feed on the grass by the irrigation ditch. This will allow you to get away some time each day."

"This is good, Silk Fan. I have helped my second aunt with her chickens. Tending fowl is not hard work, but surely I am wasting my professional training as a baker. When I asked if there was a bakery here, my mistress became angry and yelled at me. She does not like for me to talk. I think she believes me critical of her village."

"What would you like to do, Beautiful Moon?"

"I really enjoy baking bread. I make very good rolls and sweet cakes too. I would also like to paint, and sometimes I write poetry. Isn't that silly? Painting lovely pictures of flowers and birds in this drab place of grays and browns?"

"Do not give up those ideas yet. We can purchase some nice paint and paper with our first egg money."

The two young women work together on their project for two hours. Schoolboys stop to watch. They think it amusing that these foreigners are making such work of a chicken pen. Many people just allow their fowl to run free in the yard, courtyard, road, and in the house.

Silk Fan finally says, "We still need some more long sticks. Little chicks can get out of small places."

"Thank you, Silk Fan. I have taken enough of your time. I

see how the work is done. I can finish it now." Beautiful Moon examines her scraped and dirt-packed hands. "No one would ever guess that I am a baker now, but would you please ask to see whether there is an oven anywhere in the village?"

"Yes, I will. There seems to be plenty of wheat here. Some hot, baked bread would be a luxury."

"Good-bye, my friend."

"Farewell, Beautiful Moon."

The enclosure is not elaborate but will serve her well. Her new chicks and ducklings will not be chased by the neighbor's dogs, nor will they be stepped on.

After washing my arms and hands in the pump, I will write a poem. She finds herself alone in the house, so she takes out a small notebook and writes.

VILLAGE SOUNDS
Ducks quacking,
Chickens clucking,
Children shouting,
Pumps grinding,
Water splashing,
Wheels squeaking,
Brides crying.

BIRDS
The small brown bird is busy building her nest.
Shiny blackbirds chatter in delight of spring.
The graceful blue heron stretches his long wings to fly away.
The yellow bird flies from place to
place searching for a home.
Oh, why could I not be born a bird?

MUSICIANS IN THE
MARKETPLACE

Some days at the market are boring after the first rush of customers, so villagers bring busywork to occupy their hands. They spin, knit, or work on needlework or carving. Other market days are exciting with visiting jugglers or traveling merchants in colorful ethnic costumes, selling their wares of rich rugs or beautiful fabrics.

Silk Fan sits quietly next to her friends. She has nothing to sell but comes to keep her friends company. There is much work in her vegetable garden that pleads for her attention, but she remembers her vow to be a sworn sister to these fellow victims. As her young friends sit, awaiting customers for their eggs, Silk Fan patiently carves on a piece of soft wood. The work is slow, and no one thinks it resembles a doll yet, but Silk Fan works with steady movements of her knife, letting small slivers of fragrant wood chips fall to the ground. When it is sufficiently shaped, she will wrap it in wool and sew miniature clothing in a tradition of mothers who make dolls for their daughters. She has already finished a carved toy duck for her son.

They examine every new figure on the horizon, fresh hope springing with each man who comes along. Surely some official with authority will come soon. Even though they all are living as wives, surely their parents must know how desperately they wish to return home.

Today there are new faces at market. Two local men are speaking to a group of young people whom the brides do not recognize. Three boys and two girls about their own ages, as well as an adult man, stand talking.

"Who do you suppose they are?"Walks with Grace asks.

Silk Fan answers, "I have no idea. I have never seen them."

The musician, White Flowering Tree, exclaims excitedly, "Look. They have musical instruments! I wonder what pieces of music they played in their spring concert. Let's go ask them."

"White Flowering Tree, wait!" It is too late. These visitors are the most interesting people to come here since she was captured. Lightness in her step, she quickly walks past the card-playing men to meet with the strangers.

"Beautiful Moon," Silk Fan says sternly, "you stay right here."

With a smile glued to her face, Silk Fan walks the few steps to where White Flowering Tree speaks eagerly with the group of visiting students, thrilled to find fellow musicians with their instruments. She is watching a girl remove a three-stringed musical instrument from its case when Silk Fan stands close and firmly takes her arm. "White Flowering Tree, I'm sure these people don't have enough time to answer all of your questions. Let's go now."

"Oh, but they are all music students. They have been living in town with an uncle and are home for the season. They have just finished their spring concert. He plays the one-sided drum and gong, and she plays the lute, and he plays—"

Silk Fan tries to dismiss the visitors. "Welcome to our village. Please excuse us. We must go now, my friend."

White Flowering Tree pulls away from her friend Silk Fan and asks with a frown, "Why are you doing this? I have not finished speaking with these musicians."

Everyone at the marketplace watches this brief and harmless exchange between teenage secondary students. Pure, White Flowering Tree's mother-in-law, looks up to see her standing in the middle of a group of young people with a man talking and laughing and acting as she were a single girl! Pure's friends, the older women of the village, glance at her sideways but say nothing. Now it appears as though that foolish bride is arguing with her friend. What a spectacle!

The old mistress marches over to the group and pulls her astonished young relative by the arm and drags her down the street toward their home. The three eggs remain in their basket awaiting a buyer. Their mats are unclaimed as Pure hurries her charge away from this place of public humiliation.

"What are you doing? Where are you going? You are hurting my arm."

When they reach the gate of their modest home, Pure is out of breath and still furious. Pulling White Flowering Tree up the step, she still hangs on to her arm while she looks around for a whipping cane. She seizes a thin bamboo cane used for staking beans in the garden and begins to swing wildly, shouting, "Why do you disgrace me so? You made a public spectacle of yourself in front of the entire village. What will your husband think? Oh, what money I wasted on you! Everyone is laughing at me now."

"Why are you so angry? I was only talking to them! You did not allow me to introduce you to them. They must think you quite rude!"

"You were talking to men right in the street."

"They are students from the next village. I wanted to know what music they played for their spring concert."

"You are a married woman now! You cannot just run up to strange men in the street!"

"Those people are boys and girls my age. I wanted to meet them. You have friends. Why can I not have friends?"

Pure is furious. "They are men, you little fool!"

"They are just boys and girls like me. I went to school with people just like them until I was stolen. You do not understand. They are music students. I was an excellent music student, and I would have played a solo in my spring concert if you had not paid to have me kidnapped. I never did get to play in my concert. I wanted to hear about their concerts."

Pure jumps up and down and screams, "Shut up about that useless music. You have dishonored us!"

Perhaps it is the sight of seeing the old mistress jumping up and down. Perhaps it is her disappointment or the absurdity of the entire affair. Who can say? White Flowering Tree, still a girl, giggles and points her fingers. "I dishonored you? You did not allow me to finish my education, and I have dishonored you? You did not ask my parents' permission for my marriage, and I have dishonored you? You have broken the law, and I dishonor you? This is too funny! You do not care for my most basic needs, and I am a disgrace?" She speaks through compulsive giggles while being whipped by her angry mother-in-law.

"You hired criminals to kidnap me, and I am the disgrace? You stole my belongings, and you are upset?" She snickers at the absurdity of the charge.

Pure, red-faced and cursing, screams, "Daughters-in-law are supposed to be quiet and obedient!"

Trying to turn to look directly at her attacker, White Flowering Tree continues, "You do not respect me as a family member, and you are dishonored?"

Swinging the cane again, Pure hits her on any part of her body within reach. White Flowering Tree is driven out into the courtyard, still laughing. She goes for a drink of water from a bucket but spews it from her mouth in a fit of laughter. She walks around the courtyard trying to regain her composure, but still the laughter explodes.

"Oh, it is so funny. You think that I have disgraced you!"

The tears are tears of laughter, and still giggles come. "I have been an obedient slave, and you think me a disgrace?"

When her husband arrives home that evening, he is puzzled to find his new wife sitting on the stone floor of the courtyard with countless red marks all over her body, holding both hands over her mouth, laughing, and drenched in water. He almost gets the next bucket of water in his face as his mother throws it on his wife, who is lost in a fit of giggles.

Pure corners her newly arrived son with a furious question, "Whatever happened to proper Chinese girls who knew how to be quiet and behave in public? Listen to what happened today in the marketplace. I was so ashamed."

Throughout the night, the neighbors on the small triple courtyard hear giggles and wild laughter. The pretty girl who dreamed of playing a solo in the spring concert in her senior year of high school does what others have done before her when faced with no choices in a totally unreasonable situation. She wanders in insanity for a time.

My dear Pride of His Father,

How I miss you. The wind from the hills is blowing steadily now. I kiss the wind to send you a message of my great love for you.

I cooked rolled dumplings in soup today and then could not eat them while thinking how much you enjoyed them. My throat closed up with grief. I will always love you.

Please make Strong Wind wear a hat and shoes when he is outside.

Silk Fan

MOUNTAIN ROCKS

Walks with Grace sits on a box in the courtyard, pondering. *I must find answers before long. Silk Fan urged us to find something we enjoy doing. I have tried to see this place through new eyes. I miss so much about home. I miss using my mind. Where can I find something to read? I miss being around loving people. I miss having meaningful work to do, and now I must plan for a baby. I dread these waiting months.*

The high, irregular tones of tinkling bells break the dullness. The tinny sound is unlike any other. She rises from her seat and heads toward the narrow dirt road. She recognizes the goat herder plodding by her gate as he does each day with the same matted skin cape covering his shoulders, molded to his form.

Today, I will make a business deal with him, one which will keep my hands busy and give me work that I find pleasing.

A friendship of sorts has developed between them because they are both considered second-class citizens. He knows about the villagers who shun her in their attempt to make her more submissive, but he is his own person and speaks to everyone. Today as he passes by, he carries a small, leggy kid in an ageless leather sling hanging from his neck.

Yes, today I will offer to knit him a pair of warm wool socks in exchange for some wool.

She greets him, "How was your day on the hills, sir?"

"Oh, the evil gods do not like my goats. Today I have a new kid with no nanny to feed it."

"Ah, the little one is so cute! Is it a male or female?"

"A little female. But she will never make it a week without help."

"How I wish I could own such an elegant creature."

In surprise, the goat herder asks, "You would really like to be keeping such a nuisance?"

"This small beauty would be no nuisance. She will be good company in this unfriendly village."

"Then I will give her to you. A good thing it is for us all. I will bring you some milk each evening on my way home. If you will bring me a bowl, I will give you some now."

"Oh, thank you!" She hurries to bring a bowl. While he milks a goat, she declares, "I promise to take good care of her. And sir, if you will bring me a supply of wool from your goats, then I will knit you a pair of warm socks for the winter."

The man's weathered brown face breaks into delight. This is a very lucky day after all.

The tiny, spotted animal brings the first day of smiles to the unhappy captive bride. Now she has pleasant work and something that needs her care. She can postpone thinking of her nightly humiliation in the lack of privacy afforded in the one-room house.

Two children who are cutting grass for their mothers' cooking fires stop their work and stare at the wide-eyed animal. The older boy offers some fresh grass for it to eat. Walks with Grace tells them, "Thank you, but she is just a newborn. She does not know how to chew grass yet, but she does need some soft grass for her bed."

When she clears out a corner of a garden shed, the two boys abandon their assignments to cut grass for this wobbly-legged creature's bed. The children are pleased to be allowed to help. They gaze through the doorway at the sleepy kid. The younger boy tugs on her pants legs and looking up into her face asks seriously, "What is its name?"

"She does need a name, doesn't she? Hmm. She is from the mountains, and she is gray and white, just as the mountain rocks are in winter. What do you think of the name Mountain Rocks?"

The older boy pronounces, "That is a fine name." His younger friend nods his head in agreement.

"Very well then, her name is officially Mountain Rocks. What is your name?"

"I am called Uncut Jade."

"What a wonderful name you have been given. Uncut Jade, do you know how to feed a very young animal when its nanny drives it off?"

"No, auntie. But I will ask my grandmother. She knows many things."

Walks with Grace watches him running toward his home. *What an ambitious name he has. I wonder if his parents will make interesting neighbors. Where did these hill people learn of the ancient name meaning "great potential?"*

The boy returns breathless and hands her a small bottle. "You must put the milk in here and stuff a rag into the top. It will work."

And so it does. The kid sucks noisily on the dripping bottle as often as she is offered any milk. Walks with Grace still lacks anything to read, and she is still a humiliated, captive bride, but she now owns the fuzzy kid that gives her meaningful work as well as something of her own to love.

After chores, as she sits on a box in her unkempt courtyard, she cards wool and watches her growing pet poke her head into everything. It had never been a fine garden or sitting area, just a utilitarian kitchen courtyard. She is glad that there is nothing for Mountain Rocks to destroy.

One evening when she has enough wool carded and ready for washing, she decides to take her pet goat on a walk with her to the waterspout. Old men smile at the pair, and children play with Mountain Rocks. What a difference the small kid makes in the outlook of the homesick captive. She can think of something other than her own grief.

Steadfast, the man who bought her and claimed her as his own, watches her working. His only comment is, "So you like goats, do you?"

Black Pearl grumbles. The old grandfather smiles at them. In the evening after her first walk with her pet in the house on Glorious Prosperity Lane, the bride makes a cheerful comment.

"Mountain Rocks will be the start of my own herd. I will be able to weave my own wool and knit warm sweaters and socks." She purposely fails to include a baby blanket in her list. She needs time to adjust to the idea of her own pregnancy.

The old grandfather does not hear what has been said, but he smiles anyway at the pretty new bride in his family. The old mistress mumbles, "You will need a billy goat." Steadfast looks up briefly and continues eating.

The months move on and Mountain Rocks grows into a pretty, inquisitive nanny goat. Uncut Jade remains a faithful friend, coming daily to speak softly to the growing animal and bring her a fresh supply of grass and leaves.

Noticing how much the child needs a friend, Walks with Grace shares her sharp-hoofed pet with the quiet boy. By midsummer, she finishes knitting the woolen socks for the goat herder. Black Pearl complains and pouts because the socks were not made for her. Walks with Grace still wears her threadbare clothes she wore to classes in the university. She works in the fields when communal chores are required and helps her mother-in-law with daily tasks. She should be too weary to care about anything, as she cards more wool and sorts it, making preparation for spinning, but having a weary body does not make her mind cease to function.

Sometimes she asks the same questions repeatedly. *Will my family come for me? Did they receive my letters? What must my fiancé at home think? Would he find another love? Why is Black Pearl so disagreeable and critical of me? Why has no one seen to my needs? How can I get any more clothes? Why does no one speak to me? And worst of all, why did Steadfast not understand how severely I am humiliated by sleeping in the same bed with the entire family?*

Watching the antics of Mountain Rocks is the best part of her day. Uncut Jade considers it his great privilege to share the pet with the pointed ears, gray back, and inquisitive nature. He guards his task jealously, lest another boy be allowed to walk and stroke the kid.

One day, Black Pearl allows Walks with Grace to go shopping alone. "When you go to market today, you must buy fresh greens. Get cucumbers and peppers too. "

"Who will sell cucumbers this late in the season?

"You just find some! You may wait until the men come home from the fields with vegetables for their families. Watch the coins and get the food we need. And sell that wool of yours!"

At the market, Walks with Grace seeks the vegetables. Among the men she notes an older man reading a newspaper and translating it for his neighbors. It is in English! Taught by missionaries decades ago, he regularly shares with his friends.

As the abacuses click, the sharpening stones spin, and the live fowl cluck, Walks with Grace meets her friend White Flowering Tree and visits for a time with her.

"This is the first time old Gripe and Grumble have allowed me to go this short distance alone. She gives me no freedom and no privacy. She still sleeps on the same bed with her son and me."

"These people are so insensitive."

"When will your baby arrive? You are growing so large!"

"It will be in four more months I suppose. I just wish my mother could be here with me. I finally got a tradesman to take a letter, but I doubt that she received it. I know that she will be so worried about me."

"Yes. I am sure she is." She gives her friend's hand a squeeze.

"Have you seen any cucumbers? I must do my shopping before the vegetables are all sold. My mistress told me to especially find cucumbers."

"No, I have not seen any cucumbers today."

"Can you believe that she actually told me to sell my wool? Here I am wearing my only worn-out suit, winter is coming, and she wants me to sell this little bit of wool I have prepared. I am going to weave a baby blanket for the winter, but I still need new clothing."

"I do not understand either, my sister. I must go now. I am tired."

"Good-bye. I will return home now, even without the cucumbers. I will see you soon."

As she approaches her house on the way home from the market, Walks with Grace spies her friend Uncut Jade waiting for her. He is crying, and the closer she comes to him, the more he cries. Suddenly, he runs away. She frowns and takes her produce into her house. The grandfather sits smoking on a bench by the door.

As she enters the house, her mother-in-law greets her with an unpracticed smile saying, "Dinner is almost ready. We will have a treat tonight."

Her new husband looks up from his seat. Nothing is said about the length of her stay at the market.

Whole roasts are cooking on the fire. We never eat this well. Is this a festival celebration I do not know? Then, in an instant, she sees hanging from a beam quarters of undressed meat still in its gray and white fur!

"No! No! It can't be Mountain Rocks."

The neighbors hear her scream. "How could you do such a cruel thing?"

"Oh, I just saved you the task. You don't appreciate anything."

Steadfast says nothing. This is between the two women in his life.

Sobbing aloud, Walks with Grace seizes the cooking meat and runs outside with it where she drops it into the neighbor's pigpen. Next, she runs back inside and screams, "You will never be a whole person."

Crying uncontrollably, she lifts the uncooked quarters of meat from the hook and darts outside again. Unsure what to do with it, she runs to the home of her friend, the Han widow, and tries to explain it.

"What is the matter, my friend?"

"This is too much! I cannot love such cruel people. She slaughtered Mountain Rocks, and he did nothing to stop her. He just sat there. She sent me to market while she did her dirty work."

"Come and sit down. Here, wipe your hands and face with this cloth. That was truly a mean deed."

"Why do they hate me so? I have done them no wrong. I work hard and show them both respect. Why would they do this? Mountain Rocks was mine!"

"Where love is absent, hate takes many forms. Take a sip of water."

"Please use this meat. It is for you. Look at it. There is so little meat on a kid so young. The purpose of this slaughter was not for food. I do not understand this."

"You sit and calm yourself. Here is some good bean soup. Eat it."

When her sobbing abates, the captured wife sits for a while and then eats the soup offered by her friend. Looking up, she asks, "Do you know where the sheep keepers go for pasture?"

"They pasture the sheep over that hill to the north country.

The path starts by the large evergreen tree by the goose pen. There are only children with the sheep now. Why do you ask?"

"I cannot return to that hateful house tonight. Next, I will be the one slaughtered."

The old widow, who has lived a long time and seen much, only releases a long, sad sigh. "Let me make up a pack for you. You will need this food. Here are some cakes made with corn and some freshly made wheat noodles. Are you sure that you will not just stay here with me for the night?"

"Yes. I would like to stay here with you, and I have never been to the high pasture, but my grief drives me. Who are the children who watch the sheep?"

"The boy is He Who Is Trusted, and his cousin, Pink Sunset, may be with him. One of their fathers brings them food each week."

The widow hobbles about her home helping Walks with Grace prepare for the trip, showing more concern in one evening than her family has in the months she has lived here.

"Here are nine copper coins and one silver coin. It is so little, but you will need this money to buy vegetables from the mountain folk. Take this walking stick with you for defense against the dogs. You do not even have a jacket. You will need one in that cool mountain air. Take that old black coat hanging in the corner and this blanket. Please return them when you come back home. Here are some verses to dwell on while you grieve." The old woman places two pieces of paper in her coat pocket.

Walks with Grace nods, takes the walking stick and bundle, and carries them into the darkening evening. Summer heat still clings to the north China hills when the pretty nineteen-year-old walks the dirt road out of the village. Although she has never been on this trail, her rage empowers her to keep moving. Just when she thinks that she might have missed the path, the moon rises and brightens her way.

Turning to look behind her, she realizes no one is following.

She pauses to rest at a turn in the winding path. *Why didn't he stop his mother from slaughtering my pet goat? Is he afraid of her? Why did he not follow me or try to comfort me? What kind of a marriage have I been forced into? How I wish that I were safely back at home with my family and my dear fiancé. What must he think? Will he realize that I did not leave willingly?*

Drying her face on the back of the sleeve of her borrowed jacket, she walks more slowly, noticing moonlight playing on wild plants growing by the way. The sight does not charm her, nor does the cool, fragrant breeze.

Her grief at the loss of her beloved pet, her one and only dear possession, consumes her emotions until she thinks again of Steadfast, her young husband. He is not her darling fiancé from south China, but he is not ugly or ill mannered. She has been trying to think of him as her husband, but this incident both puzzles and angers her.

Climbing farther, she sees an enormous, star-filled sky and knows this must be the high meadow where the children watch their families' sheep. She spends the remainder of the night by the hillside path; not wishing to startle the children, she sits down to wait. When she hears children's voices, she approaches the two young shepherds. Their working dog moves toward her with an inquisitive bark.

"Hello, He Who Is Trusted, my name is Auntie Walks with Grace. Do you remember me? You petted my little goat. Hello, Pink Sunset. May I sit here with you?"

Two weeks later, she and the shepherds have settled into a comfortable routine. When Pink Sunset's father comes the first week to bring them food, Walks with Grace knows that all in the village are aware of her secret location, but still she stays. Pink Sunset is only eight years old and afraid of the night, so she welcomes the company. Both children snuggle down beside their adult friend each night. Even though the sounds are strange and she is sleeping out under the stars, she feels a quieting calm as she sleeps in the summer nights. In the mornings, she awakens to the realization that when she returns she will still feel furious and helpless. She reads the verses her friend placed in one pocket. They speak of God always watching over her. She speaks aloud, "Where are you now, God?"

As she visits with the two children, she collects sheep's wool from the rocks and shrubs where they lose stray bits of wool, unaware she is collecting what is reserved for beggars.

Nothing seems to abate her anger. She enjoys the different scenery, the lack of a critical boss, and working with the wool, and it is good to have the two children nearby. But as she considers her life, she fails to see any answers to her situation. Anger turns to frustration and bitterness.

One morning, Pink Sunset runs to where Walks with Grace sits spinning yarn and announces, "A man is coming."

It is Steadfast.

"Hello."

She looks up at the man who purchased her. She does not get up from her place where she sits with her back to a smooth, rocky outcropping. She continues spinning curly sheep wool in slow, even movements. The movement should be soothing.

"It is time to come home." Steadfast sits down near his bought wife.

Turning her drained face away from him, she looks straight forward and says, "I know that I have been a disappointment to you. I realize that I have not fit in your family. If this is to be my place in life, then perhaps I will learn. When we have a child, I will do as the parents of these two children and send them up into the hills while they are still so young that they fear noises in the night." He tries to interrupt her, but she continues. "I will not make fine linens for him when he is born. Anything will do for him. After he learns to walk, I will begin the task of preparing him to live here in the land of his people. He needs to learn early that he needs no privacy. I will tell the neighbor children to laugh at him and exclude him from their games. He must not feel that he has any friends. He must learn to depend on himself. He must never know the disappointment I found in trusting people.

"When he laughs, I will frown and tell him that life is not funny. When he jumps for joy as little ones do, I will tell him how foolish he is. When he throws a rock, I will tell him that he will never do anything right. I will not teach him fine manners or to respect his elders. He must learn early the futility of such ideas.

"I shall give him gifts, and when he has learned to love them, I shall take the gifts away from him so that he understands that he has no right to own anything."

Steadfast tries again to stop her speech. She has never had so much to say, and she has never spoken nonsense like she is doing now.

"When he falls down, I shall not go to him with comfort; I shall ignore him. When he grows into a fine-looking boy, I shall invent some imaginary flaw. I shall tell him not to speak because his teeth are funny looking, or his hair is coarse, or his hands are too large. I will prepare him to live in this world that I find so harsh."

Steadfast waits for her to go on. When she does not, he says, "My mother did not know how you felt about the goat. She was doing you a favor to butcher it for you."

Walks with Grace throws her wool down and turning to look directly at him screams, "Do not insult me! That wicked woman knew exactly what she was doing! Such devious, evil planning I cannot imagine! I now understand why you are so fearful of her. She is your own Empress Wu. She sent me away for the day so that I would not stop her."

They both sit in silence now. She turns back to look into nothingness while she continues her speech.

"I shall not teach him to read and write or work numbers. No one cares how much he knows. He must not think that he has any choices in life. He must learn early that he is not special and that no one will love him."

He stares at her as she continues, "I shall never sing to him. Songs do not belong here. You will have to beat him. I do not think I can do that. He will belong here. He will be strong and hard."

Steadfast looks at his young wife for a long time as she gazes into space with an old, dreary face he does not remember. *Where is the tender, young face that delighted so in a simple young goat?*

This husband and wife never had time to court or learn to love and appreciate each other. There was never a happy celebration of their marriage or even a choice of a lifetime partner. There is no close understanding or tenderness in this most unnatural of bonds. A courtship never happened. A love affair never existed. The marriage never had a chance. As a family, it spells disaster.

Steadfast wearily pulls himself to his feet. Shaking his head from side to side, he slowly descends the hill toward his farming village. This is not what he expected. People told him to control his bride and she would accept him in time. Once she had a child or two, she would not want to leave. People said that is the way it is with women.

"What am I to do?" he asks the wind.

As he retraces his steps down the shepherd's trail, he hears her voice over and over in his head. *He must not think he has any choices in life. He must never know the pain I have known by trusting people. He ... how could she speak so? She is always respectful and agreeable. All she ever asked for was to write her parents and a marriage room for privacy. My mother said that she would get used to us. I really have begun to feel that she is mine. What am I to do?*

As he stumbles on the rocky path returning home, he spies clumps of bitter herbs growing and stoops to pick a bunch. *She likes bitter herb soup,* he thinks. *Men will laugh when I return without my wife. Should I take a stick and beat her as my mother instructed?*

The next morning, he takes the bitter herbs as he leaves his house. His mother, Black Pearl, berates him. "I don't know what the fuss is all about. Why didn't you make her come home? People will laugh at us. What she needs is a good whipping. What do I tell the neighbors?"

As he walks away, she can still be heard grumbling.

Taking a deep breath, he walks to the home of the old Han widow. It is in the middle of the village, so people will see him going there, but he has decided to seek other advice.

The old widow hobbles to the door where Steadfast stands with a gift in his hand. The old woman is surprised to see this young man at her door. "Hello."

"Good day to you, widow. I have some bitter herbs for you."

"What a nice day for visiting. Thank you."

"Do you have a few minutes to spend with me this day?"

"Of course I do. Sit there on my bench. I shall be with you in a short time."

Steadfast has known the old widow all of his life, but this is the first time he has consulted her concerning anything. He sits obediently, waiting. His neighbor was an educated Han bride and has other reminders beside the stumps of bound feet to indicate that she was an expensive bride of fine breeding. She must be properly dressed. Wrapping a clean robe around herself, she ties it neatly and then slowly hobbles to her door in black felt shoes. She allows him to tell the purpose of his visit.

"Madam, you have lived a long time and know so much about these things. Please tell me what am I to do with a wife and a mother who do not understand each other."

"Yes. You do have a problem. The entire village knows about your wife's pet goat, Mountain Rocks."

"Yes. But what is the answer?"

"It is an age-old problem. We old women are jealous of the young."

"But..."

"What have you done to solve your problem?"

"I do not know what to do. I went to the hills to get her, and she said such strange things."

"What gifts have you given her?"

"Gifts?"

"Do you really want her?"

"Yes."

"What is her favorite color?"

"Her what?"

"Her favorite color. Have you bought her a warm new winter coat in her favorite color?"

"No. My mother says that she will get one for her."

"How much money do you give to her each week for her needs?"

"Money? For what?"

"She should have money for whatever she wants. What wedding gifts did you have for her when she arrived?"

"What do you mean?"

"Wedding gifts to welcome her into her new home. Does she have pretty things of her own now?"

Steadfast, the handsome young man who thought that he was ready for a wife, stares at his wise, old neighbor as if she is speaking a foreign language.

The elderly widow persists, "What does she want? What does she need? What has she asked for?"

"She wants to write a letter to her parents, and she wants a private bedroom to sleep in where my grandfather and mother cannot watch us."

"Well, what have you done about that?"

"Uh, uh."

"All she has asked for is a privacy room and to contact her parents. That certainly is not much to ask."

"But we are poor farmers."

"Do you want a slave for your mother, or do you want a wife?"

He hangs his head, wrings his big farmer's hands, and answers quietly, "I have never been around girls before. I don't know how to treat her."

There is a pause hanging heavily in the morning air.

"Well, do you want her? Do you like her?"

Steadfast lifts his head quickly. "Yes! I do. She is so … pretty."

"Very well then. You must make an effort to win her affections. What do you plan to do about a marriage room for privacy?"

"That will cost money. How can I manage?"

"You found a good amount of money to pay your cousins, the pirates. Your mother always has money left for pipe tobacco, and you have a bicycle that you do not need. She has worked hard all of the months she has been here. This all spells money to me."

His mouth opens to protest. Then relenting, he responds, "I understand." After a moment he says, "One more thing, Madam."

"Yes?"

"What is a good gift for her?"

"Why don't you start with a new bed covering and a length of warm winter cloth for a new outfit, new yellow towels, and some writing paper?"

"I understand."

"When you talk with her, you must ask her, 'Do you write poetry? Do you paint? Do you want some nuts from the market? Would you like to take a walk to watch the moon rise?'"

"Yes. I see now. I thank you for your time and wisdom. Madam, is there anything that I may do for you today?"

"Yes, there is, Steadfast. If you will bring that heavy load of coal up the steps to my cooking place, I will thank you."

He jumps up, glad for a task he can handle. He finishes his task quickly and hurries away.

I must locate a buyer for my most prized possession, my bicycle. The farmer who lives beyond the common field owns eight pigs. He could certainly use a bicycle for taking feed to his pens each day. Perhaps he will pay a good price for mine.

Steadfast goes to the home of Hero and Silk Fan, where he

asks politely, "Madam, I have need of your farm cart. Would you be so kind as to allow me to rent it for five days?"

Silk Fan is amused that the only time she is spoken to in this hated place is when someone wants something from her, but she answers with dignity, "What use do you have for my humble cart?"

"I need to bring some wood from the hills for a new room for my house."

"Surely it will be broken with the weight of heavy wood."

"I promise that I shall return it in good shape. If it is damaged, I shall rebuild it for you. I need the lumber to build a room for my wife, Walks with Grace."

"If it is for Walks with Grace, then I will rent it to you. You are at least six months late thinking of your wife. My rental price will be a new wooden bench for two people."

Steadfast smiles and agrees to the price.

It is twelve days later when Walks with Grace returns to the village with the two young shepherds. Their fathers and the children with their flock of fat sheep are welcomed in a noisy ritual ending the summer. Walks with Grace bids the children good-bye and invites them to come for a visit. Pink Sunset's father notices the bond and realizes that he owes her something for her weeks of watching his sheep and his child. He promises her a portion of the wool when it is sheared this week. This is better news than she hoped for. She will have wool she needs for weaving a winter blanket.

Steadfast did not come back up the hills to command her to return with him. She feels more in control of her own life for having come home in her own time, not his. She brings some herbs tied in a bundle, a lambskin, and a small amount of wool yarn with her. She is calmer now than when she left a few weeks earlier, but she sees no choices in her young life. She has no money, does not know where she is, or how to return home to her parents. If she solved these problems, she knows that her captors will not allow her to leave the region.

After returning the borrowed coat and blanket to her friend, she trudges toward her home. The approaching cold makes the house seem appealing until she realizes that the winter will mean being closed up with those three strangers, where she is the caged animal, kept for the amusement of the owners. As she walks with reluctant feet, she does not see the many heads that turn to take notice of her. The local policy of silent snobbery has cheated the gossipers of their firsthand news.

Walks with Grace looks twice at the gates to her house. *Is this the right place?*

Bricks and lumber are stacked up, buckets of sand are on the ground, and Silk Fan's cart is piled with tools. To her astonishment, there is the definite outline of a room being added to the house. She stands for a moment, studying the project before she realizes that there is someone on the outside laying bricks. She walks gingerly through the mess to find her husband standing on bamboo scaffolding, placing wide bricks on the wall while mortar drops down on him.

"Steadfast?"

He is obviously pleased as he yells, "Walks with Grace, how do you like it?"

"How do I like what?"

"Your room. How do you like your marriage room?"

"What do you mean? Is this for me?" She walks slowly around the room, noting each detail of the construction, and quietly begins to cry.

"What are you doing?" He climbs down from his precarious perch and walks around the side of the half-finished room to find her sobbing into her hands.

"Why are you crying? I thought you would like this."

His hands are wet with dirty mortar, and he feels awkward. He reaches out his hand toward her, but he has never touched her to comfort her before, and he drops it to his side.

"You are building this room for me?"

"Of course! It is for you!"

She sits down on the ground, folds her arms around her growing form and weeps again. After all of the hurt and pain, kindness is her undoing.

Steadfast stares in disbelief. "I'm sorry. I've never been around girls. I've never been married." He turns around, shrugs his shoulders, and throws up his dirty hands and begins again.

"I want to get finished with it before cold weather. Soldier's Son and Trumpeter both helped me, but it is taking time. Please don't cry anymore. I am trying. It is built against the kang wall so that it may share the heat. That allowed me to build only three walls. Did you notice?"

He shrugs his shoulders again, checks the time by the setting of the sun, deliberately ignores the inquiring eyes of his neighbors, and returns to work.

"I'll just finish this one row before dark tonight." He looks through the half-finished room at the tall, graceful girl sitting on the ground.

Walks with Grace thinks, *He built this for me! Perhaps he really loves me.*

So one of the couples in this village of kidnapped brides seems to have a chance at marriage. He is willing to learn how to treat women and meet a real need, and she is perhaps willing to think of him as her husband.

The women have learned a new way to cope. When they meet, they try to exchange words about something good. At the widow's sewing lessons, they learn that they can thank God, but these ideas are new and hazy. Silk Fan tries to change their thoughts into positive ones.

They ask each other, "What good things do you know?" The answers vary with the seasons.

"Last night the moon shone like silver," Walks with Grace answers first.

BARBARA NOWELL

"My onions are growing well." It is the farmer, Silk Fan, who announces.

"We had fresh pears to eat." Beautiful Moon lists fruit as something good.

"I dreamed of music practice." White Flowering Tree dreams of home.

"I met someone new. She is the bride of the leather worker." Silk Fan smiles.

"I have finished weaving my baby's wool blanket." White Flowering Tree almost smiles.

Beautiful Moon adds, "My spinning is progressing quite well."

"The wild mallard has a lovely flock of ducklings," Walks with Grace says.

They all make a real effort to think positively.

One October morning, two of the brides meet. "Good morning, Walks with Grace."

"Hello, White Flowering Tree. I must go for coal for my cooking fire. This old basket will not carry much. Will you help me make a new heavy-duty basket when we return from this errand? My mistress says that we must store up fuel for the winter."

"Yes. We both need new baskets. A whole load will surely split the bottom out of this basket too."

They walk together to the end of the village, where a clerk of the fuel commune marks down the weight of each load, and they begin their way home, their burdens of black coal making them walk slower this time.

"This is so heavy." White Flowering Tree attempts to hold her load with both hands. "I do not really mind this hard work. My parents always worked hard."

"I like to work too. It is good to feel productive, but I miss using my mind. I do believe that my brain will turn to dust if I do not find something to study."

"Did you see that man on market day? He was reading a

newspaper where the old men sit to play games. It was in English! And there is *nothing* for the young people in this forgotten village to read."

"The barber's daughter is friendly. Perhaps she can tell us where we can get a book or a newspaper."

"How can we pay for it?"

"Silk Fan says to bargain. We offer to do something in exchange for the books or newspapers."

"Would you be willing to carry a few loads of coal in exchange for reading material?"

"I'd be willing to carry it now before ice and snow covers the path."

"I will speak to the barber's daughter."

A few days later, as the kidnapped brides walk through the village with a load of wheat straw for building fires, they pass the home of the barber. He is sitting near his door on a four-legged stool where he plies his trade when not working his field.

"Greetings to you."

"Greetings to you also." The brides nod in surprise at being spoken to.

"My daughter tells me that you are interested in books."

"Well, yes, we are."

"Can you read well?"

Walks with Grace smothers a giggle and answers, "I read well enough." She knows that it is rude to brag.

"Can you read the classics?"

"Yes. Do you have some classical books?" The astonished university student tries to keep the excitement from her voice.

"My mother has a few ones, but alas, her eyes are also old. My daughter cannot yet read such difficult words, and my wife and I were cheated of our education during the time of the great revolution." He stops speaking and shakes head over this part of his country's history, such a few years ago. "Would you be willing to read to her some time each week in exchange for the loan of some ancient books?"

The two homesick southerners exchange looks. They are thrilled. They do not even have to carry coal for the books. They only have to read! They both readily agree to find time each week for Grandmother Rose Bud.

As the weeks pass in the fall time of that first year, they fall into a routine of reading aloud from the book of her choice. If the only time the readers can find to read is after dinner, then the barber, his wife, and his mother all three sit on the kang while young Red Rose sits on a stool at the young neighbor's feet. They sit silently listening to poetry, history, and legends. Nothing is mentioned about breaking the village code of shunning new brides. This family is too pleased to have found their own private source of entertainment and education to worry about village traditions.

True to his word, the barber allows Walks with Grace and Beautiful Moon to borrow a book. They select an old leather-bound copy of a history of the dynasties. Neither of the young brides has read it, so they are pleased with the arrangement. The first reading for the family is a most happy day to be counted among the list of good things.

THE WIDOW HAS A VISITOR

T rue Friend is an athletic young man who has a big problem. His new wife is unhappy, and he is puzzled. It takes
much courage for him to seek help, but his neighbor,
Steadfast, told True Friend how he went to the Han widow for
wisdom concerning his new bride, and this gives him courage.
So True Friend sets out for her sturdy two-story house in the
middle of the village.

"May I speak with you this fine day?"

"Come in, young man."

"You are a wise woman."

The widow nods and waits for him to continue.

"This girl I have is not happy. She is not peaceful in my
house."

"What do you say to her?"

"What do you mean? Just ordinary things. 'Can we have
boiled onions for dinner tonight?' or, 'Lock the door,' or 'When
will you wash my shirt?'"

"So you speak to her as a master to a servant?"

True Friend is startled.

"What does she say to you?"

"What she always says, 'I want to go home.'"

"Then what do you say?" the widow persists.

"Nothing. There is no point in discussing it. You know that nothing can be done. She is here to stay." True Friend is impatient with this question. Everyone knows that brides cannot be returned.

"You refuse to talk about her capture or her family, and you wonder why she is not cheerful and sociable?"

"My mother said that she would accept us in time, but—"

"Was your mother right?"

"Uh, no. Will she ever look me in the eye?"

"Why should she look at you? She hates you."

"Why? I never beat her."

"You don't have to. You captured her, hold her prisoner, and your mother uses her whip when she fails to work fast enough."

"So what can a working farmer do?"

"First you must decide whether you want a servant for your mother or a wife."

"But all Chinese women work."

"That is not the point. Your wife works quite hard."

"So what will make her a good wife?"

"Why not start by talking with her?"

"What do I say?"

"Do you know her name?"

"Her name is White Flower."

"No. Her name is White Flowering Tree. Why not ask her what she would like to be called? Call her by her name. If she wants to speak about her imprisonment here, you must allow her to do so. You must allow her to get over this subject."

"My mother will not permit it. She always hushes her if she starts talking about her parents' home."

"Is she your mother's servant or your wife? Send your mother for water, or the two of you can take a walk to watch the moon rise by the canal."

"Uh, what if my mother wants to come along?"

"If you want a wife, you must start treating her like a wife. She is not your mother's wife." He nods and leaves shortly.

The next week, the young man known as True Friend comes again to visit the Han widow.

"Good evening, True Friend. How are your crops this week?"

"My crops are growing as they should; thank you, madam. Are you feeling well?"

"I feel as well as old people feel, thank you."

"Here are two small melons for you. They are the orange meat melons we grow."

"Thank you, True Friend. Have a seat on my bench."

There is an awkward silence as she waits for him to begin.

"How is your bride, White Flowering Tree? Did you speak with her?"

"I tried to, but she walked away from me."

"Tell me about it."

"I decided that she needed some laughter, so right after dinner, I began telling this funny story about getting all wet in the canal. She did not even wait for the funny part. She went outside to sweep the courtyard. It did not need sweeping."

"Tell me about your conversation with her concerning her capture and marriage."

"I did not do that."

"Hmm. What does she say when you are eating your morning meal?"

"The only thing she ever says, 'I want to go home.'"

"You do not want to discuss anything with her about her kidnapping, but she may not be able to get past this rude event until you talk about it without your mother present. She may not be able to get this cruelty out of her mind until you discuss it with her."

"This is hard. My mother is always present."

"She is a lovely girl. Do you want to keep her?"

"Oh yes."

"Have you brought her any wild flowers from the hills?"

"Wild flowers?"

"Yes. Any flowers will do."

He says nothing.

"Have you bought her any sweets or nuts from the traders?"

"No."

"Do you know her favorite color?"

"Favorite color? Why?"

"So you will know what color shirts to buy for her."

"I give all of my earnings to my mother. She will do that."

"You are saying that you do not want to give gifts to your wife? She had neat clothes when she came here. Have you looked at her lately?"

"She is a farmer's wife. What need does she have for fine clothes?"

"She is young. The young like pretty clothes." He hangs his head.

"Do you ever thank her?"

He just shakes his head.

"Do you give her money for her needs?"

"No."

"Do you really like her?"

"Oh yes!"

"What do you find pleasing about White Flowering Tree?"

He smiles slightly and answers. "I like the dainty way she walks. She is so graceful. And have you noticed her hands? Her hands are small and pretty."

"Have you told her any of this?"

"No. There is never time."

"Do you mean that there is no time when you are alone with your wife?"

"After dinner I sit with Mother. I am a respectful son."

"So you are a respectful son. Are you a respectful husband?"

The startled young husband asks, "What do you mean?"

"This lovely graceful bride of yours does not feel loved or respected. She is heartbroken."

"Why? She has me!"

"Yes. She has you who will not speak to her, who will not take any time with her, who will not buy even the necessities for her, you who do not know the first thing about her. What did she do in her home? What are her skills? What does she miss? You will not discuss her parents with her, and you allow your witch of a mother to dictate the climate in your home. You are a prize of a husband. You allow your mother to whip a homesick girl who works every day in worn-out clothes."

"But I always sleep with her."

"That is the main reason she hates you. You steal her from her home, do not allow her to speak, then do not get to know her, but instead you rape her. When intimacy is between a husband and wife who love each other, it is an act of sweet giving and caring. When it is with a stranger, it is rape. You are a stranger!"

"I am her husband."

"You don't act like a husband."

He gets up and walks to the door. Returning, he says, "My mother said that it would all work out. She said that she would forget about her childhood home and be a good wife."

"Was your mother right?"

"Uh, no. She said that once we have a baby, White Flowering Tree will smile and sing."

"So you will use a baby like a strong rope to tie her here where she is not loved or respected."

"I don't know what to do."

"Yes, you do. If you want a wife, you must treat her with respect and tender attention."

"Will she ever smile at me?"

The wise widow looks down at her own aged hands. After a long wait she answers, "That is up to you. Will you give her any reason to smile?"

"Thank you for sharing your wisdom with me."

"You are always welcome, True Friend."

The young man adjusts his hat and walks in the direction of home, where his miserable wife is washing and cutting up wilted cabbage leaves. Her dainty musician's hands roll each leaf and then slice it into even parts for cooking.

As the months pass, this man who shares her bed is still a stranger. As the chorus "I want to go home" echoes through her mind, other thoughts now haunt her. *Why does True Friend not speak to me? Why does he not care for me?*

True Friend does not return to the widow's home again for advice.

A NEW BABY

White Flowering Tree, who has just given birth to a son in this remote farming village far from her home, bears little resemblance to the happy schoolgirl who was brought here. The girl who wore her long hair in a single braid was a popular, laughing student who played the polished stringed instrument in her school.

As the midwife leaves, new grandmother, Pure, hurries out of the house holding the newborn tightly bound in a blanket. Grinning ecstatically, she dances about.

"We have a boy. A boy! My son has a boy!"

This child is the reason for the money she spent on the gang of kidnappers who brought the young captive bride to her home. Their expensive plan is successful. The family has a baby boy. Her friends rejoice with her and share her delight. A man who is walking past, balancing his loads of onions on his shoulders, hears the news and stops to make the traditional salute.

"Long live the baby boy! Ten thousand years to this family!"

Young children stop their play to watch. Never have they seen such a happy face on this old mistress. Neighbors from across the courtyard and road soon join the noisy celebration. There will not be a hundred-day celebration as properly performed in large towns, but there will be happy food, drinks, and fireworks as the entire village rejoices.

No one asks about the young mother. Everyone knows to whom the baby will belong. The happy grandmother will proudly care for her son's son while the young mother will pull the plow and work by the side of her husband preparing for the planting of crops. It is the time-honored custom.

True Friend sees the small bundle bound tightly in blankets and held proudly by his mother. He bounds into his home and says loudly to his wife, "So you had a boy!"

The exhausted young mother who has just given birth to her first child lies on the kang with her eyes closed. He has never been very talkative with her. She hears the excitement in his voice but knows what she wants to say to him. She has practiced it in her mind a hundred times while she grew larger and larger with this baby she carried.

"Now that I have given you a son, when may I return to my home in the south?"

"What are you talking about?"

"This is what you wanted. You have a son now. Your mother is very happy."

"But he is your baby."

"He is not my son, he is yours. Did you ask me to marry you? Did you ask me if I wanted to make this baby?"

"But he needs a mother!"

"Your mother has already claimed him. Do you see him here with me?"

He stands staring at his young wife. What she says is true. He struggles to express himself. "But this is where you belong."

"Why? You and I have both done our duty to your mother. Your son will be strong and help you in the fields."

"But he will need you."

"So he will. I shall stay one more year to nurse him. Then I will leave when he has learned to walk and drink from a cup."

"But you cannot leave!"

"Why?"

"Because I need you!"

"I will save all of my duck and egg money and my earnings from the common field this entire year, and you can purchase a real bride whose parents approve of the marriage. Perhaps it will be a girl your mother will like. She is never pleased with any of my work, and the boy should not grow up hearing all of that criticism and rebuke."

"But I want you here."

"Why?"

"Because it is you I want. Don't you see?"

"How can I see that? You do not defend me from your mother's abuse. You do not talk with me. You have never once told me that you love me, and that part of me that feels and loves has been dead for so long. You cannot love me, because I am not really me. I left my soul back in that warm land in China with my innocence and my mind."

"This is China also."

"I don't know who this is you are speaking with, but it is not me. I am a good girl who laughs, dances, plays music on my instrument, and studies so hard that I win prizes at school. I have friends at school who like me, a warm family that loves me, and teachers who tell me how proud they are of my work. I would like to find that girl."

"My mother said that it would all work out."

White Flowering Tree, who has been so confused and distant for the past year, sits up on the kang and says clearly, "It has worked out fine for you both! When will it work out for me?"

She lies down with a painful cry. No one has come to give her a drink of traditional herbs for new mothers. No one gives her any water from a thermos. She is so thirsty and tired, but he has not offered her anything, and everyone knows that wives are to serve husbands, not the reversal.

True Friend looks at her in confusion. There is celebration outside over the birth of his son. Why is there no glad celebration in here? What a mystery this young woman is. He shrugs his shoulders, turns from his wife, and goes out his door to see his new son.

My dear Pride,

My last letter must have been painful for you, my dear one. Perhaps that letter was lost or stolen. I will repeat it. You need a wife and our children need a mother. If you can, try to find a woman who is a Christian. They love and forgive so well.

No one has successfully escaped from here. I made round wheat noodles today.

Please begin teaching our little ones to write their characters and numbers.

Silk Fan

PAINTING

The sun sinks low in the sky as Walks with Grace waits her turn at the public water pump in the center of the village. Other daughters and daughters-in-law push ahead of her so that they may fill their buckets and hurry back to warm homes. Standing away from the splashing flow, she listens to her young neighbors' conversations, straining to understand their dialect.

"Tomorrow I must purchase some red envelopes."

"My brother will have the largest firecracker to be found."

"Will you make spice cakes?"

"No, my mother will make rice balls with sweet filling. I could eat them all!"

"I must hurry. There is much cooking to be done for our celebration."

"I need to visit the scribe. He writes such flowing New Year's wishes."

"I need some black ink."

"My first aunt always wrote our New Year's Day wishes when I lived at home."

"How much does the scribe charge to paint a door banner?"

"With his paper and ink, it will be a reasonable price, but so many people will ask him that he may not have time to make everyone's banners."

"If only my grandfather were not so particular about its painting. It must be done so properly."

Walks with Grace speaks quietly to the group, so near her own age. "I will paint your New Year's good luck banners for the same price as the scribe." She is surprised at the sound of her own voice.

Three wives just leaving pause with their water. They know that she is a newly captured bride, and they work beside her in the fields, but she usually has so little to say. They turn to ask, "What did you say?"

"I will paint your New Year's Day banners for you, and they will be properly done. You must bring your own paper and ink."

The three other water drawers do not immediately respond to this neighbor who suddenly finds her voice. After a few minutes, one decides to break the silent treatment and asks, "Are you sure you can paint the banners correctly, according to tradition?"

"My work will be excellent. Bring your paper and ink to my home tomorrow as soon as we have finished feeding the chickens."

The three local young women look at each other. "We know where you live. You are the wife of the man called Steadfast."

A second asks, "How do we know that you are able to write properly in the traditional manner?"

"If it is not satisfactory, then you need not pay my fee." Walks with Grace answers confidently.

"I will come to you tomorrow. May I come early? The work crew will cease work early, as it is New Year's Eve."

"Yes, I will expect you."

She steps forward and quickly fills her water buckets. The weight of her pregnant body makes her task awkward,

I wonder what sort of celebration will be held. At least they celebrate with banners and red envelopes. I wish I was a child again and knew that something good would be in an envelope under my pillow in the morning. Perhaps I really am still in China.

The three water carriers bid her good-bye. Balancing her water buckets on her shoulder pole, she makes her way back home. She walks in a slow pace to avoid spilling the precious cargo. *If I have a nice small brush, I will be able to write, "Good Fortune" on the red envelopes also. How I wish that I still had my schoolbag that those pirates made me leave in that shed. My pen and paper were in it.*

The next morning, Walks with Grace is trying to make a makeshift table from a barrel and a vegetable cutting board outside in the courtyard when the old grandfather sees her efforts and asks what she is doing. She nods politely at the elderly, bent man with the courtly manners and explains that she is preparing to make New Year's Day wishes. She can't help feeling some fondness for the courteous old man.

"So you are educated in writing? Can you make classical good wishes?"

"Yes, Grandfather, but I need supplies. I will gladly make you a fine greeting if I have some paper and black ink. Some neighbor women are coming today. I told them to bring their own paper and ink, as I do not own any."

"I understand, my child. I shall speak to my grandson about this matter."

He climbs slowly up the single step into his own home and returns shortly with a plastic, retractable, ballpoint ink pen. "Here, Granddaughter, you may have my pen. You have more use for it than I. It has black ink and will work fine for the red envelopes."

Tired from his short trip inside, he perches his bent body on a bench and yells for Black Pearl, his daughter-in-law.

"Yes, Grandfather? What do you need?"

"My granddaughter-in-law needs paper and ink for New Year's Day banners. Get her some. Why has Steadfast not taken care of this matter? We must have a fine celebration this year now that we have a new daughter-in-law in the house."

The old man is delighted to discover that he will be entertained today. Resting both hands and then his chin on his walking cane, he begins an address to any who will listen about the proper way to celebrate the New Year. Two young women approach the courtyard, and he accepts them as his new audience. After greeting him politely, they conduct their business with Walks with Grace while he continues his speech.

No one seems to be listening to him, but it does not matter to him. He is lost in pleasant memories of a long life.

"On the last night of the Spring Festival of the New Year, we celebrate by walking into the road with paper lanterns on poles. They look like firebugs all across the hills and fields. We give our families and friends fine New Year's Day wishes. After the fireworks, we go back to our homes and eat those rice treats like the ones my mother made when I was a boy. What do you call them?"

Walks with Grace bends over the board, painting a large banner in perfect characters, "Good Fortune."

"Do you mean the sticky, round rice balls, Grandfather?"

"Yes, the ones with a sweet filling."

"We call them yuan xiao, Grandfather."

"What did you say, daughter?"

Spring Clouds whispers to Walks with Grace, "We call them tang yuan."

"Well, they are called yuan xiao at my home in the south. Will you please answer him correctly? I am almost finished here. The ink must dry for a time."

After bowing to the grandfather, her client answers him politely.

Walks with Grace and Truth stands up, stretches her tense

muscles, and asks, "Do you have any envelopes for me to write on?"

"I have a few. Can you make each read, 'We wish you good luck'?"

"Yes, of course. Do you want to have my grandfather approve of the work?"

Spring Clouds takes her first red envelope to Grandfather for approval. Slowly scanning the characters, he reads aloud, "We wish you good luck."

Turning to Walks with Grace, the patriarch says proudly, "So what other surprises do you have for us? This is indeed fine work. It is in the best traditional style."

She smiles at the judgment passed on her work. If the oldest generation is satisfied, then others will accept it. Black Pearl standing in the doorway watches and listens but says nothing.

Walks with Grace speaks with two neighbors and wins respect for her skills. She continues writing on the red holiday envelopes the correct traditional New Year's wishes: "Good Luck," "Good Fortune," "Long Life," "Good Luck in Marriage," and "Much Success."

"Grandfather, what do you want your wish to read? I will write a neat one when I buy a piece of paper." He still sits on his bench, but his eyes are closed. He is asleep.

The visitors leave, and Steadfast comes to read her work.

"Would you write me a New Year's wish?"

"What do you want it to read?" she asks.

"Love from my love," he answers with a grin.

Walks with Grace makes a small New Year's wish on a scrap of paper. It reads, "Love from my love."

They look into each other's eyes and smile. Any public display of affection is unheard of, but they smile wonderful smiles.

"Come in, my pretty wife. You should rest now. Our son might come tonight."

Dear Pride,

I have something very difficult to write to you. You know how proud I have always been of you and how perfectly I have loved you all of our marriage. I love you so much that it pains me to watch a door and realize that you will not be coming through it each evening.

My life here is hopeless. I cannot find any way to escape. You, my dear Pride, need a wife, and our little ones need a mother. My hand is shaking as I write this, but I must. If you can find a willing and loving woman to marry, please try to find the price and marry her. I know that you suffer as much as I.

Hug our children and tell them that I made these clothes for them.

Weaving keeps my hands busy and helps me make it through the days.

Silk Fan

164

HARVEST TIME

Stands Strong and his friend Uncut Jade eat their noodles with chopsticks while standing in the doorways. They feel the excitement of the entire village. All who had any part in the planting, watering, and weeding of the community cabbage field will take part in today's harvest. Everyone will return home with their baskets piled high with the rich, green cabbages.

One of the oldest members of the community, the Han widow, walks with two canes to ease the pain on her bound feet. She will tally the names and number of baskets that each person takes home.

Both the older and younger cadres from this area wear their official hats and make official-sounding noises about where to deposit the vegetables.

Beautiful Moon and White Flowering Tree left home with their families and now walk together in the tide of humanity moving toward the cabbage fields where they worked all summer. Each of them is grateful to see a friendly face.

They fall in line behind a woman who is wearing an apron around her waist, full of steamed rolls. She is having difficulty managing two large harvest baskets. One is properly strapped to her back while she carries the other for her daughter, with whom she is having an animated conversation. As the mother gives her instructions, the girl dances away from her, staying at arm's length, avoiding her mother. Other village women watch and listen as they parade in line with the entire village.

"Here, child, take this basket."

"I do not want to wear that big basket."

"Do not argue, just take it. You will need it when we arrive at the common field."

Mother, I will see you when we get there."

"No. You must stay with me and work next to the other women and girls."

"I want to walk with Father and First Uncle Mountain Man."

"No, daughter! Stay with me."

"I want to walk with Father and Uncle." With a last disobedient protest, the girl runs off with shining, straight hair bouncing in the morning sun, without a basket.

Beautiful Moon and White Flowering Tree exchange glances and note that the mother is more than embarrassed. Her brow creases in concern.

Later, as the harvesters eat their noon meal together, the two brides witness this same family together. The mother still wears a worried brow as she squats in the shade of a willow tree feeding her husband some steamed rolls. As they eat, a handsome young man with a wide smile showing white teeth comes up. Riding on his back is their daughter, laughing and calling happily, "Look. I have my own horse." With a smooth sweep of his arms, the young man lifts his niece off his back and deposits her on the ground.

"This horse is tired. Let's eat now."

The mother has nothing to say to either of them as she hands both the horse and its rider a steamed roll. As she eats, she leans over and removes her daughter's shoes. Taking the strings out of both, she returns the shoes to their owner.

"Momma, what are you doing?"

The mother continues until she has both strings tied together into one long, dusty string.

"Momma, what have you done? Now I cannot run to keep up with First Uncle! Put my shoestrings back into my shoes!" The spoiled only child thinks that is appropriate for her to give orders to her parents. They always cater to her needs.

The mother calmly ties the length of shoestrings to her daughter's arm, and a friend ties the other end to the mother's arm.

The village group begins to disperse as they return to work, and still the mother and daughter are arguing. Tears now cover the face of the rebellious child as she answers her mother's questions with demands. "Momma, Father and Uncle Mountain Man are leaving now. They said that I could help them today. I must run to catch up with them."

The well-dressed child sits on the ground, wiping her face with dusty fists. She does not understand why her mother, who is always so kind and unselfish, is acting in such a strange manner in front of everyone they know. The other children will be laughing at her when they see her tied to her mother like a toddling baby.

"Momma, why do you need my shoestrings?" The vivacious demands have melted into a tearful whimper.

"You would not listen to me this morning. What did I say?"

"Momma, please. You are embarrassing me. Everyone is looking at us."

It is time to return to one of the most important workdays of the year. The other workers are now replacing their baskets upon their backs. The mother's friends walk slowly in order for their friend to attend to her child.

"What did I say to you this morning?"

"Momma, why are you shaming me so?

"What did I say?"

"I don't remember."

"Get up then. We must be on our way. Place your basket on your back now. It will be awkward with one hand tied to me."

"Momma, please."

"What did I say to you this morning?" Pitiful sniffles and more wiping of tears do not move the calm-mannered mother. "What did I say when you would not listen?"

"You said that I was to carry my own basket."

"Yes, and what did you do?"

"I did not take it."

"And what else did I tell you that I wanted you to do?"

"I don't know."

"As you wish. Keep walking. We can wear this string all week if you like."

"Momma, no. Everyone will see me." She strains to see if Stands Strong sees her.

"What else did I say?"

"You said that you wanted me to walk with you and the other women and girls."

"That is correct. And what did you do?"

"I told you that I wanted to help Father and First Uncle Mountain Man."

"You told me. You did not ask my permission."

"Why are you so angry? I was with Father."

"You deliberately ran away from me and disobeyed me, so now you must be tied like a baby that has not learned to obey."

"Oh, Momma, I will obey. Please take the string off my arm."

"Will you walk with me and take care of your own basket now?"

"Yes, Momma."

The girl's mother holds her head high and continues her

work. Ignoring the many stares, she continues on her way. Raising children is such a public activity.

Beautiful Moon and White Flowering Tree are busy cutting and packing the vegetables into their own baskets, but they cannot escape hearing the conversations next to them.

"Who is he?" The women friends are discussing the drama.

"A brother-in-law."

"Will he stay here after this week of harvest?"

"I do not know."

"Where does he live?"

"He lives with his family in the third village."

"Why is he here now?"

"He went to Shanghai to work with the other men and hoped to use his money to return home with a wife. But he returned without a wife."

"He is handsome. Didn't he meet any potential wives in such a large city?"

"You know how it is. None of the city girls wants to be a farmer's wife. They know that he will return to work in the city and leave her alone to farm with only his mother for company."

"There are so few girls here, even for a handsome man."

"Surely they will not allow him to stay in their home. She is their only child."

"How does one say, 'You not welcome here'?"

"She will simply have to speak to the child."

"How can you explain such a danger to her? She is only nine years old."

The patient mother decides that this is her chance to speak with her daughter while they are both walking the dusty paths through the long rows of the communal garden.

"Daughter, you are too old now to climb on uncle's back. He is a man now, and you are growing up. You are not a small child anymore. It is not suitable for you to climb on him like you did when you were a baby."

"Why, Mother? Mountain Man likes me."

The mother sighs. "What I am telling you is very important, my child. First Uncle Mountain Man needs to spend his time looking for a young woman to marry. If he spends his time with you, then he will never find a wife. You must stop holding his hand and sitting in his lap, and you certainly must stop riding on his back and clinging to him. It is not proper."

"But Momma, he likes me to be his special friend."

"Daughter, you are not listening to me."

The two new-bought wives hear their neighbors' conversation concerning their neighbor's dilemma. They are not a part of the conversation, but they hear and see.

"She still does not understand the danger."

"How can she understand? She is still a child."

"And then it will be too late."

Beautiful Moon looks at her friend, White Flowering Tree, who raises her eyebrows. She is no longer a child, and she does not understand either. Her mother did not discuss incest with her, and she too fails to comprehend the scope of the problem involving a visiting relative. Nice families do not discuss even normal marriage relationships until the girls were ready to be sent to the homes of their new husbands. Why cloud their innocent minds with such fears?

"Momma, we are almost to the end of this row; please untie me. The other students from school will see me and laugh. I promise to stay with you."

"Do you promise to listen carefully to everything I have to say to you and to think about it now and later?"

"Yes, Momma."

"There is much I need to tell you, but I shall remove the strings for now. Rays of Dawn, will you please untie us?"

When her friend unties the shoestring, the crowd melts around them and moves steadily on. The mother waits while her daughter hurriedly laces her shoes and repositions her empty harvest basket. The child thinks that this episode concerns only an issue of carrying her own harvest basket.

The two stolen brides hear the mother speaking quietly with her only child.

"Daughter, I need to speak to you concerning your body. You own your body and are entitled to your privacy. No one has the right to touch you on your private places. Do you understand?"

The child is busy placing the fat cabbages that her mother cut into her own basket and turns to look blankly at her mother.

"Because you are so special, some men or boys might want to hold you and hug you and touch you in your private girl places. I want you to know that no one, no one, has the privilege of doing that. Do you understand?" The nine-year-old girl stands with her mouth slightly open and stares at her mother. She has no idea what her mother is trying to explain to her.

"Do you understand, my little girl?" She speaks so softly that no one is sure what she says.

"Daughter, when anyone tries to touch your girl places, even if it is someone you know or someone in the family, you must yell as loud as you can and scream, 'Stop!' You should come to find me or another auntie nearby. When you scream: 'No! Stop!' the boy or man will probably leave you alone."

"Yes, Momma."

As they reach the end of the row, where they empty their baskets, the child, her mother, the two new brides, and eight other neighbors, too are all strangely subdued.

HAPPINESS FOUND

I t is the second year since the gang of criminals attacked the five southern females. Summer Rain, youngest of the victims, returned to her home at the instruction of the official who declared her too young for a legal marriage. Afraid of the powerful gang, he took no action on the status of the other four women.

The brides continue to send letters to their families at home in south China. No answer from any of their families gives hope that all were confiscated before they leave the valley. It is a constant effort to find a traveler who might be willing to post a letter from another district. Yet they cling to this thin hope that a letter will reach some bride's family and all four will be rescued.

They find some comfort in their joint friendship to which they swore themselves, and each of them has found useful work, but none has accepted the situation, and only one is happy.

Silk Fan remains the leader and comforter of the small band of captives. No official or neighbor is concerned that her marriage is not legal because of the fact that she already has a husband in southern China. After one year, the snubbing tradition is lifted, and people consent to speak to the four newcomers.

Silk Fan amazed her friends, her neighbors, and Hero by purchasing a young girl from the child's uncle. She could not afford the orphan, but she refused to allow this child whom she had just met to be sold into prostitution. Silk Fan loses some of her despair as she sews for Humble, serves meals on time, helps with schoolwork, and generally takes the place of a loving second mother. Hero reacts with pleasure at having two much younger females in his small home. He is most pleased one day when Humble asks, seriously, "Grandfather Hero of His People, may I call you Second Father? My first father is with the ancestors now." Hero, who has little to say on most days, smiles and replies, "Humble, I would be pleased to be your second father."

That simple conversation seals a relationship that is meaningful for both. She shows little attentions that would make other men jealous. Humble asks his approval of her math homework and many characters, so carefully practiced in ink, and she goes to meet him as he returns from the fields. Smiling happily, she walks the last few yards from the village with his hoe over her shoulder or his fresh, dirty vegetables in her arms.

A dutiful student who makes friends easily, Humble keeps Silk Fan company with her simple, girlish ways. She begins her first weaving project, a wool blanket, with enthusiasm. On one warm day in the second fall, Humble tumbles breathlessly into the courtyard with several other children at her heels. They all talk at once, so at first, Silk Fan, who is weaving outside her door, cannot understand anything.

"Everyone, please be quiet. Humble, what is the problem?"

"Mother, you must come with us. You must come. It was asleep, but not now."

Several children speak at once. "Yes, we woke it up, but we did not mean to. We did not know what was there."

"You were too noisy!"

"Where, Humble? Who?"Silk Fan tries to understand their problem.

"We do not know its name, but it is in a box by the side of the road to the school. We saw it when we came out. Please come with us, Mother." Silk Fan laughs at the excited group of schoolchildren who cannot tell her what they have found. "I am coming, Humble, but what is that you have found?"

"It is a baby, Mother. A real, live baby! No big person was near. Why would someone leave a baby by the school path?"

The children were correct. A doe-eyed baby sits in a box, leaning to one side, surrounded by a blanket and baby cloths.

"I do not know that answer, Humble. Who wants go for the cadre?" Immediately, three boys say that they are each the fastest runner, and all three leave in puffs of dust.

All ages of school students demand answers.

"Whose baby is it?"

"Why is it here?"

"What is its name?"

Silk Fan tries to answer the children's queries. "I do not know to whom this baby belongs, but I think that it was left here so that you would be certain to find it when you left school." Silk Fan kneels beside the baby.

"Where are the mother and father?"

"We do not know that, children."

A bored cadre, officer of the government in this valley, arrives with an escort of schoolboys.

"Hello, cadre."

"Hello, Grandmother Silk Fan. What do we have here?"

Silk Fan smiles at the salutation. As Hero is a grandfather, she is being correctly addressed.

Unperturbed by the noisy children or her posture, which is slipping with every minute, the infant stays in the well-made box, sucking on its fist. No one touches the baby. The cadre lifts his eyebrows, but he does not touch the newly discovered child.

"What will you do with this baby, cadre?"

"When I write my report this week, I will make a note. Who found it?"

All of the children claim credit for the find. The man nods his head and turns to return to his home. He was sharpening his harvest knife and does not want the bother of this foundling.

"Aren't you going to do something, sir?" The astonished Silk Fan has summoned the highest official in the village and can barely believe his lack of concern over this small perfection of humanity.

"You cannot just leave the child here!"

"You take it," he says to no one in particular as he strides away.

Two of the children whisper then run home. They return soon with the news that neither of their mothers will allow them to bring a baby home. When the baby finally falls on its ear, the softhearted Humble picks it up and begins a lullaby.

Silk Fan bends down, searching for a note or name, and then sadly acknowledges that no one will ever return to claim the baby. It is another case of people caught in the governmental ruling that limits each family to one child.

How much more grief must we suffer? I wonder who actually put this lovely little one here. Mothers cannot do this cowardly deed, so other family members usually take the baby, always a girl, and leave it while the mother is away selling her eggs at market or washing the laundry in the canal. Oh, that poor mother.

"Well, Humble, what are we going to do with this tiny one?"

"May we keep it, Mother?"

With a small, laugh Silk Fan answers, "I do not have the nerve to ask Hero for another child, my dear."

"May we keep it if he says yes?"

"Humble, we are not rich people. Other people can give it a better home."

"May I just ask Hero?"

"Humble, there is a government policy about how many

children a family may have. We probably will not be allowed to keep it even if Hero allows it."

Silk Fan decides the children do not need to know the law will allow men to have more children if he wants, but not with the same woman.

Humble does not release her tight hold on the bundle of baby while the crowd of schoolchildren waits for Silk Fan's answer.

"We will take the baby home with us for the night and find some official who cares for abandoned babies." The children nod their heads. "Who wants to carry the box to our house?"

Uncut Jade is the first to stoop over and to pick up the box, most probably the baby's crib. He says nothing but follows his friend, Humble, who is still holding the baby dressed in warm clothing and wrapped in a colorful blanket. The children follow in a somber parade of honor for the foundling.

"You know that we are only going to care for this baby until we can find a home for it. It is not our baby."

"Yes, Mother."

"We do not have the money for its care, and Hero will not allow it. Do not think of it as 'our' baby."

"Yes, Mother. I am naming her Happiness Found."

"We do not even have a goat for milk."

"Yes, Mother."

HOMESICK

People in the village now speak to the kidnapped brides, but the friendships here in this select group of second-class women are built on shared experiences of horror and grief. Today, on a day when snow blows in great whirls, the group meets at the home of Silk Fan to weave baskets.

"When the days are warm and the trees are budding pale green and people bustle about eager for spring work, I think of home." Looking off at a distance, White Flowering Tree continues, "My home in the south is such a lovely place."

Even her friends sometimes refuse to listen as she reminisces about her lost childhood home, so she speaks for her own benefit. As the wind-driven snow howls outside, her friends allow her to speak. No one mentions the inconsistency in her memory of the seasons.

"The city was such an exciting place for a young girl. Before I was stolen at the railway station, I saw only good things in my home city. Our school had such fine teachers. We read many writers of poetry and philosophy. We worked hard painting our characters and studied some ancient art each year. When we cut out blocks for printing, our teachers took us to watch the fabric printers at work. Those artists are so skilled.

"Our paintings were only the paintings of schoolgirls, but our teachers were patient and encouraging. I still remember the varied shades of pink in our paintings of peonies."

Dreamily, White Flowering Tree continues, "I played in the string orchestra. I liked the feel of the varnished wood in my hands as we played the old music. I made the notes come at my bidding. That pei-ke-hu was such a fine instrument. If I had it here, I could play soothing music for my baby."

She stops working and is lost in her beautiful memories. Since her captivity, she has a problem holding on to her sanity. Now her friends exchange glances. When is it a kindness to allow her to talk, and when are they encouraging weeks of retreat into another world? Her friends do not know.

"May I tell you about my home? I think I can do so now with no tears."

Silk Fan whispers to White Flowering Tree in an attempt to keep her attention on the present time and place. "That is the wife of the leather worker, our new friend."

She is the latest captured bride and thus an immediate member in their circle of friends. She begins, "I lived in the capital city of our district. Most people have shiny black hair and pleasant faces. They are not thin and hungry looking, just well-built farmers. People helped their neighbors. If there was a flood or an illness, or if a man did not return from his fields, he knew that it would not be long before a kind neighbor came to help him. At evening, a widow we know would come by after her day of begging. My mother always gave her rice."

The others smile in acknowledgement of a homeland with which they can identify.

"My girlfriends and I took our watercolors and sat on a wall to paint the hazy skies. Even the cold breeze seemed exciting as we waited on the mountaintop for the wild cranes to fly over-head. We counted them each year. We were farmers' daughters, but our whole families did cultural activities together. My grand-mother told us stories of history. My father recited long verses about ancient dynasties. My mother taught us how to paint lovely pictures and to cut tiny figures out of paper. How I miss the sim-ple pleasure of kind people and real Chinese culture."

"Thank you," Silk Fan says. "Please tell us again about liv-ing in your hometown, Walks with Grace."

A small smile creeps over the face of the displaced student. "I did not come to live in town until I was eleven years old. My parents allowed me to attend school in the city as a special privilege because I studied so hard. They could have used my help at home on the farm, but they wanted me to have a fine education. I lived with my cousins during the school week and went home on the weekends."

As thoughts of her parents come to her mind, she hesitates. To prevent this from becoming another time of tearful remem-bering, Silk Fan prompts, "Tell us about the city streets."

Homesick, Walks with Grace reminisces, "The streets are always alive, every day, not just on market days. Women who worked in the offices in town look very neat as they travel to work. At the university we dressed simply but also presentably." The blanket on her infant son slides down over his face. She gently moves it and continues with her memories.

"Sometimes I dance in my mind while wearing a lovely silk costume. At times, I am a flower girl in an opera, and other times I am my real self, dancing in class to authentic music at my university class."

Beautiful Moon sighs. "Where could you go?"

"Many businesses are right on the sidewalk. Four or five of us girls would take time just to watch the artisans at work. One friend always wanted to watch the sign painters or prayer writ-ers at work because they painted such fine letters and ancient quotations.

"On one side street there is a row of sewing machines all lined up early in the morning. These tailors would sit and sew all day long. They could make anything to fit anyone and make it exactly as a person described."

Walks with Grace gives her small son a toy for teething and continues. "A bowl of hot tea is so cheap that we could always buy some at a sidewalk shop. The teahouses were really for adults, just a nice place to meet and visit. People said that at night these same teahouses are used for gambling and for meeting boys. I do not know for sure; I was never allowed to go out at night without my family. That is not proper. At night I studied. The book sellers were places I dreamed about. There were so many books to see. I only had money enough for my university textbooks, but I liked to look."

"May I tell you about the bakery shop where I worked?" Beautiful Mon says.

"Oh yes. Please do," they chorus.

Silk Fan announces, "Our time is spent. We will hear from Beautiful Moon another day. Tomorrow is our day to sew with the widow. Do all of you think that you can come?"

"Yes. I think that I can come," White Flowering Tree answers.

"Walks with Grace, do you think that the barber's mother will allow you to bring her book for us to read while we sew?"

"I do hope so. I have stayed too long with you. I must read for a time to her now if I am to borrow the book. Since it is so cold, the entire family listens. I hope that old mumble and grumble will allow me to go out again."

Each young woman takes her unfinished basket back home. The unfinished baskets will serve as busywork during these most dreaded hours of being shut in with their captive families.

After an evening meal of wheat noodles with lamb, Walks with Grace goes to read to the almost blind neighbor, Grandmother Rose Bud, who is wrapped in her quilts waiting for the treat of a private reader. Her small granddaughter, Red Rose, sits close by. She smiles at her neighbor and indicates that she is to sit next to her. The entire family waits respectfully as the old mistress of the house speaks, "I want to hear about Jeremiah."

"Do you want to hear from one of the psalms, Mother?"

"No, I want to hear the book of Jeremiah. It is after the book of Psalms."

The barber sits in his chair while Walks with Grace finds the unfamiliar section of the large leather-bound book. Walks with Grace begins reading aloud.

Little Red Rose giggles. "What funny names! I am glad that I do not have a funny name."

"Shh, child. We want to hear this old story." Her father takes her into his lap and nods to their reader. Walks with Grace smiles at the child and continues reading the amazing story about Jeremiah aloud through all the parts about God's promise to punish his people for abandoning him to worship idols.

"Madam, this is the end of chapter one. Shall I continue reading?"

"Yes. Continue reading until you read God saying, 'I will not give you up. I will plead for you to return to me, and will keep on pleading.'"

So the reader repositions the volume and continues reading to the perfect audience, one hungry for the old stories remembered, and the others hungry for a new, intriguing tale.

"In those days Israel was a holy people, the first of my children. Even their priests cared nothing for the Lord, and their judges ignored me: rulers turned against me, and their prophets worshiped Baal and wasted their time on nonsense. But I will not give you up—I will plead for you to return to me, and will keep on pleading; yes, even with your children's children in the years to come!"

Jeremiah 2:9

"Young mistress, read that verse again. Children, listen and repeat it after her. God is making a great promise here. We have hidden this book too long. I have held on to this promise. You must know about this great God who loves his people so much."

Walks with Grace reads the verse three more times while the family repeats it in ancient rote style.

"But I will not give you up—I will plead for you to return to me, and will keep on pleading: yes, even with your children's children in the years to come."

Jeremiah 2:9

After reading the verse for the third time, Walks with Grace is released. She is anxious to return home to see her husband. Following such a difficult beginning to their marriage, the young couple is discovering each other as partners. He seems eager to please, and she is making real attempts to think of him as her husband. As she wraps her tiny son in wool blankets for her return trip home, she ponders the new verses she has just read. Somewhere in her past, she remembers dimly the words from this book. She remembers that it was her own dear grandmother who gave her a Christian name. During the fearful years her family dropped the last part of her name in an attempt to save her life. Walks with Grace now becomes Walks with Grace and Truth as her grandmother named her.

WHERE ARE WE?

Walks with Grace and Truth and Silk Fan are working with a group of women cutting stalks of bamboo. "These stalks are so thin that they seem useless. At home, we grow large, strong bamboo."

A short young woman in a faded blue suit frowns at Silk Fan. She does not understand what is being said. Rejecting short stalks, she bundles her choices into a huge pile and motions that they are to gather only long stalks. Silk Fan smiles her thanks and says to Walks with Grace and Truth, "I still do not know where we are or who these people are. Perhaps they are another kind of Hans."

"We are Hans! They are not like us!"

Silk Fan tries to calm Walks with Grace and Truth. "You are correct, but this girl is trying to be friendly. She says that these bamboo stalks will be used for new bed mats."

"Do you think that we are still in China?"

"I do not know."

"Do you know why Beautiful Moon is not with us today?"

"No, I have not seen her this week."

The two captured wives join a line of other women returning home with large bundles tied to their back, just like a parade of pack animals. As they return to their homes, the village seems unusually quiet. Neighbors watch the young women returning and then glance away. Uncut Jade is waiting for Walks with Grace and Truth and Silk Fan. He delivers a message and immediately runs to the home of White Flowering Tree.

"This seems like such an urgent message from the widow. Perhaps she is ill. I am going there now to see her," Walks with Grace says.

"I am coming too," Silk Fan agrees.

They deposit their loads inside their courtyards and both walk quickly. Behind them, the running feet of Uncut Jade and White Flowering Tree draw closer.

"What is the matter? Why does she want us? She has never sent for us before."

"We do not know."

Uncut Jade knows the cause of the summons. Sitting down on the worn steps of the widow's home, he waits with his chin in his hands.

Beautiful Moon was caught trying to run away again. She was severely beaten and crippled in not just one leg but in both legs. This is an ancient cruelty reserved for runaway slaves and wives. The old people from remote places know of this custom, but it is too horrible for the young people to believe. The widow informs the brides of Beautiful Moon's fate.

Walks with Grace and Truth and White Flowering Tree scream aloud, and all four weep openly. The young girl who helps the widow weeps for the bride, shamed that this atrocity happened here in her village.

The widow composes herself first and asks the local girl to find a clean piece of cotton fabric in the storage chest. As she rips then folds the strips of fabric into tight rolls, she speaks quietly. "She will need these clean bandages. If they put dirty rags on her, she might die."

Silk Fan speaks first. "I will take them to her."

Walks with Grace and Truth speaks next. "I will go also. She needs friends now."

The widow nods and instructs, "Take this food."

Silk Fan speaks angrily, "This is meant as a message to each of us, you understand."

"Do you mean a threat?" Walks with Grace asks.

"Yes. Of course it is," Silk Fan states with a firm face.

"Then I am coming with you. I want those evil warriors against girls to know that I am not afraid of them." Walks with Grace and Truth growls.

"Well, I am afraid, but I want to come along." White Flowering Tree is not brave.

"Madam, may I go with them?" Her helper is only eleven years old, but she wants to join this group. She takes a jug of water and says quietly, "I can wash her wounds."

Silk Fan addresses their hostess, "Madam, I need something to impress these monsters. Something official looking. May I borrow the brass rod from your scroll?"

"Will this serve your purposes?" The widow sees danger in Silk Fan's request.

"It will do well. Now do you have something with cords or fringes, or bright ribbons, or a flag, or a hat? I need something more."

"You see what you can use. My gold-colored sash with the green tassel is in that tall chest. I have only some bronze bracelets and my father's war awards. One is quite fine."

"Oh, madam, I do not want to use his medals of honor."

"He would be pleased, and I am also." The elderly woman smiles.

"These silk ribbons are pretty. May I use them? They will flow in the wind as I carry it. They are perfect for a funeral curse." Silk Fan is persistent.

"Will you wear them?"

"No. I shall tie them to the brass rod, holding it up before me as a symbol of whatever authority Beautiful Moon's mother-in-law imagines us to have."

"Please be careful, my young friend." The widow shakes her head in warning.

"I shall be bold today. They have not appreciated good manners or hard work. Their own superstitions will speak to them today." The lead sister makes bold plans.

"Walks with Grace and Truth, why don't you carry my best walking stick? I thought it too fine for use. Now I think that today is a good time to bring it out." Remembering when a fine stick such as this one brought dignity and authority to its owners, she takes the dark, wooden stick embellished with metal and simply nods.

As the subdued band of young women descends the outside stairs, Silk Fan asks, "Does anyone know where the duck man and his nephew are this time of day?"

Uncut Jade, who has been waiting for them, answers quickly, "I know. They are in the common cornfield."

"Good. We need to borrow his nephew and his dog."

Uncut Jade runs to find Golden Treasure, the ten-year-old boy whose daily job is to guard his uncle's large flock of ducks as they forage the grain fields. His long hair and worn clothing announce that he has been beyond his mother's reach for months. He misses childhood friendships, so he is flattered to act as guard today.

At the end of the rod, Silk Fan ties the gold satin sash pinned with the official war medal. The green tassels swing from the sash while the two bronze bracelets clang and the thin silk ribbons wave in the breeze. Silk Fan leads the way, carrying the long brass rod made for holding a painted picture of swans and flowers, a wedding gift from the widow's youth.

Close behind her marches Walks with Grace and Truth, holding the fancy walking cane in one hand and a gift of bread in the other. Her recent tears have left her eyes red and her face streaked, but anger sets her jaw in firm resolve

Next marches White Flowering Tree, a fresh green pear in each hand. Beside her, the local girl carries a jug of water while taking long strides in order to keep up with the adults. Behind the young women marches the shabby boy holding his guard dog on a short rope. He wears a self-confident expression on his serious face. Uncut Jade follows at the rear of the parade, carrying a basket filled with rolls of cotton strips for bandages. He does not know what will happen next, but he is loyal to his friends on this day of great sadness.

From the group a voice is heard saying, "My insides are quivering."

Another voice declares, "I wish we had a large, black bird with us. They bring years of good luck." The local girl knows local traditions.

"What shall we say?" The young girl is now frightened.

"Just allow Aunt Silk Fan to speak." Uncut Jade does not plan on speaking.

Stern-faced, the parade makes its way to the home of Beautiful Moon. Village housewives watch. Some follow a short distance behind. As the brutalization of the loveliest bride in the village was never a secret, this is watched as the next scene in an ongoing drama.

Double Joy is washing a batch of red peppers outside in her courtyard. She is startled at the sight of her visitors. Without hesitating, the oncoming group bears down on her house. She runs in the direction of her own door. "What do you want?"

"We are here to see Beautiful Moon."

"We do not need any company today."

Silk Fan and White Flowering Tree brush her aside. Walks with Grace and Truth ushers the servant girl inside and nods to the two boys. She takes the basket of bandages from Uncut Jade, and the two boys position themselves in the doorway. At a word from his owner, the guard dog growls a warning.

The visitors immediately see their friend lying on a mat on the kang with bloody rags covering both of her ankles. Silk Fan is not prepared for the bloody scene. "Oh, Beautiful Moon, what have these evil monsters done to you?"

The servant girl who so bravely offered to bathe her wounds is too shocked to do so now. She silently hands the jug of cool water to White Flowering Tree.

Silk Fan asks gently, "Have they given you anything to ease the pain?"

The beautiful girl who wanted to open her own bakery shop shakes her head. Her mouth is clenched in pain and moans escape her lips. As her friends cry at the sight of her injuries, she rolls over slightly so that they can clean the bloody marks on her back. As she moves, she screams in pain, and both of her feet dangle at strange angles. There is much scrambling about as they try to place her feet firmly on the kang. Silk Fan gasps in horror. "They have cut both of her tendons! These heartless animals have crippled our Beautiful Moon!"

No amount of sympathy, pain-dulling herbs, bandages, or assistance from these friends can help her. Silk Fan sends the servant girl to the widow for some herbs for their crippled friend. The three young wives do what they can and sit for a time, holding her hand. None has imagined anything this horrible. The servant child returns quickly, having run the entire way. She hands a small bottle of dark liquid to them.

"My mistress says it is good for pain and for clotting the blood." A sip is given to Beautiful Moon, and the bottle is hidden under her mat. She is bathed, her wounds are bandaged, and she is dressed in a clean gown, but these friends realize that it is beyond their abilities to help her. As she continues to moan, their united anger rises.

Walks with Grace and Truth speaks, "One of us will come back tomorrow to see you. Here is some food. We are placing it under your bed cover. Please try to eat something." Beautiful

Moon does not answer. Tears roll from her eyes as she grits her teeth.

As the brides leave the house, they hesitate at the sight of the crowd gathered in the road. The two boys and the dog still stand at the threshold. None is willing to challenge their right to be there. Their brave leader, Silk Fan, says, "Just ignore them and stay with me."

Turning around and facing the doorway of the house from which they have just emerged, Silk Fan raises both of her arms and points the brass picture rod at the door. She shouts in a commanding voice, "We curse this house and those who own it. May it be as inhospitable to them as it is to this innocent one, today and forever."

Walks with Grace and Truth points the impressively carved walking stick, and White Flowering Tree and the servant girl as well as the two boys speak in echo as if they have practiced their lines. A loud chorus is heard to say, "Today and forever."

Without turning around or looking at the dumbfounded owner of the house, Silk Fan instructs, "Just follow me westward."

The group follows Silk Fan and stops at the western corner of the square stone house, where she points her hands toward the corner of the roof. The long brass rod sways with its imaginary symbolism. The others join in the gesture and point their hands upward. Walks with Grace and Truth holds her fancy walking stick high, pointing it at the roof.

The crowd in the road hears the shout from Silk Fan. "From this time on, this house shall be known as the House of Hatred."

An echo follows, "The House of Hatred."

The friends move behind their leader to the southern corner of the house. Silk Fan stands with firm resolve on her young face and announces, "Their ancestors cringe with shame, as all will know that there is no honor here. They howl in grief at your lack of humanity. There is no honor here!"

Brave, lusty voices shout, "No honor here."

"May the souls of these mean people wander forever seeking peace."

The choral echo underscores the curse, "Wander forever seeking peace." Groans arise from the crowd. Did she really curse their souls to wander forever?

As the young people head toward the eastern corner of the house, the crowd breaks into a run to follow the action. They want to see and hear. Silk Fan waits until all of her small group is in place and resumes her speech.

"May the sun hide from you. May your bones feel the cold of winter and your hands and feet turn blue with chill. May the wind blow ice down upon you as cold as your hearts."

The chorus repeats at the top of their voices, "As cold as your hearts."

The crowd pushes and shoves for a good place to view and hear every word. This scene will be described repeatedly for years. Silk Fan, the usually proper housewife, waits until her entourage and audience are in place at the northern corner of the House of Hatred.

Shaking her brass rod in the air, she shouts out, "May your eyes cry for sleep but your nights be haunted by terrible dreams of vultures chasing you. We curse you to a weariness not eased by rest, a thirst never quenched, a hunger never filled, fears which chase you, and possessions that will never make you happy. We curse this house!"

The echo rings out, "We curse this house!"

Double Joy, so brave when she and her relatives cut her beautiful daughter-in-law, is now being publicly mocked and cursed. She tries to break up the group and send them away, but the duck guarding boy understands his role. He speaks a low word to his dog that responds with a menacing growl.

All three of the children wait for their cues, thinking only of the moment. The adults are aware of all sorts of repercussions but bravely follow Silk Fan's lead. The audience rushes to face the only door of the house. Again, Silk Fan lifts her hands with a flourish and is mimicked by ten other hands pointing to the roof of this building that is bearing all of the blame of its owners. With an authoritarian voice that would do credit to an important party cadre, the usually quiet and well-mannered Silk Fan screams out again, "The friends of this house will be as corrupt as its owners. May their old age be cursed with loneliness and suspicion."

"Loneliness and suspicion."

A neighbor woman gasps, covers her quivering mouth, and backs away. She has just voiced the fears of elderly people.

The crowd, which has grown in size as people return home from the day's work, stands with huge eyes and open mouths. The bold words they hear amaze and frighten like the curses spoken of by their ancient ones.

Silk Fan turns on her heels and for the first time addresses the crowd. "I curse the women of this land, you who have murdered your own daughters and hated the daughters of other women. You are guilty of a cruel hatred against the young and innocent. We curse you to live in your own hatred and never know the harmony of a loving family and to have your vicious souls spend eternity wandering in search of peace."

"Wandering."

The crowd shrinks back in horror. One woman leaves, shaking her head; two other women sob, while an old man quietly takes the arm of his family member and walks home.

Double Joy protests in anger, "You can't say those things."

Ignoring her reaction, Silk Fan marches to the gateway to the road and lifts her arms once more. "I curse you men of this village for being afraid of your old mothers. Curses be upon you for consorting with criminals, stealing innocent girls and women, and treating them with such hatred. You have created a place void of love and honor."

The loud refrain repeats, "Void of love and honor."

Their anger has fueled their courage thus far. Silk Fan leads them on the way back toward their homes. White Flowering

BARBARA NOWELL

Tree wants to turn around to see what weapons will be used against her. She carries the widow's breadbasket that now holds Beautiful Moon's bloody clothes. *At least Walks with Grace and Truth has a fancy walking stick with which to defend herself.* She tells the young servant girl, "Do not turn around." The girl moves closer to her and clasps her shaking hand.

Uncut Jade carries the empty water jug and walks with his friend, who still holds his dog on a tight rein.

Silk Fan changes the brass rod to her left hand. Her right arm is tired, but she still holds the picture rod up like a battle flag leading her troops. Her hope was that the brass rod would embody any superstitious fears held by Double Joy, but as she leaves, she realizes that her mighty curses held more command than any physical symbol. She waits expectantly for the first rock or mud clod to hit her in the back, regretting involving the children but not her words.

A mother in the crowd stands with a strange look of triumph on her face as her tears roll down onto her clothes. She holds the hand of her young son tightly and smiles. No one came to protest her kidnapping when she was brought here.

A group of men stands smoking and watching silently as the young people pass by. Beautiful Moon's mother-in-law is fuming. She throws her fresh red peppers down in the dirt in frustration, but the crowd looks only at the retreating band of young people. The curses have stung their ears, and the truth of their words silences everyone.

At the widow's house, Silk Fan carefully replaces the picture of the swans and flowers on its brass hanging rod; White Flowering Tree folds the satin sash and returns it to the drawer with the ribbons and bracelets and the treasured war medal. Replacing the fine walking stick in a stand, she asks, "Who wants to go to the water pump and refill the water jug?"

The children leave on this errand, and the brides try to tell their versions of the afternoon's events. Silk Fan thanks her elderly friend and excuses herself. "I doubt that this affair is over, but we have given them something to think about. Their own superstitions will keep them awake tonight. I must go to prepare the evening meal for my family now."

The elderly widow who befriended the stolen brides sits at her place in her padded chair and shakes her head. Where will this end? Will the community allow the young women this vocal protest? She sighs.

A short time later, Hero comes home, a dusty jacket over his shoulder and a bunch of turnips in his hand. Silk Fan is crushing herbs on a stone in preparation for the dinner meal and speaking to her baby daughter, Happiness Found, who is gently swaying in a hammock.

Without a word of greeting, he asks, "Was it you?"

Silk Fan stops her work, turns to look him squarely in the face, and answers, "I am not ashamed to say that I spoke with everything that is in me!"

Humble, who sits on the kang working on mathematical calculations, jumps at the emphatic declaration. She has never heard Silk Fan raise her voice. Hero was so sure that they had been mistaken. It could not have been his polite, talented, and thoroughly proper Chinese wife, Silk Fan, they were talking about.

"Did you really put a curse on the entire house?"

"Did you know that those monsters cut both of Beautiful Moon's ankles so that she can never walk again?" Hero does not answer. He simply walks out, shaking his head. Returning to stand at his door, he asks, "Did you really curse their souls to wander forever?"

"I certainly did!"

Hero washes his face and dirt-dusted hands in the chipped enamel basin outside his door and returns to look at his wife. He shakes his head again and sits down heavily in the chair in his courtyard.

FLYING HORSE

The farmer in the faded blue slacks and the sweat-stained shirt known as Flying Horse is not old, but he walks with a bent back and shoulders that seem permanently bowed down with the care of an old man. His hat indicates that he is not without resources. He does not, however, strut about with self-importance or brag among the men who sit playing dominoes about how fine his father's family line or how many generations have lived in his house. He especially does not brag about how much his fields will yield this season, ashamed to do so, thinking that his neighbors can read his mind and discount any braggadocios statements he might make. Everyone knows of his burden, the reason for his creased brow and bent back. He does not want to have to speak to any more people than necessary because of his shame over his only son, Honorable Integrity. When the boy was born, he was named as ambitious a name as they could imagine because it was immediately apparent that he would always be an embarrassment to his entire family. The boy is a child whom every family dreads, one who would never help in the fields, whose legs would never grow straight, and who would never walk!

People know that boys like this have no hope and have always been shut away behind closed gates, away from gossip and the cruel taunts of other children.

Today, Flying Horse walks with his head down and a lit cigarette hanging from his lips. As he passes the home of Hero of his People, Flying Horse notices that his young wife, whom everyone knows to be kidnapped and sold to the highest bidder, is busy in the courtyard.

What is happening? There is definitely a baby tied to her back, and she is singing! She must be slightly unstable. He knows that she has nothing to sing about living as she does with an old man who is not even known for his industry.

Silk Fan is not unstable; she just had no time to worry about gossip. Her bought daughter is in school this morning, and this new baby whom her bought daughter found is a happy addition to her family. Silk Fan is busy planting food for her expanding family. Bending over with the warm body of her found baby on her back, she carefully thins out the new plants of sweet greens. She smiles to herself. It is a good joke on these people who disposed of their own daughters. In short order, she has acquired two lovely girl children. Sometimes she sees another infant's face and hears another child's voice calling her as she holds and feeds this foundling, but she shakes her head and realizes that her two birth children are not here.

When Flying Horse and the other adults of the community understand this new family, they will pronounce loudly that Hero is the one who is unstable. A wife to care for him in his old age is understandable, but two female children to feed is another. Is he senile?

Flying Horse walks on, unaware of how this busy, stolen housewife will change his life and the lives of all of his family.

The next day, Flying Horse bids his wife and his son good-bye and once again begins his slow journey with deliberate steps and bent head and back. In his hand, he carries a basket with a hinged top for transporting baby chicks. The footprints in the road indicate that several children came this way running to their daily classes at the village school. Flying Horse sighs deeply.

My only son should be attending school. There is no harmony in such cruel daily reminders that he will never be able to run to school and sit among the other children learning. I was denied my own education in the time of the revolution, and now my only child will never learn to read, write, and figure like other boys. Life is too harsh.

He knows that the government will allow another child in his family because of this deformity, but the gods have not sent another child to cheer the house nor ease the workload.

A neighbor rides past him on a bicycle loaded down with farming tools. Flying Horse tries not to feel any guilt. He knows that it is the season for preparing the earth and planting early food. This major task will have to wait. He still has not found any young fowl for his son. As he walks in his habitual manner with his head bent, he hears the childish song before he sees the singer. He knows that it is Hero's bought wife. Why is she singing? Oh. He spies the baby tied to her back and remembers the scene from yesterday.

Flying Horse is aware of a housewife in her courtyard shaking out the night linens. She spreads the wrinkled linens on her low enclosure wall and gives him a nod. Now he cannot pretend that he did not see her. He greets her with a slight nod in return.

He strains to hear the song she sings.

"Two caterpillars, four, six caterpillars, eight, now ten caterpillars crawling down the wall. All right, little one, count with me. Two, four, six, eight, ten ... " Silk Fan pauses when she realizes that Flying Horse is staring at her.

"I do beg your pardon. I thought that perhaps you were teaching a child, but I see none except your baby."

"You are correct. I am teaching my baby to count by twos."

"But she cannot even speak; how can you teach her mathematics?"

"She can hear, and perhaps she will remember some of these lessons when she is older."

Silk Fan gives her neighbor a lovely smile and continues with her morning work.

He began the conversation, but where are the traditional greetings? One usually gives one's own name and then asks, "Where are you from? How is your health?" Then, "How old are you?"

The man is embarrassed to be caught staring at her. He mumbles, "I am Flying Horse."

"I am Silk Fan, wife of Hero, and this is my found daughter, Happiness Found."

He nods at her and then hurries on his way. *Oh, I did not ask whether or not she has any baby chicks.*

When he arrives at the marketplace, the old men are already assembled on one side of the road, and a game of mahjong is already in progress. He greets them and quickly goes to inspect the goods for sale or trade. He finds no chicks. Looking very disappointed, Flying Horse starts walking away but sees one of his wife's friends. He knows that she keeps chickens in the shed with her family's pig.

"Good morning, Yellow Butterfly. Are you well today?"

"Yes, I thank you for asking, Flying Horse. Are you well?"

"Yes."

"How is your family today?"

"Everyone is healthy. We welcome the springtime. How are your family members?"

"We are all doing fine, thank you. What brings you to market today?"

"I am searching for chicks for Honorable Integrity. He wants to care for them this year."

Yellow Butterfly did not plan on selling any of her chicks this year, but for the sake of her friend, Regal Peony, she changes her mind. She hesitates a moment and smiles. "Since they are for your son, I will part with a few. Come to our house at midday."

Elated, Flying Horse does not know how many a few could be, but he smiles for the first time in weeks. "You are a true friend. I will be there today."

Now I can plow. I have double happy news for my family. Our son will have his own baby chicks this year. He is a good child. He needs something of his own-. I wonder if he can count by twos.

THE LATEST VICTIM BRIDE

The meetings at the home of the Han widow, whose feet are crippled from childhood by the tradition of binding girls' feet, have lost all pretence of being sewing lessons and have become a meeting place for mutual friends. The aged woman is grateful for the company of young people who love her, acting as daughters to her. In a land where families are traditionally cherished, she acquires a family she treasures. The short verses that she copied so carefully from the radio broadcasts have become important for the survival of these kidnapped wives. As they sew household linens and children's clothing, they seriously discuss the Bible verses.

Pale Orchid, the latest kidnapped bride, is immediately accepted into their circle, welcomed as a friend in need of encouragement. She was purchased by a retired soldier for his only son, Brick Wall. A product of the new, exciting spirit of China, she is a Christian willing to risk her life and endure the harassment of officials in order to share her experiences in worshiping God. Her parents both spent time in prison for breaking the laws against meeting in private homes for songs, prayers, and Bible study.

Grandmother Rose Bud now allows Walks with Grace and Truth to borrow her eighty-year-old, leather-bound Bible each week. She reads aloud, and the others copy favored verses while Pale Orchid interprets the meaning. Their new sister is making comments on the book of Mark from the old Bible.

"Oh, Silk Fan, Jesus was so good, and yet he was treated so badly. They beat him, and mocked him, and spit on him. This book says that they held illegal trials and that the Roman soldiers nailed him to a cross!" Walks with Grace and Truth shudders.

Five sets of hands stop work at this revelation. Then in a quiet voice, White Flowering Tree asks, "Do you think he knows how badly we are treated?"

There is silence as the sad, young faces contemplated this thought.

Pale Orchid explains what she understands. "I believe that this is one reason for his suffering. God wants us to know that he understands our pain."

Walks with Grace and Truth adds a question, "So you say that the great God of creation sees and feels our pains?"

"I am sure of it, my friend." Pale Orchid smiles.

White Flowering Tree gasps, "Oh."

The widow speaks next. "Please read John 14:6."

Pale Orchid thumbs through the book and finds the familiar passage. "It reads, 'I am the Way, yes, and the Truth and the Life. No one can get to the Father except by me."

Silk Fan sums their collective feelings, "These ideas are larger than I am."

"Thank you for allowing us to visit today, madam. I am so glad that you welcome me here. Now I not only have friends but sisters with whom I can worship and study the word of God." Pale Orchid smiles sweetly.

The latest victim bride brings more than biblical knowledge; she also brings with her encouragement and spiritual hope to her new friends. As the days pass, she continues to teach and share her joyful faith.

Another day, women work and their young children play outside where the weather is a pleasant relief from the long winter. The central courtyard behind the homes of Silk Fan and White Flowering Tree is the scene of weaving mats.

The discussion turns to the subject of Pale Orchid. She has been befriended as "one of them," but they are puzzled by her lack of anger and her constant good humor. White Flowering Tree asks, "How can she be so happy all of the time? She was stolen from her home just as we were."

"She does wear a smile most of the time," Silk Fan comments.

"Why?" Walks with Grace and Truth asks between tying knots in her mat.

"I do not know! I am still so angry that I have forgotten how to smile." White Flowering Tree is lucid today but bitter.

Silk Fan answers in a gentle voice for her angry young friend's benefit. "I will ask her when she comes. She said that she would try to come today."

It has been three and a half years since the attack on Silk Fan. She still bears scars from being dragged to the boat. It has been three and a half years since she saw her precious children and husband.

It has been three and a half years since Summer Rain, the twelve-year-old schoolgirl, pleaded her case with the marriage official and was sent home. Her friends here do not know that the local gang members took the small pieces of paper with their names and addresses as she left this village. They hoped that her contacts with their families would result in their rescue. They no longer look for their families each morning, their hope wearing thin as time moves steadily onward, using up their very lives.

It has been three and a half years since strong-armed thugs

knocked Walks with Grace and Truth down in the train station while she was on her way to calculus class.

It has been three and a half years since White Flowering Tree and Beautiful Moon were beaten and bound. It has been three and a half long years since they last saw their parents, their lives changed forever.

Pale Orchid has not been in these hills that long, but she was kidnapped and purchased by a stranger here. Each of the young women has settled into a routine in her life, which she did not choose, but only Pale Orchid displays any real happiness. The sisters suspect that Walks with Grace and Truth has accepted her husband, Steadfast, but they are too polite to ask personal questions.

"Mother, are these stitches tight enough?" Humble sews busily on a new pair of slacks. Silk Fan stops her mat weaving long enough to inspect the rows of hand-sewn stitches.

"They appear to be fine. Are you back stitching every few stitches to strengthen the seam?"

"I am trying to remember to backstitch. I do not understand why we do not just go to Faithful's house and borrow her grandmother's sewing machine. It is old, but it works well and is very quick."

Silk Fan answers quietly, "Humble, will you tell me why?"

"I know. It is to teach me sewing skills to last me the rest of my life."

"That is correct. Now finish these slacks. You will enjoy having something new."

"Yes, Mother." Silk Fan smiles proudly at her oldest daughter.

"I see Pale Orchid coming down the road," Humble announces before sitting back down on the stone courtyard.

Walks with Grace and Truth's small son, named Strong Bamboo, runs on short, baby, legs in the direction of the approaching visitor. He knows that she will meet him with a happy smile and swing him about with glee.

"Hello, everyone! It is so good to see you all."

"Good day to you, Pale Orchid." Walks with Grace and Truth likes Pale Orchid.

Silk Fan greets her with a smile. "Hello, Pale Orchid. I am glad to see that you have come today."

"Hello, Aunt Pale Orchid." Humble enjoys her company. "We were just talking about you."

A small voice says, "Hello, singing Auntie."

"My goodness! What a big boy you are. Do you grow in your sleep?" Pale Orchid picks up the two-year-old boy and swings him around in her arms. Squeals of laughter declare the game a huge success.

"Swing me too, Auntie." Happiness Found remembers Pale Orchid.

White Flowering Tree's son is quiet.

"Do you want to see me jump?" Strong Bamboo asks eagerly.

The latest kidnapped bride to join the group is not particularly pretty, nor does her hair shine, but the children all gravitate toward her. She acts as if she knows that she is beautiful. The three young mothers continue working as she plays with their children. "Do you remember the song that I taught you?"

"Yes." Little Happiness Found bounces in happy anticipation.

"Then let's sing it."

Three children's voices join in singing with the smiling Pale Orchid. They each sing on their own key and pace, but she sings on and they join in.

> Jesus is my friend, Oh what a good friend.
> Jesus loves me every day. Jesus is my friend.
> Yes, strong Jesus is my friend and your friend too.

"That was good singing. Now let us sing 'God Made Me So Special.'"

The small children sing with practiced movements of dancing bodies and sweeping gestures with chubby fingers that point heavenward and then back to themselves with each line.

God made me so special. There is no one else just like me.
God made me so special. Just look at me!
God made my face, my hands, my tummy, and feet.
Look how special he made me.

"What fine singers you are," Pale Orchid praises the children.

"She makes me feel guilty." Walks with Grace and Truth watches her.

"Why?" White Flowering Tree asks.

"Because that is the way motherhood should be."

"You are a good mother. You take care of your child."

"Yes. I do all the necessities. But watch her; she bubbles with energy and laughter."

"I see what you mean. One would never suspect that she is here against her will."

Pale Orchid laughs. "That was fine music. Now I must do my work."

"Sing just one more song, Auntie." Strong Bamboo holds on to Pale Orchid's pants leg and begs.

"I must work now. Can you show me how the wind blows the trees? You are the willow tree. The wind is blowing you."

Pale Orchid blows an imaginary wind on the three children while she settles down with her yarn. The children lift their short arms to the sky and turn and sway in a dance with the wind.

"What a blessing from God these children are. You are so fortunate to have little ones." She takes out a pair of knitting needles and a skein of bright purple yarn.

"Ooh! What a royal color!" Humble exclaims.

She smiles and says, "It is pretty, isn't it? Who is going to teach me how to begin my second skin? My mother taught me how to knit, but I do not know where to start."

Walks with Grace and Truth shows her how to begin her project of knitting her long winter underwear, and Pale Orchid joins the group of young women working.

The children return to entertaining themselves. The group

waits until Pale Orchid has her knitting needles clicking at a regular pace before they ask the question that are on all of their minds.

"Pale Orchid, we want to ask you something," Walks with Grace and Truth says seriously.

"Yes, what is it?"

"How can you be so happy all of the time?" Walks with Grace and Truth leans forward and speaks for the group.

A big smile spreads across her face as she answers, "My God has put a song in my heart."

"Which god is that, Pale Orchid?" White Flowering Tree questions her.

"He is the Lord God almighty! He made this earth, and I talk with him every day. He loves me!"

All four of her friends stare quizzically at her.

"Is this god like the god of the people of Israel? He did miracles for them."

"White Flowering Tree, it is the same God. He loved us so much that he sent his one and only son to earth to show us how to love."

"What is his son's name?" White Flowering Tree demands an answer.

"His name is Jesus."

"Pale Orchid, we have heard of Jesus, and we know many stories about him."

"Yes, we have memorized many verses, but we are not as happy as you." Walks with Grace and Truth joins in.

"You have verses? Do you have Bibles?"

"What do you mean, Bibles?"

"The entire holy book from which these verses come is called a Bible."

"None of us have an entire book. We only have verses copied from the radio programs," White Flowering Tree explains.

"Grandmother Rose Bud, the barber's widowed mother, has a Bible," Walks with Grace and Truth interjects.

"Oh! Great joy! I have missed reading my Bible. Forgive me, please. I am so excited to hear of a Bible that I have failed to answer your question. Do you know that verse that reads, 'My purpose is to give life in all of its fullness'?" (John 10:10).

"I read it one time to the barber's family, but I do not know what it means." Walks with Grace and Truth is as puzzled as the rest.

"It is the most wonderful quotation from the Lord Jesus himself. He explains why he left heaven to come to earth. He loves us so much that he wants us to have a life filled with love and happiness here while we live on earth and afterward when we die. He promised that we can live with him in heaven."

The group of women gazes at her with uncomprehending faces.

"Isn't that wonderful?"

"I do not understand." Silk Fan speaks for them all.

"It means that we do not have to be miserable here. Jesus said that he would leave a friend here on earth to comfort and encourage us. This comforter is called the Holy Spirit of God himself. My happiness came to me since the Spirit of God came to live in my soul. In the Bible in the book of Galatians, we are told, 'The Fruit of the Spirit is love, joy, peace, longsuffering, gentleness, goodness, faith, meekness, and temperance.' Isn't that the most wonderful news you have ever heard?" (Galatians 5:22).

"This spirit of God gave you all of this? He gives love and joy and peace?" Silk Fan asks earnestly.

"Does this mean that even after we have been mistreated and so unhappy we can still be as you are, joyful and peaceful in our hearts?" White Flowering Tree finds this news difficult to believe.

"This is what Jesus meant when he said, "My purpose is to give life in all of its fullness" (John 10:10).

Quietly, Walks with Grace and Truth responds, "Do you really think that this promise can change our lives? We are not even the same people we were a few years ago."

"You must learn to trust in this Jesus you have been learning about."

Walks with Grace and Truth holds her string out, ready for another knot, but she stops in midair. "That is all?"

Pale Orchid answers simply: "The Bible says it this way, 'For God loved the world so much that he gave his only son so that anyone who believes in him shall not perish but have eternal life. God did not send his son into the world to condemn it, but to save it'" (John 3:16).

"I have that verse that the widow copied from her radio," Silk Fan says.

"You still have not told us why you are not angry at these people who stole you from your home. They are criminals!" White Flowering Tree cries.

"Yes, they are indeed cruel people who are living outside of the law, and they do not deserve fine wives such as us, but the Bible teaches, 'Love your enemies. Do good to those who hate you. Pray for the happiness of those who curse you; implore God's blessings on those who hurt you'" (Luke 6:27–28).

"I might pray that they all die horrible deaths very soon." White Flowering Tree refuses to believe this verse.

"Pray that God will touch their hearts and make them kind. Keep praying for them. Thank God each day for his son, Jesus."

White Flowering Tree fails to understand faith. She knows only that she is angry. "These dreadful people are the ones who need to learn how to live and pray!"

"Yes. Of course they do."

They all sit thinking about the amazing news that their new friend brings. Pale Orchid sees how difficult the lesson is for the group. "I have learned to thank God for this time in my life."

"What did you say?" White Flowering Tree shouts at her.

Silk Fan quietly adds, "I know that this place was not in your plans."

"No. This place and these people and my husband were not in my plans, but God answered my prayers of thanksgiving in the most unusual way." With a new smile, Pale Orchid brightens. "God told me this is an opportunity."

"Did you say, 'an opportunity'?" Walks with Grace and Truth asks incredulously.

"Oh yes. God told me that this is the opportunity for which I have been praying. My family and I had been praying for ways we could tell some new people about the love of God. This is good news."

Four faces stare openly at their new friend.

"I have a chance to tell all of these people that God loves all of the people of the earth. This is the news about the great love of God who was willing to give up his son. This God loves us so much. The government outlawed the worship of God. I am telling everyone I meet that I have given all of my problems to Jesus, and I trust him to take care of me," answers Pale Orchid.

No one speaks for several moments after the newcomer makes her astonishing speech.

"But, but you are still here!" White Flowering Tree voices their confusion.

"Yes. I am still here among my enemies, but Jesus gives me this peace and joy I've never known."

Walks with Grace and Truth speaks next. "I have a verse which I kept because it sounded so pretty, but I never knew what it meant. It reads, 'I am leaving you a gift: peace of mind and heart. The peace I give isn't fragile like the peace the world gives. So don't be troubled or afraid'" (John 14:27).

"You are so fortunate to have that verse. God was preparing you for when you would understand. I have a peaceful heart, and I am joyful. I never stop marveling over the grand plans God has for us."

Ten productive hands come to a rest. After a time, Walks with Grace and Truth asks, "Pale Orchid, teach us how to get this peace and joy. We need help. Our children suffer because we do not know how to have peaceful souls. We are still so very angry."

White Flowering Tree's voice breaks as she confesses, "Yes. Help us. I look into the small face of my child, and I see the face of his father who paid criminals to capture me. I hate him and his mother, and I do not want to hate this innocent baby. He should have a mother like you, Pale Orchid, one who sings and smiles and makes him happy too."

"My friends, I think it is time for us to pray to the Father, God."

Silk Fan sees a ray of hope in their new friend. "Pale Orchid, will you pray for us? We don't know how to talk to God."

"Yes. I will lead you, but each of you needs to pray in your own hearts also."

"What harmony. We can do that."

"Oh, mighty God, we praise you for including us in your plan of love. We thank you for caring about girls and our unhappy souls. Father God, we are tired of hurting. We are tired of being angry and hating. Please forgive us for our sins against your goodness, and show us how to please you. We trust your son, Jesus Christ, and his loving ways, and we want to be like him. Thank you, God."

The group of friends sits quietly for a few moments before Silk Fan speaks for them all. "Pale Orchid, what a beautiful prayer. Thank you."

"You are welcome, my friends. You must pray this prayer often. May I see some of your verses? I am hungry for the verses that promise us so much."

Humble jumps up, saying, "I will get my verses for you."

She returns with a handful of much-used slips of paper rolled up and kept in a small cotton bag, the yellow one in which she packed all of her belongings when she came to live with Silk Fan.

"Pale Orchid, in my home district, many of my neighbors and teachers and even my aunt and uncle were beaten and sent to prison. We never saw my uncle again, but I remember my grandparents singing songs. Do you know a song that says, 'And

I shall see him face to face?'" Walks with Grace and Truth had a Christian grandmother.

Pale Orchid closes her eyes and sings the hymn in anticipation of the reality of this promise. The other girls listen, and the children stop and look at her.

"Who is this you will meet face to face?" White Flowering Tree asks the question.

"The song is speaking of seeing Jesus face to face when we die and go to heaven, or if he comes to earth again before we die."

"Will we see him too?" Walks with Grace and Truth voices the question all want to ask.

"This is a promise Jesus made several times in the Bible. He even promised one of the thieves on the cross who died with him that he would be in paradise that day with him because he believed in him. These promises are speaking about people who believe in Jesus." Pale Orchid is a natural teacher for hungry students.

"Does it mean us?" White Flowering Tree asks with in astonishment.

"It speaks to all people of all ages from all over the world who believe in Jesus. Won't it be a fantastic meeting in heaven?"

"Please, Pale Orchid, teach us a happy song about Jesus." Silk Fan yearns for a happy expression of her growing faith.

As the afternoon wears on, the four young women continue their handwork while their babies sleep on mats nearby. A new sound is heard as they sing words that the aged people heard many years ago.

Walks with Grace thinks, *I wish Steadfast was here to hear this lesson. I must try to explain all of this to him.*

An elderly neighbor remembers the hymns and thinks angels are singing.

Pale Orchid sings one line and the others repeat it, "When we've been there ten thousand years, bright shining as the sun, we've no less days to sing God's praise than when we first begun."

Only White Flowering Tree does not join in the singing. She has drifted into another world, staring into space, sometimes talking to herself, sometimes just sitting.

"Pale Orchid, please promise that you will continue to teach us what you know. We need encouragement."

"My friends, I promise. We all have so much to learn about God's goodness."

COUNTING STONES

Two children prepare for school one autumn morning. The young child is a girl who is so painfully shy that she refuses to attend the local school with her cousin. Her parents are very pleased and relieved when one of the new-bought brides, Silk Fan, accepts her into a half-day class that she teaches in her home.

As the boy marches off happily to school, the shy girl speaks to her mother.

"Mother, we must find five smooth stones."

"You took stones to school yesterday."

"I need five more stones today."

"How silly. Why do you need more stones?"

"Mother, we are learning to count stones."

"Oh. Well, let us get busy and find more stones."

The bought bride named Silk Fan is a welcomed teacher for the parents of three small girls who would not otherwise get any type of education. Silk Fan, who foolishly took in not one but two foundling daughters, seems to be doing an excellent job of teaching. The three local mothers sought her acceptance for their own small girls into her afternoon teaching session for her second daughter, Happiness Found. The wise teacher asks a small payment for each afternoon, sometimes paid in produce and sometimes in a few coins.

The extremely shy girl draws in the dirt with slow and careful strokes.

"Look, Mother, this says 'fish.'"

"Yes, I see, child."

It is not until her nephew comes home from school and asks about the drawing in the dirt that she realizes that it really is the correct symbol for the word *fish*.

"Is cousin really learning to read and write? It is written correctly."

In surprise, the girl's mother answers, "Then I must find some way to pay her teacher more. I only give her the price of two onions each day."

The four small girls are all happily counting stones, singing songs, and learning the first of their country's very long language. Parents and students are happy with their own private class.

Silk Fan smiles at her class of four small girls but has trouble keeping her mind on their lessons. *Today I saw the face of Strong Wind and heard him say, "I know the answer, Mother. Call on me." I wonder if my own two little ones are learning to count and read.*

WASHING WOOL

White Flowering Tree and Walks with Grace and Truth are washing newly sheared wool. They are expecting their new friend, Pale Orchid, to come visit with them. She promised to find time to teach them about their verses so carefully written. She does not have any verses, but they do. They do not really understand the meanings, but she does. They all look forward to sharing with each other. With cold water dripping down their arms and onto their shirts, they smile when they see Pale Orchid. She helps them wring out the tightly curled wool.

Walks with Grace and Truth suggests: "Let us sit here beside the canal while our wool dries. We can speak as we wish here. We must watch the little ones. The water is too cold for swimming if we must rescue a baby today.

"Please explain this verse. 'Let not your heart be troubled. You are trusting God, now trust in me. There are many homes up there where my Father lives, and I am going to prepare them for your coming. When everything is ready, then I will come and get you, so that you can always be with me where I am. If this weren't so, then I would tell you plainly'" (John 14:1–3).

Walks with Grace and Truth persists, "Who is speaking in this verse? Who is preparing a home? And where does his father live?"

"My friends, this is a beautiful promise. Jesus is saying that we can go to heaven to live with him and his father, God!" Pale Orchid teaches with patience and joy.

"I will need time to digest such a wonderful promise. Those verses written on crumpled yellow paper are all from our friend the widow or from the barber's widowed mother. They have been giving us verses for years now. They have tried to encourage us, but we still did not understand many of the verses."

White Flowering Tree explains about their faithful friend, the old Han widow. "The widow is so ancient and frail now. She was singing something last week when I took her some noodles. The words were something about, 'Abide with me. Fast falls the eventide. The darkness deepens, Lord with me abide.' I do not know, but it sounded like a death poem. She had her eyes closed, and she smiled while she sang."

Pale Orchid smiles and answers, "The old Christians were so frightened during the liberation that they were even afraid to sing their songs of faith. They did not want their families killed."

Silk Fan says, "Our two elderly friends, the Han widow and Grandmother Rose Bud, gave us those small verses to give us hope. When I heard some of those same verses being read over the radio last spring, I began to understand, but there are mysteries in some verses. Can you explain them to us?"

"It is the same Lord she is singing to in the song. The Lord Jesus is speaking in that verse when he promises to come back to earth. She wants to live with him. He is the son of the almighty God and lives in heaven now. That is why our friend the widow smiles. Her spirit has lived with the Lord Jesus for many years now. She is not worried about her death because she joyfully anticipates sitting down with Jesus in heaven."

Walks with Grace and Truth is surprised. "Oh, Pale Orchid, we did not understand all of this. Why did she not teach us these songs?"

"She was afraid for her life and for yours also. Christians were persecuted so brutally by the young thugs. There is still a government department of controlling religious groups. Believers lost their homes and jobs, so their families starved. So many were put in prison and beaten. My own father was in prison for almost all of my life for sharing the good news of Jesus's love with other people. His body is bent and thin now, but he is a triumphant man who praises our God every day. His courage and the courage of our Lord Jesus have given me strength to see my future in a new light. Since I have been able to thank God for this time, he has given me a joyful spirit. I see now that this is an opportunity to share the good news of the love of Jesus."

Walks with Grace and Truth pleads, "Oh, Pale Orchid, do you really see your life in this place as an opportunity?"

"My friend, I am sure of it. God is going to use me to tell these people about his love for them."

"Even the mean people who took you from your home and those who paid gangs of thugs to capture you?" White Flowering Tree asks incredulously.

"Especially those people. People who hate the most need love the most."

There is silence as this new attitude challenges them. Could this be the secret to their survival here? Next, Pale Orchid makes another statement that the brides do not yet understand. Pale Orchid smiles sweetly and says, "I think that God has placed us in these last days to wage war so that the number of survivors will increase through us. Does anyone have verses from the book of Revelation? We need to think about that next time we meet."

"I will look in my memory verses to see if I have a verse from Revelation," Walks with Grace and Truth tells her.

"I saw a young woman about our age going toward the hills today. I do not know her name, but she was quite upset and would not look at me. She wore a red sweater and black slacks. Do you know her?" Pale Orchid inquires.

"Did she have long hair tied in back with a ribbon?" Walks with Grace and Truth replies.

"Yes, who is she? And why was she crying so?" Pale Orchid wonders.

"She had a baby girl this year, and her husband has not returned from working in the city this spring. His cousin brought a letter and some money for his mother but nothing for her. The neighbors think that he will not return to her and that he will find a wife in the city who might give him a son."

"Perhaps I can find her. She needs a friend now. I will speak with you another day, my friends. May God keep you." Pale Orchid packs her things in order to leave.

"Good-bye, Pale Orchid."

"White Flowering Tree did you understand that Jesus wants us to live with him in heaven?"

"No."

"Neither did I. What awesome words! I will share this with my family. I read a verse to them each evening."

Two young wives with new ideas to ponder sit on the ground, watching their children while their clean wool dries in the sunshine.

PAINTING PRAYERS

Strong Bamboo, a very young boy, the son of Walks with Grace and Truth and Steadfast, plays in his courtyard with a green beetle and a stem of wheat straw. He is a happy child, too young to understand that his name is an ancient one, describing how the strong bamboo plant survives by growing where it is planted, bending, but rising again in the wind. Today, Uncut Jade comes into his courtyard but does not play with him. He stands by the doorway, waiting for Strong Bamboo's mother to finish hanging out her wet laundry.

"Good morning, Uncut Jade."

He hesitates to speak to his favorite adult neighbor. After a moment, he replies. "Hello, Auntie Grace. You are looking well today."

"Thank you. Is there something I may do for you? "

Lowering his head, he speaks too quietly. "My mother asks how much you will charge us to paint a funeral blessing."

"Of course I'll paint a blessing for you, but who died?"

"It is my second cousin. I did not know him, but my family knew him. They are all weeping now."

"Tell your mother that I will write it now and that it will be dry in two hours. The cost is six copper coins. Do you know what sort of blessing she wants?"

"No, Auntie."

"I will paint a fine one for you."

"Thank you. My mother said that you would. Here are some coins for you."

Walks with Grace and Truth accepts the coins for her work and, drying her hands on her apron, looks for her paper and ink. She still lacks a proper table for painting but clears off a place on the kang and spreads out the smooth white paper. Hesitating before the pot of rich black paint, she searches into the depths of blackness with memories of another time when she sat in a class, watching a teacher demonstrate the proper method of painting.

Black Pearl asks, "What message will you paint?"

"I know only an ordinary funeral blessing. What do you suggest?"

"An old one says, 'Happiness with Your Ancestors.'"

"That will do well. He was a cousin in Uncut Jade's family."

Black Pearl steps down the one step from her house to the courtyard. She will gladly watch her only grandchild while his mother paints her fine characters. She does not tell her daughter-in-law, but she is proud of this distinction she brings the family. No one else in her family or among her friends is able to read and write so well.

Walks with Grace and Truth earns a few coins for her own use, and the neighbor's family will receive the needed funeral blessing, but more important to her, she knows that she is now accepted as a vital working member of the community. Children speak to her, and adults call upon her in time of need. The young kidnapped bride finds this comforting. She views each contact as acceptance. If she must live in this foreign place, she needs to feel accepted. Her friend Silk Fan was correct when she encouraged her to scrimp to purchase the proper paper, brush, and ink and become a scribe, earning money for her needs. Her husband's grandfather was the first to recognize her talents, and now she is a recognized scribe. Steadfast, her husband, is the proudest man in the village. His pride mingles with his love for his talented wife.

The ancient characters she paints appear to be fine art. They are of no comfort to the departed man, but they will comfort his family.

Uncut Jade returns with another question. "Do you know where the white paper flowers for a funeral may be purchased? They must be white."

I wonder if they are just getting the boy out of the house with all of its funeral talk. Surely they will know better than I where to get the traditional flowers.

"No, my friend, I do not know who sells the white paper flowers."

With a nod, the boy returns to his home, and the young wife who still misses her friends and professors from the university returns to her task. Strong Bamboo captures the escaping green beetle and places it back on the brick floor of the courtyard. His proud grandmother, Black Pearl, smokes her pipe as she watches him play. Her daughter-in-law has not only proved herself worthy of being spoken to but has brought calm and dignity to the house. She honors the older generation and serves the family with good humor. If the old woman is ignored at times, it is because her son Steadfast and his wife, Walks with Grace, now spend time together playing happily with their son.

A SMALL BOY AND A GOOSE

The winter has been long and wet with hard ice crystals on the ground. Strong Bamboo stands on a stool to gaze at the landscape outside his window. It is the springtime excitement with promise of new life that has this boy eager to help his mother on this cold morning while the mist still clings to the sides of the hills. Snow has not fallen in days now, and he is anxious to go outside to play. This morning he runs outside on the pretext of gathering pinecones for his mother's fire.

His adventure proves invigorating but short on pinecones. Returning with only three pinecones in his mitten-clad hands, Strong Bamboo bursts into the house with a cold rush of air and a happy smile. His hat is askew, his eyes shine brightly, and his voice is lively as he bounces into the two-room house and backs up to the fire to warm his small body.

"Mother, may we go to look for a baby goose today? Will you go with me now? Their feathers are strong, and we can make, what do you call those pens that we make with goose feathers?"

"We call them quills, son."

"Quills! You said that we could find a baby goose and raise it. Ice is still on the water, but I saw some mother gooses. Can we go today?"

Walks with Grace and Truth smiles at him lovingly and admires his round face and his healthy skin, recognizing his father's good looks in their son's image. She succeeds at motherhood the way she does as a university student, wife, scribe, math teacher, and dancer. But talent and determination are not answers to this family's peace and happiness. Since the arrival of Pale Orchid in their village, the entire family has a wonderful change of attitude. Their acceptance of Christianity has made their lives totally different from their former ones. Perhaps the most surprising is Black Pearl's demand that she be read to each evening from the collection of Bible verses. She shares her new knowledge with her neighbors.

"Strong Bamboo, I told you that we will find a baby goose later when the wild birds leave their nests. It will be a few more days."

"I want to tell Father about the mother geese that I saw."

Bursting into his parents' bedroom, he finds his father still enclosed in his warm bed. He climbs onto his father's resting form and eagerly proclaims his news. "Father, I saw mother geese outside. Get up and help me look for baby geese."

Walks with Grace and Truth enters the room to find the two playing and tossing about on the bed in her marriage room.

"Come on, my son, leave your father alone. We have rich goat's milk to drink with your bread this morning. Come, sit down to eat."

As he scrambles off the bed and runs to his waiting meal, his father addresses his mother with an inviting grin. "Come here, my pretty dove, I have something to tell you."

Dancing away from his outstretched hand, she laughingly

says, "Not now, you shameless man. I shall not get back into your bed until nighttime."

Blowing him a kiss, she escapes his hand and returns to her young son.

"I want to eat like Father does. He dips his bread into the milk. Help me pray like Aunt Pale Orchid does." The beloved boy bows his head to pray before his meal and follows his mother's lead as he prays. "Father in heaven, thank you for this good food and for baby geese. Amen."

The old grandmother calls out to her only grandchild. "Strong Bamboo, you forgot to pray in the name of Jesus, who taught us how to love."

The child with milk dripping from his mouth stops to say, "In Jesus' name we pray. Amen."

"Grandmother, the water is hot now. Shall I bring you some? The house is still chilly. Do you want to eat where you are, or do you want to get dressed first? Your grandson just had to go outside. He is ready for spring."

"I shall get up now and eat properly. I do not want to spill my milk."

As Walks with Grace and Truth hangs her son's wet mittens to dry, she remembers a pair of colorful gloves she was given years ago by a young man she planned to marry. He was the one of whom her parents approved, the one she loved.

I wonder what work he does now. Did he find another girl to marry? Does he love her as he loved me? I wonder if she is pretty. Dear Father in heaven, let him find happiness and your peace. And Lord, thank you for teaching me to forgive and love Steadfast.

"Strong Bamboo, the mother goose will not allow her baby geese to leave the nest until they grow some warm feathers, but there is much we can do to prepare for your goose. We need to make a pen for him and start collecting a supply of goose food."

The little boy nods his head.

Black Pearl looks proudly at her family and says, "You are such a good daughter, and he is such a fine grandson. How was

I ever lucky enough to have such a fine family?" Walks with Grace and Truth smiles gently and tells her mother-in-law formally known as grumps and grumbles, "Mama, Christians are not lucky. It is not by chance that we are happy. This happiness is a blessing from God."

A simple nod is her response.

Black Pearl is an extremely happy grandmother. Strong Bamboo is a blessed boy. Walks with Grace and Truth smiles at them both. She is content, and her husband is the proudest and happiest man in the village.

THE WISDOM CONTEST

The doors of the school are closed for the day. Pigs and chickens have been fed, and the families' dried laundry has been taken inside. Cooking fuel has been placed where each mother and grandmother may reach it. Water has been brought into each house. Now the village children of all ages are free to be children. The irony today is that when left to themselves, they labor diligently on what looks much like schoolwork.

Several teenage girls are busy in one courtyard weaving a belt. Morning Sunshine weaves and pulls the fibers taut with nimble fingers. She knows she will need it soon to hold a cumbersome basket on her back. She does a woman's work when she is not in school. Two others sit listening while a fourth girl, Joyful Day, is reading aloud to them from a notebook with handwritten pages. She reads, "Create in me a new, clean heart, O God, filled with clean thoughts and right desires" (Psalm 51:10).

Three small children play jumping games while a boy nearby

dutifully tutors a younger boy. Nearby two other children play a game of cards. The most noise, excitement, and dust originate with a group of eight boys who are playing a game that consists of trying to keep an old copper coin in the air. No longer in circulation, the hole in the center of the coin has been stuffed with duck feathers, and it serves as a toy. There is much pushing, shouting, and dashing about as the boys play their unsupervised game. The game always ends up in front of the house where the girls are weaving and playing cards. The boys know that one purpose of their activity is to impress the few girls in their village.

Amid much sweaty arguing about who scored the last point, the boys rest on a wall by the side of the road, when a laughing girl named Red Rose runs from her home and hurries to show something to the other children her age. It is the barber's daughter, clutching a small silk bag containing a new treasure.

"Throw it high." Girlish laughter fills the air.

"Throw it again." The small child swings her arms as high as she can but still does not succeed.

"My arm is too tired. I cannot get it up on the housetop," Red Rose whines.

"I will throw it for you."

"No, she must throw it herself." Other girls agree on the rules.

Some of the boys drift over to watch. They have not been invited, and watching the game is certainly not as appealing as joining the older girls, but they are older than these little girls and might have an opportunity to show their superiority here. One of the largest and most vocal boys is named Tiger.

As Tiger marches over to the younger children, the owner of the special bag sees him and bursts into tears. Clutching her treasure to her body, she wails loudly. He understands why and tries to console her, but he is not to be trusted. Her loud crying brings two mothers and one old grandfather to their doors and the four older girls to her side.

"You bully!" Morning Sunshine rebukes him.

"Why don't you leave them in peace?" Joyful Day joins in.

"What is wrong, little one?" Humble asks.

"He did nothing to her!" a friend defends Tiger.

One of the older girls stoops down to her level and asks her gently, "Why are you crying?"

"Be … because he is always mean to me."

In front of all of his peers, Tiger tells the little girl, "I will not be mean to you anymore. I was just going to help you."

"No you won't. You will tease me and laugh at me." Red Rose is very brave in speaking to the neighborhood bully as long as she clings to her friend Humble.

"I will not laugh at you. Do you want me to help you?" he tries again.

"No."

"You may sit on my shoulders to throw your tooth onto the roof."

"You said that you would not laugh at me!"

"I am not laughing at you. My grandfather told me the same thing when I lost my top front teeth."

He tries again to convince the younger girl of his harmless intentions. "I think that the bag you have it in is making it fly like a kite. Let us try taking it out of the bag. It might be easier to throw."

"Do you think it will matter if I sit on your shoulders? They said that I had to throw it."

Humble and Tiger both assure her that it is a legal method for throwing teeth, so she climbs on his shoulders with the help of the older girls. With her left hand clinging to his ear, Red Rose makes a mighty effort to throw her newly dislodged baby tooth onto the roof of her home. The chorus of cheers indicates that this time the tooth lands on the shingled roof.

The children begin to disperse.

"Humble, why was Strong Boy so nice to me today?"

"I think the reason is that he has met Aunt Pale Orchid."

"I think that Tiger has met Jesus." Morning Sunshine nods her head and smiles.

Red Rose answers. "Is it the same Jesus who is in my grandmother's book?"

"He is the very same Jesus, Red Rose."

"And you think that Jesus made him kind to me?"

"Yes."

"Thank you, Jesus."

"Why did you say thank you to Jesus?" Joyful Day asks.

"I thanked Jesus because he made Tiger kind to me. He did not laugh at me or tease me in front of those boys. It is a miracle, like the miracle when Jesus made the blind men see in grandmother's big black book."

"Yes. He is still making miracles today."

"I do not understand all that you are speaking about." Joyful Day responds.

"Oh, you do not know our friend Aunt Pale Orchid or our friend Jesus. We will tell you all about them."

"What does Aunt Pale Orchid have to do with this miracle worker Jesus in the big book?"

"She can tell us all about Jesus because she knows him like a friend. She talks to him as if he is sitting beside her. She explains how powerful Jesus is. You will see. You will understand when Pale Orchid smiles and tell you how much Jesus loves you."

"Is she the new aunt in the village who always wears a smile?"

"Yes. She is the one who smiles."

Some of the children nod their heads. They have met the new neighbor, Aunt Pale Orchid, the one who smiles.

Like a wolf pack descending upon its prey, the group of eight boys moves on. Harassing the two boys who are studying, one of the group asks, "Why are you still in your books? This is a time for play."

"We are working on quotations for the spring wisdom contest."

A groan escapes the wolf pack like a primitive howl.

"Do you want the other schools to win the contest again this year?"

"You know that one proverb is not enough to win the competition!"

"How many do you think we will need?"

"All the students together did not remember ten in class today."

Sea Swimmer states emphatically, "I would like to win this year's contest. Those mountain boys have beaten us every year that I can remember."

Humble smiles at her little friend. She knows what the boys do not. "Why don't we practice now? Morning Sunshine can be the judge."

In a unanimous voice, the group calls over the oldest girl to judge the correctness of the contest. Morning Sunshine is in her last year of school and has been reading her teacher's best books. Because she is one of the prettiest girls, the boys obediently agree. Putting down her weaving, she comes to where the group waits. She seldom gives them a notice, so the boys are pleased.

"Let's see how many we can think of. Perhaps we can remember enough to win the wisdom contest this year."

A ten-year-old boy struts around the dirt yard and says, "Boys are always wiser than girls." Several boys laugh in agreement. No one seems to notice when Humble whispers to the barber's gap-toothed little daughter who sneaks away from the crowd and runs back home. The children name all of the proverbs they can recall.

"People who know when they have enough are rich."

"A journey of a thousand miles begins with one step."

"Why feed a horse for twenty years for someone else to ride?"

"That is a mean proverb!" Joyful Day says angrily.

"Yes. That one is what people say to girls to be cruel and

make them cry. Is that the best one you know?" another of the older girls agrees.

"It is an old proverb. My uncle often says it to my cousin." He is defensive.

Tiger speaks up, "Let's say that they can't be mean sayings even if they are old classics."

"That is a very good idea."

"'Children obey your parents'" (Ephesians 6:1).

"Rotten wood cannot be carved. I have forgotten what it means."

"Vegetables from another's garden taste best."

"'The heavens are telling the glory of God; they are a marvelous display of his craftsmanship. Day and night they keep on telling about God'" (Psalm 19:1–2).

"'If you are looking for advice, stay away from fools'" (Proverbs 14:7).

"That is not a classical proverb. Where are you getting those quotations?"

Little Red Rose, the small daughter of the barber, smiles a shy smile with a missing tooth and shows a thin strip of paper to the doubters.

The boys demand, "Morning Sunshine, is it a real traditional proverb?"

"Red Rose, is this from your grandmother's book?"

The child nods her head. With a pocket full of slips, she plans on using them all in this neighborhood session.

"How is it that we have never heard them?" Tiger asks loudly.

"Are they from Mao's red book?"

"No." She smiles mischievously.

"Red Rose, will you read some more to us?"

Humble speaks up, "She doesn't have to read them. She knows them all."

"Then tell us some more!" the boys demand in chorus.

"'A good man's mind is filled with honest thoughts; an evil man's mind is crammed with lies'" (Proverbs 12:6).

"'The Lord is my light and my salvation; whom shall I fear?'" (Psalm 27:1).

"These sound like proverbs. What if the teachers will not allow us to use them in the spring wisdom festival?"

Tiger looks at his male friends in surprise, but it is Morning Sunshine who understands the potential of Red Rose's quotations.

"Do you think your grandmother will bring her book the day of the contest?"

Red Rose answers innocently, "I will ask her."

"Are they the same quotations that the man on the radio reads? My uncle copies them all into a notebook," one of the boys volunteers.

"They are the same verses from the same big book." Humble says emphatically.

Tiger turns to Red Rose and asks, "How many more do you know?"

With a huge grin, the little girl who was so recently afraid of her tormentor laughs and answers, "Many more!"

Tiger speaks to the little girl politely, "May I have just one?"

"Me too. Just one?" Sea Swimmer asks quickly before all slips of paper are taken.

So the village that has not won the wisdom contest in many years prepares for a win with many narrow strips of paper containing quotations.

"This one reads, 'In my distress I screamed to the Lord for his help. And he heard me from heaven; my cry reached his ears'" (Psalm 18:6).

"Which god is that, Humble?"

"That is speaking of the Lord God almighty, the one who made the universe."

"How do you know this?" Uncut Jade asks.

"I know because I have many of these papers in my pockets and my memory too. Let me tell you about this Lord God almighty. He is the God of creation and love. One of my favorite verses reads like this, 'For God loved the world so much that he gave his only Son so that anyone who believes on him shall not perish, but have eternal life'" (John 3:16).

Uncut Jade stares at Humble. "That sounds like a great quotation. May I use that one in the contest?"

"Yes. It is for anyone to use."

THE SPRING WISDOM CONTEST

A few weeks later, three village school teams assemble for the annual Spring Festival of Wisdom. None of the schools is large or wealthy, but each team represents its village, and the competition holds the key to its reputation for the coming year. Students and teachers from the two visiting mountain schools start out very early while the morning mist still hides most of their homes. A visiting government cadre rides his bicycle, and four other older adults, respected for their age and learning in the classics, come in a wagon pulled by a long-eared mule. All want to be on time for this important school competition.

The excitement makes everyone fidgety. Girls giggle, and boys whisper and point to their visiting opponents. When three of the oldest members of the village arrive, the room becomes unnaturally quiet. The local teacher greets her visitors respectfully and guides Red Rose's almost blind grandmother, Grandmother Rose Bud, to her chair. She is an honored judge today. Grandmother Rose Bud's entrance commands attention as she slowly walks to the teacher's chair, wearing her special festival robe from many years ago. It is golden-colored brocade Qipao, still amazingly beautiful.

The teacher's chair and two long, wooden benches are placed on the west side of the schoolroom for the adult visitors. When the visiting adults arrive, two boys chosen for the honor serve them cups of water from a thermos.

By the time the teacher gives a short speech of welcome, some parents slip into the door and find a vacant corner from which to watch the event. As traditional songs are sung, a crowd gathers outside the building in order to hear the children's voices as they compete for the academic honor of their village.

The children wear their best shirts, and many have fresh haircuts in honor of the day. Students of all ages think that they are prepared for the contest, but the presence of so many adults and visiting students rob many of them of their confidence. These solemn-faced judges will rule on the legality of each quotation. The mood inside the familiar schoolroom is strangely somber, even as the parents jostle for places outside, chatter, and laugh. A grandfather opens the window so those outside may hear the contest.

Memorization is a favorite method of learning in China. Small children and old scholars alike commit basic characters and long passages to memory, lending dignity to the practice of study. Today's contest is intended to honor learning of traditional material. Younger students are allowed to begin. Each child has learned a few proverbs, and it is important to them and their families to be included in the contest today.

A beaming, round-faced, six-year-old boy stands very straight and shouts the first offering of the day, "To go too far is the same as not to go far enough." He sits down immediately. He does not wait for the judges to rule on his quotation. He knows that it is correct. He is content that his family will beam with pride. He is glad that he has been allowed to begin because he learned only four proverbs. If another student uses his few lines first, then he may not use it again.

A judge from each of the three schools nods. They will not challenge recognized pieces.

The second student is a visiting child with a long face. He speaks in a high-pitched voice that does little to hide his discomfort. "If you want fish, then go home and make a net."

The first student from the farthest mountain school is

dressed in boots and a colorful tunic in an ancient traditional pattern. He is aware of his fine image. "No state can exist without the confidence of the people."

A girl wearing a colorful sweater smiles as she repeats quietly, "Talk does not cook rice." Her parents smile approvingly as she sits down.

The visiting cadre leaves the room to go outside and quiet the crowd of parents and neighbors. "You sound like a bunch of cackling chickens. You must be quiet. The judges must be able to hear the students. Do not laugh so loud or cheer for your children. Have some dignity!"

The crowd is ashamed to be corrected by a visiting cadre, but their manners do not improve. They are soon crowded in front of the open window again, talking aloud and cheering their local children.

Stands Strong continues, "Vegetables from another's garden taste best."

The line of contestants should be thinning down by now. The two visiting teams eye each other. They both had planned on winning this contest easily.

Humble speaks up with this simple saying, "Nothing is achieved without effort."

A large-shouldered boy looks only at the judges when he quotes, "Let things run their course."

A mountain boy with an impressive-looking belt says, "Women and servants are most difficult to deal with. If you are familiar with them, they cease to be humble. If you keep a distance from them, they resent it."

Morning Sunshine has one benefit from her beauty; she has experience in dealing with rude young men. With calm composure, she quotes from Confucius to answer and insult this mountain student who thinks so little of women and servants. Her opponent has correctly quoted from the Analects, but with hundreds more to choose from, she considered him in bad taste.

She quotes, "The superior man is broadminded, but not partisan; the inferior man is partisan, but not broadminded."

It is only after a ripple of smiles and light laughter roll across the room that the boy in the impressive belt realizes that he has been mocked.

A ten-year-old boy does not understand the laughter and is afraid it is at his expense, but he stands to give his quote, "A man who reviews the old so as to find the new is qualified to teach others."*

The older students are impatient. They exchange glances. The senior boys and girls think the young students have had their time of glory. Now they should sit down and allow them to shine. Everyone knows the purposes of this day. This contest is important for village pride, but it also has many personal purposes.

Seniors from all three schools worry.

As the sun climbs high overhead, the number of contestants is narrowing down to fewer and fewer students. Now the competition is becoming serious.

"People who know when they have enough are rich."

Joyful Day calmly states, "'God orders his angels to protect you wherever you go.' Psalm nine, verse eleven."

Tiger recites his last proverb aloud, regretting that he has not studied more and defended the honor of his village more bravely. "This proverb is from Solomon, King of Israel, to his sons, 'A gossip goes around spreading rumors, while a trustworthy man tries to quiet them.' Proverbs eleven, verse thirteen."

The judges have quizzical expressions on their faces. After consulting with Red Rose's smiling grandmother, they nod. These new proverbs from the ancient writings of King Solomon will be accepted.

A pretty visiting girl with long, shining hair braids quietly quotes, "A journey of a thousand miles begins with a single step."

Her beauty is not wasted on the numerous boys in all three

schools. There are so few girls in any of their schools that they find it difficult to think of her as the "enemy."

Humble recites with confidence, "'Children, obey your parents; this is the right thing to do because God has placed them in authority over you.' Ephesians six, verse one, from the Holy Bible."

A boy with very short hair says clearly, "Just stay at the center of the circle and let all things take their course."

Judges and old grandparents alike nod. How satisfying it is to have students learn the old sayings of the Tao.

Many faces with jaws set reflect the seriousness of the contest now. As expected, the senior students are among those left in the competition. This is one of the last times they will be able to shine as students. None of them will continue to high school and college for an advanced education. After this season, they will take their places beside the adults of their communities. The unusual characteristic of today's event is that so many children from the local school are left in the competition.

A thin boy by the name of True Promise proves his preparation in the classics when he quotes a time-honored proverb, hoping that the girl with the hair braids notices his composure.

"The superior man extensively studies literature and restrains himself with the rules of propriety. Thus, he will not violate the way."

All of the judges smile in approval. They are proud of the manner in which these children are honoring their ancestral learning.

The next turn belongs to Humble, who smoothes her hair down with both hands and then holds them behind her back in order to present a quiet and orderly impression. "'O my soul, why be so gloomy and discouraged? Trust in God! I shall again praise him for his wondrous help; he will make me smile again, for He is my God!' This is from verse five of chapter forty-three in the book of Psalms of King David."

A visiting girl in a colorful green outfit recites a popular, ancient quotation, "No state can exist without the confidence of the people."

A visiting judge speaks quietly. "I am sorry to inform you, but this proverb has already been used." The girl looks embarrassed as she sits down.

Little Red Rose now looks out of place with all of the older students, but she still smiles, displaying her empty gum, awaiting the emergence of a new tooth. She recites her next bit of wisdom with ease, picturing it in her mind as it is written in her yellow notebook.

> "About this time the disciples came to Jesus to ask which of them would be greatest in the kingdom of heaven. Jesus called a small child over to him and set the little fellow down among them, and said, "Unless you turn to God from your sins and become as little children, you will never get into the kingdom of heaven. Therefore anyone who humbles himself as this little child is the greatest in the kingdom of heaven."
>
> Matthew 18:1–4

The two visiting judges and their teachers look at each other with alarm. How are they to know whether this is a true proverb? One judge with lines of age across his brow and white hair creeping from under the sides of his traditional, embroidered hat asks Red Rose to stand up again.

"Little scholar, how do you know this wisdom? What is its origin?"

"Sir, it is found in chapter eighteen of the book of Matthew in verses one through four of the Holy Bible."

The visiting dignitaries do not expect this small girl to be able to answer so quickly. They confer again, and the same judge asks again, "We have heard of this book, but how can we know that what you have said is a true quotation?"

Red Rose's teacher smiles. How can she, a young woman, argue with such learned old men? Grandmother Rose Bud turns her dim eyes toward the judges and says quietly, "It is as she says. It is written here in this book. I can no longer see to read its pages, but we can send for someone to find each quote for you, and you can read it to make your ruling."

As the teacher whispers to Tiger to go to find Pale Orchid, the two men bend their heads together again. If they fail to question the validity of these quotations, their entire villages will attack their learned standings. If they accept all of these unfamiliar sayings, they will both surely lose the competition, and to girls! It was acceptable to allow girls to enter this traditional contest, but surely even the teacher, as young as she is, should know that it is only proper for a boy to win such an honor. The venerable judge nods and says that he would like an assistant.

"Would you like to examine my volume?" Grandmother Rose Bud hands her precious Bible, still wrapped in folds of faded, red silk, to the startled man seated next to her. He carefully unfolds its contents to read the old Chinese characters for himself. He reads for a moment until he realizes that the entire room is watching him and that the contest is halted while he examines the newly found treasure. He clears his throat and pronounces, "Let us continue. We will consult an assistant when he arrives."

A visiting boy named Horse Roper stands, waiting to be recognized. He carries his chin with an arrogant air and is ready to contribute his part again. With a bold voice, he quotes, "Set your will on the way; have a firm grasp on virtue. Rely upon humanity. Find recreation in the arts."

Uncut Jade tries not to smirk at the proud visitor named Horse Roper, but he now has another reason to defeat this team from over the mountains. He does not like Horse Roper's arrogant air.

"'Jesus said, go home to your friends, and tell them what wonderful things God has done for you; and how merciful he has been.' This is from the Holy Bible in the book of Mark in chapter five, verse nineteen."

Tiger interrupts the Spring Wisdom Contest by entering the classroom with Pale Orchid in tow. When she sees the assembly, she regrets not having questioned him further about why she is needed. She has been picking berries and is embarrassed about her unkempt appearance. The old judge is surprised that his assistant is a woman.

"Auntie Pale Orchid, will you do us the honor of finding the verses in Grandmother Rose Bud's Bible, which our students quote?"

"You know that it will be my great joy. But first I must wash my hands. I might stain those precious pages."

As she washes and dries her hands, a bench is placed next to the judges.

"This will allow you to rest the book on the bench while you turn the pages."

The scholarly old judge reluctantly yields his treasure to this young woman with the berry-stained hands who smiles so broadly. *Who is she? She appears so young, yet she is addressed as a married woman. She certainly is not from these hills.*

Morning Sunshine stands waiting patiently while the latest arrangement is made. She waits for her teacher to nod to her before saying,

> "The eyes of the Lord are intently watching all who live good lives, and he gives attention when they cry to him. But the Lord has made up his mind to wipe out even the memory of evil men from the earth. Yes, the Lord hears the good man when he calls to him for help, and saves him out of all his trouble."
>
> Psalm of King David, chapter thirty-four,
> verses fifteen through seventeen.

The two judges and other guests listen intently to the text of the quotation.

Now the judges are amazed to see that this young woman called Pale Orchid knows where to find the Psalms of King David, and she offers its printed page for their proof of the reading.

This will go down in history as one of the most astonishing Spring Wisdom Contests in memory. Where has this book been hidden? Who is this young woman, and where did she learn so much about this old volume?

The next visitor is worried as he recites. He is running out of material.

Little Red Rose stands with both hands to her sides. She has lost all fear and is enjoying herself. She does not even see that Tiger, who is no longer in the contest, is her silent cheerleader. She speaks clearly as she recites, "'Commit everything you do to the Lord. Trust him to help you do it, and he will bring it to pass.' The Holy Bible, the book of Psalms, chapter thirty-seven, verse five."

Pale Orchid surprises the visiting judge by immediately finding the verse and handing it to him. He eagerly reads the passage and informs the other two judges of his acceptance. The teacher approaches the three seated judges, speaks with them for a moment, and then announces, "We will take a break for one hour. You may study if you wish, but please be back promptly."

There is a rush as the students scurry out with suddenly freed tongues. They leave the adults sitting in the room on hard, wooden seats. Their old bodies need to rise and stretch, but their minds hold so many questions.

A committee from the village parents arrives to offer refreshments of steamed rolls filled with lamb and spices. The visiting judges and teachers accept the food politely. They know that it will be delicious. Their many questions will have to wait.

After the hour, a small boy under the direction of his grandfather and his grandfather's watch bangs on a brass gong hung on a pole. It is not a very large gong, but then he is not a very large boy. He sounds the gong to indicate that the hour is spent. The contest must be completed soon, as the return trip for the visitors must not last into darkness.

A local boy begins the second session. He speaks slowly, "'They asked Jesus: What should we do to satisfy God? And

Jesus told them, 'This is the will of God, that you believe in the one he has sent.' This is found in the Holy Bible, the book of John, chapter six, verses twenty-eight and twenty-nine."

The broad-shouldered boy named Faithful Friend stands next and quotes, "Only the most intelligent and the most stupid do not change."

Uncut Jade speaks quietly, as is his habit. "'Better to be poor and honest than to be rich and a cheater.' This is a proverb of King Solomon, chapter twenty-eight, verse six."

The students continue to display their learning, each following the last student from opposing schools. No one says the obvious, which is the local students are the only ones giving their references, but the judges and the most astute visitors are now interested in hearing these new quotations. Everyone has heard the old classics of the Tao and Confucius, but these are new and interesting. More than once, the most scholarly judge wants to stop the contest to ask in ancient tradition for an explanation or discourse on the verses, but the event continues.

Morning Sunshine stands to recite one of her favorite verses. "'But when the Holy Spirit has come upon you, you will receive power to testify about me with great effect to the people in Jerusalem, throughout Judea, in Samaria, and to the ends of the earth, about my death and resurrection.' This is found in the Holy Bible in the book of the Acts, chapter one, verse eight."

Morning Sunshine sits down and is unaware that two elderly people in the room quietly begin to weep. They have heard these words before, years ago, when they were young. In these same hills, before their world spun out of shape, they knew these very same words. Tears come unbidden, down lined faces that have many regrets.

The pretty girl from the mountain village hesitates as she tries to recall the words of her last piece. "A ruler who governs his state by virtue is like the north polar star, which remains in its place while all the other stars revolve around it."

The solemn boy is visibly shaken. This is his last proverb,

and he wants to repeat it perfectly. "The way of the superior man is threefold, but I have not been able to obtain it. The man of wisdom has no perplexities; the man of humanity has no worry. The man of courage has no fear."

Red Rose is alone among the older students now. She quotes, "'Then Peter replied, I see very clearly that the Jews are not God's only favorites. In every nation, he has those who worship and do good deeds and are acceptable to him.' This is from the Holy Bible, the book of Acts, chapter ten, verses thirty-four and thirty-five."

As Pale Orchid finds the passage and shows it to the judge sitting next to her, the thin young man who has presented his last quotation leans over and says in a loud whisper, "They do not know the real classics." The local students hear, as intended. They do not acknowledge the other team but rather smile to each other.

Faithful Friend quotes his next lines perfectly. "Man is born with uprightness. If one loses it, he will be lucky to escape with his life." With an embarrassed expression on his face, he says, "Honorable judges, we regret to say that we have recited all of the proverbs that we have prepared."

"Thank you. You must not be ashamed of your scholarship."

With the elimination of one team, there is a murmur in the room followed by the quiet of unusually attentive children. The crowd outside passes the word around, and then it too is restrained.

Uncut Jade stands at his full height and proceeds to present a difficult piece from Confucius. "The man of wisdom delights in water; the man of humanity delights in mountains. The man of wisdom is active; the man of humanity is tranquil. The man of wisdom enjoys happiness; the man of humanity enjoys long life. This is found in Analects, chapter six, verse twenty-one." With a direct look at the thin boy, Uncut Jade sits down.

The next student has lost his arrogant expression as he resorts to a quote from Mao. "Women hold up half of the heavens."

Morning Sunshine is beautifully poised as she presents the next piece for the benefit of the boy who accused them of not knowing the "real classics."

"If we are not yet able to serve man, how can we serve spiritual beings? If we do not yet know about life, how can we know about death?" She ends by saying, "This is from the Analects, chapter eleven, verse eleven."

A groan is heard from the remaining opposing team. The thin boy is firmly slugged by his friend, who realizes several things: The local team does know the classics. They have just used up two of the ancient sayings, ones his team could have used. And last, girls could possibly defeat them!

Horse Roper jams his hands into his pockets in order to concentrate better. "I transmit, but do not create. I believe in and love the ancients."

Uncut Jade chooses a short but famous verse, "The way of our master is none other than conscientiousness and altruism. This is from chapter four, verse fifteen of the Analects."

Red Rose quotes: "'Don't let evil get the upper hand, but conquer evil by doing good.'" With a smile of the innocent, she finishes, "This is from the Holy Bible, the twenty-first verse of the twelfth chapter of the book of Romans."

Horse Roper bites his lip, closes his eyes, and then recites, "A superior man in dealing with the world is not for anything or against anything. He follows righteousness as the standard."

His team feels his struggle. They wring their hands, willing him to carry them to victory.

Morning Sunshine quotes slowly, "'Come and hear all of you who reverence the Lord, and I will tell you what he did for me. For I cried to him for help with praises ready on my tongue. He would not have listened if I had not confessed my sins. But he listened! He heard my prayer! He paid attention to it! Blessed be the God who didn't turn away when I was praying, and didn't refuse me his kindness and love.' This is found in the Holy Bible in the book of the Psalms of King David, chapter sixty-six, verses sixteen through twenty."

From somewhere can be heard a firm one-word exclamation, "Yes!"

Horse Roper does not look at the judges when says, "When cranes fly overhead, it is time to plow your field."

The judges make no comment. Each waits on the other to question it. No one does, so the quotation is accepted.

Little Red Rose looks at her grandmother and speaks to her as if she were in her own home sitting by the fire and reading to her.

> "Ask, and you will be given what you ask for. Seek, and you will find. Knock, and the door will be opened. For everyone who asks, receives. Anyone who seeks, finds. If only you will knock, the door will open. If a child asks his father for a loaf of bread, will he be given a stone instead? If he asks for fish, will he be given a poisonous snake? Of course not! And if you hardhearted sinful men know how to give good gifts to your children, won't your Father in heaven even more certainly give good gifts to those who ask him for them?"

"This is from the Holy Bible, the book of Matthew, chapter seven, verses seven through eleven."

No one is sure where the applause began, whether it was outside the window, or with her own team members, or with the two women who are crying, but it is a loud applause for the small gap-toothed little girl standing among the senior students today.

She looks around, puzzled, and turns to her teacher for instruction. Her teacher, who has joined the praise, goes to her student and explains that the applause is in appreciation for her memory work. Only then does the small six-year-old girl grin, place both hands over her mouth, and sit down. Tiger, her former tormentor, now supporter, sends her a huge smile and a victory sign.

Horse Roper stands and gives what he knows to be an accurate quotation.

"It is man that makes the Way great, and not the Way that can make man great."

Morning Sunshine, the fourteen-year-old senior student, is the only student from her school who still stands undefeated with little Red Rose today. She has saved this last quotation for the end of the day. She has chosen it with care. Folding her hands, she lifts her chin and calmly recites,

> "So now, since we have been made right in God's sight by faith in his promises, we can have real peace with him because of what Christ Jesus our Lord has done for us. For because of our faith he has brought us into this place of highest privilege where we now stand, and confidently and joyfully look forward to actually becoming all that God has had in mind for us to be. We can rejoice, too, when we run into problems and trials for we know that they are good for us—they help us learn to be patient. And patience develops strength of character in us and helps us trust God more each time we use it until finally our hope and faith are strong and steady. Then, when that happens, we are able to hold our heads high no matter what happens and know that all is well, for we know how dearly God loves us, and we feel this warm love everywhere within us because God has given us the Holy Spirit to fill our hearts with his love."

"This is from the Holy Bible, in the book of Romans, chapter five, ver—"

Before she finishes giving credits for the quotation, a man from one of the visiting schools stands up and interrupts Morning Sunshine. "Please, judges, could she please repeat that piece? We have never heard it."

The two women who cried and three local people who had been standing in the corner all day join in the plea. "Oh yes. Please may she recite that last one again?"

The head judge looks at both of his colleagues.

"It is the turn of the other team, and it is getting late. Horse Roper, what do you have to say? Do you have any more quotations to give?"

"Sir, I do have one more, but I now believe that these scholars have an unlimited supply. Let her speak again."

"This is still a contest. How many quotations do you still have, Morning Sunshine?"

"Sir, I know four more from Confucius, three more from Lao-tzu, and several more verses from the Holy Bible."

"It has been said then. You may begin again."

The lovely girl named Morning Sunshine looks at the old judge. He agrees with the crowd. They all want to hear this amazing verse again. So she begins again to recite the verse she herself has come to hold so dearly.

She continues with her memorized verses while the audience sits quietly.

In a remote school somewhere in northern China, two schools of mostly male students are defeated today by a small village school and bested by two of the most remarkable girls they have ever heard. The students could have been disagreeable and loud in defeat, but this day does not lend itself to that show of bad temper and rudeness. The old judge himself leads the tone of the crowd; the students sit as still and as quietly as do the judges and other visitors. This is from an ancient book, but it is new to most of them, and they want to hear it at least once more.

As the judges stand to award the honors, Morning Sunshine and little Red Rose bow politely to them. After the judges give the prizes to the winners, they linger a few minutes too long, speaking to the two girls, the aged grandmother, the teacher, and her amazing assistant. There are so many questions that plead for answers.

How reluctantly the visitors leave to return to their villages this afternoon. How many make promises to themselves that they will return. It is an extraordinarily harmonious day full of surprises.

After bidding their guests good-bye, the local students explode in celebrations of victory. What an astonishing day! This day will live in the village history. Boys and girls alike retell each incident of their victorious contest with shouts and dances of joy. The school that has never held marvelous goals or dreamed of fame and glory suddenly possesses more pride than it can hold.

The village adults who were not invited but knew enough to invite themselves rush off to find any audience available.

"Let me tell you what our children did today."

"You will never believe what happened in the Spring Wisdom Festival today at the schoolhouse."

THE CADRE

The heavy loads of water hanging from their shoulder poles make Silk Fan and Pale Orchid walk slowly as they move toward a central point in the common field. They will serve water to the entire village when the workers reach the halfway point. As they walk the two friends talk.

"Pale Orchid, how are you getting along with your husband? He seems quite happy. Are you?"

"Silk Fan, I am learning to love him and his parents. He seems proud of me and listens as I read from the scriptures that Humble copied for me. He is proud of his position and is grateful to his father for obtaining it for him, even if it was through a bribe."

"Pale Orchid, is your father-in-law difficult?"

Laughing a small response, she tells what everyone in the village knows, "He tells me that I should be grateful to live in an old house of his ancestors where he receives a soldier's pension and Brick Wall receives a salary for his government position."

"I hear that your mother-in-law is pleasant. Is that so?"

"I do not know how to plant the vegetables as she does, but I am learning. She is patient as she shows me her way to work."

As they round the curve of the field, they notice a man with a dark notebook in his hands standing by the irrigation ditch, write, then progress toward the workers, spread across the field of growing turnips.

"Silk Fan, who is that man?"

"I do not know him. He appears to be a visiting cadre checking on our work."

"Perhaps it is because we had such a grand harvest last season. Brick Wall said that the big city authorities were quite impressed with our production and want to make us an example to inspire other villages."

As the man with the notebook nears, he spies Brick Wall working with the rest of the villagers pulling weeds with his hands. The women hear him spit, "Stupid fool! How can he earn respect if he works like a common laborer?"

There is little about him except his hat and his commanding attitude that would indicate that he is a man of authority. He travels the farmland on dirt roads shadowed by yellow hills, passing modest homes with small private plots, feeling superior to the local population who work the land.

Hoping to surprise slackers sleeping in the shade, the visiting cadre's visit is unannounced for the purpose of catching slothful workers. He finds none but is startled to hear a noise coming from the direction of a group of workers who are weeding the crop. He hears no instruments, so it cannot be a radio, but he definitely hears singing. The old party line songs are almost never heard now except at public parades, and the words he hears are not a familiar party song written to encourage workers at their tasks, but these people are singing all together as they work.

He stops momentarily to listen. Silk Fan and Pale Orchid notice his confusion.

"Nearer my God to thee, nearer to thee! Even though it be a cross that raiseth me; still all my song shall be, nearer my God to thee."

Brick Wall notices his superior standing alone at the edge of the field and rises from his bending position, wiping his hands on his trousers while marching to meet him.

"Greetings, Cadre!"

"Hello, Cadre Brick Wall. Do you beat them or bribe them?" he asks abruptly.

"Neither. I do not need to. If I had known you were coming, there would have been refreshments prepared for you."

"Do not concern yourself with that. I have come to inspect your fields, and I find you working like a common citizen."

"Yes, I do work with them."

"How can you watch for laggards and quitters?"

"That is not a problem here."

"And what are those workers doing singing? It will steal their energy, and they will not finish the day's work!"

"Those are just hymns of faith that Christians sing."

"You allow Christians to work on your field teams? You know what our central government policy is toward religious groups!"

"This group is different. This is the work group that produced such a high yield of corn production last year."

"What do you mean that it is different? They look like ordinary farmers to me."

"Yes, they do. But they come to work on time, never fight among themselves, do not take the crop for themselves, and they do not use vulgar language in front of the women. They are the same people who have lived here for years. They have only become cooperative and honest since they have become Christians."

"That is strange. You may keep them if they really are productive. Now I must see the storage bins. Oh, try not to let the news of your work crews' strange habits get around. I do not want to have to explain this Christianity thing to my superiors. They have enough worries at this time with the terrible earthquakes and the upcoming Olympic Games."

It is year five since the captured brides came to this northern farm community, and some peace has come to most of them, an inner peace they call the peace of God. They are a part of the labor group that sings as they work. The group continues with their task as their local young cadre meets with the visiting official.

The number twenty cadre shakes his head and follows the path away from the unsupervised workers with their odd work habits. How will he keep them a secret? Their production numbers are bound to draw the attention of other officials. In his haste to make his connection with the truck, he might have made a mistake.

Silk Fan and Pale Orchid are both experienced enough to know the possible repercussions of a visitor who asks about Christians who sing without permission from the national department in charge of controlling religious groups. Just when they feel free to sing praises as they work a new worry creases their brows. As they serve their neighbors water, both wonder whether their harmonious village will have further visits from authorities.

THE FUNERAL OF
BLACK PEARL

It is a new day. The dawn breaking sun startles the sky with a red glow across the east. A little boy named Strong Bamboo is already dressed. His weary-faced mother is taking him to the second room, his parents' bedroom, for his morning meal. He does not understand why he must eat his wheat cereal here. His tall, pretty mother calmly tends to his needs. As the child sits on a wooden bench eating, his mother says quietly, "May my spoken words and my unspoken thoughts be pleasing even to you, O Lord my rock and my redeemer" (Psalm 19:14 TLB).

She smiles at her son and goes to stand beside her husband, Steadfast. He acknowledges her presence with an affectionate squeeze to her hand. Steadfast loves his educated wife dearly and has even defended her from his old mother's negative attacks in the last few years.

The couple has had little sleep in the last few weeks and is now too preoccupied to eat. Steadfast has done his duty to his mother by being present during her final days on earth. The obedient Chinese son has kept the ancient tradition of listening to his mother's last labored breaths.

Now it is time to prepare her bent body with the wrinkled skin for burial. As the morning sky turns slowly from a brilliant red, to a fiery pink, to yellow, and finally to a dull gray, the neighbors come to visit and acknowledge the death of the old mistress of the house. The older women come to prepare the body in the time-honored manner.

Walks with Grace and Truth has been the proper daughter-in-law for five years. Captured from her home many miles to the south, she was an unwilling bride who was engaged to a nice young man of whom her parents approved, yet she has fulfilled the traditional role of a peasant wife and daughter-in-law to the family she did not choose. She had her own plans, education, and life interrupted but has done the bidding of the old mistress, been her own personal servant, and worked long hours in the fields and home, doing as she was instructed. Her time, her body, nor her child are her own. She became the traditional young Chinese wife with little status, much work, and few choices or possessions.

The only parts of her life, which she claims as her own, are her mind and her soul. Her hunger for some sort of distraction and mental challenge led her to knowledge of God and his plans for the world. This enlightenment has changed her attitude from that of an angry victim to that of a victorious woman with a peaceful spirit. A gentle kindness now inhabits her days. She has a glow about her personality that brings a smile to her lips and soft words to her husband and child. Her mother-in-law benefited from this change in her last years. Never fully comprehending it, yet she welcomed the gentleness and good humor in the last, helpless days of her life.

As the neighbor women assemble to wash the body in preparation for burial, the talk is all feminine business.

"I will bathe her feet."

"We need a tie to hold her hair in place."

"Tell your husband to get a long board for laying her out. Don't let him take down a door for it. She must have a proper burial board."

"Bind her ankles together now. She must not be allowed to wander about the afterworld."

"Where are her festival clothes?"

"Yes, she must go to meet her ancestors in her best clothes."

"If I had a silver coin, I could go to buy her a real belt."

"Black Perl never owned a real belt. This tie will do."

"Now fold her hands correctly in the traditional way."

"Close her eyes neatly. Yes. She looks fine."

"I shall miss Black Pearl. She was my friend and neighbor for most of my life."

"Walks with Grace and Truth, you have served her well. I thank you. Now you are the mistress of the house."

Walks with Grace and Truth nods politely to her elderly neighbor.

The oldest grandmother present, one who had refused to speak to her the first dreadful year, speaks next.

"Yes, you fed her with a spoon when she could no longer feed herself, and you carried her on your back when she could no longer walk. You have brought honor to this house."

"We will go now to cook rice for an offering. We will walk with you to bury her."

"Shall I tell her son that he may come in now?"

"Yes."

Keeping tradition comforts the oldest generation. So much has happened in their tumultuous lives. They remember so much pain and suffering of wars and hunger, but it is the breaking of tradition that haunts them the most. Their parents wore their hair in long traditional styles, wore time-honored clothing, and had as many babies as came. Gangs of thugs even tore down their temples and burned their holy books. The worst times of persecution of the teachers, priests, and mayors is over, but an ever-present fear still rules their lives.

Now an official from the central government forces the one-child policy. The committee on family planning often visits this remote mountain village. Their private lives and the number of children they have is the concern of the central government.

As the women work together, no word is mentioned of the way in which Walks with Grace and Truth came to live among them. They were all a part of the conspiracy to keep the kidnapped brides prisoners, bound to this place by fear, poverty, and their own children.

No apology or retribution was ever made. No one seems to feel any guilt or responsibility to the younger women who now work and produce children for them. People in this part of the world have always preferred boys to girls, so this just becomes another chapter in the history of the mistreatment of girls and women.

The neighborhood men file into the house to pay their respects to the dead. They stand solemnly for a few minutes. Many have never been inside before as the house is small and usually a place for women. A man who reads notes the beautifully painted scrolls hanging on the walls. His neighbor turns to him and asks, "What is the message?"

"It reads: 'For I know the plans that I have for you says the Lord, They are for good and not evil, to give you a future and a hope. In those days when you pray I will listen. You will find me when you seek me if you look for me in earnest'" (Jeremiah 29:11 TLB).

"What does the scroll by the window tell you?

The room is quiet while the neighbor reads aloud again, "'I am the true vine and the Father is the gardener. Yes, I am the vine and you are the branches. Whoever lives in me and I in him shall produce a large crop of fruit. For apart from me you cannot do a thing. You did not choose me! I chose you! I appointed you to go and produce lovely fruit always, so that no matter what you ask of the Father, using my name, He will give it to you'" (John 15:1, 5, 16).

The visiting neighbor men want to ask a hundred questions, but they know that this is not the time for questions. They will ask Steadfast later. Walks with Grace and Truth is only a woman, but she obviously knows much. As they leave to return home to dress in their best clothes, a friend turns and asks his lifelong friend, Steadfast, "Do you object if we ask Walks with Grace and Truth to read for us some time? I do not understand those writings on your walls."

"I will ask her later, my friend."

As the men leave the house, two young women come up the road. White Flowering Tree is pushing Beautiful Moon in a homemade bamboo cart. With only their friend Walks with Grace and Truth present, they speak freely.

"So is it over now? Is she really dead?"

"Yes. She died this morning as the day was beginning. The old ones have bathed and dressed her."

"So when may we dance on the old tiger's grave?" White Flowering Tree asks.

"Yes, that would be appropriate. I would like to dance anywhere. I would like to just be able to walk!" Beautiful Moon has ample reason for her bitterness. "Now you will have some peace."

"I already have peace, but it is not because Black Pearl died and ceases to rule and criticize me. I have a quiet soul now. The peace is a gift from the Holy Spirit of God. It is a wonderful gift that I have received."

"What is wonderful is having her out of this house and out of your life."

Walks with Grace and Truth smiles at her crippled friend, Beautiful Moon, who still lives in the House of Hatred with her husband and mother-in-law.

"Things have been different around here for many months now. I have forgiven her. I am at peace."

Beautiful Moon is astonished. "But my friend, she was a monster! She made your life miserable."

"That is true. She allowed hate to rule her life. She loved power and loved to hold a grudge, even when there was no cause. She enjoyed being angry about anything. That hate and anger cannot rule my life any longer. I will not allow that hate to rule me from the grave. My eyes stayed red with weeping and my soul hard with resentment for too many years. The Christians taught me how to win over such misery."

Beautiful Moon is amazed. "You mean this, don't you? I do not understand how you can be so calm and so happy! You have been this way for over a year now, long before her death. How is it possible? She paid for your kidnapping, kept you a prisoner here, and used you as a slave. She gave you to her son to be used as a breeding mare!"

"That is all true, Beautiful Moon, but I have found a new way to think that brought me much relief. I depend on the power of God to forgive. I could not do that alone. This is the answer to my joyful spirit. All of those wise sayings of Confucius did not bring me peace of mind, or the sayings of Mao. The Buddhists just wanted me to erase myself and accept the horrors."

"How then? I do not think that I can survive much longer. I have drawn my own blood as I clinch my hands in anger. I also broke a tooth when I gritted my teeth in anger as I cried out in hatred at all those who use and abuse me. They will not even bring me water for bathing when they know that I will never walk again. I will never accept this."

In sympathy, Walks with Grace and Truth wraps her arms around her friend. "You are correct. There is nothing fair or good about our situations. I am only telling you that God forgave me for my hatred through the power of his son, Jesus Christ. I learned to forgive her hatred. This has changed my life, not her death. Our friend, the old widow, helped me by letting us copy all of those verses from the radio. Those slips of paper were more than an exercise in memory. They saved more than my mind. They saved my soul."

"I do not understand all of this. You have changed so much. I would just like to change my address."

"We know, Beautiful Moon. The house will be quieter now. We can talk while we weave. You are welcome anytime. We will talk about this new peace I have found. Please find Pale Orchid and bring her with you. She knows all about this peace. She is a Christian!"

The two friends leave, and Walks with Grace and Truth dresses in a clean outfit of dark blue wool for the trip up the mountain cemetery. It is not a fine set of clothes as she should have for the occasion, but it is clean and it is her best. Since the funeral will take most of the day, she is anxious to begin the trip. She packs some food and takes the hand of Strong Bamboo, who wants to ask his little boy questions.

Steadfast and his friends lift the long burial board as a line of friends and neighbors walk respectfully behind them. The old women walk together, some holding the hand of a daughter or daughter-in-law. Children run in and out of the line as it makes its way up slowly up the trail. For the children still living in innocence of grief and death, today is a holiday.

The new mistress of the house firmly holds her son's hand and seeks her husband's face. She not only accepted Steadfast as a husband, but she now loves him. The marriage room that he built for her was the first step he made to win her affection after she ran away. She will not release Strong Bamboo because he is too young to run with the older children and would very shortly be at his father's feet, hindering him as he carries his burden.

Walks with Grace and Truth must pay attention to the steep path, so she seldom sees Steadfast's face. She is concerned for her young husband. She wonders what he is thinking.

He sheds no tears. I wonder if he will be relieved to live without his mother's constant presence. He did not demand obedience as the old proverb said was his privilege. He will have to learn how to manage the money for the household and make a thousand other decisions that Black Pearl made for him all of his life. It will be a new way to live.

Before the burial, the crowd dutifully places gifts of food, flowers, and painted prayers on graves of their ancestors. After this ritual, the men who carried the body dig the grave and then sit and rest. A traditional meal is eaten. The men are mostly farmers who have never left this region. They are here for their friend and neighbor, Steadfast, but they hesitate to speak, not knowing the proper words to say about the death of a neighbor and mother of a friend. They purchased prayers written on white paper to place on the earth, and their mothers or wives placed the envelopes properly, but what is an acceptable thing to say?

The younger men are relieved when an older man offers a traditional saying, "The old proverb says that a diamond with a flaw is preferable to none."

Another man responds, "Yes, Black Pearl was a good, hard-working woman."

The men relax, thankful that appropriate comments have been voiced. Steadfast answers, "Yes, she was, and we honor her today, but I tell you that my diamond without a flaw is my wife, Walks with Grace and Truth."

The funeral crowd looks in embarrassment at the sudden turn in the conversation. The sweetness of spirit and the bold use of her talents go beyond the demands of an obedient wife. Her service to the community is not lost on the people of the village.

The men and their wives and mothers who served them food simply nod their heads.

The captive wife of many talents shines as a flawless diamond that they do not deserve since Christianity changed her attitude. Hard work and obedience were expected, but joy and peace were not, and the mountain village is now learning how to react to such a treasure.

A CHINESE OPERA

Five years ago, Silk Fan and Walks with Grace and Truth were attacked, kidnapped, and brought to this northern village. Today, they are both very busy. It is impossible to keep the preparations a secret at the home of Hero and Silk Fan. Their home is now called the House of Learning. Oral recitations are a part the noises of each afternoon as the school prepares for its first parents' night presentation, their own Chinese opera.

Concerned parents, nosy neighbors, and any curious party need only to walk slowly by the House of Learning in order to hear the drill of mathematic tables or the childish voices of poetry being memorized. It is an unusual combination of serious learning and sounds of happy giggles that often fill the afternoon air.

The wall around the House of Learning also provides a backdrop for a proud display of her students' work. It is not as fine a wall of dizabao that could be found around university campuses, but it has already been useful. Several young women took great delight in making a wall-sized poster of the human body, indicating functions of major organs. The poster was hung across the brick wall, where other pieces of student art hang. Everyone knows that the students are learning that teeth are for chewing food, the lungs hold air, and the esophagus takes food from the mouth to the stomach. Any thinking person must know that the purpose of the poster was to proclaim in large public letters that the male's sperm determines the gender of his child.

A local young woman who was beaten for producing daughters willingly paid for the large poster paper and paint. The same young woman rescued the poster from the mud after a heavy rain. The biology poster on the wall about the House of Learning lasted for weeks.

The musical instruments used in this tiny school are limited to those that Silk Fan borrows or scrounges. After all, she thinks, their sweet voices will make up for the lack of professional tones of the instruments.

Silk Fan is assisted in the children's production by her friend, Walks with Grace and Truth, who comes to the school one afternoon each week to teach advanced mathematics to her only student, the crippled boy, Honorable Integrity.

Honorable Integrity knows that he is surely the star of the program, as he is the narrator. His head bounces with joy as he reads the text. After being excluded from the village school, he will read aloud before everyone, proclaiming his skills. This is the biggest event in his young life, and he insists on inviting not only his parents and his grandparents but also six others. His angular face has been wreathed in smiles for weeks.

His parents purchased him a fine new suit for the event. He glows as he relates to his teacher, "Teacher Silk Fan, my father even bought me leather shoes!"

His parents, who have borne the grief of their crippled son, want the village to see him as they do, smiling and competent. His mother, Regal Peony, is a quiet woman who comes tonight in her best clothes with a pleasant expression set on her face. She is much more nervous than her son. When Honorable Integrity was born, his family named him the most ambitious name they could imagine, knowing that society would avoid him and deny him so much. After years of disgrace, tonight, Flying Horse holds his head up in pride of his truly honorable son.

Silk Fan thinks that accepting this shunned boy into the tiny class was the right decision. He is now twelve years old and most helpful. When he finishes his work each day, he willingly drills the younger girls on their lessons and treats all of the little girls in the class with masculine respect.

Flying Horse was the boy's tireless sponsor in having him accepted into Silk Fan's half-day classes for little girls who are not in the local public school. He often recalls Silk Fan's accusations that, "Boys do not know how to show respect to girls." The amazing farmer's wife/teacher used this reason for weeks when refusing his inclusion in her select group of outcasts. What a wonderful day it was when she agreed to allow him to come to classes for a one-week trial. Honorable's parents warned him against teasing the girls, and especially the little shy girl. His experiences would be unlike other boys, but his father is so happy that he is receiving an education that he often reminds him of Silk Fan's statement.

Four little girls all squirm as Silk Fan fits newly sewn, white, flowing gowns onto their small bodies. The student performers are the daughter of the soldier's wife, disapproved of by her finger-counting neighbors, a blind beauty rejected by the system, the extremely shy daughter of a neighbor, and the throwaway baby whom Humble claimed, brought home, and named Happiness Found.

That evening their entire families try to push into the small courtyard to claim the choice places for viewing their children in their first school production. The waiting crowd reads the poster aloud,

A Baby Comes to Town
A Chinese Opera
By the students and friends of the House of Learning

The impatient crowd waits until Humble lowers the poster and announces, "You may come in now." She is almost knocked to the ground by the wave of humanity that pushes its way into the triple-family courtyard.

Knowing the family nature of Chinese gatherings, Silk Fan expects a crowd, but her mouth falls open when she sees how many visitors are here. People are sitting upon her privacy wall, on the neighbor's wall, and in her plum tree! They are all awaiting her small students' big night. The crowd moves in and stands shoulder to shoulder. Many in the audience are unrelated to any student, just local people anxious for entertainment. A busy chatter fills the air.

Silk Fan steps to the center of her courtyard where she daily teaches little children and prepares vegetables. She quiets her neighbors with her serene smile."Thank you for coming tonight. Your children have worked very hard on this opera. Our narrator tonight is Honorable Integrity, son of Flying Horse and Regal Peony." With a wave of her hand, she directs attention toward the smiling boy so formally dressed. He sits at a stand with his script in front of him and a lantern at his shoulder. The crowd hushes in anticipation.

Honorable Integrity rehearsed his lines in loud projected tones. When he complained that he was yelling, both teachers reassured him that this was proper theater technique. Tonight, he speaks slowly and clearly as he begins his story in a voice that he still considers too loud.

"Our opera tells the story of how the creator God sent his son to earth. His son is named Jesus and he was equal to God and was also a creator. His life brought hope to everyone. It happened like this: A very long time ago in a small town called Nazareth God himself sent his angel, Gabriel to see a girl named Mary. She was a good girl engaged to a carpenter named Joseph, whose great, great-grandfather was the poet David.

The angel said to Mary, "Greetings, Mary, God loves you very much."

A gasp and ohs and ahs escape the audience as a light brightens the first scene. Humble is draped in a bed covering gracefully drawn over her head. She kneels, waiting patiently for the angel to speak. A volunteer, Gabriel, a masculine figure in white, strolls toward Humble, who plays the part of Mary.

Lanterns sway and the drums and flute play as the angel Gabriel walks in and speaks.

"God has chosen you over all of the women in Israel. Don't be afraid. God cares about you and will be gracious to you. You will become pregnant and have a baby boy. You are to name him Jesus. He will be called the son of God and do great things."

A murmur flows through the crowd, so the narrator hesitates before continuing.

"He shall be very great and shall be called the son of God. And the Lord God shall give him the throne of his ancestor David. And he shall reign over Israel forever; his kingdom shall never end!"

The crowd strains to hear Humble speak Mary's famous lines as she asks the angel, "But how can I have a baby? I am not even married."

Gabriel said, "You will become pregnant by the power of The Holy Spirit; so the baby shall be holy from the time it is born because he will be the Son of God."

Mary said, "I am ready to follow God's plan for my life. I will gladly serve him. I am willing to do whatever he wants."

The sudden eruption of excited voices from the audience gives evidence that they listened and understood the actors and their speaking message. Questions and comments fill the air. They quiet down as the lights are covered, and the area is relatively dark. When the light comes on again, the opera continues. Mary and the angel are gone, and a man in strange clothes is lying on a bed, apparently sleeping. A loud whisper from the audience asks, "Who is that?"

Honorable Integrity ignores the whisper and continues. "Joseph, a good man, had a dream and saw an angel standing beside him. Joseph, son of David," the angel said, don't hesitate to take Mary as your wife! For she is carrying a baby conceived by the Holy Spirit. And she will have a Son, and you shall name him Jesus (meaning Savior), for he will save his people from their sins."

The audience murmurs and sighs. Some have heard the story, and others have not, but all agree that it is an awesome one.

"When Joseph awoke, he did as the angel commanded and brought Mary home to be his wife."

On stage, Joseph leaves his house and returns with Mary, who carries a bundle of her belongings. Tears dampen a few faces as the lights are darkened again.

"About the time that Jesus was to be born, the emperor of Rome ordered everyone in his territory to register for taxes. They had to register wherever their father's family came from. So Joseph had to go to Bethlehem and Mary had to go with him even though it was time for her baby to be born. When they got there, they tried to find a place to stay, but there were no rooms left."

A figure holding an extra large mask of a man in an extraordinary ancient emperor's hat demands the attention of the crowd. The narrator says Roman emperor, but this mask is definitely old China, and the audience is delighted. Silk Fan, holding the mask in front of her face in proper operatic form, speaks her lines in a mock male voice.

Then the light moves to the couple on stage.

The next scene seems to be in slow motion. Joseph takes Mary on a long, slow, courtyard-crossing trail to Bethlehem while the lone dancer's moves depict painful travail of the overburdened Mary. On the half-dark stage, long, purple paper streamers blow and whirl from the arms of the dancer. The old people smile and chatter.

"I remember these dances. This is really old China."

"She is so graceful. Where did they find an opera dancer?"

"How did they know the proper makeup for her to wear?"

Four children are in the center of the courtyard stage wearing masculine masks and holding bamboo doorframes. They sing a song about no more rooms left to rent. One older auntie in the audience stands up from her seat on the ground and yells, "Oh, give them a room. Can't you see that she is in pain? Her baby is coming."

Her companions shush her, and she covers her face, ashamed that she has gotten carried away with the little opera.

"So they found a stable where animals were kept and that is where Jesus was born. Mary wrapped him up in long cloths and laid him in a manger, a box where animals were fed."

The audience gazes sympathetically at Mary sitting on the wheat straw in the barn.

"Some shepherds were spending the night in the nearby field with their sheep. Suddenly the sky lit up and an angel appeared among them. They were badly frightened, but the angel reassured them. 'Don't be afraid!' he said. 'I bring you the most joyful news ever announced, and it is for every man, every woman, every boy, and every girl everywhere! The Savior—yes, the Messiah, the Lord—has been born tonight in Bethlehem."

The two small children with whom Walks with Grace and Truth stayed on the hilltop when she ran away are playing their natural roles as shepherds. Wearing their everyday clothes, they hug their live lambs to their bodies for comfort. They walk in slowly, awed by the sight of the angel who was not so impressively dressed at this afternoon's rehearsal. Pink Sunset is startled and jumps when the drums and bells announce the army of angels.

"You will recognize this baby because he will be wrapped in swaddling clothes and lying in a manger. Suddenly, the whole sky was full of angels praising God and singing, Glory to God in the highest and on earth peace and goodwill to people everywhere."

Four little girls dressed in long, white dresses with ribbons tied around their shining heads dance onto the center stage and look expectantly toward their neighbor, math and dance teacher. They are holding hands for the benefit of the blind child, but the audience sees only four lovely dancers in costume. With long ribbons trailing, each girl follows the chief angel of the Lord and dances with expressions of joy and grace. The stringed instrument plays lightly, and the bells tremble sweetly.

Applause breaks out as the angels step in elaborate displays of praise and the young shepherds shrink back in fear. The chief angel, Walks with Grace and Truth, the angel Gabriel, Teacher Silk Fan, and even the narrator all join in with the small angels to add strength to this song of Glory to God in the highest heaven and peace on earth to people everywhere. The dancing angels bow in a reverent benediction of peace, and a large, beautifully written scroll is presented. "Peace on Earth."

The scroll of ancient Middle Kingdom style is unrolled by someone sitting on the roof. It is so dramatic and beautiful that all eyes look upward to read the new wonder. Some in the audience read it aloud and the action on stage freezes until the audience is satisfied. It is hung by one slight stage assistant on a roof usually reserved for Silk Fan's laundry pole.

The audience cheers loudly. This is a beautiful performance, and by their own children!

The angels leave, and the two shepherd children are left alone with their lambs under the lights. They look truly frightened and forget to project their lines. Silk Fan shushes the crowd and prompts the children to speak loudly as they repeat their first lines. Looking ashamed, the adults listen as the children begin again.

The small girl shepherd, Pink Sunset, asks, "Who were those people?" Her cousin answers. "I don't think that they are people!"

"What were they?" she asks in little girl awe.

"I … I think that they must be spirits, cousin."

"Oh, what kind of spirits? They praised God and told us great news, and they were so beautiful!"

"They were spirits who bring good news, like the letter carriers."

"Why did they sing pretty songs praising God?"

"I … I think that they are God's own special spirits to do what he says."

The girl sits for a moment with her eyes still wide with wonder and then says, "Can we go to see the new baby? I'll be so quiet. Can we?" Pink Sunset speaks her lines well.

"Yes. We will find him. Come on, hurry."

The two shepherds get up and walk around the crowded courtyard and come to where Mary and Joseph are watching the baby Jesus in the manger. The flute and strings play a sweet lullaby as the narrator speaks again, while colors exploded in waving flags behind the scene. No one seems to care that the very young musicians play the same five notes over and over. It is delightful music to all who hear it.

"Then they saw that the baby was the savior. So they went into town and told anyone who would listen what had happened especially about the baby born in a manger. Those who listened to the shepherds were amazed. Mary treasured everything in her heart and thought about it often. The shepherds went back to tending their sheep and praised God that the angels told them about the baby."

The proud narrator closes his script and smiles broadly at the audience as the lights remain on the two shepherds. He did not make any mistakes and spoke his many lines clearly. The crippled boy is very happy, and the neighbors are amazed.

The exuberant audience breaks into loud applause and cheers. The crowded audience cheers the children and the two stolen brides/housewives/mothers/teachers. With happy congratulations to each other, the parents find their own children and try to return to the familiar road. Walks with Grace and Truth is still dressed in her dance costume, drawing much attention, when she realizes that the shy child, one of the little girl angels, is in a state of panic with the crowd pushing and talking at once. With gentle hands, she bends down and picks up the fearful child.

"I am so proud of you. You did so very well tonight. You danced beautifully. I heard you singing too. Your song was a beautiful gift that you gave the baby Jesus."

She holds the child in her arms, not mentioning the terror in her eyes.

An older grandmother, who knows proper tradition, looks for someone to pay for the wonderful night's performance. Seeing Silk Fan, she presses some coins into her hand, smiling her thanks for the evening.

Will this farming village ever be the same again? Will the people ever be able to see the children and their teachers without remembering this wonderful night? Will the scrolls be left up long enough for people to copy its lines? The audience erupts in chatter.

"My sister did not come. She is going to be so upset that she missed this opera."

"I liked the last scroll. It is so different from the New Year's wishes of wealth, health, and good luck. It just said, 'Peace on Earth.'"

"That is what the angel said."

The audience has so many questions and comments as they leave.

"More of the village children should have been at this opera."

"Where would they have stood?"

"Flying Horse, your son did a wonderful job as narrator. I know you are proud of him."

"Yes, Honorable Integrity is a fine spokesman."

"Did you notice that the angel told them that they would

find the baby Jesus wrapped up in long cloths, just as we wrap our babies?"

"Yes, I did."

"Mother, may I keep my angel dress?"

"Where do you think that crippled boy learned to read so well?"

"Is this baby Jesus the same Jesus who is spoken of on the radio messages?"

"It must be the same. I have never heard another story so astonishing."

"I am going to tell everyone I know about this opera."

Never have such young children presented such a grand message.

Steadfast stands holding his son, Strong Bamboo. Waiting until the crowds have dispersed, he smiles broadly at his costumed wife and says, "You are the most beautiful thing I have ever seen. Stay in your gown. I want the whole village to see my wife the beautiful dancer." She laughs at him and says, "You silly man. Come on, let's all go home."

THE SKY IS EVER CHANGING

D ouble Joy, the old mistress of the house that is known as the House of Hatred, places a carrot in front of the porcelain kitchen god of wealth. In this small house, there is a place reserved for these miniature figures of gods.

Beautiful Moon is seated on the family kang, where she spends her nights and days. Her young friend Humble often comes by, but today is a school day, and she will not see her until later in the afternoon.

Carefully and slowly, she inches her weight to the wall so that she may sit up to perform her kitchen tasks. When she hears her mother-in-law's steps approaching, she carefully folds her unfinished sewing project and places it aside.

"You were no help in planting or picking these spring peas, so you must snap them! Save some small tender shells for eating."

"I need a pan for the peas."

"Here, place them in this basket."

Beautiful Moon smiles at the fresh produce and thinks to herself, *What a lovely shade of green these peas are. The fields must be pretty this spring.*

She never reacts to the absurd statement that she has not participated in the planting and picking of the fresh green peas. Eating two small peas while Double Joy's back is turned, she realizes that she needs to go to the latrine, but it is not time yet. It seems as though she needs to go so often now. For a modest young woman, it is humiliating to ask for assistance in this necessary body exercise. The old mistress is never sympathetic and complains at the task, so she is seldom asked.

She picks up the shiny green shells that hold their treasure of five peas nesting in a row and imagines that they look like pearls. With a small smile, she realizes that this moment qualifies as a good thing in Silk Fan's project of fighting depression. She continues with her task. As the mound of green peas grows, she shifts her weight from one side to the other, being careful not to move her crippled feet.

She cannot wait for the schoolgirls to come to her aid. She must relieve herself. It has been eight hours since she went this morning. If either her husband or the old mistress had paid attention to the lovely Beautiful Moon, they would have noticed that the shape of her body had changed over the winter months. Her dainty waist has grown, and her pretty face has become fuller. Double Joy is not interested in this failure of a daughter-in-law.

Humble comes by after school and helps Beautiful Moon. It has been so long that she whimpers when she relieves herself. If she had been pregnant before or if she had a caring mother to help educate her, she would have realized that this was a very serious medical situation. There is a nurse available for the village, but the mistress's cousin who held the runaway bride down while she was being mutilated fears the governmental reaction. There are legal consequences of being reprimanded or fined for cutting Beautiful Moon's legs, so the nurse is never called to this house for any reason.

Beautiful Moon knows that she is expecting and sews tiny garments for her baby, but she knows nothing of caring for her body during pregnancy.

Daily performing the task assigned to her, she speaks respectfully to her mother-in-law and does not complain. Today she is whipping the eggs into froth and then sifting the brown wheat flour together, creating smooth egg noodles for the family's meal. As she stirs the batter, she realizes that there is something wrong with her besides her crippled legs. She does not feel well. She drops her small hands into her lap and closes her eyes.

In the last few months, she has grown quieter and often wears a sweet smile on her pretty face. She no longer speaks the plaintive cry that characterized her first years here. She no longer tells her captors or her friends, "I want to go home." Do they know that no man will want her with such crippled legs?

Although obviously ill, Beautiful Moon assumes a pleasant countenance and a sweet smile. Her friends find her a joy to visit and share the news of her first baby to be born in such a short time, even when her family seems oblivious to it.

Humble and her friend, First Star of Evening, always bring their latest poems for Beautiful Moon to read. First Star has written a new poem for a school assignment, but she wants Beautiful Moon to review it first. The schoolgirls come to help her but stay to visit because she always encourages their poetic efforts. The love of poetry and their shared work has created a strong bond between these schoolgirls and the crippled wife. She shows respect for the schoolgirls' work and even shares one of her own latest poems. It is unlike her earlier ones, so dark with despair. This new poem is an energetic one that shows promise and hope in God. It is titled "The Sky is Ever Changing."

It is later in the afternoon when the two schoolgirls come by to visit their friend. They are on their way home from school.

Double Joy is not at home when Humble and First Star of Evening come to the House of Hatred.

Humble calls out at the only door, "Hello. It is I, Humble, with First Star of Evening."

There is no answer.

"Hello?"

Slowly, she enters the familiar house and sees her friend Aunt Beautiful Moon in her usual place on the stone bed. She is lying down with her head on a pillow. Her eyes are closed, and even in the dim light Humble can see that her skin has taken on a strange new hue.

"Hello, Auntie Beautiful Moon."

The sick young woman opens her eyes but does not sit up.

"How are you feeling today?"

"Thank you for coming. I have not felt well for several days now. I do not feel like getting up but know that I must relieve myself."

Humble looks at her pregnant friend and then turns to First Star of Evening and instructs her, "Go quickly to get my mother. Tell her that I need her. If you cannot find her, get Aunt Walks with Grace and Truth. Run!"

Both women answer the alarm and quickly come to help Humble and First Star of Evening with their sick friend. Silk Fan has seen this puffy, yellow skin on pregnant women before.

"How much water have you drunk today, Beautiful Moon? Have you used the bucket today?"

By the next day, Beautiful Moon does not answer when her friends come to call.

Three of the kidnapped brides lay out the body of their friend on the bed where she has spent the last years of her life. None of them has ever buried anyone younger than a grandparent, and not one of them is prepared to bury a friend, so dear and so young.

In her cold hands, her friends find her small green notebook, in which she wrote her poems, expressing on paper thoughts she was not allowed to speak. Her most recent composition, from the last weeks of her life, speaks such beautiful lines that they feel joy, not grief. It reads simply and beautifully, revealing the new condition of her soul. After failing to find peace in this foreign land, her friends learn that in her final days she has found peace with her creator, God. Her final poem is not dark and disturbing but a joyful declaration that God sees and knows her.

Walks with Grace and Truth reads the last entry of the green notebook aloud to her friends.

THE SKY IS EVER CHANGING
The sky is ever changing and yet he sees me.
The mountains soar out of sight and he sees me.
The trees are tall and too many to count and God sees me.
He makes new clouds every day and knows where I am.
He blows swells and waves across the
water and still hears my voice.
He gives flight to countless birds and
still feels my every breath.
His eyes see everything and he still sees me.
His voice speaks creation and he speaks courage to me.
The great God who created all calls me by my name.

The three women whose friendship was forged out of common need have never had this kind of challenge to their sisterhood. Each bears this condition of imprisonment in her own way, yet the death of one of their own is such a new grief that they shed no tears. White Flowering Tree, the bride whose sanity is so fragile, speaks first.

"May I read it?"

So her friend hands the notebook to her. She reads the poem again, slowly and deliberately, like the radio reader has done for so many years when he reads the short verses they copy. When she finishes reading it, White Flowering Tree says quietly, "I like the line where she says, 'The great God who created all calls me by my name.'"

At this point, all three young women who have come to minister to their dying friend, Beautiful Moon, embrace each other. The tears seem to be for Beautiful Moon, but they realize that it is also joy over the fact that White Flowering Tree understands the poem and relates to its truth.

As they stand about the still body of the lovely woman who only wanted to be a baker and marry a man who loved her, Walks with Truth and Grace voices a prayer, "Dear Jesus, We thank you for the life of our friend, Beautiful Moon. We also thank you for her death. Thank you for taking away her pain and all of her earthly grief. We thank you that you have made such wonderful place for Beautiful Moon and her baby. We trust you with their care until we join them in your heavenly home. We now thank you for giving White Flowering Tree a glimpse of your Father's love. Amen."

Silk Fan takes a blue plastic bowl and begins to wash the battered body of their dead friend. White Flowering Tree brushes the long hair from the tear-stained face of her friend. She will need a proper brush to make it smooth.

Walks with Grace and Truth states, "We must find a proper burial dress for her. She does not have one fine enough. It must be as beautiful as she."

White Flowering Tree asks, "May I take the notebook home with me? I want to copy these lines. Here is another poem in her old style. Let me read it to you."

Silk Fan is afraid that the old style is the one of grief and bitterness. White Flowering Tree reads it aloud,

GOD
God knows me.
God loves me.
God hears me.
I can rest.

Walks with Grace and Truth responds, "It is Beautiful Moon's old style, but both of these latest poems sing the new song in her soul. We must read them both at her funeral."

"Yes, we must read her new, happy poems when we put her to rest."

The old mistress of the house, Double Joy, comes in as her friends are ready to leave. She does not know that her daughter-in-law, Beautiful Moon, is dead.

WINTERTIME

It is the fifth winter in this farming village so far from Silk Fan's home in the Chang Jiang Valley. As she slips into her old fashioned, knee-high shoes, she whispers a prayer for her own two children who are growing up without her, "Almighty God, I pray that you will care for my two children. Please be their shepherd today. Lead them in green pastures and besides quiet streams. Let your goodness and kindness follow those two little ones. Thank you, my Lord."

Blowing the dry grass and coals into a flame, she shivers.

By many standards, the house never becomes warm enough for comfort, but by wearing layers of clothing and frequently stoking the fire, people survive as they have for generations, going about their lives and awaiting spring.

Fourteen-year-old Humble snuggles on her soft, goose down-filled pillow next to her younger sister who still sleeps. She begins to repeat the words of this week's Senior Day presentation for school. She already knows all of the lines and will repeat them with confidence, but she says the words over again to herself. The graduating seniors have all prepared for this big day. Many keep their part a secret to be revealed only on this day. Those who will recite a literary piece choose the most difficult to be found.

Humble knows that her friend, Morning Sunshine, will present three of her finely woven belts, but she does not know what the other seniors will present. She is excited about her memory work. What she does not know is that when she stands to recite the verses from the Psalms, she smiles, and her eyes sparkle as she speaks with joy. It is the perfect classical piece of literature for the schoolgirl to present. This is her last year in the local school. There is no high school available in such a remote area. Since her formal education will be completed at the end of this term, she wants her presentation to be impressive.

"I am so glad that we knitted this fine new sweater this winter. I will remove my heavy coat and look my best when it is my turn to recite. I do believe that it will be the prettiest one in the entire school. Not even the teacher has one so fine." She stretches her arms out and smiles with pleasure at her new sweater made in soft blue wool.

"Perhaps you should not wear it today if it will cause you to think of yourself instead of the words of the Psalm."

"Oh, Mother, you are right. Please come pray with me now."

Silk Fan stops her breakfast preparation and sits by her bought daughter while she prays. "Dear God, thank you for making me. Thank you for this dear home and my precious mother and father. Give me courage, and let me honor you today in what I have learned. For the sake of Jesus, amen."

Silk Fan adds her mother's prayer, "Thank you, Jesus, for making this child so lovely in your sight. Give her a clear mind and a humble spirit today. Amen."

"Thank you, Mother."

"You are welcome, my daughter. The water was frozen in

the pan. It will take a while to melt. This cloth has enough water on it for you to wash your face."

Excitedly Humble bounces out of bed and dresses for school.

"When Hero awakens, we must thank him for the large supply of heating coal he brought into the house. He worked all day to bring us this fuel for such a cold time."

Silk Fan is not surprised that he is staying in his bed later this morning. There is little work that demands his attention this time of year. With yesterday's work done, he will stay in bed until the chill leaves the air and his dutiful wife prepares his morning meal. Hero is acting much older this year. He is no longer the muscular farmer who purchased and married Silk Fan five years ago. He now looks like the nearly seventy-year-old man that he is, with a wife who is not yet thirty.

"Mother, may I recite my memory work for you one more time? You look here at Psalm 139 and correct me if I say any of it wrong."

"Yes. Just try to be still. Hold your hands together and do not dance."

"Yes, Momma."

The orphaned girl clasps both hands behind her back, smiles, and begins to repeat the psalm for her second mother.

"I am supposed to look at the audience, so look at me, please."

Silk Fan nods and Humble begins.

"This is a song written by the poet King David many years ago. 'O Lord, you have examined my heart and know everything about me. You know when I sit or stand. When far away you know my every thought. You chart the path ahead of me, and tell me where to stop and rest. Every moment, you know where I am'" (Psalm 139:1–3).

She continues with the long song of David until she finishes the entire piece.

"Humble, my dear child, that was perfect. I know that God himself is as pleased as I am."

"Thank you, Mother. I want to eat now. I am hungry."

Silk Fan places dried fruit in front of her and stirs her red bean soup in the wok.

"This should keep you warm as you walk to school this frozen morning."

After eating, Humble checks her pocket for a pencil with a point on it, wraps warmly in a wool hat, and buttons her heavy winter coat all the way up to her chin.

"May the Lord bless you and keep you."

"And you also, my dear mother."

Silk Fan places a long-sleeved shirt and warm slacks for Happiness Found near the fire to warm them and sits down to wait on Hero and her youngest daughter to awaken. While she waits, she sews a straight line of fine stitches on a new pair of child's summer slacks. The red color gives no clue as to the identity of its future owner. A package of newly finished children's clothing is sent each year to Silk Fan's home in the south. No word has ever been received from her true husband. Some people say that the letters are intercepted before they leave this village. Are the packages of mother-made children's clothes also taken before they reach the needy children for whom they were sewn? Silk Fan does not know these answers. She only knows that children of a farmer will need new clothes each year, and she must do what she can to provide them. The faces of a laughing one-year-old boy and a happy three-year-old girl with straight black hair interrupt her thoughts too often to forget. How she longs to hear their childish voices and see their beloved faces.

Silk Fan folds her sewing when she hears Hero calling.

"Why is the house so warm? Silk Fan, come here. I feel quite strange."

When Humble returns home from her special Senior Day activity, she carries a leather-bound book. It is first prize for the important event. As she enters her home, she is surprised to see Hero's friend, Steady Traveler, giving Silk Fan instructions for boiling the bark of willow trees with the roots of mountain shrubs. Hero is groaning loudly, and Happiness Found is crying in chorus. With the entire household in chaos, there is no celebration of her winning first place on her school's Senior Day.

"Humble, would you please take Happiness Found for a walk to visit Strong Bamboo?"

"Come little sister; allow me to put your coat on you. We are going outside. Would you like to see your friend Strong Bamboo?"

It has been one week since Hero frightened his family and neighbors with his strange groans of pain and odd requests. Even in the subdued light of his home, it is evident that his face has a strange gray color as he moves about, trying to find a comfortable position. He holds his hand over his chest and often grimaces in pain.

Every day, he has something new to ask of Silk Fan. Every day, he sends for the herb collector. Every day, Silk Fan is instructed to boil barks, herbs, and dried leaves into a dark tea for him to drink, even as he frowns at the strong odor. Every day, he asks for the neighbor's son, Stands Strong, to come in and help him. He even had the boy help him bathe on the last time he summoned his daughter and her family. When his family comes into the house, he speaks quietly to Stands Strong, "It is time now for you to bring the old scribe here."

To his bought daughter, Humble, he indicates, "Go now to bring Walks with Grace and Truth here. Tell her to bring her best paper and ink. Ask her to bring a good piece of banner paper left from New Year's Day if she still has a piece."

To Silk Fan he says, "My old friend, Steady Traveler, should be here. Go to fetch him now. One of the old women of the road should also come. You may find anyone you wish."

The quickness with which he is obeyed indicates how serious they think the situation is. As Silk Fan takes her coat from its place and exits into the cold air, she thinks to herself, *How does he think all of those people can fit into our small house? What does he have in mind? He has never invited people in, and now that he is old and ill, he wants half the people of the village to come. I wonder if he wishes me to serve tea and sweets? I have not prepared such treats.*

As the two scribes and the other two old people are summoned, his family gathers nervously around him.

Heaven Sent tries to ease her father's pain. "Father, may I help you sit up?"

"Are you hungry?" Silk Fan asks.

"Are you warm enough?" Humble holds one of Silk Fan's warm woven blankets.

He shakes his head at their questions and attentions. Turning to his grandson, he commands, "Come here, my grandson. I need your help. Go outside and find my young neighbor, and tell him that I will not need him anymore today. Give him these coins. He has earned them. His name is Stands Strong."

Courageous takes the coins and immediately leaves to find the neighbor. He does not want to miss what he senses will be an important event, so he hurries on his errand.

Small Happiness Found climbs up onto the kang to sit close by Hero.

"Father, do you wish me to sing you a song? I can sing about the blue butterfly. Shall I count to ten for you? I will say the numbers slowly, just as you taught me."

The old man just smiles at the refreshing sound of his youngest daughter.

His married daughter, Heaven Sent, reaches for the busy little child. "Come, let us not bother him now."

But Hero holds her tightly. "No, do not move her. She is my own small butterfly. She is the joy of my old age. Let her be. It was a double lucky day when she was found."

Courageous returns and obeys immediately when his grandfather summons. "Come here and stand by me, my grandson. I want to look into your eyes."

The boy walks slowly to stand by his grandfather. It does not seem right to have him in bed in the middle of the morning with so many people coming into the house.

The door is held open too long as people shuffle in and greet each other in surprise. Hero shivers and asks for more heat. Six hands vie for the privilege of placing more coal on the fire.

"Heaven Sent, roll up that quilted cover and place it at my back. I want to see people's faces." He is accommodated and made more comfortable as he sits up against the heavy quilt before he speaks to the crowd assembled in his small house.

"Humble, move into the corner; we must make room for the two scribes to work at the table. Silk Fan, make them space to sit while they write."

Hero clears his throat and begins his speech. He is amazingly composed for such a quiet man. "I realize that this is a bitterly cold day, and you have paid me homage to come. I thank you for that. As you can see, my body is trying to leave this earth, so I have called you all here to witness my words. My oldest friend, Steady Traveler, is here to be my first witness. We have been friends since we were younger than Courageous. If you two fine professional scribes will write down my words, I will pay your usual fees and give you our gratitude. It might be that I shall remain here for many more months, and it might be that I shall die today where I lie."

The old neighbor woman and his daughter both murmur, "Oh no."

"Whichever the time, I am ready to go. I have lived longer than my father and mother. If I am still alive when spring arrives or when the next winter's wind howls, then this paper we write here today shall still be my word.

"Heaven Sent, may this crowd here today hear me say that I am proud of you. You are a loyal daughter. You have a fine son and a good husband." Turning to look at his son-in-law, Steady Worker, he says only, "You are a good man.

"Courageous, my grandson, you have an honorable name and honorable parents. Take care to keep your name so. We have no great wealth to give you, but you have never gone hungry, and you will never be sold as a slave. Listen to your father well and learn all that your teacher has to teach. I regret that I will not live to see you grow into a fine man. I want you to have my steel-harvesting knife with the leather sheath as a reminder that all work is honorable. When you work in the fields cutting wheat or grass for the fire, let it remind you of your old grandfather." None answer him.

"I want this all written properly. Do I need to stop speaking while you record this?"

The old scribe with tobacco-stained fingers nods as he paints clearly. Walks with Grace and Truth does not lift her head but continues to write neatly. She is using the long paper for New Year's Day wishes. If Hero continues so, it will require the entire length.

No one speaks as the words turn into graceful black characters on the two pages. Heaven Sent cries softly. The children look around the room. Happiness Found does not understand the event, but Humble remembers the death of both of her first parents and bites her lower lip at the news she hears today. Courageous is composed until he sees his mother crying. Then large tears, unfitting for an eleven-year-old boy, roll down his face and fall onto his shirt.

At a nod from the old scribe, Hero continues his speech.

"Humble, come here and stand before me." She crawls down from the kang and smiles shyly as Hero takes her hand. "You have been a good daughter. You have been worth every bit of money we paid your uncle for you. Your second mother, Silk Fan, knew that you would be a good daughter. Learn from her. Keep working on those roasted peppers. You will make a fine cook one day."

Humble beams at the words of praise but finds it hard to look at him directly. She loves him and does not want to cry in his presence. As she looks at her feet, she is pushed aside by her little sister. Happiness Found squirms onto Hero's lap and, taking his face in her two tiny hands, asks the innocent question: "Am I a good daughter too, Father?"

Hero pulls the child to his chest and buries his face in her shoulder, holding her closely. Slowly pulling away from her face, he says quietly, "Yes, my little Happiness. You are a very good daughter."

Looking around his crowded home, Hero seeks the face of the young woman who changed his life so much in the last five years. She is standing by the door.

"Silk Fan, come here."

The neighbor woman, his old friend, and family move aside to allow Silk Fan to move to the center stage. She looks into his eyes and says simply, "Yes, Hero?"

"You have been a faithful wife. No man could have asked for a better cook or a more even-tempered woman. You have put most of these people to shame with your constant farming, sewing, cooking, and teaching all these children. When I go to join my ancestors, this house will be yours. It is free of debts, thanks to you. All of my fields are yours. You have farmed them better than I. You are free to stay here the rest of your life, or sell them and go back to your family. No one will stop you."

A low murmur buzzes across the crowded space. It has been said.

The proud Silk Fan takes the stance of a proper Chinese wife. She says nothing as she continues to stand in front of him with her eyes politely downcast.

"Will all of you please write your names on my paper? You are my witnesses. Now I am tired. Silk Fan, thank our guests." Hero frowns at another pain in his chest and lies down on the mat of the bed where he has slept all of his life.

Steady Traveler would like to spend time now with his lifelong friend, but not with this crowd of people present. "My friend, I will come again soon." With an awkward touch to Hero's arm he nods and then marks both documents and makes his way to the door.

"The ink will be long in drying. It is a lengthy document."

"I do not write with much grace."

"Just write your name."

"Why are there two scribes?" the neighbor woman whispers.

"One is for the government official, and one is for Silk Fan."

"Oh, I understand."

"Hump! You know why there are two scribes. Even now in the middle of freezing time, there is to be no question about what he has said. The house and the fields belong to Silk Fan." Hero's son-in-law grumbles.

"He waits until his dying days to say all of that. I have never heard him speak so eloquently." The old neighbor woman pushes her way to the front to make her mark on both of these remarkable documents and hurries out. This valuable piece of gossip will not wait until market day.

"What a morning! He has set Silk Fan free! And she may sell the house and land and leave or stay here in her own house. I must tell someone."

Silk Fan calmly goes about the task of serving the family a hearty meal as her mind races. The watch now begins.

Just how long will he live? Will Heaven Sent stay to help with the daily tasks of caring for a sick and dying man? Will she make a scene about the possession of the house and fields? Will the neighbors give her trouble for Hero's plain-spoken bequeath? How will I manage with no one to do Hero's work? Do we have enough fuel to finish out the winter? I wish that he had spoken to me about his plans for today.

As all of these thoughts whirl in her mind, Silk Fan commands herself, *you cannot think about them now. You can think about them later.* But in spite of tasks to be done, people to feed, and a calm face to present, her hands shake as she hears a tiny black-haired girl ask, *"I'm not as dirty as the piggy, am I, Mother?"* *She will be eight years old now. And my little son, Strong Wind, will you even recognize me?*

My dear Pride of His Father, how I long for you. Have you received any of my letters? Will you allow me to come home again? Oh, how I wish to speak with you. Have you taken a new wife? It has been such a long time. Have you forgotten about me? Do you want me back? Is my shame too much for you to bear? I cannot forget you all.

A tear rolls down her face as she ladles the warm stew into bowls. She finally permits herself to cry.

The weeks of nursing a dying man are busy ones for Silk Fan. She finally allows little Happiness Found to visit a friend's home some time each day because Hero's painful groans upset their small daughter. The once-strong man is uncomfortable in the role of a sick patient. This is not how he wishes to spend his time. He and his friend, Steady Traveler, discuss the amounts and virtues of various herbs making an effort to be in control of his own life until the end.

Silk Fan sits quietly to the side, allowing these two lifelong friends time together. Her lips move in silent prayers as she sits knitting a new pair of warm woolen socks.

"Father God, thank you for Hero's life. Thank you for giving him a kind heart that has made him kind and loving to Humble and Happiness Found. Thank you for giving me the spirit of grace so that I could endure living here these five years. Thank you for making me an obedient wife. Thank you for Steady Traveler's friendship. Dear Lord, please ease Hero's pain. Amen."

DECISIONS

Hero's death brings an immediate change to his household. Happiness Found does not understand why his body was taken away. He was the only father she remembers, and she misses the attention that he lavished upon her. Humble understands about his death. She loved Hero. He seemed more like a grandfather than a father because he allowed her all the time she wished for study and friends.

Silk Fan must now do all of her household work as well as his. She has labored here for five years, honoring this man who paid kidnappers to steal her from her home in the south because the brutal torture and death of her friend, Beautiful Moon, convinced her that escape was not an option.

In the last weeks of winter, she is busier than usual. She spends long hours sewing many garments of various sizes. She will not make too many inquiries concerning the availability of more fabric. In this community of gossips, she dares not allow other women to see that she is accumulating too much new fabric. She cuts out a new pair of slacks for Humble and sits her down to stitch her own clothes. From Humble's outgrown school clothes, Silk Fan cuts and sews a smaller outfit for a younger girl.

From Hero's best shirt, she cuts a boy's new shirt. She is pleased to be able to recycle the clothing because she still has many garments to produce in a short time. When the electric current is not available, she labors as she has for years, straining her eyes to see by candlelight.

Why do my hands tremble and my knees turn to rubber? This is the time for which I have waited for so many years. Why do I doubt my plans now? Where is my courage? I will finally be united with my Pride of His Father, my true husband. Oh, my darling little ones! What will they think of me? Will they have a stepmother? I will not think on that possibility. I must concentrate on leaving.

Even now, a picture of two small children playing envelopes her mind.

How I wish that there were some way to avoid involving my friend Walks with Grace and Truth. I want her to have my fine woven wool blankets, but this must not betray our plans. If we are seen taking things to her home, people will be suspicious. I shall make a list and have it witnessed and recorded. Oh! I cannot do that! No one must see this until I am gone. Nevertheless, I shall write this down and leave it here in my house.

This is my official statement signed on the
fifth day of the third moon in the year of 2008.
Silk Fan, widow of Hero of His People.
My house now belongs to a woman named Persistence.

She continues listing every item in her home and the recipient of each.

Why should the smallest decision be the most difficult? Why do I worry about everything? Stop, Silk Fan. Think. You must give away all of your Holy Scriptures and hymns. You do not know what lies ahead.

My students understand that this is time for spring plowing, so they will not come for their classes. That is one detail about which I will not have to be concerned.

The bright voice of her daughter interrupts. "Mother, here is the morning water. Morning Sunshine was drawing her water also. She wants to come with us today. May she? Precious Pearl wants to come too. I told her no. She would just hinder our work."

"Are you sure that Morning Sunshine wants to go? Does she know that we will plow today?"

"Yes, Mother dear. She knows. The three of us can get much of the lower field plowed today if we all work. Shall I find a friend to watch Happiness Found for the day? She will be in our way and unhappy too."

"No, Humble. We will take her with us. She can play as we plow. It is not fair to ask others to watch little children when they have work of their own to do."

The overburdened mother has her own reasons for deciding who will be with her this week on the first days of spring plowing. They have never plowed without a man to push the heavy wooden plow. Perhaps the two girls can manage to jointly pull on the wooden shaft while Silk Fan manages to push with all of the strength of her slender shoulders. It will be an arduous day of physical labor but necessary for Silk Fan's plans. The village must know that she is plowing and planting her fields.

"I will go tell Morning Sunshine now. What will she need besides a water bottle and some lunch?"

"She will need some work gloves, a basket for collecting herbs, and a headband to keep the perspiration from her eyes."

"I will tell her, though she may not want to wear the headband. It does not look very clever, you know."

Silk Fan laughs at the teenager's concern for stylish headgear while doing this strenuous work. Placing the food and water bottles on one end and her work tools on the other, she balances her pole gracefully on her right shoulder and smiles at her youngest daughter, Happiness Found. They begin walking toward her lower field to prepare the soil for her spring crops.

It is rather early, but she wants to establish the fact that she is not only going to work her own field but is anxious to get about the task.

Two different men who do not have wives note with disappointment that Silk Fan is confident. Perhaps she will be less confident tonight when she is exhausted. She is aware of the eyes that follow her, but she ignores them and continues on her way. *I wonder how many days I will need to carry out this charade,* she thinks.

The day's task is more difficult than any of them imagined, but they dutifully continue with their work. The furrows are not straight, and some are not deep enough, but they continue with the spring plowing. When they arrive at the halfway point of the field, Silk Fan declares it too wet for plowing.

"Come, let us sit down here and rest. I think that we have worked enough for today."

"We have not finished, Mother."

"I know. We will rest now, daughter."

"I am so thirsty."

"I am so dirty! Look at my legs." The two older girls laugh at their legs covered in the soil they plowed.

Wiping the perspiration from her face, Silk Fan speaks to her assistants, "Here, drink some water. Morning Sunshine, you worked very hard. I thank you for coming to help us."

"You are my good friends. I gladly help you."

"You are the good friend, Morning Sunshine." Shy smiles are exchanged.

"Humble, you worked like a grown woman! I am proud of you both."

"Thank you, Mother. What shall we plant here, Mother? Is this the place for pretty spring peas?"

"I think that is a good spot for beans to grow in the high hills in the sunshine.

Silk Fan has other plans for her precious spring pea seeds, but she does not reveal them to Humble.

The next morning, the two men who would like to have Silk Fan as a wife are discouraged to see that this morning she is already in her field, carefully working her way across a newly plowed furrow with three girls as helpers, planting rows of seeds.

After planting only part of the upper field, Silk Fan announces that it is time to quit work. "We shall leave my carrying pole and trays here for tonight. No one will bother them here on our field." She looks sideways at the girls who are busy with their own thoughts and do not question the lack of logic in this decision.

"As we walk home, look for some new greens to pick for our dinner. They are so tender this early in spring."

As they walk slowly home carrying their supplies, she casually asks Humble if there is anyone she would like to visit.

"Yes, I would like to show my friends the new slacks we made and the nice shopping bag we made with the rope handles."

"Let's not show the bag just now, Humble. They might think that you are bragging. Why don't you just visit them?"

"You are right, Mother. You always think about the feelings of others."

But this afternoon, Silk Fan is not thinking about the other girls' feelings. She is allowing her daughter to spend time with her friends. The two teenage girls wash their dirty hands and legs at the central water pump and stroll to the home of another friend, Joyful Day, for a time of visiting.

How can I be more careful? I want to tell my friends good-bye. I dare not. The entire village must believe that I am staying here and planting my vegetables.

Silk Fan washes the wild greens they have harvested along the way from their field and prepares the evening meal for herself and her dearly loved daughters.

I dare to hope that my dear husband, Pride, is waiting for me at our farm. I am so tired. We must retire early and rest before we start such a long journey. Hmm. What can I sell along the way? Perhaps I can take a notebook, or a pen, or my best stirring spoon to sell in another village. Either would bring some cash for our trip.

Months earlier, while formulating plans for this exciting trip, Silk Fan made the decision that they would take Humble's wool blanket with them. It was Humble's first weaving project. She washed the wool and dyed it using wild roots. The weaving is tight and well done, if uneven in some rows, as expected from a girl's first work. They will need the blanket for warmth while sleeping outside on their journey, and she loves her oldest daughter too much to leave it. While the two girls are outside, Silk Fan folds and refolds the blanket, fitting it into the bottom of her largest harvest basket. It fits well and leaves space for the food, a cooking pot, pea seeds, and clothing for all six family members.

The young woman who visited one market day seemed quite serious about not returning to her own village so deserted by its younger generation. She said that this small house would be just the right size for her and her grandmother to share. Silk Fan was reassured when she mentioned her grandmother. A strange young woman would need a proper chaperone if she plans to live and work in a new place. The grandmother will cook the meals, wash their clothing, and grow a few vegetables, as well as keep her granddaughter safe and the family name clean.

The young visitor wore an elegant dress in bright green that was obviously not homemade. Her hair, dyed the color of oranges, declared that she was not to be considered as a possible wife for a local farmer. She lived in the city for five years and disclosed her plan to open a factory using fine lamb's oil for manufacturing her grandmother's popular hand cream. The sheep are plentiful here, and she wants to live away from the city. One field will serve her purposes well.

Silk Fan waits until this visitor named Persistence returns from her own village with her parents' blessing and savings before she makes firm plans for leaving and returning home to her farm home, where she desperately hopes that her other two children might remember her. She tries not to entertain the thought that Pride of His Father has given up on her return and found another wife.

"He is too poor," she speaks aloud. "He will not be able to afford a new wife, nor find one willing to take on the rearing of our two small children."

As if convinced by the sound of her own voice, Silk Fan opens the door to her root cellar and begins to move food up to her cooking area. *God has truly provided for our needs. I will warm thousand-year-old cabbage with greens, dried apples, and rolls for dinner.*

Next, she prepares several foods that will travel well. While she boils eggs, she stuffs sausage into rolls, fries corn cakes with peppers and herbs, and packs dried fruit.

My girls will be surprised to discover that the bread has unusual additions cooked in them. It is all good food, and we will need the nourishment for strength on our journey. These treats can be eaten as we walk.

Opening her door, she calls her children in to eat their last dinner in this house.

"Hello, my dears."

"Mother, Red Rose let me play with her rope."

"That is good. Red Rose is a nice girl. Please wash your hands."

"Ooh, the house smells so fine."

Silk Fan sets the corn cakes to cool and replaces them in the hot pan with plump bundles of glistening wheat rolls stuffed with dried green peppers and every sweet herb she can find.

"Is this a special celebration meal, Mother?"

"It is a celebration of God's goodness to us. Let us thank him. Dear gracious God, we thank you for loving us, caring for us, and giving us this food. Amen."

The three enjoy their meal while Silk Fan keeps one eye on her steaming rolls as she eats. None must be allowed to burn.

The tasks are ones she can handle, yet she almost chokes on her food. It is difficult to appear calm when her entire body strains with fear and excitement.

She consciously slows her eating and smiles at her daughters. How good, indeed, has God been to them all. Pretty Humble was saved from a ruined childhood of being sold into prostitution. Young Happiness Found was saved from death, and Silk Fan has been blessed with the gift of two precious daughters. Through hard work, there is adequate food. All three thrive in the love of their family. This summary of her five years of captivity in this northern village calms her.

There is still much to do.

"Let's get a nice bath and go to bed early. You must be tired from your hard day of working in the field."

"I am so tired, Mother." Humble worked hard and is weary.

"I will take care of cleaning up the kitchen, my dear. Why don't you go to draw a bucket of water for bathing?"

Silk Fan has already packed the new clothing that she sewed for both of her families. The new garments are in the bottom of her large harvest basket that she plans to carry on her back.

We cannot risk being brought back by angry villagers. We must be prepared to leave. We cannot afford to find more things that will weigh us down and tire us out.

Resisting the temptation to collect more items to take, she looks around and sighs. She is getting cold feet.

"There you are. I thought that you might have decided not to draw any water."

"Mother, Humble let me pump some water all by myself."

"You are already wet from the pump. I am glad you have started on your bath."

Their bathwater is cold and baths are quick for the three who have worked in the field today, trenching the earth with a wooden plow. It is still light outside when sleep claims their weary bodies.

It is four o'clock in the morning when Silk Fan awakens.

Both of her daughters are sleeping soundly. Silence is the peaceful music of the farming village as dark holds the sky. Excitement and dread fight for control of her mind. This is the day! The large harvest bag is packed, and food for the trip is prepared. The neighbors have all witnessed her preparation of her fields.

Silk Fan, why are you hesitating? Get up. This is your opportunity to return to your beloved Pride of His Father. Why are you hiding in this warm bed? Do you want to grow old in this cold place with colder people who beat and steal girls and women and murder their daughters? Just a few more moments of rest. You cowardly woman! Get up!

Obeying her own orders, Silk Fan moves her legs from the warm covers and slips on her house shoes. Looking out her front window, she notes the lack of activity in the still sleeping village. She decides not to stir the fire embers but reaches for her clothing, so carefully set out a few hours earlier. She dresses in two layers of underwear and two sets of ordinary clothes. After putting her only shoes on over her warm socks, she sits down on the kang and watches her children sleep.

We really should wait until I see smoke from someone's fire, or at least hear a rooster crow. The rolls will make a nice breakfast that we can eat while walking this morning. This is silly. Why does my stomach hold rocks and my skin shiver like a willow tree in a windstorm?

Silk Fan sits up until the sun rises and the neighbors can be heard outside her door. She stares at nothing as she loses her courage, stands up to remove one set of clothes, and returns to her bed. *We will leave tomorrow.*

"Dear Jesus, thank you for the time of rest. You know how frightened I am. Please guide us this day. Amen."

On this day when Silk Fan planned to leave, she seems to live as one in a fog. After telling her daughters that this will be a day of rest, she sits for hours staring into space. She is already packed and ready for her longed-for trip, so she avoids any serious work. She feeds her chickens and reads a few lines to the girls from her collection of Bible verses, and then she simply sits on her kang, searching for courage. In truth, they all need this day of rest, but that is not the reason for this delay. Silk Fan, the brave survivor, allows her doubts and fears to overcome her resolve. The girls entertain themselves as she quietly fights her doubts.

Taking out a pen and her best paper, she writes a letter to her husband.

Dear Pride of His Father,

The old man who purchased me has died. According to his will, I am now free to leave. Since I know about the local tradition of capturing girls and women, this will be very difficult to do. These men who steal and sell us would rather kill us than allow us to leave this area.

I am determined that they shall no longer control my life. I will leave this spring after people are convinced that I am preparing my fields in readiness for planting. I am frightened because I do not know the way, and travel is so dangerous, but I am leaving this place. I will not post this letter until I am three days' gone.

It is quite cold here and still too early for the swans to return to their nesting grounds.

Please give Strong Wind and Shimmering Sunrise hugs from me. I pray for you all each day.

I am coming home.

Your desperate wife,
Silk Fan

She reads her own letter again and smiles at her last statement. Taking courage from her statement that she is coming home, she folds it neatly, addresses an envelope, and places it inside a pocket she sewed into her coat. She makes a hot meal for the last time in this house she never quite felt was hers and calls her two children. After a quiet meal, she retires early and once again plans to leave this place where she has lived for the past five years.

"It is time to arise, my darling daughters. We had many fine hours of sleep. It is time to begin our day. We are going to play a game. First, dress in the clothes I have laid out for you. Then put your work clothes on top of them."

Lord, you know how frightened I am. Help me to stay calm and rely upon your strength while on this trip. Lord, you know the way. I do not. Lord, please watch over these precious girls whom you have given to me and keep us all from harm. And Lord Jesus, please care for my dear family at home. Thank you, Jesus.

Silk Fan begins each morning with this prayer as she walks steadily to put as much distance between her traveling family and the village.

It is almost light when the mother and her two daughters leave their home and move toward their newly plowed field. If anyone notices anything odd about the early hour, they must surely rationalize that after two strenuous days of work, Silk Fan took yesterday off for resting, and now she is returning to her field. Today, they stop at her lower prepared field and collect her carrying pole with the two trays. After distributing some of the load from her huge harvest basket, the three make their way around the curve in the lower part of her field, and they continue walking down the dirt road that leads south. They do not seem to be in any hurry but continue walking. Humble balances the loaded pole as gracefully as any adult, and Silk Fan wears her utilitarian harvest basket on her back. Happiness Found bounces along with her hooded jacket on, buttoned against the cool spring air. It is early for most of the neighbors, and no one questions their destination. Silk Fan tries to smile. It is difficult to do while holding her breath. By midmorning, they have covered a few miles and left the boundary of the village behind. Ahead lays unfamiliar land. With a forced smile she says, "This is going to be a great adventure today, my daughters."

Aware that they need to cover as many miles as possible on

their first day of travel, Silk Fan walks at a steady pace. She does not stop long for any reason. She gives one of her special rolls to each girl, and they eat while walking along the same path that Silk Fan traveled when she was brought into the village five years ago. When she explains the purpose of their adventure to Humble, the surprised teenage girl laughs.

"We are really going south to your own farm? We really are going?"

Silk Fan smiles reassuringly at her and continues walking as fast as little Happiness Found will go. Humble is quiet for a time as she digests this amazing information. The first three days of walking, they travel all day long and into evening.

She does not bother Humble with the very real fear she has of being caught and returned to the village. She knows that even after five years, her escape is a threat to their dirty secrets. With a strong resolve, Silk Fan refuses to continually turn her head to check behind them for an army of approaching bicycles. When the village gang comes for them, it will be on bicycles.

Lord Jesus, it is getting dark now. Please help us find a field that is not newly plowed for our bed. And Lord, please do not let it rain tonight.

A sheep shed is their hotel for the third night. In the shearing room they are dry and warmer than they would be in the open air. When Happiness Found is sleeping soundly, Silk Fan decides that it is time to speak with Humble.

"Humble, my dear one, I know that you are disappointed that I did not tell of my plans to leave the village. If anyone knew about my plans, I was afraid that we would not be allowed to leave."

"Is that why you suggested that I visit with my friends? Did you know that it would be a farewell?"

"Yes, daughter."

"Thank you. I trust your judgment, Mother. I was just so surprised the morning we left to learn that I had paper sewn into the lining of my coat. I can laugh now, but I was so surprised."

"Shh. You must not mention it and remember not to finger it."

"Will you please explain to me about the money? I will not mention it to anyone."

"Yes. But be quiet. We do not want little Happiness to know about it. It would be a heavy secret for such a young one. If she awakens, please speak of something else."

"I will."

"Persistence, the young woman whom we met a few weeks ago—"

"Do you mean the lady with hair the color of oranges and a dress for an empress?"

"That is the one about whom we speak. She paid us the cost of our house. This is the money we have sewn into our clothing. You must not think of it, speak of it, or even look in that direction. You know that there are thieves who would gladly do us harm and steal our money."

"Oh, Mother, you are so brave and wise. This frightens me more than leaving home in the morning mist with only the moon for light."

"I am sorry that you are frightened, but you need to know of our secret. If something happens to me, you must know my plans. This is all of the money we will receive for our house and land."

"Is it a great amount of money?"

"A great amount? Probably not by city standards, but for us it is a good amount that will solve some problems. We might have to purchase another house in which to live or build another room onto our small farm house. Or perhaps we will find a secondary school where you may attend. This will cost money."

"Oh, that is too much to ponder. I shall never sleep tonight. Do you really think that I might get to attend high school?"

"We do not know what our future is hiding from us."

"Mother, do you think that we are safe here in the sheep shed?"

"We will be safe if we are quiet. Shh. Go to sleep."

As the family begins their fourth day of walking, they notice that other families are traveling the same direction. More people with baggage and loads of hand crafts share the road each day. They are going to a city to sell the winter's crafts.

Today, she will undertake a new safety measure. The new precaution is for Humble's safety, but she tells her daughters otherwise. She knows that no one will steal a four-year-old girl, but they will readily steal an attractive teenage girl like Humble.

"We are going to do something different today, my girls. There are so many people walking and riding on the road now, so we are going to just use this trick so we can stay together. First, I will attach my strong carrying band onto your belt, Happiness Found. Then I will tie the other end to your big sister's coat. That way, no one will have to hold your hand, your arm will not tire out, and we will always know where you are. We do not want you to get lost in the crowds."

"May I still hold on to your coat if I want to?"

"Yes. You may certainly hold on to either of us."

"What if I want to stop and pick up pebbles, or a flower, or perhaps a little frog?"

Humble smiles at her sister's concerns and never questions the wisdom of her mother's plan. "I will stop when you tell me, Happiness Found. This will be fun."

"All right, sister."

"I wonder what new things we shall see today, my daughters. This is such an exciting adventure. We have never been here before. What do we want to see today?"

"I liked seeing the wagons and carts yesterday. I wish we had a cart." Happiness Found is serious.

"I like seeing all of the different styles of clothing people wear. Did you see the girl wearing the red dress yesterday? She was lovely."

"Oh no. I stepped in a mud puddle. Now my shoes are dirty," Happiness Found complains.

"We are sorry, sister. Do not worry. We will all be muddy by the end of this day. Mother, may I speak to people now? We are a long way from home."

"Our speech gives us away, my dear. Let us wait a few more days. We do not want to draw attention to ourselves. However, we will have to ask some questions about our location."

"How I wish I had known what your plans were; then I could have asked my teacher for help in drawing a map for our use."

"Then everyone in the village would have known that we were planning to leave."

"That is true. I would have given your secret away."

"Just try to listen for any hints as to what town or village is near. It would be awful if we walk in the wrong direction."

"I will try to listen, Mother."

The young mother and her two daughters continue on their journey walking down hilly paths, crossing streams, passing through timeless villages and by endless fields. They are joined by other people who stoically carry their loads and walk beside them.

On the third week of traveling, the group moves to one side of the muddy road to allow a few young people wearing backpacks to pass by going the opposite direction. Silk Fan thinks they are university students returning home from the winter session. She stops one young woman and asks, "Please tell me where you have been."

The weary-eyed student answers with the name of a place Silk Fan does not recognize, and she droops when it is not a name she knows as one of her destinations.

"Please wait one moment. Are you hungry? I have some food."

As Silk Fan lifts her weighty harvest basket from her back and draws out some hardboiled eggs for the students, the young woman's face lights up and then changes to disappointment. "I cannot pay you, Auntie. I have no money."

"Do not concern yourself with pay. Eat these eggs. They will nourish you. You have something I need very much."

"We have very little, just gifts for our families."

"What I need is information. Please tell me how far it is to a train station."

"It is only a day's walking journey."

"Does this train go to the central city where many shoes are manufactured?"

"Yes. It travels south."

"Can you please tell me how many days' journey I must travel on the train before I reach the city of shoes?"

"Auntie, it is only three days' journey. Is that all you need to know?"

"Yes, thank you."

"Thank you for the eggs, Auntie."

A smiling Silk Fan hoists her basket again and rejoins the crowd walking in the direction of the train tracks.

"Children, I am not sure of the names of the next towns we will pass, but I now know that this is the direction we want to go."

As they begin their way again, the young university student runs back in order to hand Silk Fan a small packet wrapped in delicate, clear plastic.

"You will need these, Auntie."

With a smile, she runs to catch up with her fellow students who are going home for the season to eat at their families' tables.

"Mother, why did you give those people our food?"

"What did you notice about them, Humble?"

"They are not too much older than I."

"Yes, they are, and they all are too thin. They have not eaten enough this winter."

"Why not, Mother?"

"Because people are anxious to send their children to the city university, but they fail to provide enough money for food."

"Why?"

"Their parents think that in such large cities there will be many jobs available for their children to earn money for food.

Often, it simply is not so. There are too many people looking for jobs."

"I am glad that you gave them our eggs, Mother. What did the girl give you?"

"I do not know. It is just some small gift of thanks."

She tucks the small plastic package into a pocket.

"We were concerned about our dialect leading to our capture, and now we have spoken to just the right people. God has provided us with direction and assurance."

As the trio stops for a drink of water, a new group of people walk past, traveling north. In spite of her own warning to Humble, Silk Fan stares along with both of her daughters. All of the people, men and women, are all wearing strange little white masks on their faces.

"Why are they dressed like that, Mother?"

"I have no idea."

"I am frightened of them." Happiness Found grasps her mother's hand.

"I do not understand their faces, child, but they do not seem to mean any harm."

What are we going to see next?

Fingering the package in her pocket, Silk Fan removes it and gazes uncomprehendingly at carefully packaged white masks wrapped in plastic.

Automobiles occasionally pass on the road, and the travelers move aside but give the car and driver their full attention. These people are not farmers bringing their produce to market, nor do they seem to be government officials. Who are these wealthy people?

Humble asks innocently, "May we sing some songs now that we are far from home? Surely no one will come this far to return us."

"They came this far to capture me and the other prisoner brides."

"My dear Mother! You spoke of this part of your life so seldom that it is difficult for me to believe it. You made our lives so happy."

"You, my dear daughter, made these last few years bearable for me." Silk Fan smiles at her. "Humble, I have neglected to speak to you on this subject because I wanted you to have a carefree childhood."

"What subject is that?"

"The subject I want to discuss is your safety, my dear. You are a lovely girl now. Many men will be interested in you."

"I am only a schoolgirl, and boys at school have already flirted with me, Mother. If they are ill mannered, I just ignore them."

"I am going to explain something else, Humble. Did you notice how many more boys there were in your classes than girls? One result of this is that there will not be enough young women for wives when it is time for them to marry. You are young, strong, and so smart. Many young and old men will want you for a wife. They all want pretty wives who know how to work hard on the farm."

"Why is this problem of safety? Isn't it good that we will have many choices of a groom?"

"Yes, it could be very good, but you must be aware of evil people, a widower, men, or a woman seeking a wife for the son of the family."

"But Mother, I am too young to marry!"

"Yes, you are, my dear. These people have been paid money to capture a wife for the bride market. They will not ask how old you are, nor if you wish to marry, or, like me, if you are married."

"Oh, my dear Mother! I am so sorry. I have not been sympathetic with you. I have thought of you as Hero's wife."

"I have stayed alive to return to my true husband and my other two children, but some wives are not so fortunate. Those who could not reconcile themselves either run away and are beaten or they lose their minds. I am now trying to prepare you for your own survival."

"Yes, Mother."

"When I was captured, I was just coming to the aid of a woman who was acting as if she was in great pain. Men came and drugged me and tied me up."

"Why would a woman take part in such an evil scheme?" Humble frowns.

"Some people will do anything for money. Remember also that the mothers of the future grooms manage the family funds and have paid for the capture of their future daughters-in-law."

"Oh what a horror! How can the new bride love and respect her new husband and his mother if she knows this ugly scheme?"

"They seem only concerned with their own needs. Remember that the young wife is expected to do much heavy farm work also. She is a necessary part of the family economy."

"I have much to think about. Now I will be suspicious of everyone I meet."

"This is why I have not warned you before. You were relatively safe in our old village where we knew everyone, but now you must be aware of the dangers."

"Mother, would I be safer if I tried not to smile, looked unattractive, and always dressed in poor clothes?"

"Those tricks would probably not save you, my dear child. We must try to be cautious and wise, but we will not cringe in fear. You must try to live your life in confidence and avoid constant worry about life's dangers."

TREACHEROUS JOURNEY

After walking many tiring days through unfamiliar places in the company of strangers, Silk Fan begins to feel that the train station toward which they have faithfully trudged is an unreachable goal. The fear of being recaptured drives her for the first three weeks. She does not dare allow herself to be discouraged now because she is pushed on by the hope of seeing her true husband and her own two children. She remembers that on the trip north five years ago, she had the benefit of trucks, car, and a train. Now, their physical strength is challenged.

Her shoes and those of her children are almost rags. Cold mud seeps through the holes in their shoes, causing their feet to ache. One of the creature comforts for which Silk Fan yearns is a bath. She has a change of clothing, but she has not yet found a place where she feels safe enough to stop and bathe. She keeps promising herself that they will stop and rest for a few days, but the fear of the kidnapping gang and angry villagers chasing them forces her to keep a constant pace.

Humble proves her maturity and good nature by bribing her little sister with a piggyback ride each afternoon. She carries Happiness Found on her back while the rope shopping bag she carries bounces on her hip. They carry their loads while moving on the unpaved road, always leading southward. Silk Fan wears a knitted brow and carries her extra load of the two loaded trays balanced on her pole while her basket weighs her down every mile. She tells herself, *When we find the train, we will rest our feet and backs.*

This strong young woman who thought she had put fears to rest now finds new monsters creeping around the shadows of her composure. The countryside looks startlingly unhealthy, and the people here can be considered hostile. People are now grumbling and shouting loudly. She is not only fearful for their safety, but worst of all, she is totally out of food. She has not yet told her girls that she has no food left in her harvest basket. Fellow travelers are no longer moving ahead. A noisy confrontation blocks her path.

The travelers share their news. "They say that we may not go through here."

"They cannot stop us. The road goes through this place."

"We have always gone this way to the railway station."

The villagers shout, "You have germs! You must go around our village."

The travelers ask, "What is he talking about, germs?"

A traveling man yells, "Get out of my way. I must catch my train."

A woman is alarmed. "Stop pushing!"

"He is hitting that man!" Humble stops and cries out.

A traveler yells, "Get out of my way. I'll take care of the bully."

A woman traveler screams, "More people are running toward us. They have hay rakes and poles, and they seem so angry!"

Silk Fan asks in alarm, "What is wrong here?"

The villagers yell at the crowd, "Go back. We do not want you here. You bring sickness."

"Mother, where are you?" Humble cries out.

The villagers attack with hay racks. "Get out of here, you dirty drifters."

"Happiness Found, where is Humble?"

"Why are these people fighting us?" Little Happiness Found is frightened.

"Oooh, Mommy, where are you?"

Silk Fan shouts, "Come back here, children!"

The travelers beg, "Stop beating us. We have done no wrong."

"Be gone! You all bring bad luck." The villagers are unrelenting.

Confusion and violence reigns as the throng of travelers meet with villagers. The travelers loaded down with market-bound goods find themselves attacked by the local villagers armed with farming tools. There are no officials, only very angry citizens determined to prevent people from walking on the same worn roads they have used for years.

Family farms held for generations by the same families spread out with fields of brightening colors fanning toward the south. Fruit trees just budding with delicate shades of green rise to the north. The travelers look nonthreatening. They are not even armed. What could the problem be? Travelers have tradi-tionally been welcomed when they purchase food and drinks at this stop on their journey.

Men running to join the conflict knock her small daughter down, and now the child lies face down in the filth of the road, crying pitifully. She reaches out to pull Happiness Found from the path of struggling adults.

"Mother, why did those mean men knock me down? Now I am all dirty."

"I do not know, dear. Are you hurt?"

She holds her crying child while frantically searching the

crowd for Humble. A sad sight greets her eyes. There in the road is her dependable daughter, crawling in the dirt on her hands and knees while tears stream down her face. She strains to reach Humble but does not wish to release the sobbing Happiness Found.

"Humble, we are over here. Come here, dear."

"Ohhhh."

"Humble. We are on this side of the road. Come here."

The weeping girl lifts her head to see her mother and sister, but she continues to crawl the mud crying.

"Please stop crying, Happiness. Humble needs our help." The small child stops her sobbing at the sight of her sister's distress.

"Happiness, will you please stay right here while I go to help your sister? It will only be a minute."

The four-year-old nods her agreement because of the pathetic sight of her sister, so dirty and so unhappy. She temporarily forgets her own ills as she watches her mother cross the road.

"Oh, Humble, please get up. Are you injured? Here, let me help you."

The teenager is truly distressed. She sobs. "Mother, they took my carrying pole, and I cannot find my travel trays. My book is in one tray. These horrible people just grabbed my pole and threw my trays aside."

"Get up, dear. We will look for your things."

"Mother, it held my book, the prize book I won." Tears continue to roll, and the girl continues to cry while searching for her prize book that she won for her performance on the seniors' special day. This weeping girl crawling on the dirty road bears little resemblance to the poised schoolgirl of this spring who recalled ancient quotations and helped her school win the district school's Wisdom Contest, or the senior girl wearing her new sweater in the Senior Day Program such a short time ago.

In the middle of the muddy road, she sees her new trousers

that she has carried all of the way wrapped up in a bundle on her tray. She picks up her garment and cries aloud again, "Look how dirty my new slacks are!"

Refusing to sit down with her family in the new grass beside the road, Humble walks down the way where the crowd still fights and argues. She finds one of the trays and wails louder when she discovers her precious book torn and being trampled by the unruly crowd.

"Look, Mother. That man did not ask for my carrying pole. He just grabbed it and threw my things aside!"

Silk Fan guides her miserable teenager by the elbow back across the road to where little Happiness Found sits. Hugging her sister's legs, she offers her sympathy and renews her tears, this time on behalf of her beloved sister. The conflict continues in an angry and noisy confrontation. Silk Fan takes each of her precious daughters by the hand and reverses their steps. Her heart sinks at the thought of losing any of the miles they have already claimed on the way back home, but she knows that nothing good will come from staying here. Perhaps even more problems await them. Examining both girls, she tries to determine the extent of their pain.

"Are you injured, Humble?"

"He just knocked me down, Mother!" Humble explains as she wipes her tears with a very dirty hand.

"Hello. Come this way."

"I am so sorry, my daughter. He was rude to you. He wanted to use your carrying pole as a weapon."

"Well, he could have asked me!"

"Hello, Auntie! Come up here."

Happiness Found tugs at her mother's slacks and says, "Mother, I think that girl is speaking to us."

"Come to my orchard. There is a way just beyond the plum tree."

Silk Fan's gaze follows the voice and sees a young girl motioning to them from a break in the line of fruit trees on the hill bordering the road.

"Come, girls. I do think that God has sent a ministering angel to rescue us today."

"Do we know her?"

"No, we do not, but she is friendlier than her neighbors. We will rest here."

"Come. Sit down here in the grass. I will bring you some water for washing." With that promise, the girl disappears into the fruit trees.

"Thank you, Lord, for this angel of mercy."

"Mother, can we stay here for the night?"

"We will see. Help me take the basket off my shoulders. Now we will put everything into my harvest basket. Just shake the dust off your things. Your new slacks will wash clean, my child."

Humble does as she is instructed by placing her few remaining possessions into her mother's harvest basket, but now she stands with a very perplexed expression on her grimy, tear-stained face. She realizes that all of the food they brought with them is gone.

"Look, the girl is returning and she is bringing us a jug of water," Happiness Found says.

The young owner of the fruit orchard makes no comment about their poor and dirty appearance.

"Oh, thank you. You are so kind. Drink some water, daughters, and then we will wash off some of the road that we are wearing."

Humble wants to laugh at her mother's joke, but she is too startled by the sight of her young hostess.

Mother always taught us that it is rude to stare, but the young girl who brought us water looks pregnant!

Silk Fan removes a washing cloth from her basket and bathes the face of her younger child as their hostess stands and watches her. The girl says wistfully, "I remember my mother doing that for me."

"Mother, may we stay here for a while?"

The girl answers Happiness Found's question with a smile. "You are welcome to spend the night in my orchard if you like. My uncle is not home today. No one will bother you here. I will return shortly. I must check on my cooking fire." She walks awkwardly back up the hill toward her home.

Slowly turning the wrinkled and torn pages of her precious book, Humble asks, "Did you notice?"

"Yes."

"But she is so young."

"Yes, she is."

"She appears to be my age."

"I expect she is your age."

"Why would her parents allow her to marry if she is so young?"

Silk Fan does not answer with words, just a sad expression.

Humble gasps. "Do you mean that she is not married? Oh!"

"Do not question her. She is coming now and carrying something. Go to help her with her load."

"Mother, this is the saddest thing I have ever seen."

"Put on a smile, dear."

Humble gets up from the ground and runs to help the girl who is returning with a bamboo rice steamer in one hand and four round bowls with chopsticks in the other. Humble takes the rice steamer from her and smiles at their benefactor. The two teenage girls laugh and chatter as they return through the knee-high grass growing between the fruit trees.

The sounds of the crowd are still heard, but here in the orchard, the scene is of a picnic dinner.

"I thought that you might be hungry."

Wide smiles brighten all three faces. "Thank you. This looks like a grand feast."

White steam rises from the bamboo basket as the girl, heavy with her unborn baby, divides the rice into the four bowls.

"I am glad that you happened along. I enjoy seeing company."

Humble smiles widely as she and her mother eagerly accept the food they dared not anticipate.

Quietly, Silk Fan addresses her young hostess, "We thank our God before we eat. We would like to do that now."

"I understand."

"Humble, would you like to voice our thanks?"

"Dear God in heaven, we thank you for your constant protection. We thank you for this warm food and for the generous heart of our new friend, and we thank you for this clean place to rest. In your holy Son's name, we thank you. Amen."

"A woman who sells tea on market day speaks of a god with a holy son. She says that the son is also God."

Humble and Silk Fan both smile at her. "You must continue to see her and learn from her. This is the one, true, loving God we learned about. You will be so glad that you did."

Humble smiles and nods her agreement with her mother's advice. The girl adds, "Sometimes I sell my herbs to her. I will have some sweet herbs this spring, and then I will ask about her God."

The four picnickers sit in the grass and lift their bowls toward their mouths, eating with chopsticks, while the noise of the conflict continues as if in another world. The sounds drift up to the orchard.

"We appreciate the food, and we appreciate your rescuing us." The girl just nods her head. "What is your name?"

With a shy smile she answers, "My name is Pink Peony."

"What a pretty name!"

"My mother used to tell me that my name meant springtime. She and my father are gone to live with the ancestors now."

A renewed series of shouts draws their heads in the direction of the ongoing confrontation. The noise does not alarm

Pink Peony. Finally, Humble asks, "What is that all about? Why are they fighting?"

Sighing, she answers, "There are frightening things happening in our village now. Many of the animals are sick, and now some of the farmers' children are also sick. Government officials came here from the city and made us kill all of our ducks and chickens. The people here blame you travelers with bringing the sickness with you."

A frown crosses the attractive face of Silk Fan.

"We have no ducks or chickens now. I need eggs for cooking."

No one knows how to answer this young girl, so helpful and so very pregnant. She has just explained the unexpected trouble the travelers had today, but the wider news is quite disturbing. What terrible thing is wrong here, and how far reaching is it? With a look of horror, Silk Fan thinks, *What if this illness reaches all the way to my home in the south?* Suddenly, she looks very tired.

Pink Peony reads the worried faces and slowly rises to her feet.

"You may stay here. If you wish, I can lead you around the town. We will have to wait until after dark, but I can lead you back to this road farther along the way."

"Can you really do that?"

"Yes. I know my way about this place. I have always lived here. The moon is not too bright tonight. We will walk beyond the road through the farm fields. I will return after dark, perhaps at midnight. Do you think that the little girl can be quiet?"

Silk Fan is still trying to comprehend the wonderful offer that Pink Peony is making. She answers, "Yes. We can all be quiet. Are you sure that this is safe for you? We do not want to put you in any danger."

"Just be ready when I return."

"Thank you. We will be ready."

She turns to leave. "Wait, we want to pay you for the rice."

Removing some coins from her pants pocket, Silk Fan asks, "Is this enough?"

"Yes. That is what I usually charge for rice when people come to meet the train."

"Do you have any extra rice to sell? I do not wish to cause you a shortage, but we need some more for our trip."

"I have enough to sell. I am prepared to sell to many travelers, but with the trouble and sickness, I have not sold much this year."

With a smile, Silk Fan thanks her young hostess. "You are very kind. We need the food, and we need to return to the road."

"I will prepare you a package of long rice. I must go now to move my sheep. I have only two." Knowing that two sheep are considered so small a flock as to be a joke, she smiles and adds, "They will grow fat on this spring grass." Turning awkwardly, she says, "I will see you when the moon is high."

After such a tumultuous day, the grassy bed is a blessed relief to the feminine family of brave travelers.

Happiness Found falls asleep. Humble sits quietly with her mother.

"Humble, do you still have the small pair of scissors I gave you?"

"Yes. They are right here in my coat pocket. Do you think that we will need a weapon for protection?"

"It is to our advantage that we are three in number, but we must always be alert. We will look for another place for sleeping after midnight. We do want to get beyond this dreadful place."

"Thank you, Mother, for being so wise."

"Let us talk later on."

Humble is not quite ready for sleep. "Mother, do you think that it would cost too much to have my book rebound? My teacher told us that there are places called book binders that do such work."

"I do not know. When we get to the city, we will try to find such a place. You must realize that our money might be needed for our living."

My lovely daughter, Humble, what I cannot bring myself to tell you is that I fear all of our money will be needed to purchase a house for us to live in. If Pride has another wife or if he rejects me after years as another man's wife, then I will have more problems than dangerous travel to consider.

"Mother?"

"Yes?"

"After seeing Pink Peony today, I think something worse than losing my book could have happened to me."

Silk Fan nods her head at her daughter's newly found insight. "Get some sleep now. We must get up within a few hours."

Humble snuggles down under a peach tree that is just beginning to show promise. Silk Fan relaxes as she lies between her two daughters and thinks to herself, *I wonder how long it will be before I can sleep with both eyes closed. Lord Jesus, please protect us and let me in truth to be calm inside and not just pretend for their sakes.*

A peace descends upon her. She relaxes as she sleeps in peace under some fruit trees in deep springtime grass under the open sky.

The sound of footsteps awakens Silk Fan. Even in this darkened and unfamiliar place, she realizes that it is her young hostess coming to escort them around her hostile village.

"Auntie, are you ready to go?"

"We are almost ready. Please give us one minute. Humble, Happiness, come. It is time to get up."

"I have brought you a package of uncooked rice and three steamed rolls. You will need them later."

"May God bless you. Here is some money for you."

"Even in the dark, I can feel that it is too many coins."

"Please keep them all. Purchase something for yourself and your baby."

Relieved, she tucks the rolls and the package of rice into her harvest basket.

"Thank you. Now we must go quietly."

Humble hoists the huge basket onto her back, freeing her mother to handle her sleepy sister.

"Do you remember that we are going to be very quiet now? We are pretending to be little mice sneaking through these farms. We do not want the cats to see us or hear us."

"Mother Mouse, I have to tee-tee."

Pink Peony laughs softly at the family. With sure feet, she leads across her orchard in a westerly direction walking on a path beaten smooth by centuries of foot traffic. Turning onto a road where a few houses are darkened, she passes a gray stone house that is guarded by a lone dog. With a low growl, he announces his ownership.

Pink Peony whispers, "Warrior! Be quiet."

Happiness Found hears the growl and immediately climbs her mother like a tree. She is afraid of dogs. She whispers to her mother, "Do dogs eat mice?"

Silk Fan whispers back into her ear, "You are safe, little one. She is the dog's friend."

The child nods but keeps her arms locked tightly around her mother's neck and her legs wrapped about her body. The parade of four moves on in a silent march with Pink Peony leading the way.

At a fork in the road, she turns southwest and stops.

"This road leads to an old temple. You may sleep there if you wish. Travelers often do. No priests live or work there now. Just follow the road. It will take you back to the main road leading to the railroad."

"Is there another orchard on this road? I would rather not go into a place in the dark where other people are already sleeping. We might startle people who are armed."

"Yes. You will see fruit trees on the hilly side of the road. I will leave you here."

"Thank you, and may God go with you."

Pink Peony smiles, nods, and turns to retrace her steps to her home.

"Do we still have to be as quiet as mice?"

"You were a good little mouse. We are going to walk a bit farther to find another bed under the fruit trees. Do you want to continue playing the mouse game?"

"Yes, but I cannot see very much."

"Mice walk in the dark. It is fine because the mother and sister mouse are always with her. You must walk now. Little mice do not ride in mother mouse's arms. We are a family of three mice taking a walk at night."

An ancient stone pillar marks the entrance to the grounds of the abandoned temple. The family of mice walks silently by. After traveling a distance down the road, they decide that they have traveled beyond the troubled village. Locating the new orchard as Pink Peony told them, they climb through newly growing spring grass and lie down for the second time this eventful night.

"We can still get some more rest here, girls."

"Sleep sweetly, Mother Mouse." Little Happiness Found quickly falls asleep again.

"Humble, how many shirts are you wearing?" she asks with a laugh.

"I have on all three of my shirts, plus my blue sweater. Do I look funny?"

"No. You look fine, just a little heavier than usual."

"May I remove my top shirt now? You said that I needed it to convince the neighbors that we were going to plow our field. It is my oldest and really is dirty now."

"If you wish, you may remove it, but it is still to our advantage to appear to be a poor farming family."

"Why? We are a long way from home now."

"We do not know these people with whom we are traveling,

and we will see more people than we can count once we get to the city. We do not want to be beaten by those seeking money."

Humble shivers at the thought of being attacked and beaten by bandits. "I will wear all three shirts. They keep me warm at night sleeping outside."

"Let us sleep now."

A noisy rooster wakes the travelers the next morning. His unmelodious crow indicates to Silk Fan that they are near a farm and are probably sleeping on private property.

"Good morning, girls. I have a surprise for you. We have steamed rolls to eat."

"Must we get up now?" Humble is still sleepy.

"You must get up only if you want your roll."

"Oh, yum!"

Happiness Found says, "Look! The clouds are made of flowers." All three laugh. It is a beautiful sight.

"Mother, the clouds smell beautiful too."

Silk Fan prays, "Thank you, Jesus, for this food and for the safe night."

Happiness Found adds her prayer, "Yes, thank you, Jesus, and thank you for the flower clouds."

The family eats their breakfast rolls while Silk Fan retrieves some of her money from hiding.

Happiness Found asks with a mouth full of roll, "May we pick some of the pretty white flowers?"

"No, little one. The flowers grow into plums. If we pick the flowers, then these people will not have fruit from them."

"Then I do not want to pick them, even if they look like pretty clouds. Mother, are we almost there?"

FINALLY

The train station is in sight. Although this is not the end of their trip, it is symbolic of freedom because it means that they have successfully outrun the gang of kidnappers and their village vigilantes. Finding the train station means that they have escaped the place of imprisonment.

The area on the platform and all about the tracks is filled with experienced travelers. The benches are full, and the ground is crowded with all sorts of private property piled around family groups. Smoking steel woks are being tended by vendors who regularly earn money from selling food to these travelers. Silk Fan breathes a deep sigh of relief when she sees the food vendors.

Locating a place as close to the train platform as possible, she sits her family down with her basket and bag. The girls are in awe at all of the many people, sights, sounds, and fragrant odors, but their eyes keep returning to the food and drinks so close and so tempting. Silk Fan follows their eyes and answers their pleading looks.

"I know you are hungry, my dears. I am too. Other people will come, and we do not want to be pushed farther back away from the tracks. Stay here while I purchase our tickets and I will return as quickly as I can."

Happiness Found slips one dirty hand into her sister's protective one and gazes in wonder at a bright-eyed boy wearing a colorful hat who waved his wares: cucumber pickles. A man smoking brown cigarettes announces loudly that he has red peppers for sale. Bent older women stir steaming pots of food. Humble does not know what the pots contain but is willing to buy and eat whatever boils there. They ate the puffy rolls on the day that Pink Peony sold them to them and enjoyed the long rice that Silk Fan cooked in her small cooking pot, but the rice lasted only two days, and now they are hungry again.

When their mother returns with three train tickets in her pocket, she hands them six hardboiled eggs and smiles at her beloved girls.

"Thank you, Lord Jesus, for this food, and thank you for guiding us here."

She leaves and returns shortly. Humble laughs at the variety and amount of food Silk Fan brings back, hands full of rolls wrapped in paper and meat-filled treats. A pretty girl follows her with a tray containing three cups of steaming soup with noodles. She serves the soup to her customers sitting on the ground.

Humble exclaims, "Thank you, Auntie, thank you, Mother, and thank you, Jesus."

"Oh, Mother, what a delight!" Happiness Found squeals.

"We still need some water, but this is a good start, isn't it?" The hungry girls just nod their heads. They begin eating as Silk Fan carefully packs some of the food in her basket for later.

To arrive safely at the train station is victory, and to find food is an answer to prayers. The family eats heartily while waiting for the next train moving south.

"While we wait for the train to arrive, Humble, I want you to memorize these two addresses. If we become separated, I want you to know the name and address of my second uncle and aunt and of my Pride of His Father."

Silk Fan muses, *Oh, how different this train ride will be from the last one I took going north. I was pushed, dragged, beaten, kicked, and cursed. Now the same sights that grieved me will entertain my weary daughters.*

THE BIG CITY

"The train is so huge, and ugly, and noisy!"

"Yes, it is, but it is also wonderful. We shall rest."

Riding on the huge, ugly, noisy, wonderful train provides much-needed rest for the three. They watch the scenery through dirty windows, and then they sleep.

After days of riding on the southbound train, the twenty-eight-year-old Silk Fan faces the challenge of navigating the city in a southern province and finding the roads that will lead back to her small farm farther south.

Lord God above, please hear my prayer. Quiet my pounding heart, and calm my soul. Give me strength to find my way home. You know the way, Father. Please show me.

The wave of humanity sweeps them along like a high tide, moving them away from the train. Silk Fan holds the hand of Happiness Found and says, "Humble, dear, please help me look, and tell me if you see a stall that sells shoes. We all need new ones. This is a blessing to be in a place where we can purchase shoes, food, and other things."

"I will try to help you, Mother."

"We want to be certain that we are always walking south. We do not have energies for becoming lost or backtracking."

"Mother, there are so many wonderful things to see. Where do all of these people live? Look at their clothing! Did you see the hats those men were wearing? May we stop to look at this stall? Silk! Oh, how beautiful!"

Sidewalk salesmen cry out, "Would the young woman like to see our wares? We have the finest hand-woven silk in the world."

"Silk. Silk! We sell wonderful silk!"

"This does not look like the market in our old village. This is a grand show."

"Humble, let's talk for a moment. I am going to allow you to purchase a few items, but not silk. It is lovely and fun to see, but it is not suitable for us. We need to buy a few gifts to take home, and I will let you choose them."

Smiles fill the girl's face at the prospect of actually purchasing anything in this exciting place.

Happiness Found asks, "May I decide too?"

"Yes. You and Humble need to choose a small gift for your cousin, Quiet One, as well as a gift for Strong Wind and Shimmering Sunrise. We will see many things, so shop carefully and try to remember that we are walking southward."

Happiness Found asks, "Sister, what is a good gift for cousin?"

"Let us look for hair bands or pretty hair clamps."

"What fun! I will look for hair bands." Happiness Found takes her sister's hand and dances toward the outdoor displays.

After the girls debate over the colors and design of dozens of selections, they purchase red hair bands for Quiet One and green ones for Shimmering Sunshine. They are pleased with themselves and their purchases, and they then look for just the right gift for Strong Wind.

Humble notes the various items offered and says, "Mother, we can't give little brother hair bands. What can we buy for him?"

"Would you like to buy him a book?"

Happiness Found squeals, "A book! Oh yes, let us find a book for him."

When they discover the many bookstalls, they find that the prices are far beyond what they wish to pay, and all are disappointed. To the vendors at the stalls, it is apparent that these are poor country farmers just visiting the city.

"Have you been to the stalls on Three Scrolls Street that sell used books? Books there are much cheaper, and some are quite nice. "

Silk Fan smiles broadly at the helpful vendor and responds, "Thank you, Grandmother. Where is Three Scrolls Street?"

"It is not too long a walk. After the tobacco sellers, turn to the left, and you will see them on the next street over."

"Oh, thank you, Grandmother."

The vendor smiles at the enthusiasm of the girls. They find Three Scrolls Street where a variety of secondhand goods are for sale.

Humble is impressed. "How can we choose when there are so many books?"

"Does he like books about animals?"

"Do you think that he will like a book with stories?"

"I like this one about heroes, but it is not clean."

"This has pictures, but the stories are short, and the pictures are all of trucks, trains, cars, boats, and motorcycles."

"It may be just what a boy would like, my daughters." So the choice is made at the secondhand bookstall to buy a book about all things that move, a boy's dream book.

"If you can agree upon a book, we can purchase one for you also."

"These are so many grand books. I did not know that there were this many books on earth."

"I can't decide. I want them all," Happiness Found confesses.

"Mother, why don't you choose one for us?"

"No. I want you to decide."

"Do you like this one about all of the things that people make? It has colorful pictures about making silk, cars, and designing modern clothing."

"Does it tell stories?"

"Yes. It seems to have quite a few stories."

Happiness Found decides. "I want this story book."

"You have made a good choice."

Humble is still looking around. These books are for children. She is searching for something else. Happiness Found is happy and hugs Silk Fan for the wonderful gift of a used book with pictures and stories.

"Have you found one for yourself, Humble?"

"Not yet."

"There will be other stalls. We will keep looking. Put both of our books in my basket. Now we must look for a place selling shoes. There are stores and stalls too. Let me tell you if the price is too high. We are all going to have new shoes!"

"This city is the grandest place. We will buy new shoes, and new books, and gifts for our cousin. It is a place of triple fun."

"We have turned corners. We must return to a southward direction."

"What is that man in the white coat selling?"

"Are you thirsty? We will buy something."

"Sir, are you selling water?"

"Certainly! I sell water, tea, and fruit drinks."

His attitude is impatient. He has seen enough of these peasants coming to town to sell their wares but not to buy his.

"How much do you charge for a fruit drink?"

He waves impatiently at his posted sign of prices.

"I want three fruit drinks please."

Taking out her money, she sees the large plastic jugs from which he is pouring the juice. There are numerous clean white plastic jugs on a shelf behind him. The poor housewife knows immediately the value of such treasures in places without running water.

Silk Fan asks him, "How much do you charge for the plastic jugs?"

"How much do I charge for the jugs? I use them to hold my water, tea, and juices." With a laugh he asks, "How many do you want?"

"That depends upon how much you charge. I would like to purchase four."

He hands the three drinks to Silk Fan and takes her payment, and then he looks about at his stall as if counting his jugs. With a condescending smile he says, "I can allow you four of my fine jugs for four copper coins."

Tying two together with a cord, he hands her the four empty plastic jugs, grinning at her all the while. Silk Fan acts as if she does not notice his grin and accepts the jugs with a proper thank you.

"Girls, look what we have. We have new water jugs with tops. We will not get wet by splashing water. What a wonderful find."

Humble does not miss the snub. "Mother, why did that man laugh at you? Was he flirting? Or was he laughing at you for wanting the empty jugs?"

"Do not pay him any attention, my dear. He was probably laughing because we look poor and not dressed as city people."

"I did not like him! It is rude to laugh at honest people."

"You are correct, my dear. It makes some people feel superior to laugh at others."

"Do you mean superior to us? He does not even know us. There is no woman in all of China who is better than you, Mother." Humble is indignant on behalf of her beloved second mother, Silk Fan.

There is still much to see, and they have not found the shoe aisles, but Humble is angry, and a deep frown now creases her brow. As they walk, she removes her outer shirt, which is her oldest one and the one she has worn the entire trip. Saying nothing, she rolls it up and throws it into her mother's basket. Making a decided lift of her young head, she slips her coat back on. She is now wearing only two shirts, plus her blue sweater under her coat, and they can barely be seen, but she knows the difference. She will not be a laughingstock.

Silk Fan stops at a stall that sells kitchen goods. Stacked in tall towers are countless items. *I had not planned on spending much money, but I do not want to return to this city until necessary, and these bowls are just what my house will need.*

Halfway through her anticipated delight in such new utensils, she remembers that she still does not know whether or not Pride will accept her. She may need all of this money for a new house in her new life. She hesitates, and then with resolve, she tells herself, *I will need these necessary bowls wherever I live!*

"Count out eight of these rice bowls, Humble."

"Did you say eight, Mother?"

"Yes, eight. And examine each one. We do not want any cracked bowls. Stand right here with my basket, Happiness Found. I am going to buy us a new soup pot and two new vegetable knives. The prices here are better than those of the peddler who comes by our door."

They help stack the small rice bowls and knives into the soup pot, and smiling broadly, they deal with the owner of the marvelous collection of kitchen goods. Humble's eyes widen in amazement at the boldness of Silk Fan's purchases.

"The Lord knew that we would need this space in our basket."

"Now we must look for shoes, my daughters."

"May I ask someone where shoes are sold, Mother?"

"Yes. Ask a woman."

Silk Fan realizes how sheltered Humble is because of her life in a small village. Allowing her to speak to people in public is one way of building her confidence.

"Mother, she said that shoes are about four more lengths down this same way."

"There are so many different types of shoes, Mother. Who wears these flower-covered slippers with such high heels? These are silly shoes." Happiness Found dismisses the high fashion shoes.

Laughing, Silk Fan allows the girls to admire the various shoes on display, remembering her own girlhood visits to this same place. "Look at the prices, my dear. Find some shoes that we can use for plowing."

Silk Fan chooses some sturdy, enclosed ones for Happiness Found. Her tiny feet have turned blue with cold too often on this trip. Humble chooses a pair that charms her. For her own use, Silk Fan chooses a pair of sturdy plastic ones that will be easy to wash when clogged with mud from the fields. She also chooses a pair for both of her own true children and is looking at suitable ones for her husband, Pride of His Father.

Humble tries to help shop. "Those are too large for you, aren't they, Mother?"

"They are too large for me but just about right for my darling Pride."

"Do you remember his size, Mother?"

"I remember the size of his foot, the length of his arms, the size of his shirt, his large, gentle hands, and the way his eyes shine when he smiles at me. Yes, I remember."

This rare insight into her soul surprises Humble. As if returning to earth after a time, she asks simply, "Do you see any stall selling socks? Happiness must have a pair. If the price is fair, we will buy a pair for each of us."

They laugh in delight as they pack the six pairs of shoes and socks into the harvest basket, which is becoming heavier with each purchase. Looking for a spot where they can all stop to put on their new shoes, they pause at a bicycle stand. Oblivious to the crowds around them, the three refugees slip off their worn-out shoes and put on their new ones, right onto their travel-worn, dirty feet.

"Humble, take your shoestrings out and save them. You might need them." She nods, does as she is told, and looking to the sky says, "Mother, it is going to rain soon."

"Let us seek shelter, dear."

Humble quickly removes the two books from the open basket and slides them under her coat. Vendors quickly pack away their wares, fold their tables, and then roll lengths of plastic down over their outdoor shops as the spring rain begins to sprinkle and then fall steadily. The shoppers move toward shelter.

"Auntie, you may come here into my space."

A middle-aged woman with a pleasant face is turning her tables on their sides. Next, she lowers the green canvas visor that covers her stall. She is prepared for rain. She welcomes the family. "This area stays dry when it rains. You may sit down here between my cases. You may stay the night if you need to. Some of the other vendors sleep here in their stalls, but I have a place to stay. Here is my broom. It will serve to bop any drunken man in the head. Just scream if you must. I think that you will be fine here."

"May God bless you."

"Thank you, Grandmother." Humble smiles at her.

Silk Fan is relieved. "Thank you, Lord, for providing shelter. This is a blessing. If we need to, we can sleep here. It is dry enough. Take off your coats and shake them. We want them to dry before we sleep in them."

They shake out their coats. Silk Fan reaches into her well-filled basket and discovers Humble's old shirt in it. She says nothing but understands. Humble wraps her arms about her body and exclaims, "What wonderful things we bought! Will we buy anything more?"

"We must buy more gifts. We need to find some things for second uncle and aunt, for my grandfather, and something very special for Pride of His Father."

"What is something special?" Humble asks.

"A flashlight would be a great gift," Silks Fan answers.

"A flashlight! Oh joy! A flashlight!" Happiness Found is thrilled at the thought of something so grand.

Humble is also surprised. "Will it be just like the one the government cadre used?"

"Perhaps. We must look for them. We also need to find a store selling paper. School note pads and practice paper for character painting will be sold here somewhere. "

Humble understands that Silk Fan's mind is focused on the needs of her true family, her husband, Pride of His Father, and her two small children.

"What else will we buy?"

"We need to buy a few more things. We need needles, candles, thread, and a nice gift for second aunt. She would really like to have some fabric. She has four people to clothe."

Happiness Found says excitedly, "May I choose the fabric? May I?"

"We will all help to choose it. Remember that it is not for us."

"May we buy some for ourselves? Not silk, but something pretty for sewing?" Humble looks about at myriad of colors of fabric.

"We will need to make bedding and clothes too. Fabric will be so heavy to carry that we will have to shop carefully. Oh, how I wish that we had a cart and a mule to help take our things home."

"Are we buying a cart and a mule?"

Silk Fan shakes her wet face and laughs. "No."

Actually spending money is a new game for Happiness Found, and she takes this wish for a cart and mule seriously.

"Perhaps we can buy you another pole and tray set for taking our treasures home. Neither of us can lift all of this, plus the other things we need. I really do want to be on our way tomorrow morning. There is time left in our day to shop if it will cease raining. Look, dears. What a nice gift. We shall wash our feet and hands in that little puddle of clean water streaming off the canvas cover."

Retrieving their small white cloths from her utilitarian basket, the three dirty travelers use the privacy offered by the upturned tables and rolled-down canvas sun visors to discreetly bathe some of their body parts in clean rainwater.

Humble laughs. "Ooh, that is chilly but so good. May we wash our hair too, Mother?"

"I am afraid for you to do that, dear. Your hair would not dry, and you might be chilled all night long. We do not want sick girls."

"Here, sister, let me help you wash the mud from your face."

"Mother, may I wear my new socks now that I have bathed my feet?" Happiness wants to wear her new socks.

"Yes. That will feel grand."

As the spring shower of cool rain ceases and the stream of water running off the canvas visor come to an end, the girls are eager to return to the delightful world of shopping. Vendors remove the long sheets of plastic from the rows of colorful fabric as the sky clears.

At one stall, a woman looks at the wet shoppers and turns her back on them, mumbling something about country people being too shabby to trade here. Silk Fan ignores the snub and continues down the line of merchants. At another stall, a young couple rolling up their plastic covers smiles a welcome.

"We have man-made fabric, linen, and very fine cotton cloth. We have cloth for bedding, baby clothes, school clothes, and grandmother's clothes. Look and see."

"Thank you. May we purchase a length for suits, or must we purchase the entire roll of cloth?"

"You are welcome to buy enough for each garment, but Auntie, if you purchase a roll, we will have the big brown truck deliver it to your door."

"I do not understand."

"We hire the men in the big brown trucks to deliver our

orders to your home. They will also deliver your harvest basket if you want them to."

Silk Fan looks confused. *Is this pleasant young couple trying to make fun of us?*

"We do not know about the big brown truck. How many lengths are in this roll of cotton?" It is difficult to hear the answer to her questions as both girls ask excited questions.

Humble asks sweetly, "May I have some of this one?"

Happiness Found jumps up and down. "I want the pink cloth. It is so pretty."

Laughing, Silk Fans asks, "What do you think of this color for the gift for second aunt?"

Humble frowns. "It is so dark."

"It is just a dark blue. Do you think that she might want something more cheerful? This dark blue fabric is fine for making slacks for everyone in the family."

"I understand," replies Humble. "May I choose a color for blouses?"

"You may choose three colors. And Happiness, you may choose three colors of this medium-weight cloth. It must be suitable for blouses for all of us girls."

The clerks willingly cut off six different lengths of fabric for the six blouses that will be sewn at home. The two girls are giddy with excitement. They have never seen such choices and have never seen their mother spend money so freely. Humble forgets her ire at the sneering city clerks.

"May I have the green one for myself?"

"We will try to please everyone, Happiness. You may have the green piece if you wish. Please do not handle it. We want to get home with clean new goods."

"Does Auntie wish to purchase any other of our fine fabrics?"

"Oh yes. They are beautiful, but we cannot carry anything else. We have a far distance to walk."

About that time, a man in a brown uniform comes by and asks the young business couple if there is any business for him.

"Yes, sir. May this customer look at your truck? Auntie, if you will follow this driver, he will explain his business to you."

All three city people are polite and patiently explain how the delivery business works. The family admires the man's brown delivery truck.

"We work very much like the postal service. Does the postal service deliver to your home?"

"Yes. We also send letters and packages for a fee."

"That is how we operate. For a fee, we deliver packages right to your door."

Silk Fan, who has been in too remote an area to keep up with modern business that is sweeping China, is at first very suspicious of this offer to deliver her purchases but begins to believe it is not a scam. She is still unwilling to trust anyone else with the handmade clothing she has prepared for her family.

"Will you deliver this heavy soup pot, bowls, my shoe purchases, and books too?"

"Of course I will. My truck is large and carries many things to many people."

"Will you tell me what your fee will be for all of my purchases?"

"Let me allow the clerk to weigh your fabric." The truck driver is polite.

"Miss, I have decided to allow this man to deliver my goods, and I want to buy some more sheeting fabric if you please. How much will this entire bolt cost me?"

Feigning surprise at the stated price, Silk Fan shakes her head and looks down. The clerk suggests a lower cost, and Silk Fan counterbids with her own lower cost, both experienced at the game. After a time, they agree with smiles and nodding heads.

Both clerks smile broadly as they wrap up the farmer's clean, new, cotton fabric. She has enough new fabric to sew bedding for a school! Silk Fan writes with a smart ballpoint pen on a form:

To: Farmer Pride of His Father
South Dragon Road, Farm # 12
Village # 26 South Central China

Silk Fan removes the full price from the secret pocket of her slacks and thanks the three businesspeople who are amazed at the country woman who is so lost in the city but so confident in making her purchases.

"Sir, when will your truck come to my house?"

"My brown truck will arrive at your home within five days. I have other places I must stop for pickups and deliveries before I leave town."

"Thank you very much. I must divide these lengths. I will have to deliver some of these purchases myself."

She lifts the heavy soup pot filled with bowls along with the two books and asks, "Would you please wrap this with my fabric?"

As the sales clerks and the deliveryman with his brown truck confer and pack her grand new purchases, Silk Fan muses, "This man with his shiny brown truck is going to save my weary back."

An unaccustomed giggle escapes her mouth. *What will Pride of His Father think? Clean new linens and food and gifts for the entire family will come in a big brown truck. He will think that I am mad.*

SHOPPING

"We must purchase a fine gift for Pride of His Father. He is the head of our home, and we want to show him respect."

Humble asks, "Will we buy him gifts even if he refuses to accept us?"

"Yes, my child. We will buy him gifts even if he refuses to accept us."

Happiness Found, who does not understand the issue, smiles. "I know what I want to get for him: an important-looking hat. Would that be a good gift?"

"That would be a very fine gift, my dear."

"I would like to get him a wristwatch."

"What good ideas you both have! We will price these two gifts. I have not forgotten your book, Humble. There are many other market stalls and indoor stores. We will try to find a book for you. We also need to look for paper and pens."

"I will carry the basket for you now, Mother."

"Thank you, daughter. Come, Happiness Found. Take my hand. There will be crowds."

At the first intersection of Market Street, they note the name of the next section of stalls piled high with food items. The street sign reads, "Vegetable Lane." On seeing the rain glistening on piles of vegetables, Silk Fan stops and covers her mouth with her free hand.

"Food! Why did I not worry about food? I have been so concerned about getting back home that I have not even considered the fact Pride may have a hard time growing enough food."

"Mother, you could not help him from so far away!"

"I could not help him then, but I will help him now. I will ask this vendor of cabbages if she will send her produce in the brown truck."

Marching with new energy and dragging Happiness Found by the hand, she rushes up to the first friendly-looking woman and asks, "Do you send large orders by the brown truck to places two days' walk away?"

"Yes, Auntie. What would you like to send?"

"I need to know what price you will charge me for twenty heads of cabbage, six bags of onions, and six bags of those limp carrots."

Humble slowly reaches for the hand of her little sister so that Silk Fan can bargain freely with the produce vendor. They make an agreement and smile.

She is assured that all of her purchases will be delivered to the family farm.

The piles of rice amaze her girls and thrill Silk Fan. She remembers growing rice and eating it daily. She smiles at the selection and purchases huge bags.

"Mother, you bought so much rice!"

"Yes, I did, my dear. Did you notice that there were no noodles or flour for sale? We will eat plenty of lovely long rice with good vegetables! This food must last us until our own vegetables are harvested. That will be months from now."

Silk Fan will no longer allow her mind to entertain the suspicions that the vendors and the driver of the brown truck might be criminals. She has too much to do while it is still light.

"Humble, dear, ask that young woman who sells herbs how we might find the sellers of dried fruit and paper."

As they hurry in the direction of the paper sellers, the sidewalks and the streets seem to become more and more crowded. Some are merchants, many seem to be farmers with nowhere to go, and some are rich people out for a stroll with their ever-present cigarettes and pet dogs.

At one building covered in sheet metal, a door opens and dozens of young women exit, chatting and laughing.

"None of them have books; where have they all been, Mother?"

"I think that the girls are all factory workers, not students."

"Shall I ask if they know where the paper-selling store is located?"

"That is a good idea."

Humble stops one of the factory working girls and asks directions. After a short discussion, the girl and two of her friends reply, "We will take you there. This is our time for dinner. We must return to work in an hour, but we do not have enough money to eat properly, so we will go with you. We like to study the nice things in the fine paper store."

Humble and Silk Fan ponder their answer. After telling their friends good-bye, they lead the way through several streets to a glass-fronted store, which they enter. The three young factory workers are followed by the dirty family of farmers. Customers are already in the store, but none as appreciative as these six who whisper and point to the writing sets, fine papers, and gift-wrapped stationary sets. The workers purchase nothing.

"Mother, do you see the rolls of extra long paper for announcements and banners? Auntie Grace would like to come to this store. It sells wonderful supplies."

"Yes, she would like this store."

There are pots of black ink, fine brushes of all sizes, pencils, art supplies, and ballpoint pens. Silk Fan decides that for schoolchildren, these pens will have to work. She knows that it is difficult enough to learn the over three thousand commonly used characters without having to learn the skills of painting with brushes. She knows that older scholars and scribes would not approve of the departure from traditional learning styles, but after her last five years' experiences, she decides to be practical about schooling for her three younger children.

A store clerk with her hair in a classic bun addresses the factory workers first. After being told that they are only escorting the farm family, she sighs audibly and speaks to Silk Fan in a frosty tone.

Silk Fan, now dressed in travel-worn clothing, still possesses the fine manners taught by her mother many years ago. With quiet dignity, she lists the items she wants to purchase. One of the factory workers whispers to Humble that her mother should bargain for the paper goods because the clerk's asking price is too high. She nods, and all five of the girls watch as Silk Fan calmly negotiates the price for her paper and pens.

They are amazed at the poise with which Silk Fan conducts her business. The store clerk is also unprepared for the dignity of this disheveled woman with her children and harvest basket. She was prepared to charge higher prices because of the dirty country woman's appearance. These city working girls cost her higher profits. The clerk purses her lips and wraps the items.

"Thank you for helping us find this store. Now where can we purchase some food? Is there a soup shop nearby?"

"Yes, Auntie. We can take you to a small one nearby. We eat there often."

"That is fine. We would like to invite you to have a bowl of soup with us. We appreciate your help today."

"We do not want you to repay us."

"We want to do this. You have been quite helpful."

"Thank you."

From the exchanged glances and smiles, Silk Fan knows that the young factory workers are really hungry and were going without eating because they have sent money from their meager earnings home to their families. As they all eat in the restaurant, Silk Fan questions them. "What do you make in this factory?"

"We put parts together for some mechanical toys. The toys are quite clever."

As the six emerge from the soup shop, a group of four younger girls passes by. Happiness Found is the first to respond vocally, "Who are those girls? Look at their beautiful clothes!" Silk Fan grabs her daughter's hand and quiets the child so impressed with fancy clothing. Happiness is not so easily shushed.

"Their dresses are so pretty, but their faces are all unhappy. Why do they look so sad?" The factory workers often see these girls and are embarrassed. Turning their heads, none of them answers the question.

Silk Fan says simply, "We do not know them, dear."

Humble has never seen prostitutes either.

"Friend, we must be going. We have only a few minutes to return to work."

"Can you please tell us where we may purchase small farming tools or flashlights and things for men?"

"Yes. There is a large hardware store near our factory. You can follow us there."

So the party leaves the soup shop with the working girls paying attention to Happiness Found, who is still munching on a slender cracker covered with seeds.

"Thank you, new friends. May God bless you all."

They direct the family to an amazing store that sells goods for men. Even Silk Fan, who is familiar with most farming supplies, is awed by the clothing. When she left this part of the country five years ago, farmers' wives made the family's clothing. What she sees here is an elaborate display of factory-made clothes for working men.

The boots must be made for soldiers; surely no farmer could afford them, she thinks. The shirts are available in fine cotton fabrics. The display of men's trousers holds her attention the longest. She leans over to finger the knees of these blue, cotton work pants. The fabric is almost stiff. Pride of His Father could kneel down in the dirt when planting his crops and never get dirt on his skin. The pockets fascinate her. *Oh! How many pockets do these pants have?* She picks up a pair and counts. *There are five pockets in this pair of pants.*

Boldly addressing a shopper, she asks, "Madam, do you know the price of these men's work pants?"

"Those working men's pants are called blue jeans, and a factory in the next district manufactures them. I do not know how much, but this store has an asking price above my means. The farmers in my district cannot afford such luxuries. I am sure that the asking price is quite unharmonious."

Silk Fan has found her special gift for her husband. Holding up several pairs at arm's length, she tries to imagine her beloved husband's body in each. Measuring the length and width against her own waist, she decides that one pair is exactly the right size for Pride of His Father. She smiles with satisfaction. Placing the garment over her arm, she turns to her daughters and says, "Let's look at the rest of the items. Have you seen anything you want to buy for Pride?"

The store with real walls and a roof displaying the costly array of goods is almost intimidating to Humble. She follows her mother about the store and stops at a stack of white plastic chairs.

"Mother, does Pride of His Father have a special chair?"

Silk Fan examines the chair with its curved arms and knows immediately how appealing it is to her daughter who was reared in poverty in the distant hills.

"No. We have benches and stools in our home. That is what most people use."

"Mother, you said that we want to honor Pride of His Father. This is what I want to give him. It is his own special chair to sit in when he comes in from the fields. He will rest and eat in comfort, and he will look so grand in this chair."

"My dear, how will we get it home?"

"I will ask a clerk if the brown truck delivers such chairs. Sir, do you employ the brown truck delivery service to deliver those white chairs if it is two days' walk from here?"

"Oh yes. We certainly do."

Humble smiles her thanks. "Mother, that clerk says that they do deliver these chairs."

"Did you ask the price?"

"Oh, no. I was so excited that I did not think of the price. I shall ask him."

Once again, the teenager addresses the clerk.

"Sir, what is your price for the white chair?"

At four years of age, Happiness Found is old enough to be concerned for her mother. "Mother, if Pride gets a special chair, then I think that you should get one too."

Silk Fan laughs at the sincere concern Happiness Found has. "Let us see what the price is before we get excited about the number of chairs we will purchase."

"Now, girls, since you are getting the chairs, you cannot buy the flashlight too. However, since it is such a good gift, I want to buy it for my second uncle. This handsome hat is for my grandfather." After taking a tour of the grand aisles of products, Silk Fan returns with a harvest knife with its own shiny leather sheath and the pair of blue pants with five pockets for Pride of His Father, pleased with her selections.

"Please sell me extra batteries for the flashlight. Here is the address."

"Mother, my head is dizzy with all of our spending. I do not know whether to laugh or sing!"

"You may do both if you wish, child. We must purchase things now because I will not be back in a city for many a day. We need to find two more stores, as it is getting dark and we will leave this place early tomorrow morning."

Humble is helpful. "Where are we shopping next?"

"Please tell me if you see a shop selling small things for women and girls."

"I will." Humble squeals, "Ewwww! Be careful where you step! That rude man just allowed his pet dog to spoil the side-walk where everyone walks."

Silk Fan guides the party to the other side of the walk. "That is indeed rude. So is the habit these people have of spitting on the walkway. Who failed to teach them proper manners?"

"How disgusting!" Little Happiness Found adds her comment.

"There are women coming out of that small store with the pink and purple display in the windows. Look into the windows to see what items are sold."

Humble looks and answers, "It has many bottles, linens, socks, women's underwear, thread, and small gifts."

"Good. We have a girl for whom we are going to buy some personal things."

"Who is that, mother?"

"You, my daughter, are that girl."

"Me?"

"You are old enough to have your own things. We are going to buy you a new hairbrush and a comb. You choose ones that you like."

While Humble reels from the information that she is the recipient of gifts, Silk Fan chooses a zippered nail care kit. Next she chooses a plastic soap box and a fragrant bar of soap that she remembers from her own youth. Some feminine items, new underwear, and a sewing set are the next gifts just for her bought daughter, of whom she is so proud.

"Humble, come and pick out a sewing set for yourself. Be sure that there are several sizes of needles. You also need a thimble. That is a nice one. Try it on for size. Does it feel com-fortable? We are also going to buy you a toothbrush. We grow sweet mint at home. It is lovely for cleaning your teeth. Do you see any washing cloths? That is good. Choose a towel also. Do you see anything else you want?"

"May I have a nice hair clamp?"

"A hair clamp? Get two, one for each side of your hair. "

"Thank you, Mother."

"You do not ask for things, dear. Remember that I want to supply your needs."

"Just like Jesus supplies our needs for courage and peace?"

"Yes, Humble."

"I never expected to own so many fine gifts."

Choosing more packages of sewing needles and thread, she approaches a clerk and once again begins the routine of bargaining for the purchase price of her chosen items.

Laden with more goods than they have ever seen their dear mother purchase, the girls follow their mother away from the stores with ceilings and back outside toward the stalls, where they are promised a place to spend the night under an awning.

"Humble, we still need to find a book so that we can replace your award book that was trampled and torn."

"Mother, your basket and my arms are full. Thank you for remembering my award book. We will search for another bookseller. I wish that I still had my carrying pole and trays. We need them now. Happiness is tired. Let's just find our place to rest and forget about the bookstore."

"If we see a bookstore, we will stop, but you are probably correct. I do want to buy some food to take with us tomorrow. Look for such a vendor, and then we will stop for the night."

As they make their way back toward the direction of the train station and the outdoor stalls where they camped under the awnings out of the rain, they are too preoccupied to notice that people in the crowd have watched as they pay for one purchase after another. Their spending spree is drawing the attention of thieves who specialize in attacking women.

Market Street is still filled with people, but this time, many of them seem to be milling about instead of hurrying to purchase goods. Several men are engaged in gambling.

Humble sees the new crowd and asks, "Mother, why have they stayed here? Why don't they go to their homes?"

"I do not know. Perhaps they will stay here for a few days to sell their wares."

Humble points. "I remember this place, Mother. We walked this way after the shower. Do you remember this row of bicycle racks next to the row of wooden carts? I think that this is near our shelter under the awnings. Were not the awnings green?"

The weary Silk Fan nods her head in agreement.

"May I play in my rain puddle again?"

Silk Fan laughs at the sudden interest her youngest daughter has in their location. "Yes, dear. Help sister find our place. There seem to be many stalls with green awnings over them."

"There!" She points to the spot where she played so happily just a few hours earlier.

Reaching deeply into her sturdy harvest basket, Silk Fan withdraws Humble's wool blanket. The blanket that has proved so valuable on their journey is once again indispensable. It is still daylight, but the little girl who wanted to play in the rain puddle is soon sleeping on the blanket under an awning in an open market somewhere in south central China. The hood of her jacket is still puffy with the cash her mother sewed in there for safekeeping. It serves as a fine pillow.

"Humble, dear, do you still have a few yuan in your pockets? You might need a few for purchasing food. It really is not a good idea to be seen searching for money in your hiding places when you are out in public. We have done so well on this long trip, and now we will arrive with our new purchases. We hope to be at second uncle and aunt's home in one or two days. I want to leave you two girls there for a visit with them. Your cousin, Quiet One, is a nice girl. I do not concern myself with you, but Happiness may not want to stay there."

"Do not worry, Mother. I will take care of her. I know that

you have much to say to your other two children, and also to Pride of His Father."

"You are very wise. You will not stay at second uncle's home for too long. I have no concern for your manners. I know that you will make me proud."

"Mother, my sewing kit is the only thing that fits in my pockets. I really need my pole and trays for carrying things."

"I know, Humble. Your shopping bag with the rope handles and this plastic sack will have to last another day or two. You can manage if you are careful. We are bringing a load with us."

"I am grateful for our purchases, and I pray for that girl, Pink Peony, who helped us. She was in such a bad situation, and yet she took care of us."

Silk Fan nods her head and thinks to herself, *It was the right decision to bring this sweet-hearted Humble along with me. She will have a better life here in the south.*

"May I sit outside? There is still some daylight."

"Of course, just stay nearby."

The fourteen-year-old girl carefully places her cousin's gift back into the basket. She smiles in pleasure, just realizing what a treasure of new belongings she possesses. Leaving her coat with her mother, she walks eight feet to the other side of their market stall and notices what a splinter-ridden place she has chosen to sit.

Nearby, a teenage boy is sweeping the sidewalk with a bamboo and twig broom. Seeing her hesitancy to sit down, the boy offers with a grin, "Shall I sweep off the rain for you? This will be a good place to watch once the crowd comes."

"Would you please do that for me? Uh, what crowd?"

"You will see. Storytellers come, and some people sing songs, and sometimes people play some musical instruments."

"Who are these people?"

"Oh, just people like me and you, people who have no homes. If you sit right here, you will see them. That is why I am cleaning the sidewalk. My family comes here every night."

"Why don't these people have homes?" It is an innocent question.

"You are not from this province if you do not know about the farmers."

"I am so sorry. No. We do not live here. I did not mean to offend you, but I do not understand about the farmers with no homes."

"You must have come from the moon. Everyone here knows about the men from the government who came to steal our farms. They said that they had to have our land for a shirt factory, but they never gave my father and grandfather enough money to buy another farm. There are many of us here. We have no farms, no land, no homes, and nowhere to go."

The boy whose education ended last year wears the same style of faded slacks and shirt worn by farming families across the land. He seems happy to discover another young person.

"I will be back in a short time. I want to sweep up this area before the crowd comes because some people will sit here. Do you have a box or stool for sitting?"

"No."

"I will bring you newspapers to protect you from the splinters. You can see everything if you sit on this table." He moves on, making slow, circular movements with his twig broom.

"Hello. My name is Singing Breeze. My brother said a new girl was here. This is Swims against the Current. He is our third cousin."

"Hello."

It appears by their unkempt appearance that they, like Humble, have been living on the streets. The ten-year-old girl who introduced herself and her cousin, a thin boy of seventeen, sit down beside her. The girl chatters away about a monkey act seen here last night. Her cousin has no chance to speak as the girl chatters on. Her brother returns with a fold of newspapers and his broom. Spreading the newspaper on the worn display table, he sits down with the other three to rest.

Singing Breeze turns to Humble and asks, "Can you sing any songs?"

Humble answers, "I am afraid that I do not know many songs. Do you have a favorite story?"

"I don't know any good stories. However, I liked the one the old woman told last week. It was about a miracle man who fed five thousand people with two small rolls of bread and five little fishes."

"What was the name of the miracle worker? Was his name Jesus?"

"Yes. That was his name. Some people will sing about him tonight."

Humble's face is painted in smiles. A prayer escapes her happy lips as she whispers, "Praise Father, Son, and Holy Spirit."

Singing Breeze persists. "Do you know any poems?"

"I do know a poem written long ago. I learned it for my Senior Day performance."

"Oh, please tell it to us."

"Yes. Please do."

As she cocks her head to claim the opening words from her memory, her new friends wave to three more young people to join them.

"This is from the writings of King David who lived many hundreds of years ago in another place a long way from here. It is from Psalm number one hundred and thirty-nine."

"Did the king really write one hundred and thirty-nine poems?" the boy wants to know.

"Shhh. Let her speak."

Humble closes her eyes and is back in her home, where she learned this prayer. She opens her eyes and begins the words she learned for a school recitation, the one for which she won first prize. She will not think of her torn prize book now.

"'O Lord, you have examined my heart and know everything about me. You know where I sit or stand. When far away you know my every thought. You chart the path ahead of me, and tell me where to stop and rest. Every moment, you know where I am. You know what I am going to say before I even say it. You both precede and follow me, and place your hand of blessing on my head. This is too glorious, too wonderful to believe! I can never be lost to your spirit! I can never get away from my God! If I go up to heaven, you are there; if I go down to the place of the dead, you are there. If I ride the morning winds to the farthest oceans, even there your hand will guide me, your strength will support me. If I try to hide in the darkness, the night becomes light around me. For even darkness cannot hide from God; to you the night shines as bright as day. Darkness and light are both alike to you. You made all the delicate, inner parts of my body, and knit them together in my mother's womb. Thank you for making me so wonderfully complex! It is amazing to think about. Your workmanship is marvelous—and how well I know it. You were there while I was being formed in utter seclusion! You saw me before I was born and scheduled each day of my life before I began to breathe. Every day was recorded in your book! How precious it is, Lord, to realize that you are thinking about me constantly! I can't even count how many times a day your thoughts turn toward me. And when I waken in the morning, you are still thinking of me! Surely, you will slay the wicked, Lord! Away, bloodthirsty men! Begone! They blaspheme your name and stand in arrogance against you—how silly can they be? Oh Lord, shouldn't I hate those who hate you? Shouldn't I be grieved with them? Yes, I hate them, for your enemies are my enemies too. Search me, O God, and know my heart; test my thoughts. Point out anything you find in me that makes you sad, and lead me along the path of everlasting life. '"

Psalm 139

The schoolgirl in dirty clothing finishes her recitation, but her amazed audience is slow to respond.

Ten-year-old girl Singing Breeze finds her tongue first. "Where did you learn that?"

"It is surely a masterpiece." Her audience is appreciative.

"Who is this girl who knows the Holy Scripture?"

"Do you own a Bible?"

"I want my parents to meet you. We do not own a copy of the Psalms. Some people here do, but we do not."

One of the last three to join their group interests Humble. "Did you say that some people around here own Bibles?"

"Yes. Songbooks and Bibles are sold in some of the churches here."

Humble gasps and whispers her question, "How much do these Bibles cost?"

"I do not know. My family said that whatever the price, we could not afford one."

The brother of Singing Breeze answers with quiet resignation, "The price for a whole Bible is eleven yuan. We will not be able to buy one."

A damp chill moves in on the evening air. Humble shivers and realizes that she has left her coat with her mother. She wants to share this wonderful news with her. There are Bibles for sale here in a church in this city!

"I must get my coat. Please do not leave. I will return in a few minutes."

Jumping off the market display table, Humble makes her way around the line of boxes, cases, and tables to the spot where her mother waits with her younger sister. She finds them both asleep. She slips on her travel-worn coat and returns the short distance to sit with her new companions.

"My mother and sister are resting behind this line of tables. They are both tired."

The nods indicate that the group finds nothing strange about sleeping on a sidewalk in a marketplace. They are homeless and know the reality of finding a dry place to rest.

"Where is your home?"

The other young people exchange looks. They have no

homes now. One recognizes it as a polite question and says simply, "We did live to the west of here near the coast, but now … "

"Are you selling anything?"

"My mother sells shopping bags."

"I would like to sell my brooms if I could find more materials for making some."

People begin to arrive alone and in family groups. Some bring small wooden boxes, some folding chairs, and some bring a supply of old newspapers. It is obvious that they have come for the evening. The street of vendors is becoming a community meeting place.

Several older women claim a table near where Humble and her new friends are sitting. They form a circle for a few minutes and then place their own cushions on the tables. They come prepared for the splintered display tables. Swims against the Current hurries to help the older women climb upon the tables where they want to sit.

With no announcement and no musical instruments to accompany them, the grandmothers begin to sing together. It is not a song that Humble recognizes, and the voices are neither strong nor professional, but their faces reflect joy, and the audience pays them the compliment of smiling and giving the musical grandmothers their attention. The crowd claps, and the singers wave and indicate that it is someone else's turn.

More people begin to arrive and must look for a place to sit on the ground.

One of the boys asks, "Do you want to sing tonight?"

"Of course! What shall we sing?" another boy responds.

"I want to choose!" insists Singing Breeze.

Her brother says, "As you like. What do you want to sing?"

"The best song is 'Jesus Loves Me.'"

With no cue, the five young people with whom Humble has been sitting break out with a well-tuned line of an old favorite children's song of faith.

Humble is quite surprised to find herself in the middle of a chorus and more surprised to find that the small group of young people is leading the crowd. When they finish singing, Humble can hold her question no longer. "Won't the police come and arrest us?"

"No. I think that they are just glad that we are peaceful."

"Do the cadres and other officials ever come here?"

"Yes."

"What do they say?"

"Nothing."

"They come here to hear the storytellers," the older boy says.

"And sometimes they come to sing."

Now a family band stands up and starts a song, which the crowd quickly follows. The crowd claps in rhythm as they all sing, "Praise God in heaven. He sent us his Son."

Humble sits on the table swinging her feet, enthralled with the news that people here are free to publicly celebrate their faith in God.

"My mother is going to be so thrilled to find out that there are other Christians living here and that we do not have to worship in secret."

A commotion in the crowd indicates that some other people are arriving. The crowd claps and moves to make room for the newcomers whom they recognize as the storytellers. The newcomers are moving slowly to the front when Humble hears the unmistakable voice of her mother.

"No. Stop. Uhhh. Thief!"

Humble jumps down and runs toward the voice of her mother, who screams in distress.

"Come with me! That is my mother. She needs help!"

The street-living teenage boys move quickly and meet a young man stumbling into them.

Swims Against the Current yells, "Stop!"

"Get him!" Another says.

"What did you take?" Humble demands.

"Let me go! I didn't do anything!" The thief struggles.

"Mother, are you harmed?"

Silk Fan answers, "He was plowing through our basket. Do not let him go."

"Mother, are you hurt?"

"He hit me," she replies.

"You half man! You hit this woman!" The boys immediately grab his arms and legs.

"Hold him while I look under his shirt." One boy takes charge.

"He has a flashlight, a big one."

Humble says angrily, "That is my gift to Pride of His Father! You dirty thief!"

The boys continue to search the thief. "And he also has a fine harvest knife with a leather sheath."

Silk Fan proclaims, "Those things are mine!"

"You know that you stole them from our basket. They are gifts we purchased today." Humble begins to reclaim their shopping treasures.

The boys tighten their hold on him. "How could you? You have no honor! You are a thief."

He mumbles a reply, "You don't need them. You are rich."

"Do we look rich?" Humble is indignant.

After traveling for weeks, the family of females experiences what they have dreaded: an attack. Frustrated, afraid, and angry, Humble and Silk Fan try to calm themselves and repack their precious belongs. They are so close to their destination. Tears would be so appropriate now, but they are withheld with firm jaws and feminine determination.

The noise and commotion of the theft disturbs the story-telling event, so the crowd sings another song while this business of a thief among them is resolved. The crowd is willing to wait in order to have a quiet story hour.

"Mother, are you sure that you are not hurt?"

"I am not injured. Please help me repack our basket."

"Would you look at her? She has not awakened."

There, curled up on Humble's hand-woven blanket, little Happiness Found sleeps soundly, oblivious to the chaos around her.

The boys drag the thief off. After conferring with their parents and other men present, it is decided to tie the thief to a lamppost. They do not want to waste valuable storytelling time dealing with the authorities and a thief. The sullen young man does not know what to make of his captors. He has not been beaten, cursed, or spit upon. He sits down on the sidewalk with his hands tied securely behind his back, surrounded by a crowd, waiting on one of its countries' most beloved entertainers, a storyteller.

One of the newly arrived men, one of the storytellers, stands and holds up both hands. He is a middle-aged man wearing a blue shirt.

"Tonight, we will hear an old favorite. It is a tale that your grandfathers told your fathers." The low laughter of the crowd indicates its pleasure.

Turning a collective face toward the speaker, the crowd listens to the storyteller tell a story that they all know. The story concerns a race between all of the animals in the land. The beautiful tiger is outsmarted, the pig is too lazy, the donkey is too slow, the rabbit does not like the water he must traverse, and the horse is too proud to compete. So the lowly rat wins the race by riding on the head of the oxen.

The crowd claps and laughs again at the old tale. A young woman with an infant tied to her back stands up and speaks. "Sir, we would like to hear the story of the man who read the woman's thoughts."

"Yes."

Another of the storytellers stands and smiles at his audience, saying, "If that is the story you wish to hear, then that is the story I shall tell you tonight."

There is applause as he announces his story, and some people from the rear move closer to sit on the ground, right in front of Humble and her friends. They want to be able to hear clearly.

"The man called Jesus was traveling one day and stopped at a famous old well. He was hot and tired from walking all morning. It was noontime, and he was alone because his friends have gone into town to buy some food. When a woman came to draw water from the well, he asked her for a drink. She was surprised because his people did not usually speak to her people.

Jesus replied, 'If you only knew what a wonderful gift God has for you, and who I am, you would ask me for some living water.'

She was astonished at this stranger in her town. She said to him, 'But you don't have a rope or a bucket, and this is a very deep well! Where would you get this living water? Besides, are you greater than our ancestor who dug this well for his family? How can you offer better water than this which he, his sons, and cattle enjoyed?'

Jesus replied that people soon become thirsty again after drinking this water, 'but the water I give them becomes a perpetual spring within them, watering them forever with eternal life.'

'Please, sir, the woman said give me some of that water! Then I'll never be thirsty again and won't have to make this long trip out here every day.'

'Go and tell your husband,' Jesus said.

'I'm not married,' the woman replied.

'All too true," Jesus said, for you have had five husbands, and you aren't even married to the man you are living with now.'

'Sir," the woman said, "you must be a prophet.'"

"How did he know so much about her?"
"Yes. How did he know?"
"Do you want to hear the rest of the story?"

'When she asked him a question about where to worship God, he answered her that it is not where we worship but how we worship that counts. He said that God is a spirit and that he would send his Holy Spirit to us to help us worship as we should. He said that God himself wants this kind of worship from us.

To prove to him that she knew something about the subject, she said, 'Well, at least I know that the Messiah will come, the one they call the Christ, and when he does, he will explain everything to us.'

Jesus answered her, 'I am the messiah!'

This astonished woman was so shocked that she left her water jug right there by the well and ran all of the way back to her village. She told everyone, "Come and meet a man who told me everything I ever did! Can this be the messiah?'

These people were busy working, but when they saw how excited their neighbor was, they came in a hurry to see the mind reader. Many from this village believed that he was the messiah because of the woman's report, 'He told me everything I ever did.' (John 4:3–29).

Many in the crowd want to talk at the same time. Some of the crowd has heard this story before, many have not, but they all clap tonight. The attentive crowd now erupts into happy chatter as each had his own personal story to tell others. They laugh and smile at the best story they know. The thief just sits in his place at the foot of the lamppost, confused and thoughtful.

The last of the storytellers now stands up and has a difficult time getting the crowd to listen to him. "My friends, wasn't that a wonderful story?"

People clap again to show their pleasure.

"How many of you here tonight own a Bible where this story of the mind reader is written?"

Many people think that this is a rude question. They know

that Bibles are in the city, but the price is beyond their means. Finally, one man speaks for the people.

"We know about the Bibles, and some have seen one, but none of us owns one."

All evening no one mentions the financial straits of the crowd, and now some hang their heads in embarrassment.

The speaker continues and announces, "We have gifts for you tonight. If you will make a way for people to walk through the crowd, some friends have decided to give each of you a Bible of your very own." The people do not respond at once. Surely, this storyteller would not make such a tasteless joke. Most sit in silence. A few look to the men for direction and realize that some young men are trying to make their way through the crowd with wheelbarrows loaded down with cardboard boxes. The young men politely excuse themselves. "Please let us by."

The crowd does not make a space for them to walk, as they still do not understand. The speaker asks again, "Please allow these men to come this way. They have gifts for each of you."

Slowly, the crowd moves to allow the two wheelbarrow-pushing young men to stop in front of the storytellers. To everyone's astonishment, the man opens a cardboard box and withdraws two new books that he holds over his head.

"Who is the oldest man here? And who is the oldest woman here? Would someone please help her to raise a hand?"

There is much discussion as entire families vie for the honor. It cannot be decided whose family claims the longest-living patriarch. Three elderly women and two elderly men all claim to be the eldest, so the speaker announces, "We want these honored elders to be the first to receive a new Bible. It will cost them nothing. Some dear friends have donated them so that we can read for ourselves the many stories about God."

The crowd laughs and applauds as the young men who brought the books into the crowd now deliver each of the seniors a brand new Bible. Some of them now understand. Some do not yet dare to hope that he really meant that they all would receive a valuable book of their own. Humble sits in silent awe as she watches the young men deliver each person a gleaming, new treasure.

The crowd is strangely quiet. It holds a collective breath as they watch the cardboard boxes empty. Will there be enough? Will everyone really get one? Humble suddenly realizes that her mother is not present. Forgetting to take care of the splinters under the newspaper, she slips off her front row seat on the display table and runs to where her dear mother lies with her sleeping little sister. She does not try to speak softly.

"Mother, come quickly. You must come now. Come on! You will not believe it."

Rising from her resting place on the sidewalk, Silk Fan follows Humble. She has not heard such alarm in her child's voice on this entire trip. Humble runs ahead of her, motioning her to follow.

"What is it, my child?"

"You must sit here with me, Mother. You must!"

Just as Humble is about to break into tears, thinking that the boxes are exhausted, another young man pushes his wheelbarrow toward the speaker's place. There are enough. She will receive one!

The young man smiles broadly as he approaches the table where the five young people have sat all evening. He hands Silk Fan her Bible first then gives each of the teens one of their own. Silk Fan and Humble turn to look at each other. They are both speechless. After years of copying a line or a verse, they now own Bibles of their own!

The boy who said that he could never have a Bible because his family could not afford one cannot stop grinning. He will not open the paper wrapping yet. He is happier than he ever remembers being.

Some in the crowd are weeping, some are shouting, and all are hugging their new prizes. One of the men with the wheelbarrows is trying to lead a praise song, but people will not allow it. They are busy thanking him. In the middle of the exuberant throng, a voice is barely heard. "May I have a Bible too?" It is the thief, still tied in place by the lamp pole. Two men go to deliver the book to the thief and speak with him. When the unbelievable night has quieted down, Humble speaks to her mother in the quietness of their shelter.

"Mother, I do not need to find another book of quotations. This is far beyond my dreams. I did not dare to hope that I could ever have my very own copy of the Holy Scriptures. This is everything I could ever want."

"Are you sure, my child? We can still look for you on the way out of town tomorrow. I promised that we would replace you award book."

"We have more than replaced my other book. I am sure about this, Mother."

As they lie down on the sidewalk to rest, Humble hugs her new Bible to her chest. She does not open the paper wrappings yet. In the middle of the night, Humble awakens and checks to see if the replacement book was really just a wonderful dream. It still rests in her arms.

RICE PADDIES

The sun is still asleep when the merchants who practice their businesses on the sidewalks come to open up for the day's customers. Silk Fan knows that it is time to awaken her family before they are finished with their night. A high, squeaking noise of the canvas sunroof, retreating after serving its purpose, indicates that their kindhearted hostess comes to reclaim her space. Their shelter for last night spreads its wings and flies away. The upturned tables, moved away from their place in front of the stall, reveal the family's own small hideout.

"Good morning, my daughters, we must arise now. Our friend needs her place of business again. We must thank her for giving us shelter last night."

"I am still sleepy."

"Happiness Found, please put on your shoes. We will have a new adventure today."

"What adventure is that, Mother?" Humble sits and helps Happiness with her shoes.

"We are going to ride on a bus! All we need to do is find the correct bus, one that is driving south. We will not grow weary, and the driver knows just where he should go."

"Have you ever been on a bus, sister?"

"No. This will be a first time for both of us." Humble brushes her hair back from her face with her hands.

"The nice thing about the bus is that it can go faster than our feet can walk." Silk Fan shakes the blanket and begins folding it for repacking.

"Our friend from last night told us that he would direct us to the correct bus for today's travel. I do not know what time it is, but I think we still have time to find someone who will sell us breakfast."

Their hostess who gave her permission for the use of her sheltered sidewalk is busy unloading her stock from a fortress of oblong cardboard boxes. She smiles at the family.

Silk Fan sees her and asks, "Who would like to thank our hostess for her generosity?"

Humble says, "I want to. Is she like the innkeeper in the Christmas story who didn't have a room but let Mary and Joseph stay in her barn?"

"Yes, she is. Isn't she?"

"We will both go, Mother," says Humble as she takes her sister by the hand. They offer their thanks and then wash their faces and brush back their hair. The new day begins with its own game of "Ready Or Not, Here I Come."

"Humble, that cart by the street is selling food. I see hot steam rising. See if they sell bread or rolls. We can eat while we are riding on the bus."

Returning with three treats, Humble smiles her pleasure.

Silk Fan says, "Let's get out of her way. We can stand by that bicycle rack and wait for our friend. He said that there are many buses, but we must ride the one that travels south. Humble, be sure to listen to the names of the small towns and one city we will pass. We must not go too far. We will have to get off the bus at the proper time."

"Yes, Mother." Humble pays close attention as Silk Fan recites the names of the town and villages that she remembers.

What Silk fan does not say is that she feels chills and fear rising in her body because of the nearness of the end of their journey. In only a few more days, they will actually be at home. *Oh, Pride of His Father, please forgive me. Please accept me and these two girls I have adopted.*

A broadly smiling boy eating an apple comes toward them and calls out, "Humble, my mother invites you to come and eat with us."

Silk Fan removes the package from Humble's already full hands and places her food in her overloaded harvest basket. It will be needed later in the day. The lost family, seeking directions from the big city, finds friends and food on their last day there. The host family is homeless but generous. They all share a meal prepared on a small grill in an alley and stand up to eat the food. The boy's vivacious little sister is pleased to see that her new acquaintance has a little sister too. She offers Happiness Found a large piece of bread. She smiles her thanks and eats it immediately. After all adult and teens confer among themselves, they decide that the best bus to catch is number twenty-two.

When their hot meal is completed, three teenage children who have no school, no jobs, and no homes walk the journeying family through the busy streets to a bus station where they may find bus number twenty-two. As they board the city bus, they are surprised to learn that their friends have one more gift for them. "It is a lunch. Mother packed it for you. You might need it today. Good-bye."

"Thank you, new friends. May God richly bless you all. Good-bye."

Silk Fan is thrilled to find the correct bus. It will serve to get them home quicker than walking, and it will save their waning strength. She pays the fare and thanks God for the money she carries for such expenses.

"They are nice people, aren't they, Humble?"

Happiness Found wants to chatter away, but Humble has an assignment that she takes seriously. The scenery is interesting to her mother because there is so much that she does not remember. These tall buildings of glass and steel have mushroomed up in the last few years. Humble concentrates on reading signs and identifying the names of places through which the rumbling bus moves.

Little Happiness is amazed at the city buildings. "Mother, look at those tall buildings. What are they? Those are the largest buildings I have ever seen."

Silk Fan asks her seatmate about the route of the bus.

"Where does the bus travel after the town with the shoe factory? Are the roads safe for walking women and children? Can we buy food along the way? Do you know a farmer by the name of Strong Warrior? Is there a secondary school in this district?"

She listens carefully to each piece of information.

Vigilantly counting, Humble peers through the window. "Mother, this makes town number six."

"Thank you, dear."

"The next place is called Valley of White Swans. What does it mean, Mother?"

"It is just a name, my child."

"I can see the shoe factory from where we sit. It is a sprawling, brown building."

"Thank you, Humble. You are faithful in your tasks. We will get off in one moment."

Silk Fan steps down from the city bus, positions her overburdened harvest basket on her back, and smiles. Happiness Found takes the hand of her older sister, Humble, and asks, "Why are the men pushing wheelbarrows barefoot? Where are their shoes? What if they stub a toe? May we sing on this road, sister?"

"Ask Mother."

"Mother, may we sing here?"

Silk Fan, who is scanning the roadside for signs, answers with a smile that shows only accomplishment, not anxiety. "My little daughter, you may sing. You may dance. You may skip. You may giggle and leap. You may hop or run. You may laugh or whistle for all to hear. You may count or hum to yourself. You may collect wild flowers or throw rocks. We are going home, little one, to a wonderful home."

Both of the girls look inquiringly at their much-loved adoptive mother, the worn-looking peasant woman who has not smiled lately, and notice that she wears a beautiful smile. They hold hands while swinging and dancing around her and ignore the stares of the city people who do not appreciate what a joyful day they celebrate.

Hmm. I do not remember this road being paved, and I do not remember the dirty skies, but I do remember the lovely, long, low rice fields and family farms. Oh, look what a happy scene!

Like an expanded canvas, the rural scene spreads before them. It is an ordinary scene of farmers wearing finely woven straw hats, backs bent as they plant rice in ponds mirroring their forms. It is a simple scene, typical of the region, and the charm to her is its familiar refrain. She does not think of aching backs or itching legs; she thinks only, *I remember this scene, I am coming home.*

"Mother, why is the land so flat?"

"Yes dear, it is beautifully flat, isn't it?"

Humble smiles. Her mother did not answer her question. "I will take the basket now, Mother."

"Thank you, Humble."

"Happiness Found, are you counting donkey carts? I see three."

The child is busy watching sidewalk fortunetellers.

"Did I tell you that we will spend the night tomorrow with your cousin and my second uncle, Brave Warrior? They have a nice large house and a sweet daughter. You have a fine girl cousin. It will seem like having another older sister like Humble."

"Is this cousin the one for whom we bought the hair bands?"

"Yes, she is. She is named Quiet One. She will be so pleased with your gifts."

"Do you think that she knows how to whistle?" Happiness asks.

Silk Fan laughs. "Perhaps. If she does not know how, then you can teach her."

Happiness Found stops to peer into a ditch at black tadpoles swimming in the roadside puddle of water.

Humble wants to talk about her friends whom she has left behind but does not want to burden Silk Fan with her concerns. "Mother, will you miss your friends from the village?"

"Yes, daughter. I will miss my friends. I am sure that you will too."

"I will miss the aunts and some of my school friends. Auntie Grace and Auntie White Flowering Tree were good friends to both of us. I will miss First Star of Evening because she is so kind. She never refused to go when we visited Aunt Beautiful Moon. In addition, I shall miss Morning Sunshine. She was pleasant company. Several younger children are good friends. Little Red Rose is fun to know because she giggles and because she works so hard on her schoolwork and memorizing for the contest. That is something I will never forget."

"Humble, you make friends easily. You will meet other nice young people here. I want you to know that I considered leaving you there, but I could not do it. I love you and want what is best for the two of you. You will have a better life here. We will see to it that you marry someone worthy of you. You are a fine girl, and you will find a fine young man here in the south if you want to marry. I just could not leave you there where girls and women are held so cheaply."

Humble nods her head. She thought in terms of missing her friends, not future marriage plans.

Along the way, she recognizes fireworks sellers, barefoot doctors of traditional medicine advertising their own hall of longevity, and men with overloaded bicycles selling everything from dumplings to factory-made t-shirts. She smiles at the way some things have not changed. Men pulling rickshaws still make their living as they have for centuries. Humble says nothing as they pass several empty trishaws awaiting customers.

"Did you know that your mother is a mind reader, my dears? Yes. I too would like to ride all of the way home on one of those trishaws."

Even after the rest last night and the bus ride this morning, they are already tired. It is no longer necessary to rush, but weariness slows their steps. "We will rest at the next town."

"May we open one of the Bibles we received last night? It will be so exciting to read our very own Bible. This is so much better than finding a quotations book to replace my award book. It is more than I ever dreamed of owning."

"Yes, my dear daughter. You may if you wish. Just remember that the wrapping keeps it clean. We will have all the time we need for reading it when we get home. Last night was one we cannot ever forget. Imagine all of those people worshiping together in public. I will always remember the songs and joyful crowd singing praise to God. That happy crowd taught me a great lesson. I believe that these books, our wonderful Bibles, are China's hope. If the words in this lovely book can change individuals such as the captive brides, then I believe that it can also change our whole ancient land."

"Mother, I find it difficult to realize that we really do have our very own copies of the Bible with the same words that we always copied. It requires all of my self-control not to remove the wrapping paper and read its pages. I feel like a thirsty farmer who comes home after a long hard day in his fields, who wants to drink to his fill. I want to read all day long until the sun dies and I cannot see its pages."

"I understand, Humble." They both smile. "Girls, guess what we are going to find for our evening meal?"

"Noodles?"

She shakes her head.

"Dumplings?"

"Guess one more time."

"Steamed rolls?"

"No. We are going to have rice. It is not too expensive here in the south because it is grown here. We are going to eat the best rice dish anyone sells."

The girls respond to Silk Fan's enthusiasm and to her playful spirit. They do not yet understand what freedom and returning home means to their dear mother. They think that it is just plentiful rice that excites her. She has put up a brave front for their sakes, and now she is almost home.

Tonight, Silk Fan does not look for street vendors; she looks for a proper restaurant. Since her own small village does not have a public eating place, she wants her much-loved daughters to have another experience of eating properly in a real restaurant, not just buying from vendors and eating while standing in the streets. The neighborhood restaurant she locates is not elegant enough for wealthy businesspeople, but it serves her needs well. The long rice dish with vegetables and a rich sauce is delicious and filling. It satisfies her longing for familiar things. The tired girls eat everything offered them and smile their satisfaction.

"That was so fine, Mother. We ate in an indoor restaurant for a second time. "

"We will be eating with our families very soon, daughter. Home meals are the most elegant meals anywhere."

We are almost there. Pride, please hold on for one more day. I am coming home to you.

He does not hear her thoughts, but it helps to reassure her to do as she has for years: think of and speak to her dear husband, regardless of the distance between them. *We have traveled across a continent and are safe now. We really are almost home.*

The sky is not as clean as she remembers, and the sun is low in its path, indicating that it is time for seeking a place to spend the night, but Silk Fan is no longer lost. She turns in the direction of her grandfather's farm and remembers the fact that she shopped in this town with her own mother.

Traveling on a full stomach is easier than traveling on an empty one, but walking is still walking. Weeks have passed since they left the mountain village before dawn, and all three are not only weary, but their bodies are losing reserved strength because of such extended demands that daily travel makes on them.

As they pass a narrow alleyway, Happiness Found sees a sight that delights her eyes. Several children are doing balancing acts on top of a tower of flesh. An adult stands by giving commands, but the children are the acrobats. Happiness Found stops in the middle of her path in fascination. Silk Fan patiently waits for the act to finish. She knows that her girls will not likely ever see such delights again. As they move on, a man leading a shaggy, white pony speaks to them.

"Aren't those tumblers talented? They will give a full performance in a few minutes. They will be on the courtyard in the next street."

Dancing in circles and getting in her mother's way, Happiness Found squeals, "Can we, Mother, can we? Can we see the whole show?"

"We really must find a place to stop. The sun is going to sleep soon."

"Sir, what does a ticket to this show cost?"

Turning to speak to Silk Fan, he answers. "Hello, Madam. My name is River Worker. The show is free. You may give them a few coins if you wish to, but there is no charge. You see, this is just a practice for when they perform in front of crowds in cities."

"River Worker, are you from this area? My name is Silk Fan.

These are my daughters, Humble and Happiness Found. Did we attend school together? I remember your face."

"Silk Fan, I remember you well."

He is embarrassed and wants to ask all sorts of questions but says simply, "This act is well done. These children and their parents present a professional balancing performance."

"It looks interesting, but we are traveling and must find a place before the sun dies."

"Since my animal is my companion, we must find a place outside. There are some abandoned farms near here. We try to stay there because it is safe, and there is usually water and grass nearby."

"River Worker, do you think that such a place is safe for a woman and her children?"

"I will wait to go with you. Nearby is a nice place with fruit trees and a well. I have seen this act, but I will wait for you. You will be safe."

"Children, my old classmate from school is offering to take us to a safe place for the night. We will stay for only fifteen more minutes. Then we must go."

"Oh, joy! Thank you, Uncle River Worker. Humble, we are going to see the wonderful children's show!" Happiness Found squeals.

The family claims a place on the sidewalk and discovers that excitement steals the weariness from their bodies. In a city alleyway, amazing children are working. Boys with firm limbs and bells on their clothes strut for the appreciative audience. Girls of all ages dressed in brightly colored costumes share their best smiles and then climb on the knees of their brothers and reach for outstretched hands to climb even farther toward the sky. Happiness Found gasps audibly, willing the girl in the shiny green dress to surefooted heights.

"Isn't she beautiful?"

"Yes, she is, and they are so brave."

"What if they fall?" Happiness does not take her eyes away from the children.

"Oh, look! They are dancing through hoops. They are the bravest children I have ever seen."

"When she moves, her dress sparkles. She is grand."

A small crowd that assembles claps for the family as they climb down from their perches amid bells jingling and people cheering. Many of the townspeople have seen this act before, but they watch it again with unfailing admiration. Happiness and Humble both stare in awe. Little Happiness Found has a new goal in life: to acquire the skills and bravery of the girl in the sparkling green dress.

"You may place your burdens on my cart if you wish. The path from here to the abandoned farm is not too far for walking. Just follow us."

"Whom does he mean, us?"

"He means that we are to follow him and his white pony."

Humble addresses River Worker, "Uncle, what is the name of your pony?"

"His name is Flying Hooves, but perhaps we should have called him Dragging Feet."

"Is his load very heavy?"

"No. My load from my home to the city is usually bamboo. It is not a heavy load. This load from the city to the country villages is plasticware. This load is not only beautiful but light-weight as well."

"Will he allow me to stroke his mane?" Happiness Found asks innocently.

"Wait until we arrive at our night's resting place. It will only be a few minutes. He likes the pale green herbs growing by the fence there. You may feed him some fresh herbs if you want to.

"My shaggy animal and humble cart serve me and my family well. We raised this short-legged pony from birth, and he works faithfully with us. I will sell my goods in nearby villages and towns, and then I must plow my fields. Flying Hooves is a farmer's friend."

In a short time, River Worker coaxes the animal into a road-side path by a small farmhouse. Silk Fan wants to question him about her family, his family, and all of the neighbors whom they both know. He has been polite in refraining from quizzing her about her absence, and now he has work to do.

Humble peeps into the barn as Silk Fan examines the abandoned house. The young mother looks for security where there is none and speaks aloud to herself, "Surely this is the last night we shall have to seek shelter like wild rabbits with no holes of our own."

"Sister, do you think that the family who lived here owed sheep?"

"This appears to be a cow stall, or perhaps it is where their oxen slept."

"I think that they owned a small, shaggy pony like Flying Hooves. Humble, why did the people leave this place? It seems like a nice farm."

"I do not know. Let us go to gather some fresh herbs for Flying Hooves. You told Uncle River Worker that you wanted to help feed him." Humble is dutiful.

"We have a fine place for resting, daughters. When you have finished helping with the pony, please gather some dead limbs from the trees. If you find enough, we shall have a fire."

"What grows on these trees, plums?" Happiness remembers the flower clouds of plum blossoms.

Silk Fan says, "These look like peach trees."

"Oh, I wish that I could live where there are peach trees growing!" Humble sighs.

"What a lovely wish. I do too. Come in here, girls. What do you think of our room for the night? It has a roof, and we shall have a good fire. We shall be quite comfortable."

"Mother, why is there no floor? It has a dirt floor just like the barn."

"My child, many people live in homes like this. It is not necessary to have a wooden or stone floor in a home to make it warm and safe."

"Oh. I did not think about that." Humble's education is expanding.

"Did you find enough material for the fire? It will be dark soon. If you want a fire, you must collect wood now." They all collect brush and limbs for a fire.

Silk Fan shivers. It is a cool spring evening, but it is fear that sends cold chills racing down her spine. *What if Pride of His Father has a new wife? What if Pride is too ashamed to accept me back as his wife? What if my dear children cannot remember me? What if people laugh at me for bringing two girl children home with me? These quandaries are too large for me, Holy Father. Please take care of them. Amen.*

"Quite soon now we hope to arrive at Second Uncle Strong Warrior's house. You will be able to take an honest bath, wear clean clothes, sit down for meals with hands washed with real soap, and read from your wonderful books. I am sure that Great Auntie and your cousin will allow you time for sharing your favorite verses with them."

Happiness Found stops picking up limbs and quizzes, "Do you really think we might be there tomorrow?"

"We will feel safe and free and happy at Great Uncle's house. I do not know about my own home. I never received an answer to the letters I sent to Pride of His Father. We do not even know whether or not any of my letters and packages reached him."

Humble sighs and changes the subject of the conversation for the sake of her mother. "Mother, which verse do you want to read first?"

"Let me think. There are so many verses that have strengthened me in the last few years. The thirty-third verse of chapter sixteen in the book of John promises, 'I have told you all of this so that you will have peace of heart and mind. Here on earth you will have many trials and sorrows: but cheer up, for I have overcome the world' (John 16:33). What do you want to read first from your own Bible book?"

"I want to read that verse from Jeremiah that Pale Orchid told us about. Jeremiah was a very unhappy man who was a prophet of God. He did not want to be God's servant, but he was obedient. God gave him a beautiful promise to encourage him. It reads: 'For I know the plans I have for you, says the Lord. They are plans for good and not for evil, to give you a future and a hope'" (Jeremiah 29:11).

Happiness Found lies down. "I am sleepy now. I want to lie down and look at the fire."

Her mother responds, "That will be cozy. The fire will keep us company now."

The care-worn mother and her two travel-weary daughters snuggle down on Humble's dirty wool blanket and gaze into the crackling peach wood fire. A peaceful sleep claims their eyes. The three of them are together, and the fire warms their space. It seems luxurious.

The next morning, they awake to a song sung by the owner of the shaggy pony named Flying Hooves. Young Happiness Found awakens with a smile and a question. "Mother, may I ride with Flying Hooves?"

Silk Fan's old school acquaintance, River Worker, answers, "You may all ride on my cart as far as the home of your second uncle, Strong Warrior."

Silk Fan considers the full cart. "There is no space for us, but we thank you for your kind offer."

Warming to his new audience, the traveling peddler smiles the smile of a performer and charms the girls with a laughing speech.

"I have magic powers. Watch me as I find regal seats fit for the ladies of the court of the royal empress."

Silk Fan did not know the young man well when in school, only remembering him as a pleasant boy in a class a year below her own. His jovial personality surprises her, and she smiles as he teases her daughters. She repacks her belongings, once more folding Humble's blanket into her harvest basket. As he begins the task of moving his load of goods about, he breaks into a sales song. Happiness Found stands mesmerized.

"Plastic! Pretty plastic for sale. I have purple plastic tubs for watering your pigs and green plastic buckets for feeding your hens. I have brown plastic containers for storing your rice and flat yellow plastic boxes for keeping paper clean and nice. Look and see and buy from me! Small pink tubs are for bathing your baby. Sturdy blue bowls are stacked up high, and spoons, plates, and chopsticks too. Green containers have tightly locking lids and clear ones are for Grandmom's best pickles. Come see them all. Oh! I have pretty plastic for sale!"

Both of the girls giggle at the singing peddler. Their laughter is good cheer born of the freedom of childhood. A laugh escapes Silk Fan's lips. She appreciates the childish fun as her daughters enjoy the sales song.

The rearrangement of the stacks of plastic goods does allow for seating space on the farmer's homemade cart. He now ties his stock in place with a loop of twine.

"My ladies of the court of her highness, the Empress, you may now select your seats for your carriage ride. Who would like to ride on a seat of upturned purple tubs? Designed with your comfort in mind, please find a pretty pink seat. Now the empress herself will find this fine blue seat fit for royalty. We await your pleasure."

Silk Fan laughs aloud, and Humble smiles in delight while Happiness Found looks and listens in awe.

"This looks wonderful. Where may we place our bags and basket, my friend? We do not wish to lose our own goods this late in our long journey."

"The private harvest basket and shopping bags of the empress will travel at the front of the carriage tied tightly to the bamboo side."

"This is a fine arrangement. We thank you. This ride will save our weary feet and our tired backs."

"Oh, Mother, this is a royal ride on a rainbow! I feel like a beautiful lady sitting on a pretty seat, holding on to a bamboo handle."

"I do too, Mother. This is such a wonderful storybook ride. Look at my pink seat! Do I look like the pretty girl in the sparking green dress?" Little Happiness Found is enchanted.

It is only after the family of three sits on their perches and the steady clip clopping of the faithful horse's feet mark their own regular cadence that Silk Fan breathes a long, slow sigh of relief. Her girls are safe. They are granted good childhood entertainment, and her back is resting for the first day in weeks. They are finally going home.

"Will you really sell all of these beautiful plastic containers before you arrive back at your home?"

"Sometimes I have a few items left. People are glad to see me because my goods are useful, and I charge a fair price. There are several villages where I am known. My pony and I save our customers a long trip into town. We will stop along our way home. Since it is planting season, this will be my last trip for a while, but this work earns money my family needs. I am saving money to purchase a bride."

The young man blushes at his own confession of such a personal nature. Silk Fan nods. She knows about the problems of buying a wife.

"Since it is for your bride price, we will purchase two fine rice tubs in brown plastic."

"Thank you."

The singing plastic salesman is pleasant company for the family of three refugees. All four travelers ride on the pony cart as they travel in the direction of familiar family farms. Silk Fan smiles at the happy young man and the cheerful reaction of her girls. She smiles to keep her nervous stomach calm. She is going home after five harrowing years.

SO MANY SURPRISES

As she awakens the morning after arriving at her second uncle's home, Silk Fan realizes she feels truly safe. Free to sleep later, she is up early, eager to complete her journey and to see the object of her love, her own dear first family. Last evening, she bathed in leisure, a delightful luxury after the stressful weeks of travel. It is with amazement that she notices how thin she has become. The exhausting trip has coaxed the very flesh from her body.

I refuse to wear all those layers of clothing that I have been wearing during my tramp across this land. Even if they are too large for me, I am going home in only one set of clean clothes.

Her happy aunt hovers about her long lost niece with motherly attention. "You look lovely, Silk Fan. Do not fret. Here, eat some rice cakes." Eating the food pressed on her by her smiling aunt, she prepares to make the last link of her journey back home. With her scissors, she snips her own neat stitches from her children's clothing. Removing the fold of money from little

Happiness Found's coat hood and Humble's coat, she packs her money carefully into the hidden pocket of her slacks. Her hands tremble and her fingers fumble as she makes final preparation to see her own true family.

"Second Auntie, please allow my daughters to sleep as long as they need. They have been so brave and strong."

"We know that you are all quite weary. We will bring them to you in a few weeks. Humble has already asked if she may help me plant. They will be fine here in our home. Our daughter is delighted to have them visit. Thank you for the gifts. I needed sewing needles, and the fabric is pretty."

"You are welcome. Are you sure that Pride of His Father has not taken a new wife?"

"We are sure. If he does not die of a heart attack when he sees you, he will be overwhelmed with joy. Besides, who would marry such a sad-eyed man?"

"Did I tell you that I wrote letters to him?"

"Yes, dear. You told us."

"Here are some seeds for you. You failed to plant the last ones I gave you." Her uncle smiles as he presses some seed packs into her hands.

"Do not tease her. She is tired and nervous too."

"Second Uncle, you must know that I did get to plant some of your seeds. I would have been hungry without them, and somewhere in the northern hills, your apple trees are growing today."

The proud family man nods his head at this bit of news.

"I must say good-bye to grandfather, and then it will be time for me to return home." She bends to hug her grandfather who wears the hat she brought to him. He does not want to release her. After a few minutes, Strong Warrior says, "Father, she needs to go home. We will see her again soon." He releases his beloved granddaughter, but his eyes follow her.

Strong Warrior lifts the full harvest basket on his own shoulders and calls to his brown dog. He is secure enough in his manhood that he does not hesitate to carry the basket, even though it is a woman's task.

"Second Uncle, are you planning to take me home?"

"I will walk you part of the way. We cannot have you getting lost this late in your trip. Sergeant is going all of the way with you. I am pleased that he remembers you."

"He is a good dog. I just hope that my own family will welcome me as your old dog has. Tell me, is Pride angry?"

"As we told you last evening, he tried to work with the authorities, but they were of no help. He tried to get some family men to go with him, but they all said that they did not know where to go and that many more men were needed to find you and fight for you. He was very angry and very sad for so long. He looks like he is still grieving for his parents' death, but he feeds the children each day. Do not worry. He will be thrilled to see you."

Silk Fan smiles and nods her head. She reaches down and pets the old dog assigned to guard her. Perhaps she needs a dog too. This very path is the site of her kidnapping. The narrow way holds frightening memories.

"Second Uncle, what about other people? Will they mock us? I do not want Pride to have any more grief."

"Do not act as if you have lost face, my child. Smile and go about your own work. Enjoy your family."

"I have something to tell you, Second Uncle."

"Yes?"

"I have some money."

"Did you steal it?"

Laughing, she answers, "No. The old man who bought me left me his house and fields when he died. I sold the house and fields. It is legal. His daughter is married and lives too far away to farm the fields. I have legal papers signed and stamped."

"Silk Fan, I think you will want to refer to this money as 'your wages.' Other young people who go to cities to work bring back money for their families, and they are just called wages. This might be easier to explain."

"You are so wise, Second Uncle. Although it is none of anyone's business, it will be simple to state that the unexpected wealth is wages."

"Silk Fan, do you have papers for these girls too?"

"Yes. I have the sales receipt from Humble's uncle and a tax record for both girls. Second Uncle, we will need another room built onto our house, now that we have three daughters. With the money I have, it should not be a problem."

"You wait a little while, and I will tell Pride that it is my idea."

"Your mother and father must be proud of you. You treat me like your own daughter, and I love you for it."

Second Uncle Strong Warrior nods his head in modesty.

The two family members walk and chat for more than an hour. The faithful dog leads the way on an ancient path between rice paddies and fields.

As the breeze rustles the thin leaves of the bamboo reeds growing nearby, Silk Fan smiles in delight at things not changed. The homesick girl in her joys at the lovely sight of familiar growing things. The savvy housewife part of her envisions building materials for a dozen projects.

At a familiar rice pond, he stops while removing the large, bulky basket from his aging shoulders. "I am going to leave you now, but Sergeant is going to continue with you. He might come back on his own, but I think that he will stay with you until I come back."

Strong Warrior leans down to rub the ears of his faithful dog and gives him a command to go with Silk Fan.

"Second Uncle, I want to raise two pigs this year."

Laughing, her older uncle says, "I will find two piglets for you. You will need to begin building a pen soon." The older man shows his love for his sister's child as best he can. He will enjoy his family in peace now that she is home again and delight in the presence of two more girls in his extended family.

"Come with me, Sergeant. We must see our family." With only a backward glance toward the retreating form of her elder relative, she leads the brown dog toward her family's farm somewhere in southern China. They both know the way.

Moving quickly past the stretch of the river that holds such dark memories of her kidnapping, she shivers, holds tightly on to Sergeant's neck fur, and continues walking past familiar fields, unchanged houses, and the shrine where people still leave favors to the gods. After two hours, she trembles as she spies a square stone post, marking her own land. Her eyes scan the beloved scenery as she absorbs all of the beautiful ordinary things of her farm.

She forces her body to continue marching steadily and refuses to give in to her knees that turn to rubber. Her eyes seek hungrily for the sight of her family, but she does not see them. The only person on the horizon is a single boy, too old to be her son. He is running in the spring wind, trying to make a plastic bag fly like a kite. The dog, Sergeant, leaves her side and pounces to the boy, begging to be included in the game.

"Hello, Sergeant. Why are you here? Come here, boy."

Silk Fan walks slowly up to the boy and the dog. "Are you named Strong Wind?"

He nods his head in answer but continues playing with the dog. His smiling, boyish face reminds her of the infant he was once. She speaks to him again. "May I sing you a song?" Sinking to her knees, she sings the old ballad she sang to him on her last happy day here.

THE STARS IN THE SKY

"Hello Mr. Tax Man. Greetings to you."
"Hello, Mrs. Farmer, may I sit here with you as you shell
your peas? I have come to see how wealthy you are."
"Oh, sir, I tell you no lie. I am the
wealthiest woman I know."

Silk Fan continues to sing the folk song which she sang to all three of her babies. She smiles as she sings to her son who remembered it so long ago. He listens through the entire song until she finishes with the poetic last two lines:

> And the stars in the sky dance for joy every night,
> Seeing how wealthy we are.

"I have heard that song before."

"Oh, you have heard it before? Who sang it to you?"

"A long time ago when I was a baby, a lady sang it."

"Do you remember what she looked like?"

"She was my mother. I remember her singing to me. My sister tries to sing it, but she does not know all of the words."

Silk Fan's throat closes with emotion, so she simply nods her head at her son who no longer recognizes her.

"Strong Wind, where did you get that shirt you are wearing?"

"My mother sent it to me. How did you know my name?"

The seven-year-old boy asks the question that reduces his mother to tears. She looks adoringly at him, and delight overcomes her at the reunion with her son who was so small when she left him so unwillingly five years ago. She has been absent from him longer than she cared for him. Now looking at this child, she realizes that he is almost a stranger to her. There is so much she does not know about him.

Silk Fan does not notice that a man is walking toward them, waving onions in one hand and a hoe in the other. "Beggar, be gone! Do not bother us. We do not have food to spare, and I cannot buy your wares."

It is Pride of His Father coming for his son. Mistaking his long-gone wife for a beggar, he yells at her to leave. With her large basket, now worn and dirty and overflowing with gifts and the empty plastic jugs tied to the top, she does indeed appear to be a beggar or peddler.

At his voice, Silk Fan gives a gasp and does something completely out of fashion today. She covers her weeping face with shaking hands and bows to the ground in front of her beloved Pride.

"What are you doing, woman? I am no noble lord. Get up! Be on your way!" She stays in this humble position as tears, held in for far too long, flood through her fingers and onto the ground.

Strong Wind tugs his father's pants leg and says plaintively, "She knows my name, Father."

He instructs his son to return to the house with his sister. The boy runs back to his home and tells his sister about the woman who knows his name and sang to him. He says, "She sang mother's song about the stars in the sky."

Shimmering Sunrise's eyes widen. Can it be?

As she remains bowed down and weeping, her hair separates around her ears and reveals part of her face. He knew delicate ears like that once. The shape of her neck commands memories of his darling, long-gone wife. His stomach tightens as he drops his onions to the ground.

"Who are you? What do you want?"

Slowly, Silk Fan rises from the earth and faces her beloved Pride of His Father. With a hesitant voice, Silk Fan can only manage to call his name. "Pride?"

With a shock, Pride, the poor farmer who has taken care of his farm and two children alone, has trouble believing his own eyes and more trouble speaking.

"Silk Fan, is it you? Have you returned to me? Are you a dream? Is it really you, my own wife?" He sinks to the ground beside her, and somewhere on a farm in southern China by the side of their spring grain field, he gathers her into his arms and rocks her as he has done his own children. Great, loud sobs spill from his lips.

"Oh, my dear wife." He sobs. "Oh, my sweet Silk Fan. Oh."

"Please do not cry, Pride. I am home now. I was so afraid that you might have taken another wife."

"No. No, my beautiful girl."

"I am so sorry that I have been gone so long."

"Shh."

"Oh, Pride, will you have me again?"

"Will I have you? I feared that I would never see you again. Please forgive me for not coming to get you. Everyone said that I needed an army to fight off the gang of bride thieves. The village chief told me not to go alone. He said that I would be killed and our children would be orphans. Please forgive me."

Her tears turn to smiles. "I do forgive you, my husband. I do. There are so many men and women in the gangs, and they were so cruel."

Searching every part of her face, he smiles and moves toward her lips in tender reunion, kissing her with gentleness she remembers so clearly. They smile at each other in delightful celebration.

"Come, get up from the ground."

Laughing and clinging to her true husband, she says, "We are both sitting in the dirt. I just want you to hold me. It has been so long, and I have had to be strong without you."

They stay in the field so long that their two young children chew their lips and worry about their father's strange behavior.

"What is this huge basket?"

"It is my harvest basket that I have carried all the way here. I have brought gifts for later."

As he lifts her worn basket, she clings to him. She looks about the farm, her farm with all of its unremarkable scenes, and smiles a satisfied smile. "How wonderful everything appears!"

She does not think about all of the work she will do to clean and improve it. She thinks only, *I am home again. What a marvelous word, home. Thank you, Lord Jesus, for bringing me home.*

They walk slowly to their house, where their son and daughter stand gazing in wonder at their father and the beggar woman whom he is welcoming with such unaccustomed warmth. He even leaves his hoe in the field and holds on to her. Strong Wind tells his sister again about this woman who knows his name and sang the "Stars in the Sky" song. Her eyes widen as she whispers, "Mother?"

Silk Fan and her daughter, Shimmering Sunrise, search each other's faces and hold eye contact as they approach the courtyard. Just as she recognizes her, the girl walks slowly toward her long-lost mother.

"Mother, are you truly my mother?"

"Oh, Shimmering Sunrise! My lovely daughter. You have grown so tall. Yes, I am truly your mother. I have missed you so much. May I kiss you?"

The mother who cared for other children finally engulfs her own children in her arms. First she holds them tightly and then holds them at a distance and studies each face. Laughing with joy, she kisses each child and wipes her own tears on their sweetly fragrant hair. Their natural baby aromas are gone, replaced with that of growing children.

"Oh, how I have missed you both!"

"Is this lady really our mother?"

"Are you coming back to stay?"

"Yes. Yes, little one. I am really coming back to stay."

"I am a big boy now, not a little one."

"You were a little boy when I was captured. I always think of you as my little one."

Shimmering Sunshine interrupts their conversation with a burst of joyful dancing and loud declarations. "I have my mother back!" She squeals. "Oh, joy! I have my mother!"

Dancing and whirling in circles, Shimmering Sunshine celebrates. The young girl who has taken on so many responsibilities celebrates with glee. She can finally admit how much she has missed her mother, Silk Fan. No tears for her, only girlish squeals, shouts, leaps, and dancing feet. With her thin, girl's arms flying through the air, Shimmering Sunrise expresses the elation of the entire family.

"My mother is home. I have my mother back. We have our mother!"

The joyful, exuberant dances speak for the entire family. Even Strong Wind, who is having a little boy's problem comprehending this new event. The family of peasant farmers laughs together as Shimmering Sunrise leaps onto the step, twirls, and sails gracefully out of the door. No greater celebration is ever held for a returning loved one. The joy is pure family happiness.

"Would you like a drink of water and a face cloth?" Pride has just now considered her comfort and happily fails to see the room through the eyes of his wife. She blissfully accepts the drink but does not stop smiling.

"What sweet water from our own well! What a thrill."

"Officials tell us that we must now boil our water, but it is from our well."

Silk Fan has a difficult time deciding where to rest her hungry eyes. First she wants to absorb every detail of her darling, true husband, Pride of His Father. His unkempt head holds a constant smile as he returns her adoring gaze.

I did not know that he was capable of such deep sobs. I am touched by the fact that these deep body-shaking sobs were in my behalf. I now know that he really welcomes me in earnest. Oh, great joy! My two girls were correct. A nice, white chair with arms is appropriate for such a fine man.

The long-lost wife and mother sighs deeply and giggles when she thinks of the shock Pride of His Father will experience when he sees the treasure of gifts that will soon arrive at their door in a brown truck.

Tomorrow I will tell him about the increased number of girls in our family, but not tonight. Tonight is just for the four of us. Tomorrow is soon enough to worry about the real possibility that the local government will possibility limit the number of my children who are allowed to attend school. Today is just for celebrating my homecoming.

"Mother, please sing your song about the stars in the sky. I remember it."

Shimmering Sunrise sits at her mother's feet with both

arms encircling her mother's left leg. Her precious mother has returned, and now she holds on tightly. Nothing will ever take her mother away again. Silk Fan sings her old folk song once again, with her children joining in on the parts they remember. The simple rite holds more sweetness than her family can express.

Long after the chickens stop crooning their bedtime lullaby, the family is still smiling. Long after the celebration meal of long rice and spiced vegetables, Pride does not take his eyes off his beloved Silk Fan. Long after sponge baths, happy talk, and the fire turns to an orange glow in the stove, their excited children still wiggle and talk.

Shimmering Sunrise says from her bed, "Mother, I have something to show you tomorrow."

Strong Wind joins in, "Mother, did you know that I can count to one hundred?" "Mother, I can write a whole sentence by myself if sister helps me. I want to show you what I have learned. The sentence reads, 'Big people go up the stairs.'"

All three laugh lightly at his sentence that is such a simple one to paint. Silk Fan replies with a traditional praise, "Your handwriting is your face."

He persists, "Mother, will you write us some words on cards tomorrow?"

"Yes, child, I will write many new words for you to learn."

"Go to sleep, children. Your mother will be here tomorrow." Pride encloses his long-lost wife in his arms, feels her ribs, and declares, "Silk Fan, you are so thin!"

"My dear husband, I have just traveled across this country to get back to you."

"Yes, my sweet Silk Fan."

"It was a long and frightful trip. I am only one of the captured victims who is safely back home. Who can say how many others are still held captive in places far from their homes?"

"Yes, my sweet Silk Fan."

"Do you remember how you told me that you hung the

moon in the sky just for me? Let us go to see if we can find that moon in the sky now. Our children need time to go to sleep. Come, let us go outside."

"I will if you promise not to let go of my hand."

"Yes, my good husband. I promise to be right here beside you."

The reunited married couple walks outside to search for the moon's glow. He does not let her hand leave his own. "Do you hear the sweet sound of flutes, my love?"

"Yes, I hear them. There must be a thousand flutes playing happy sounds now just for us."

Silk Fan removes her hand from his and tenderly caresses his sun-tanned face while studying his dark eyes that she has spent so much time remembering.

He sighs. "How I have yearned to feel your small hands on my face again. I had almost forgotten how sweet love feels."

"My dear Pride, hold me tightly."

He wraps his arms about the body of his beloved with an almost shy embrace. Shaking as he holds his dear Silk Fan, he buries his head in her hair, convincing himself that she is real and not another dream. Gently caressing her, he croons, "Oh, my Silk Fan, my brave, beautiful, wonderful Silk Fan." She returns his embrace with earnest feminine response, delighting in his love.

They stand for a long time, embraced in each other's arms. There is only a sliver of a moon that night, but they do not need the light to inspire them or to direct their steps as they survey their own piece of land in the great country of China.

Their two children are asleep when they return to the house.

"I want to light a candle. I want to gaze on your dear face. If I close my eyes, you might disappear. Forgive me. You must be exhausted, my little Silk Fan. You need rest. Do you promise to be here in the morning when the sun awakens?"

"Yes, my husband. I promise to be right here next to you. Come to me. Let me rub your back. I have waited so long to caress your body."

"You may rub my back another time. Let me rub your shoulders. Did you really carry that large basket all of the way home?"

With his rough farmer's hands, he gently caresses the body of his beloved Silk Fan. They both sigh in sweet contentment. He remembers all of her precious places he used to caress. He finds them again with kisses.

And the stars in the sky dance for joy this night, seeing how wealthy they are.